THE CROATIAN ISLAND LIBRARY

EVA GLYN

One More Chapter
a division of HarperCollins*Publishers* Ltd
1 London Bridge Street
London SE1 9GF
www.harpercollins.co.uk
HarperCollins*Publishers*
Macken House, 39/40 Mayor Street Upper,
Dublin 1, D01 C9W8 Ireland

This paperback edition 2026

1

First published in Great Britain in ebook format
by HarperCollins*Publishers* 2026
Copyright © Eva Glyn 2026
Eva Glyn asserts the moral right to be identified
as the author of this work

A catalogue record of this book is available from the British Library
ISBN: 978-0-00-876419-7

This novel is entirely a work of fiction. The names, characters and incidents portrayed in it are the work of the author's imagination. Any resemblance to actual persons, living or dead, events or localities is entirely coincidental.

Printed and bound in the UK using 100% Renewable Electricity
by CPI Group (UK) Ltd

All rights reserved. No part of this publication may be reproduced, stored in a retrieval system, or transmitted, in any form or by any means, electronic, mechanical, photocopying, recording or otherwise, without the prior permission of the publishers.

Without limiting the exclusive rights of any author, contributor or the publisher of this publication, any unauthorised use of this publication to train generative artificial intelligence (AI) technologies is expressly prohibited. HarperCollins also exercise their rights under Article 4(3) of the Digital Single Market Directive 2019/790 and expressly reserve this publication from the text and data mining exception.

In memory of my cousin, Roger Hubank
"It's what we do."

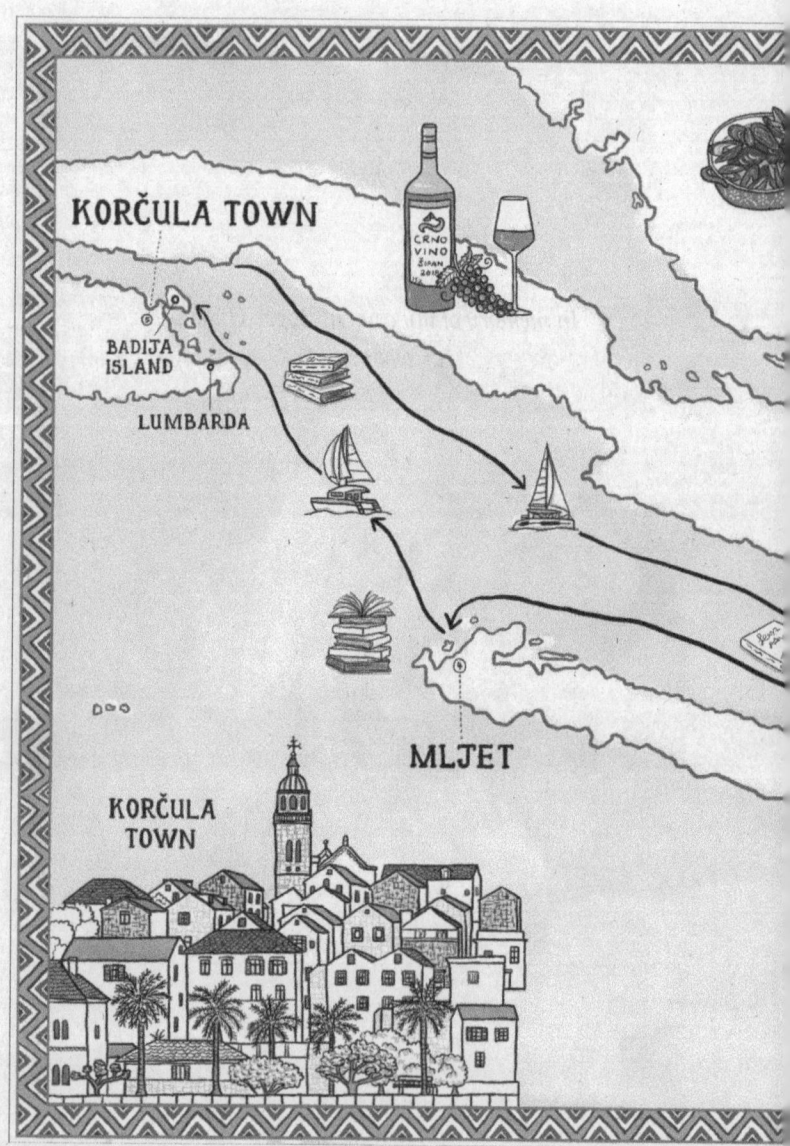

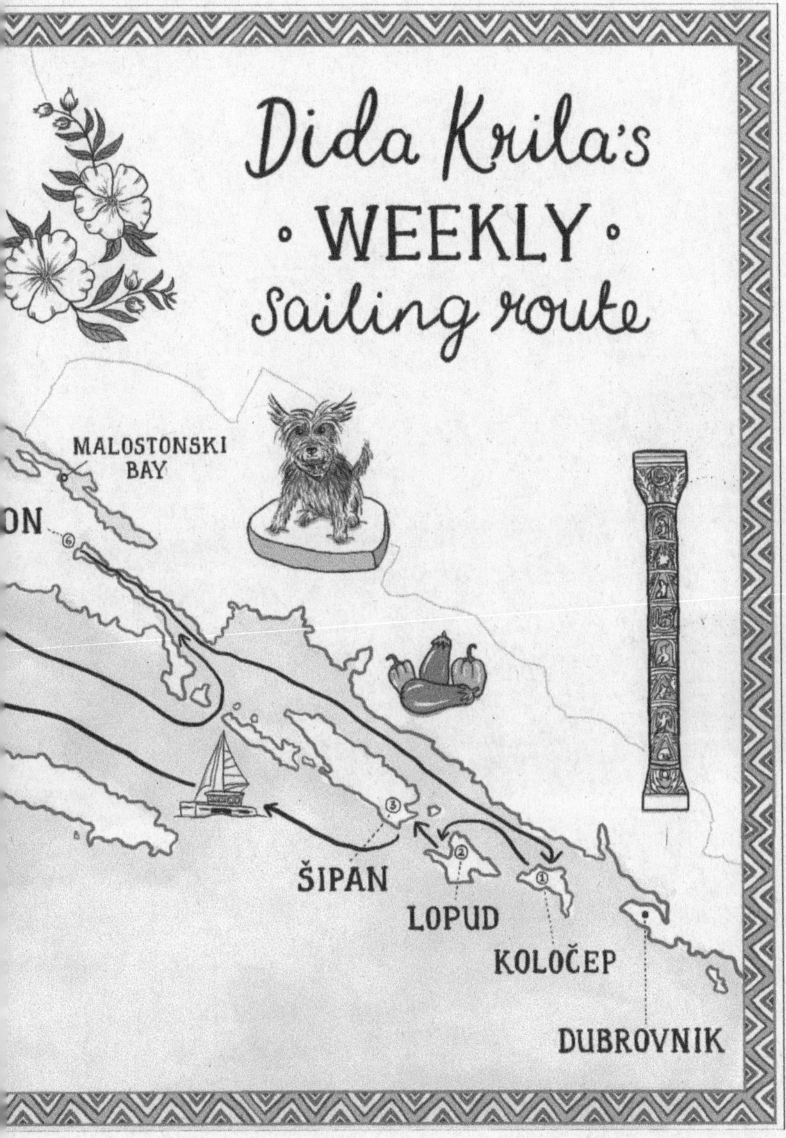
Dida Krila's
• WEEKLY •
Sailing route
MALOSTONSKI
BAY
ON
ŠIPAN
LOPUD
KOLOČEP
DUBROVNIK

Glossary of Croatian Words & Phrases

Dida Krila – Grandfather's Wings

FAMILY & TERMS OF ENDEARMENT
Draga – sweetheart, dear
Dida – grandfather
Baka – grandmother
Tata – dad
Mama – mum
Obitelj – family

SWEARING & INSULTS
Sranje – perfectly safe to use in mixed company
Tupka – dim witted
Jebem ti – only for extreme situations
Supak – anatomical insult, where the sun doesn't shine
Odjebati – extreme wording for go away
U klinac – toned down version of the above
Odvratno ponašanje – disgusting behaviour

BEING POLITE
Dobro jutro – good morning
Oprostite – excuse me
Dobrodošli – welcome
Dobar dan – good day

FOOD & DRINK

Brudet – seafood stew

Konoba – restaurant

Džezva – pair of long-handled jugs, one larger than the other; the traditional way of making coffee

Pašticada – slow-cooked beef stew

Soparnik – chard pie made with a flatbread like pastry

Pršut – dry cured ham, similar to prosciutto

Medenjaci – honey cookies

Peka – traditional meat or octopus dish, cooked with vegetables under a metal dome

Plavac mali – Croatian grape variety

Tortica – chocolate wafer biscuits

Ajvar – red pepper and aubergine relish

Ćevapi – finger-shaped meat balls

Savijača od višanja – cherry strudel

Kroštule – sweet pastry knots

Šporki makaruli – traditional pasta 'worms' with spiced beef and tomato sauce

Pekara – bakery

Burek – spiral of filo pastry, normally filled with meat or cheese

Musule na buzaru – mussels cooked in white wine, olive oil and garlic

Sir i vrnhje – cottage cheese and sour cream

Gregada – fish and potato stew

Paprenjaci – biscuits spiced with black pepper

Bijela kava – latte

Rakija – grape spirit firewater

Pogača – calzone like pastry, traditionally with tomatoes, onions and anchovies

Panceta – Croatian bacon, eaten raw

Punjeni patlidžani – aubergines stuffed with mince and tomatoes

MISCELLANEOUS
Kako se zove tvoj pas? – what's your dog called?
Barka – traditional wooden boat
Kuna – Croatian currency before the Euro
Isprazniti – empty
Razvalio – pissed, as in drunk
Sto biste? – what would you (like)?

Dubrovnik

TUESDAY 13TH JUNE

Ana Meštrović flung herself into a canvas chair outside the jazz café and glared at her friend Meri.

"You'll never, ever, not until grapes grow on willow trees, guess what they've done."

Meri sat back, the orange tiger streaks in her hair reflecting the late afternoon sunlight. "That rather depends on who 'they' are."

"Those idiots at the county education department, that's who. Most especially, sodding Ivana Levačić."

"The woman in charge of the library project?"

Ana nodded. She was about to say more when Meri flagged down the waiter, Toni, and ordered a carafe of wine.

"I'm assuming something stronger than coffee?" It was more of a statement than a question, and Ana nodded.

"The catamaran's in the old harbour, ready for tomorrow. I'm not driving anywhere."

Meri whistled. "*They* let you moor up in there? *They* can't be all bad."

Ana glowered at her. "Don't joke. They've only gone and appointed a male librarian."

"So?"

What did Meri mean, 'so'?

"You know why I got out of chartering. You know how much I hated being hit on by some leery, oversexed holidaymaker every other week."

"Not to mention how much you hated their spoilt wives and girlfriends talking down to you too."

Ana folded her arms. "At least the wives kept their hands to themselves."

Toni returned with their wine and a terracotta dish of olives, rolling his eyes theatrically. "Unlike those ladies over there!" He tossed his head in the direction of a group of Englishwomen. "They've ordered a second bottle and I'm not sure I feel safe to take it."

"Don't worry, *draga*, we've got your back … or whichever part of your anatomy you're most worried about," Meri laughed. "Now shoo! Ana and I are talking."

"All the same," she said, once he'd stalked away, "you need to be logical about this and not make assumptions. Who is this man anyway? On the vague chance you were actually listening when Ivana told you."

Sranje! Meri knew her too well. Still, she didn't want to prove her entirely right. "He's fifty-three and English, and until recently was teaching German in a London high school. He also speaks fluent French, some Italian, and even a little Croatian, which is why he got the job. The bastard's done a bit of sailing too, damn him."

"So in other words, if he were a woman, he'd be perfect."

Ana folded her arms. "But he's not."

"And he's probably not a misogynist either. For all you know he might be celibate. He may not even be straight. You can't just assume he's going to be trouble. And anyway, being this grumpy isn't like my lovely Ana. Are you going to tell me what's really wrong?" Typical of Meri to see through her blustering and get straight to the heart of the matter.

Ana sighed. "I just don't want any aggro, that's all. I need this to work – you know I do. Financially it underpins ... everything."

"And you can't lose the catamaran."

"Like I'd ever let that happen. I'd rather starve than lose *Dida Krila*."

"Oh, Ana. Like your parents would let that happen!"

"I won't take their money again." She bit her lip. If this didn't work out she might have to. The money and everything else that went with it. *Sod it, sod it.*

Meri put her hand over Ana's. "This is so not like you."

Meri was right. She didn't normally get this wound up about stuff. "I think ... I think it's because I'm nervous about having to manage people, especially people I'm going to be living in close quarters with for ten whole weeks. I've never done it before, and if I don't set the right tone from the beginning ... If we don't get on, this summer could be hell."

Meri looked up at her and grinned. "I suppose at least with charters you could have any troublemakers off the boat in a week or two."

Ana put her head in her hands. "Oh god, don't make me regret this. It was a hard enough decision to make as it was."

Meri wrapped her arm around Ana's shoulder. "I hope I didn't push you into it. It's just, when I was asked to write the press release about the project I thought it was perfect for you.

Especially as it's a pilot. You know how much emphasis the government's putting on foreign language proficiency. If it works, their grant money's there for another four years."

"And four more years will pay off the loan on the catamaran, so I won't have to worry anymore and I'll be free; free to sail where I want, do what I want. It's perfect, honestly it is. It's just so much responsibility and I'm not used to it. All I've had to do for the last few years is run my boat."

"Don't underestimate yourself. You've always skippered, you've always had crew, you've always completed logs. The only difference this time is you have a librarian and a ton of books on board, and the logs are now weekly reports to Ivana. Any stroppy customers will be down to this bloke."

"When you put it like that, perhaps it isn't quite so daunting." Ana tried to smile.

"I know you can do it. It's well within your capabilities," said Meri, giving her a peck on the cheek.

"How come you always make me feel better about myself?" Ana asked, even though she knew in her heart that this time it wasn't quite true.

"Because I'm your very best friend. Hell, Ana, aren't you the lucky one?"

At this Ana really did laugh, the knot of tension easing a little in her belly. What would she do without Meri? Knowing she had her back this summer – albeit from a distance – meant the world.

She'd met Meri almost fifteen years before, while she was studying for her degree. New to the city, she hadn't realised the jazz café was where the gay community gathered, but the crowd had been so friendly, Meri in particular, that she had felt she, too, belonged. A bond had grown between them; the combat-wearing, streetwise, single mother and the green-as-grass student. With Meri, more than anyone else, Ana could be herself.

An hour or so later, Ana circumnavigated the tourists thronging the bright square between the Rector's Palace and the cathedral on her way back to the boat. The old stones were tinged a soft golden grey by the early evening sun, highlighting the palace's elegant colonnade, and a black and white cat strolled languidly in front of her, repelling the attempts of a Japanese visitor to stroke it with a contemptuous flick of its tail. Dubrovnik would never be home, but Ana certainly appreciated why so many people came here and fell in love with the city.

Heading for the harbour, she passed into the shadows under the medieval arch of Vrata od Ponte. The fish stall beneath it was closed, leaving behind the faintest tang of the sea, but tomorrow she would buy everything she needed to make *brudet*, a traditional fish stew. It would be a good way to welcome her crew. Set that friendly tone. The youngster Natali, who she'd recruited herself and ... what was his name? Lloyd? If she was honest, she was still miffed with Ivana's choice, although she knew it wasn't fair to take it out on the guy. He'd better behave himself, that was all. And given he was almost twenty years older than her, he'd better not play on her inexperience as a manager – or try to tell her what to do.

Dida Krila's sleek form was an elegant contrast to the blue and white painted fishing boats nestling beneath the grey bulk of Sveti Ivan Fortress. Dubrovnik's old harbour was wrapped in the arms of the city walls, and it was indeed a privilege to be allowed to moor here, even for just a couple of nights. Normally only craft belonging to inhabitants of the old town and a handful of tourist trip boats were permitted, so perhaps she should stop worrying about everything and enjoy it while she could.

Ana jumped onto the wooden transom, the feeling of home wrapping itself around her. She paused in the dip of the wheel helm station, swinging the seat back and forth as she gazed at the banquettes which edged the indoor–outdoor part of the salon. The whole area was sheltered by the fly deck above and long, smoked-glass windows which gave protection against wind and sun. Now she slid them open, letting in the glorious evening light that danced across the harbour and glinted from the polished dining table.

Finally she unlocked the door to the galley, which as well as containing the navigation station, led downstairs to the four en suite cabins, two in each hull. The catamaran's spec was the best she'd been able to afford: soft, squishy seating, teak finishes; even a full-sized oven and fridge. Not that she was much of a cook, but the generous galley had proved a popular feature with her charter guests, and the charter business was why she had bought the boat in the first place.

When her grandfather had left her enough money for the down payment, buying a boat had been a no-brainer, just as it had been to name it after him. *Dida Krila*. Grandad's Wings. He'd taught her to sail and had always been happier on water than on land – a trait she'd definitely inherited. Now she liked to imagine he was still beside her on the seas. And he'd certainly be chuffed to see her moored in the old harbour. Too right he would. She wrapped her arms tightly around her chest; god, she still missed him.

Her grandfather had not just been her hero, but everyone else's too. When the Homeland War had broken out in 1991, he'd thrown in his job as a merchant seaman and rushed to Dubrovnik's aid, taking on the dangerous task of running small but vital supply boats up and down the coast to the city. Ana had been a tiny child at the time, but his exploits were the stuff of family legend. Once Dubrovnik had been freed, he'd joined the embryonic Croatian navy until the end of the war, when he'd returned home and tried his hand at fishing until the visitors began to return.

He'd instantly seen that tourists meant money, and had somehow managed to buy a small cruise ship then skippered it between the Dalmatian islands, living his life on the water and making a small fortune in the process. A fortune he'd left to his only grandchild.

But Dida had given her so much more than that. He'd taught her the ways of the ocean, sharing his knowledge and love of the winds and the tides and the freedom they brought. Her parents, although loving, had seemed just a little bit dull in comparison, with their garden and their chickens, and her father carrying on his father's business. When she was with Dida, the wings had been hers.

Dida Krila was the last link between them, and all the more precious to Ana because of it. She'd never regretted the fact she'd bought her in haste, driven by the emotion of losing him. No, of course she hadn't. It was just that over the last few years she had realised she wasn't suited to chartering. Certainly not the pandering to tourists, being nice to them even when they weren't always nice to her. That was the decision she regretted; not thinking through what it might be like dealing with the public day after day. She quite literally couldn't afford to get something so fundamental wrong again.

Her problem now was making the boat pay without those

lucrative charters. Sure, so far this summer she'd sold a few weeks to past guests she'd liked and trusted, but it wasn't enough to meet the payments on the catamaran and earn a living. The library project solved all that; her share of the government grant was sufficiently generous to meet her running costs and a modest salary for the summer. Most importantly, though, it would cover a whole year of loan repayments.

She was damned if she was going to rely on her parents for money. Not again. She was thirty-five, for god's sake. And the payback they would expect in return could end up being something she couldn't swallow.

The moment she'd told them she was quitting chartering, they'd suggested putting *Dida Krila* into the family oyster and tourism company as a luxury day boat. It was almost as if they'd been waiting for her to trip up so they could pounce and drag her in. *Sranje!* Was she being unfair? They were probably just being kind, but the idea still niggled at her.

They wanted her to take over from them one day. Of course they did. They hadn't said as much, but she knew. When Dida had fallen ill, she'd given up her job in Dubrovnik and come home to work for them. She'd done it to be close to him, but her father had called it her apprenticeship. The very thought had curled her toes, and inheriting the money had given her an instant escape route.

Except now, if the library didn't meet the targets the government had set, once this year's money ran out the family business was the best, if not the only, way of keeping her boat. But Ana still had a feeling that Dida would be deeply disappointed if she gave up her freedom.

Just as her mother and father would be deeply

disappointed if she didn't. She had to pray it didn't come to that. It wasn't as if there was any animosity between them – the exact opposite in fact; they were a close-knit family and their home had always been filled with love. That's what made it all the harder to let them down. She didn't even know whether, if push came to shove, she could do it, and the weight of their expectations added a whole level of complexity to the summer.

So the library really, really, needed to work. But honestly, there was no reason for it not to. It was simple enough. On Monday the school holidays would begin, then every week until the start of September they would sail from island to island, providing a free library service for local children paid for by the government's language proficiency programme. Worthwhile for everyone, useful for the kids and lucrative for her. A life on the water, with wins all round.

She opened the fridge and selected a bottle of her favourite Ožujsko beer, carrying it up the outside steps to the fly deck. Ducking under the boom, she stretched out on the banquette and looked up into the bluest of skies. Below her the harbour buzzed with the chink of crockery from restaurants and the murmur of a hundred conversations.

Tonight, she'd kick back and enjoy it all, alone on her beautiful boat. Just the way she liked it.

Tomorrow her crew would arrive and her work would begin.

Dubrovnik

WEDNESDAY 14TH JUNE

Lloyd Richards looked out of the window of the airport bus as it rounded the bend to reveal an open vista in front of him. Beyond a glitter of purest blue sea were the stacked terracotta roofs of Dubrovnik old town, glowing in the sun. He hugged his rucksack to his chest. He hadn't been here for more than thirty years; almost half a lifetime. Less than half of one for Jenny.

He screwed up his eyes behind his sunglasses, waiting for the red-hot prickling of grief to fade. Fifty-two, she'd been. Fifty sodding two. They'd barely even reached the age where they'd thought about planning their retirement, but they'd always assumed … go at sixty, live simply, see the world. Now all those things they'd left undone were up to him, but he still didn't know how he'd ever find the stomach to do them alone.

He'd lost his wife, and then, through his own unforgivable actions, he'd lost his job. If it wasn't for his daughter Ruth pushing him, he wouldn't be here now. And yet in his heart of hearts he knew it was time to move on. Two years wasn't enough to mourn the love of his life – perhaps there never would be enough time – but it was more than long enough to stagnate. And entirely screw up what was left of his miserable existence.

After leaving the main road, the progress of the bus towards the old town slowed, every stop and start jolting memories of Lloyd's last visit to the city closer to the surface. Even now that he was back, his fragmented thoughts were coated in a strange cloak of unreality, like that long ago summer had happened to someone else.

Then, like now, he'd only been passing through. He remembered his plan, and how excited and nervous he'd been. Freshly out of university and before his teacher training, he'd had three whole months to travel alone across Europe. So he'd flown to the furthest point – Dubrovnik – his idea being to see the famous old town, then hop on a ferry to travel up the chain of islands where his grandfather had served during the war, cross the Adriatic to Bari, and meander home through Italy and France. Except it hadn't happened like that at all.

The bus drew to a halt near the Pile Gate and Lloyd climbed down, rucksack slung over his shoulder and dragging his holdall behind him. Beyond the creamy stone of the Amerling Fountain, holidaymakers gathered in the shade of the plane trees, or on the furthest reaches of the broad piazza, photographing St Lawrence Fort high on its rock. Beyond it the sea glistened and danced; that glorious, magical, unforgettable blue, with its hints of silver and turquoise. Even through the crowds of people, watching its shift and shimmer brought a measure of peace to Lloyd's soul. Forwards. Onwards. And – hopefully – even upwards.

After filling his water bottle from the elaborately scrolled fish's mouth on the fountain, Lloyd wandered across the bridge to the Pile Gate. A tour group was milling around the top of the steps inside, so instead he walked down the slope. More people crowded below a couple of panels which looked relatively new, and as he approached he could see they mapped the damage done to the city during the siege of 1991 – a war he had only just escaped himself, but at such cost ... And he'd been one of the lucky ones.

Lloyd turned away with barely a glance and headed through the lower arch into the sunshine and past Onofrio's Fountain. As he set off down Stradun's broad expanse of shiny paving he gave himself a good talking-to. This was not about the past; it was about finding a future. He was only in the city for a few days, as he had been in 1991, and then it would be up and down the Elafiti Islands all summer, places that held no memories for him and would therefore be a blank canvas to paint however he liked.

He upped his pace, swinging his holdall to his other hand and flexing his fingers. This was no time to sightsee and dawdle, even if he wanted to. He'd been travelling all day and right now he needed a shower and a change of clothes – and quite possibly a cup of tea, assuming there was a kettle on the boat. But even if there wasn't, he was sure he could find another way of boiling water hot enough.

Emerging through an arch in the city walls and onto the bustle of the harbourside, Lloyd stopped to take his bearings. To his left were tables in neat rows under a crisp white awning, opposite a line of wooden booths plastered with posters depicting the trips available. Blue seas, blue skies, spectacular sunsets ... but the real beauty was right in front of him. No picture could truly portray the light reflecting on the water and gleaming from the hulls of the boats amassed behind the breakwater or the tantalising aroma of something meaty cooking in a nearby restaurant.

Turning the corner, the full drama of the old harbour hit him. The golden grey city walls, metres high, sheltered a rectangle of water on two sides, and the whole scene was dominated by the bulk of the fort diagonally opposite. Boats huddled in its shadow, and he scanned them for a likely catamaran. Looking around, he could see only one, moored on the far side, outclassing the wooden fishing boats around it with its sleek lines and shining white hulls. There should be at least some degree of comfort on offer, making a hot, or at least warm, shower more of a possibility.

As he approached, he spotted a woman lounging on one of the long seats on the fly deck, book in hand. He shaded his eyes and called up to her.

"Are you Ana, by any chance?"

"I am. You must be Lloyd. Come aboard." She stood, revealing tanned legs beneath knee-length cut offs. Her wavy dark brown hair skimmed her shoulders, framing a heart-shaped face lit with a pleasant smile, although Lloyd couldn't be sure it reached all the way to her eyes.

It made him hesitate on the quayside. "I'm sorry if I'm early…"

"No, no, you're not. I'm expecting you." She ran down the steps to meet him. "Would you like a cold drink?" she asked, leading him through the generously proportioned inside–outside space and into the galley. "There's a can of iced tea in the fridge. You know, because you're English …" Her words petered out.

"That is such a kind thought." Lloyd didn't have the heart

to tell her he couldn't stand the stuff, when she'd tried so hard. "But for now, more than anything, I would love a shower, if that's possible."

"Sure. All the cabins are en suite, and there should be enough hot water." She indicated a set of stairs next to the chart table. "You're down there, in the forward cabin. The aft one is where we'll store the books. Natali and I are in the other hull. I'll show you everything else once you've freshened up."

Although he had to dip his head in the narrow corridor, Lloyd was surprised that once in his cabin he could stand to his full height. At slightly over six foot, that was unusual. Never on any of their flotilla holidays when Ruth was a teenager had he been able to, but then on teachers' salaries they'd never been able to stretch to a catamaran, and this one was the last word in luxury.

Although tapered towards the bottom, the double bed was more than big enough for one person, set as it was on a high platform that fitted snugly between the cabin's walls, with polished teak shelving running along one side. Even better, the bed was facing the sea. At the moment, his view was the grubby blue hull of the boat next door, but he was sure there would be mornings when he'd wake to a glorious expanse of water. He fingered the engagement ring on the gold chain around his neck. Jenny would have loved this snug little cabin, and he was surprised and relieved that the thought was a gentle one, a kind one. Perhaps here, somewhere new, he really would start to heal.

Removing his rucksack he set it on the banquette which filled the space below the impressively large window, noticing it had cupboards beneath. Plenty of space for his belongings. The en suite was tiny of course, and the shower cubicle so narrow he would have to edge in sideways, but he was sure he could cope with that. He perched on the edge of the bed and took out his phone, twisting around to take a short video.

Have arrived and this is my cabin. Very comfortable :-) Will call this evening, Dad xx

Right. Shower. Clean clothes. Face forwards. Fresh start.

"Come on, Obi. These bags are heavy and you can't possibly need to stop to sniff every three metres."

But of course she did, as her owner, Natali Putica, well knew. Even in this quieter part of the old town, the aromas would be exquisite for a dog: restaurant kitchens mixed with dropped ice cream from Peppino's, and goodness knows what else, most of which she didn't care to think about.

She tugged gently at Obi's lead. Any amount of force would see her plant her paws firmly on the paving and refuse to go any further. When Natali had first found her and had made this mistake, it had been easy to scoop Obi up into her arms, but with a rucksack on her back, a carrier bag in one hand, and wheeling her suitcase with the other, right at this moment it would be totally impossible.

It was lucky, really, that she didn't have many possessions. Well, she did have a few more. Her winter clothes were stashed in another case under her cousin's bed at her Auntie Stela's house, where she'd been sleeping for the last few nights, and there was a box of her stuff in the hall cupboard of her mother's apartment. Her *mama* had moaned bitterly about that, but tough luck. It wasn't as though she asked her for much. It wasn't as though she wanted to.

This job on the catamaran was an absolute godsend. It may only be for ten weeks, but it was live aboard, she could take Obi, and crewing yachts was what she was trained to do. It had never entered her head that adopting a stray during the pandemic would mean she effectively put herself out of work. She hadn't thought about anything, to be honest, beyond taking care of the tiny, bedraggled tan and black creature she'd found on the dockside one morning when she went out to buy her bread and milk. Owning a dog had proved something of an education, but she couldn't be without her now. Just couldn't.

She looked down at the diminutive bundle of shining, silky fur that ran from black on her back to almost bleached blonde between her ears.

"You may be a pain in the arse, Obi, but I do love you."

The frond-like tail wagged. The chocolate-brown eyes glowed with pleasure. Natali put down the carrier bag and massaged her fingers before scratching the top of Obi's head.

"Right. Come on. We're almost there."

The harbour front was crowded with tourists, and even to Natali the aromas drifting from the restaurants were tantalising: frying fish, rich tomato sauces ... Her stomach rumbled. She hoped the catamaran had a reasonable galley – and she hoped there would be something decent for supper too. Auntie Stela wasn't much of a cook, and Natali hadn't been able to afford proper ingredients to put together a meal for them both. This job was starting just in time.

But now she could see the catamaran, her pace slowed so that Obi was forging ahead. Ana had seemed nice enough when she interviewed her, but she hoped her new boss didn't expect too much. Oh, Natali could do the job all right; she knew about boats and their engines, about sailing, about cleaning in confined spaces ... she just wasn't very good company. That's what they'd said when she'd crewed before anyway, when she wouldn't go out with the others. But what was the point when you didn't like drinking and could never think of anything to say? Luckily Obi didn't mind. She brightened. Obi would enjoy being around different people, and as long as her dog was happy, and they had a roof over their heads, everything else would be fine.

As she approached the boat she spied Ana through the open cabin window, stirring a large pot on the hob. That was very good news. Natali jumped onto the transom, then put down her carrier bag before lifting Obi after her. She wouldn't let her off her lead just yet; she needed to get the dog used to being onboard first.

Ana came out to meet them. "Great to see you, Natali. I'm so glad you could come tonight; we can all get to know each other over supper, then tomorrow I can show you the ins and outs of the boat and our weekly itinerary."

Natali smiled. "Th-th-thank you." She was acutely aware she should most likely say something else, but her mind went blank.

Ana crouched down. "And this must be your little dog. What's his name?"

"It's her. And it's Obi." Obi already had her paws on Ana's knees and was looking up at her adoringly. What it must be like to make friends so easily.

"Well she's gorgeous. So tiny too. Although I'm not quite sure what I expected. What breed is she?"

"I don't think she's a b-breed exactly, but most of her is a sort of English terrier. A Y-Yorkshire one." She always struggled with the foreign word.

"Wherever she comes from, it's a first for me having a dog aboard, but I'll try anything once. I'll show you your cabin, so you can at least put your bags down. Now, let me take your case."

Ana couldn't be nicer, Natali thought. She just wished she knew how to tell her how hard she found it to make conversation. She didn't want to come over as standoffish, but somehow, although the words she wanted to say were there in her head, her mouth wouldn't move to shape them. She was so dumb!

She followed Ana down the stairs, and once they were in the hull's passageway Ana invited Natali to take Obi off her lead. "I want her to feel at home," she explained, "and she's so small she'll be safe down here. You and I are sleeping on this side, and I've put Lloyd on the other. He's the librarian and he's English. Like Obi." Ana laughed.

"Oh." It would be even worse if they had to communicate in a foreign language. Or would it? Perhaps in a way it might be better too. Her basic English was OK, really it was, but Ana and this Lloyd person didn't know that. It was the perfect excuse not to have to say too much. This job was really important and the last thing she wanted was the others to realise how stupid she was. If she just kept her head down and did the practical stuff well, she was sure it would be OK. It had to be.

Hearing footsteps in the salon above, Obi's ears stood to attention, and she dashed through Natali's legs and up the steps.

"Wow! Can she jump," said Ana.

Natali nodded, turning to follow Obi. "She's very quick."

By the time she was halfway up the steps, Natali could see Obi clambering all over the denim-clad bended knees of a tall man with silver-blond hair, in a desperate attempt to reach his crotch. She knew it was a perfectly normal dog-thing, but all the same it was horribly embarrassing. He was taking it well though, because he slid to the floor, and welcomed Obi onto his lap, tousling the fur that formed a tan and beige curtain around her head.

"So who are you, little one?" he asked the dog in English, for all the world as if he expected her to understand and answer.

Natali hesitated. If she was going to pretend, she had to start now. "S-s-sorry. Not good English. My dog."

The man nodded, running his hand over his damp hair. He had an unusually even face, with a long, straight nose, small mouth and a high forehead, currently lined with multiple furrows.

"*Kako se zove tvoj pas?*" he asked, with a creditably good accent. Surely, surely, he didn't speak Croatian? None of the foreigners she'd met had more than a few words, at best. If he'd asked her name, well, that was a standard phrase, but to ask what her dog was called …

Sranje. Sranje, sranje, sranje. If only she'd shut up about her English. Why, oh why, did she always get herself into this sort of mess?

He was waiting for her answer. "Obi. Sh-she's called Obi."

He looked down at the dog, who was gazing adoringly up at him. "Hello Obi, I'm Lloyd." He said that in Croatian too.

Damn and damn again.

Natali retreated down the steps to unpack, only a little mollified when Obi zoomed after her.

Dubrovnik

THURSDAY 15TH JUNE

Consulting the map Ana had drawn for him, Lloyd skirted the restaurant tables that all but blocked the alleyway and emerged into the square. Yes, this was the right place; the market was in full swing. Red and white umbrellas crowded the space, covering tables spread with stacks of plump tomatoes, unruly piles of green beans, and bunches of herbs filling the air with the sweetness of basil and the sharpness of mint. He wished it was his turn to cook tonight, but Ana had insisted he would be far too busy sorting out the library.

That was why he was heading across the old town early: to collect the books before the streets became too busy with tourists. Trying not to be distracted by the delicious produce and the hustle and bustle around the stalls, he made it to the far corner and into the relatively calm oasis of Ulica od Puca where the bookshop was.

Much to his surprise, he had actually slept last night, but he supposed he'd been tired after yesterday's early start. He'd become a very bad sleeper, but perhaps not being in his and Jenny's bed would help. In the cabin he wouldn't wake half-expecting her to be there, defeated before his day had even begun when she wasn't.

As he strolled along, he admired the traditional shop frontages on either side of him. He'd never seen anything quite like them anywhere else. A stone arch with the bottom half of one side blocked off formed a window, while the full height part on the other contained the door. They were beautiful in their simplicity, and although most of them were filled with souvenirs, gifts and local crafts for tourists, there was at least a minimarket and a library amongst them.

When he reached the fine stone frontage of the orthodox church, set back a little from the other buildings behind a courtyard where stray cats dozed beneath terracotta pots of plants, he knew he was almost there. The exact location of the bookshop was given away by a flat, pull-handled trolley in front of it. Ah, so that was how he was to transport the books. Just as well Ruth had bought him a gym membership last Christmas and made sure he'd got off his arse and used it.

Although he tried his best, translating the shop's name, which was painted in gold across the top of the door, was beyond his limited Croatian. Not that it mattered. This had to be the place. He pushed the handle, greeted by a welcome wave of cool air and entered a small room lined with floor-to-ceiling bookshelves. A blonde girl of about Ruth's age looked up from counting cash into the till and said "Good morning" in English. Was he really that obvious?

"Hi, I'm Lloyd. I've come to collect the library books."

She reached out to shake his hand. "I'm Claire. Much as the order was a godsend, I'm glad they're going. It's getting harder and harder to edge around the boxes in the back rooms. We don't have much space."

The red velvet curtain behind Claire billowed alarmingly and a small, dark-haired girl wearing a mini-skirt and startling lime-green top sprung through it.

"Come in, come in. First I must show you how I have packed everything."

Claire grinned. "Lloyd, meet Luna. Our very own whirlwind."

He followed her through to a tiny kitchen, where two of the walls were completely lined with boxes, the table pushed back almost to the sink to make space for them.

"I see what Claire means," he said. "All these books must have made life a bit difficult."

"Customers never make life difficult," said Luna. "However, it is hard for me to reach the stove to offer you coffee."

"Don't worry, I've only just had breakfast."

Luna nodded. "Right. OK. Well, this is what I've done." She waved at the wall of cardboard. "Books are sorted by language and age group, so not all the boxes are full." She lifted one onto the table and opened it. "Inside each, there is a list."

As Lloyd bent over to look, the smell of new books engulfed him. He didn't even hear Luna's next words, or see the piece of paper she was waving; he was back in the dining room at home with Jenny, who was sitting in the light of the patio doors, a multi-coloured bandana around her head to disguise the effects of the chemo, sniffing the paperback by her favourite author he'd just bought her. The memory felt so real it absolutely crippled him.

Luna touched his arm. "Are you all right?"

It was hard to fight back the tears. He turned away from Luna. "My wife," he muttered. "I lost her ... Cancer... She loved the smell of new books."

"Oh, I am sorry. If you want a moment, and you can get past the table, you can sit in the courtyard."

Lloyd balled his fingers tightly into his palms and shook his head. "I'll be OK. It's been two years. It shouldn't still hit me like this but it sometimes does. Let's get on with loading them up. It looks like it might take more than one trip."

"It will. When they added Korčula to the schedule it almost doubled the order. So many more children there, I guess. I grew up on Šipan and there aren't that many; we were lucky they kept the elementary school open."

Another punch. Right in the gut, and while he was still reeling from the first. Korčula ... of all the sodding places.

"You're still not right, are you?" Luna's face was full of concern.

He did his best to grin at her. "I'll live."

And he would. It was a large island, after all. It wasn't as if he even knew whether Mirjana was still there. She could be living anywhere and probably was, given she'd been so desperate to travel. Or maybe she was not living at all. He shuddered. He knew the war hadn't touched the island, but it didn't always take a war. After all, Jenny...

No. He wouldn't, *wouldn't* succumb to this. Forward motion. That's what Ruth had told him he needed, and she was right. He picked up the first couple of boxes.

"If you can tie back that curtain, I'll get these out of your hair."

"Right guys, we need to be away first thing in the morning, so let's take a look at where we'll be going."

The briefing. Ana's first important job as skipper. She watched as Natali reluctantly sat back down on the edge of the banquette.

"It's OK," she told her. "You can finish clearing the supper things. I need to fetch the charts first."

"Sure." Natali leapt up again. It was more or less the only word she'd uttered all evening. But on the other hand, she'd cooked them an absolutely delicious vegetable pasta for supper, and earlier in the day had absorbed everything Ana had told her about the boat like a rather skinny blonde sponge. The girl really was impossibly thin, but she had a healthy enough appetite, so perhaps it was just her constitution.

Lloyd levered himself up too. "Shall I refill our glasses?" They'd seen little of him all day as he'd been closeted in the spare cabin they were using to store the library books, cataloguing everything onto his laptop. No wonder he looked pale, and it made the lines around his grey eyes seem etched more deeply into his face.

He stood back to let Ana pass through the door to the galley, and while he was busy with the corkscrew and Natali stacked dishes next to the sink, Ana fetched the charts from the drawer in the navigation station which shared the kitchen space. The dining table now clear, she spread out the first one as Natali slid back into her place next to where Obi was curled, and Lloyd put down the wine.

"Right. I think it's easier to go through our weekly schedule using the charts, so you in particular, Lloyd, know where we're going. We've only been given a couple of nights here, so tomorrow we're sailing for Ston, which is *Dida Krila*'s home port. We'll go back there every weekend because I can hook up to water and fuel easily, and it's a good place to re-provision."

"So where exactly is Ston?" Lloyd asked.

"It's a small mainland port about four hours' sailing time from here, but we'll take it slowly tomorrow as we pass three of the five islands we're going to be visiting every week. The first is Koločep and it's only just outside Dubrovnik's commercial port. I expect you know it, Natali?"

Natali shook her head, which Ana found strange, because most kids who grew up in the city had gone there at some time or other on day trips. She must have sensed Ana's surprise because she said, "W-we only went to the larger t-tourist islands on the charters I worked on."

"Fair enough." Ana shrugged. "So Koločep will be Mondays, in the main village of Donje Čelo. There's a permanent population of a couple of hundred, but a few more children in the summer as people from Dubrovnik have holiday homes there."

"We're talking quite small numbers, then?" Lloyd asked.

"That's exactly why we're going from island to island. Apart from Korčula, none of them is big enough to warrant its own library, especially one where most of the books are in foreign languages. Koločep's the smallest and it doesn't even have a permanent elementary school. But there's a real push at the moment to encourage children to be as comfortable with other languages as they are our own, and lending them free books to read is one of the best ways to do it. Hardly anyone outside the country and the diaspora speaks Croatian, and as a nation we need to look outwards."

"Some of the books seem quite advanced for reading in a second language," Lloyd ventured.

"Honestly? A lot of kids are fairly fluent in either English or German by the time they're twelve or thirteen. And of course you've seen the books in Croatian too, for the younger ones."

"So we're talking quite a small pool of children, especially when you take out the ones who aren't into reading …"

God, Ana could do without his negativity right now. The library was free. That in itself meant people would use it. But she mustn't be sharp with him. He'd seemed very keen about everything last night, but a day spent on a laptop in a tiny cabin would take the edge off anyone's enthusiasm. She wondered for a moment how much Ivana had told him about the weekly reports she was expected to file, detailing library visitors and numbers of books loaned as well as usage as a proportion of permanent population, and how closely the education department would be monitoring the results. But honestly, that was her problem not his. What she had to do right now was chivvy him up a bit, if she could.

"I'm sure it will be all right, and if it's not then we'll cross that bridge when we come to it. But for now, let's get back to the practicalities." She traced her finger across the chart, relieved to return to her comfort zone. "As you can see, Donje Čelo's in a very sheltered bay, which is just as well because we'll be anchoring off on Sunday nights, and on Monday mornings we'll have to make a mad dash to the quay to unload the library between ferries. The good news is that our pitch is only about thirty metres away, on the path to the village."

"Would it be an idea to get hold of a sack trolley to transport the boxes?" Lloyd asked.

Sranje, why hadn't she thought of that? It would certainly make life easier. "Good call. I'll phone the hardware store in Ston tomorrow." She set a reminder on her mobile. "Now the next island, Lopud, has a proper harbour so we'll head there after we close on Monday. It's only about an hour from Koločep and is a much busier destination. It's popular with tourists, some pretty high-end ones at that – the Beckhams stayed there last year – and there's also a massive hotel."

"How many people actually live there?"

Was Lloyd going to ask the same question every sodding time? "Maybe three hundred? But there are more young families, because there's work for them in tourism." Why was she feeling so defensive? Was it because she was scared Lloyd might be right? What if it turned out to be an uphill struggle to get anyone to use the damn library? That hadn't even occurred to her when she'd tendered for the project, and it could prove to be her biggest problem of all. Why, oh why, did she never think things through?

But Lloyd was at least smiling as he topped up her wine, which for some reason was disappearing mightily quickly. "Better then. What about the next place?"

"Šipan? It's bigger again. Almost five hundred people. And although there's tourism, most work in agriculture. It means they're spread out, not all in Suđurađ where we'll moor, but unlike our first two stops at least there are proper roads and cars – even a regular bus service. It's our shortest sail too," she ran her finger over the chart and the others leant forwards. "Honestly, you can see one harbour from the other."

"So we always sail the night before?" Lloyd asked.

"Not from Šipan. The distances aren't great between the first three islands, but next there's Mljet and that is a long old haul, but if we sail really early on Thursday mornings the winds coming off the mainland will help us and it should only take about four hours. Mljet's a big island, long and thin, and the education department has decided we should be right at the northern end, in the national park, so it's going to be rammed with tourists. The population's spread out and the biggest village is inland, so we can only assume they've done their homework about where it's best to be."

"So if we'll have time to sail there in the morning, what are our opening hours?" Lloyd asked.

"Ten until four. Except on Korčula. That's just a little bit shorter because the time we're able to moor up in the marina at Korčula town is limited. We'll have to be fast with the set-up there, but we'll have had a bit of practice by next Friday. I thought maybe we could have our first run-through on the quayside at Ston over the weekend. What do you think, Lloyd?"

He was looking somewhere over her left shoulder, and didn't answer. "Lloyd?"

"Yes, yes ... of course. Good call."

Ana explained that Korčula was the largest island and had a good educational infrastructure, even a high school, but they still saw value in the foreign language elements of the project, so they had been prepared to add extra money out of their own budget to be included. At least Lloyd didn't ask how many people lived there. Thankfully. Because she wasn't entirely sure she knew the answer.

"Then on Friday evening we sail back to Ston. It's a long trip again, and if conditions are against us we may have to put in somewhere on the way if we lose the light, but that shouldn't be a problem. Now, do either of you have any questions?"

"Not me," said Lloyd, and Natali shook her head.

"Right," Ana said, smiling at them both, "briefing over.

Lloyd, I think you said you wanted to see Dubrovnik at night. Natali, are you coming?"

Lloyd drained the last of his wine. "I'm sorry Ana, I'm absolutely bushed. Flight catching up with me and all that." Flight? It was only a couple of hours. He levered himself up, pressing his hands on the edge of the table. "See you both in the morning." And with that he disappeared down the steps into the hull – surprisingly quickly for someone claiming such exhaustion.

Ana looked at Natali, who in turn was looking at the wine glass she'd barely touched.

"N-not me," she said. "I need t-to walk Obi."

Something felt out of kilter; not wrong, but not exactly right either, and it made Ana even more apprehensive than Lloyd's incessant questions about population numbers.

Was she overreacting? Letting her own insecurities as a manager colour her view of the others? Probably.

She needed to get away to clear her head, and the jazz café was calling. She needed to be herself for a while, leave her responsibilities behind and have a few glasses of wine with her friends. After all, she had a glorious sail up the coast to look forward to tomorrow, and being out on the water would make everything right. It always did.

Koločep

MONDAY 19TH JUNE

"Watch out, Obi!"

Natali gripped her lead so tightly the dog was almost sitting on her feet. She wouldn't like it, but at least she'd be safe from the whirl of activity on Donje Čelo quayside; tourists wheeling suitcases, crates being stacked by local men with almond-brown skin, and weird trailer contraptions that looked like they were attached to ride-on lawnmowers arriving from the direction of the village.

Through all these comings and goings, Lloyd was pushing a sack trolley loaded with books towards the hardstanding where the library would be, about thirty or so metres away. He'd already taken the folding table and banner, while she and Obi had stood guard over the boxes – if for no other reason than to make sure they weren't lined up with the others, ready to load onto the next ferry.

Now Lloyd had taken the books, Natali was free to move away, but she stood, uncertain, nibbling her thumbnail and worrying about not really pulling her weight to help set up the library. But no way was she letting go of Obi's lead in such an alien environment. No way at all.

"I'll have to make it up later," she told the dog. "Give *Dida Krila*'s winches a proper strip down and greasing. Cook a really nice supper."

It was three long summers since Natali had crewed a yacht. To say she was grateful to Ana was the underestimation of the century, so she wanted to show it in everything she did. The last few days had been absolute bliss, finally doing the work she'd been trained for. And more importantly, it had been a great life for Obi, being fussed and spoilt by all three of them, and having company all the time. For the past couple of years she'd scraped a living taking kitchen and cleaning jobs, and the long hours had meant Obi was often alone. It was so not fair on the little dog, and there'd even been times when she'd wondered if keeping her was really the right thing to do. But there was no way she could let her go. Not now. Life would be so very empty without her.

She only wished she could get on as well with her crew mates as Obi did. Oh, they were perfectly nice just, well, clever. Not one, but both of them, had been to university, while she'd left school at fifteen.

Lloyd was especially alien. An older man who was perfectly willing to and capable of helping with domestic tasks, who seemed interested in her, asked questions, yet didn't push or press her when she couldn't find the words to answer him. Or, most importantly, when her stammer returned halfway through a sentence, he didn't try to finish it for her.

"Why can't I ever think of anything remotely interesting to say?" Even Obi wasn't listening, having left the protection of

Natali's legs to investigate an empty crate. But Natali knew the answer anyway: it was because she was stupid. And when you were stupid, by far the best strategy was to keep your mouth firmly shut.

She'd had no choice but to leave school as soon as she could, but she'd hated it anyway, and being out at work had brought so many advantages. Earning money had been the main one – saving, so she could afford to rent her own tiny bedsit away from her mother and her constant stream of boyfriends. Not being bullied and generally looked down on had been another. And on top of these riches, she had made the miraculous discovery there was something she was good at after all.

Her first job had been cleaning in a yacht charter business. For some reason, the woman who ran the workshop had decided Natali was good at mending things, so had trained her as a mechanic. All right, she had no formal qualifications, but she could fix just about anything that could go wrong on a yacht, which had led to her crewing on charters. Until Covid. Until Obi. Until the endless drudgery of low-paid jobs and living in dives, trying to stay positive, but always one step away from eviction when her money dried up or the tourists came back. But this summer, this summer, everything was going to be fine.

"It won't be if I stand around dreaming all day, Obi. Time for your walk." She eyed the steep road leading to the upper reaches of the village. It was shaded by wonderful, cloud-shaped trees and would no doubt be peaceful, but it was unlikely she'd find any shops up there and she needed bread and something for supper.

"Not today," she told Obi. "We'll explore the waterfront

instead," and she set off past the massed boxes and crates waiting for the ferry, towards the path that edged the rocky shore.

The aromas of the quayside were far too tempting for the dog, who kept stopping to look around her and sniffing the air. Natali had almost persuaded her as far as the bench in front of the ticket office, when the elderly woman sitting there clicked her fingers and Obi leapt up, scrabbling her front paws on her skirt and gazing at her adoringly.

"I am s-so s-sorry," Natali stammered.

The woman looked up at her and smiled from beneath her wide-brimmed straw hat, her face deeply tanned and covered in a patchwork of fine lines.

"It's not your fault. I did try to attract your dog's attention, and it's nice he's friendly. What's his name?"

"It's Obi … and she's a her."

The woman fondled Obi's ears. "Then I apologise, young ladies."

Obi needed no further invitation to jump onto the woman's lap, winding herself into the floral fabric of her skirt. Natali was about to apologise again when Obi's new friend gestured to the empty end of the bench.

"Given Obi has decided she needs a rest, may I suggest you join us?"

Obediently, Natali perched on the edge of the wooden seat, Obi's lead clutched between her fingers. What now? How long would she be trapped here when she should be working? But she couldn't be rude, she really couldn't.

"And what is your name?" the woman asked.

"Natali."

She racked her brain for a way to fill the short silence, but her companion beat her to it. "And I'm Baka Valentić. I've lived here forever and I'm as old as the hills. Everyone knows me, but I don't know you."

"I w-work on a catamaran. We're taking a l-library around the islands for the children."

Baka nodded. "Ah yes, I heard. My neighbour's going to bring her boy to choose a book in English, but I do wonder if he'll read it. I'm sure he would rather be swimming or on his bicycle with his friends."

Natali nodded, unsure what she was expected to say. If anything. Maybe she could just listen while Baka rambled on. More people were beginning to gather on the quay for the ferry, so maybe she wouldn't have to stay too long.

"You're a shy one behind those pretty blue eyes, aren't you?" Baka said softly.

Natali shrugged, but all the same a small surge of gratitude welled up in her. Most people thought she was rude or standoffish. At least somebody understood what she was somehow unable to say, even if it was a random old lady. In that case a shrug was a far from adequate reaction, so she nodded. It still didn't feel enough. Words it would have to be.

"I'm g-glad you don't think I'm unfriendly."

"No, I don't think that at all, but even so, a little conversation would be nice, if you can manage it."

What could she say? Her eyes darted around in panic, the increasing activity as more of the funky, motorised tractor-trailers began to arrive giving her an idea.

"You're waiting for the f-ferry?"

The woman beamed. "In a way. I am waiting for my son.

He went to America many years ago and I have not seen him since."

"But that's w-wonderful he's coming home!"

"I have missed him. Every day I have missed him. My eldest boy lives in Split, but it is not the same."

Natali fiddled with Obi's lead. "America ... it's such a long way."

"Too far," said Baka firmly, "but when he left there was nothing here. No money you see, after the war. No future. But he promised me that one day he would come back."

As if on cue the ferry rounded the headland with a blast of its whistle, and Natali stood. "I must give Obi her walk, and leave you to m-meet him. It's been nice talking to you."

"And to you, Natali."

Having chosen the lower path, Natali now had to walk past the library. Should she stop to speak to Lloyd? This could be so awkward. While ignoring him was inconceivable, he was actually working so she was sure he wouldn't want to be bothered with her. What if she spoke and he didn't reply? What if she didn't and he called after her?

He'd set up the table and brightly coloured burgundy, blue and white pop-up banner with the library's name on a small hardstanding built over the rocks that edged the bay. Next to Lloyd was a young man selling local honey and olive oil from under a huge faded red umbrella, and to Natali's huge relief they were talking to each other. A nod and a wave would be fine after all.

Obi was having none of it. She caught Natali off-guard with an excited little bark when she saw Lloyd, and he turned towards them, grinning.

"Come to see how we're getting on?"

Natali nodded.

"It's been a slow start for both of us"—he gestured towards his neighbour—"but Marin here will be busy when the trip boats come in. Not sure I'll see anyone though, with so few people living on the island."

Well, he would see Baka Valentić's neighbour and her child, but somehow the words to tell him stuck in Natali's throat. She was useless, bloody useless. She should at least try. But even as she was attempting to form the sentence, Marin asked Lloyd if he'd be here all summer, and to her intense relief the moment passed.

Continuing along the narrow path, to her right the sea was as clear and blue as she'd ever seen it, fish darting to and fro as the water lapped the rocky edges of the tongue-shaped bay. The slopes above were filled with various shades and shapes of green, studded here and there with long pinnacles of cypresses, the white-washed walls and orange-brown roofs of the houses peeping through randomly to complete the prettiest of pictures.

The tiny village square was bordered by a couple of cafés with tables next to the water, so of course Obi wanted to investigate every single one. They must smell amazing with all the things that people dropped, and Natali didn't have the heart to deny her. Thankfully it was too early for there to be many people about, although two old boys sat under an awning just outside a café door, chatting to a waiter who had a pile of ashtrays in his hand.

At the quayside a blue and white fishing boat rocked in the gentle swell, crates of octopus and mullet balanced on its stern, and beyond the cafés a squat, thick-trunked palm tree dominated the square, half hiding the tiny supermarket behind it, which was obviously her first port of call.

A rack of brightly coloured plastic beach toys and jelly shoes outside the door was topped by a metre-long inflatable crocodile, its colour faded some distance from the bright green it was meant to be. Even so, a memory stirred in Natali; yet another day from her childhood she'd tried to forget, but here it was, all the same. Some girls from her class had been messing around in the sea with a crocodile just like that, and although she'd crossed the road to avoid them, they'd still seen her, calling at her to join in, then jeering when she wouldn't. *Tupka Natali, Natali tupka.* Their sing-song voices made her flesh crawl even now.

How could she have gone into the water? She hadn't even possessed a bathing costume – there'd never been money for luxuries like that. Thank goodness one of her unofficial cousins had grown out of theirs before she'd had to take swimming classes at school. Even so, it hadn't fitted properly and after a while she'd pretended to have athlete's foot to get out of the lessons. Working on yachts, she'd often regretted not having learnt to swim properly, and although she could just about doggy-paddle she still hated being out of her depth.

But for now, she needed to shop. Which meant leaving Obi outside in a place she didn't know. If only she'd asked Lloyd to mind her, but she hadn't, so that was that. She couldn't go back now. She'd just have to trust that Donje Čelo was an honest place and tie her to the nearest lamp-post.

"I won't be long," she told her.

Trying to ignore Obi's baleful look, Natali dived into the shop's dark interior. Her nose led her straight to a freshly baked loaf, but the vegetable racks were all but empty – just a few, sad, over-squishy tomatoes no one in their right mind would buy. The woman sitting at the till saw her looking and called out that there would be more when the ferry unloaded. This ferry or the next one, she wasn't sure. So Natali paid for the bread and hurriedly retrieved Obi, who barked with delight when she saw her.

This could have been a significant setback as far as supper was concerned, but on the nearby fishing boat a man in a navy cap was wrapping something in newspaper and handing it to a woman with a pushchair. Natali brightened. The fish was for sale. Simply fried fresh mullet would be wonderful, and she was sure there were chips in the catamaran's freezer. She'd just have to hope that some salad stuff or green beans arrived on the island before she and Obi finished their walk.

Already the weird lawnmower-trailers were making their way from the quayside, laden with boxes and crates of beer and soft drinks. One headed past her towards the hotel in the far corner of the bay, and another ground to a halt in front of the shop. She saw little point in gawping at them while they unloaded, so she decided to explore a little more.

Just beyond a *konoba* set back from the path, Obi began to pant. Stopping on the scrappy piece of grass next to a children's play park, she took the pop-up dog bowl from her rucksack and filled it from her water bottle, watching as Obi lapped noisily. Around her the wash of waves and the thrum of cicadas swelled, broken only by the putter of a small boat. Now this was more like the peaceful island she'd expected, so different in every way to the bustling city where she'd grown up.

If Obi was thirsty then Lloyd might be too, so she retraced

her steps with the intention of asking him before completing her shop. But as she neared the library she saw a mother with two young children, maybe about four and seven years old, in front of the table.

Lloyd crouched down, presumably to listen to what the older child was saying. Almost immediately the boy laughed, as did his mother, the sound drifting over the gentle lap of the waves. He was clearly a natural with kids, but then not only was he a teacher, but he had a daughter of his own. Grown up now, of course, but they must be close because he'd spoken to her every night.

What must it be like to have family like that? Natali had always told herself you couldn't miss what you didn't know, but watching Lloyd with the children made her feel strange inside. She'd barely met her father, and she and her mum weren't close at all. Unsurprisingly, when everything Natali did annoyed her. Even the women she called her aunties weren't her mother's sisters; they were just her friends, their children not really Natali's cousins at all. And her grandparents certainly didn't want to know her. They had been ashamed of Mama for being an unmarried mother, so of course they were ashamed of their granddaughter too.

And as for her other grandparents in Sweden ... she didn't even know if they existed. Well, they must have done at some point for her father to have been born, but she could remember so little about him. He'd stopped coming to see them when she was about four, once he'd married and started a family of his own. A better family, she supposed. Not like her and her *mama*. The only thing she could recall was his straw-blond hair and almost white skin. The skin and hair she'd inherited which, together with the stammer, had meant she'd been mercilessly teased at school.

"No point even thinking about bad stuff," she told Obi, who looked up at her, tail wagging. That's what Auntie Stela had always taught her: stay positive, and you'll be surprised how many good things happen. And she was right. More often than not, anyway. After all, Natali had work for a whole ten weeks, and a place for her and Obi to live. If she stuck to the mantra, who knew what other good things might come her way?

As they sailed towards their berth for the night in Lopud's harbour, Lloyd closed his eyes and let the peacefulness of the moment settle over him – the wash of the Mediterranean against the catamaran's hulls, her gentle creak as she skimmed the water, the late afternoon sun filtering through the rippling sail. If he could, he would bottle this and take it with him for whenever he needed a moment of calm.

God, he sounded just like that mindfulness app Ruth had tried to persuade him to download. Smiling to himself, he took a sip of his tea. He had ten weeks to enjoy these evening sails from one island to the next and he was going to make the most of them, here on the fly deck, lounging on the comfortable sofas as Ana sat up front and steered, and Natali scurried around below them, doing whatever Natali did.

She was a nice kid, Natali, and it was such a shame she was hampered by her stammer. It was hard to encourage more than a few words out of her, and he wished he could do something to help. What wasn't useful, he was sure, was Ana finishing

Natali's sentences for her, but he didn't know her well enough to mention it just yet. After all, it was probably only because he'd spent his working life with teenagers that he was sensitive to that sort of thing.

Although they'd been few and far between, his encounters with the local children today had convinced him Ruth had been right to push him to apply for this job. He'd all but forgotten how much he missed it.

"You look happy." Ana turned to face him, the breeze licking her hair around her face.

"So do you. I'm relieved, as well, to have the first day under our belt. I'll be less nervous now that I know what I'm doing. And on an island of two hundred souls, I guess five books wasn't too bad for the start of the school holidays."

"Five?"

"Yes. The teenage lad took two fantasy novels. Said he was a fast reader." Lloyd grinned. "We had a little chat in German too. I'm not as rusty as I thought."

Ana nodded, then centred the boom before calling down to Natali to prepare the headsail to tack. They were sailing up the channel between the dark green tree-cloaked hills of the mainland and the island of Lopud, the sea sparkling around them, the sky the palest of blues above, as though it was bleached by the sun. To Lloyd's right a small harbour nestled below a random stagger of red-roofed villas on the steep slope behind it, a band of tall cypresses stretching their fingers up from the grey rocky shore.

On *Dida Krila*'s port side Lloyd could see they were coming to the end of the island. Above him the mainsail flapped, then cracked to attention as the catamaran came about in a wide arc, ready to sail around a densely wooded headland. In the middle distance, over Ana's shoulder, a long, low hillside tapered into the sea, and remembering the charts she'd shown them he knew they must be coming into the protective bay which housed both the village of Lopud and its harbour.

After a short while Natali climbed the steps and, as Ana steered the catamaran into the breeze, he helped her to pull down the sail and fold it neatly over the spar. Their peace was shattered by the motor bursting into life, and in no time they were cruising in front of the high walls of an ancient monastery, its needle-like church tower pointing skywards, the ruins of a castle dominating the hillside behind it.

The triangular harbour was already crowded with motorboats and wooden fishing craft with colourful stripes around their hulls, and Ana slowed to enter the narrow gap between the outstretched concrete moles. Lloyd followed Natali down the steps and onto the transom, waiting for Ana to steer them onto their mooring. The fenders already in place, he steadied himself while Natali jumped onto the quay, then threw the ropes after her, one at a time. She nodded her thanks, smiling in that shy way of hers, while Obi gambolled around Lloyd's legs, no doubt excited to see dry land with its endless opportunities for exploration. He'd noticed that when they were on the move she curled up in her basket under the table, which made him wonder whether the tiny terrier was in fact not the best of sailors.

The engine cut out, giving way to birdsong from the trees sheltering the kiosks that lined the landward quay, trilling above the pop music from a yacht moored a few boats away from them. His peaceful hour was over. Time to get back into the real world.

Ana joined them, stuffing her phone into the pocket of her

shorts. "I need to stretch my legs after spending most of the day on the boat. Does anyone fancy a stroll and a beer before supper?"

Lloyd told her that sounded like an excellent idea, but Natali shook her head. "I will s-stay here, prepare the fish."

"There's no need," said Ana. "We can all pitch in once we get back."

Natali smiled weakly, then shook her head again before disappearing into the galley, Obi at her heels.

"I thought she might have wanted to walk the dog," Lloyd said as they strolled past two golf buggies parked in the shade of the palm trees. Ana made a non-committal noise, then began to explain to Lloyd that as Lopud was another car-free island the buggies were used for the shuttle service to transfer tourists to Šunj Beach on its opposite coast.

"It's only a half-hour stroll, but in the temperatures we're having they're certainly needed."

"It isn't normally this hot in June?"

"No way. They say it'll touch forty degrees next week, so there's bound to be a storm at some point. Let's just hope it's when we're moored up snugly somewhere like this."

They stopped at the end of the row of trees, under a huge holm oak. The library table would be set out under its boughs, next to a blue and white painted tourist kiosk selling boat trips, so at least there would be some shade. For most of the day he'd been envying Marin's umbrella and hoping he could track one down before next Monday. At the very least he needed to buy a wide-brimmed sun hat, and given the number of shops and bars ahead of them, this could well be the place to do it.

They followed the promenade as it edged the broad sweep of the bay, a narrow sand and shingle beach fringing the sea to their right. Unlike Koločep with its steep hills, here the village was built on more gently sloping land, with space for citrus and olive groves; it was away from the coastal strip, and there were even small fields between the houses. Although most of the buildings bordering the water were traditional two-storey ones of old stone and red roofs, at the far end, about half a mile away, was a massive white creation, completely out of scale with the village, and giving the vague impression of a pair of chained cruise ships straining to break free of the land.

"I guess that horror's the hotel," he said.

Ana screwed up her face. "It brings people here, brings money, jobs – at least for the summer – so it can't be all bad."

"So the island economies are still pretty seasonal?" Shit. He hadn't meant to say "still". Hadn't wanted to mention he'd been to Croatia before. He'd been dreading Ana asking why he spoke a little of the language, but by some miracle she hadn't. She probably thought he'd learnt it online to get the job.

"God, yes," she replied. "It's the reason young people are moving to the mainland in their droves." Most likely Mirjana had done the same as soon as the war was over, so Korčula should hold no guilty secrets for him now, and the quicker he managed to convince his dumb brain that was the case, the better.

He focussed back on Ana. "So what do you do in the winters?"

"Well the first thing is to put *Dida Krila* into dry dock and get any maintenance done. And, quite frankly, when I was chartering from April to October I needed to catch up on my sleep. Then the last few years I've been helping out in my parents' business; all the big restaurants want oysters during the festive season."

Ah yes, she'd said over the weekend that her folks were oyster farmers. It hadn't been the most relaxed couple of days, truth be told, and perhaps some of that had been his fault. Very often people didn't know how to react when he told them he was a widower, and Ana, and Natali in particular, were young after all. But the fact remained, losing Jenny had been a life-changing moment and was too important not to mention. He just had to be very careful that from here on in, it didn't define him in their eyes. He needed to show them he was moving beyond it.

He returned his attention to Ana. "So is oyster farming a family business?"

"Yes. For generations back. There are only a few licences and we're lucky to have one. It's a hard way to make a living, back-breaking manual labour, but if you do it right you can earn good money. Tata and Mama have bolted on some tourist stuff too – boat trips to the oyster beds, tastings, linking up with local wineries."

"Sounds interesting."

"I'll arrange to take you one weekend, if you like."

"I'd love that, but for the moment, before we grab that beer I need to find a better hat. My baseball cap just didn't cut it today."

Ana frowned. "We need to get you an umbrella or something. I should have thought of it."

"It's difficult to know what we'll need until we've seen all the library pitches. Look, here's somewhere selling tourist garb so I guess they'll have hats."

Ana was still scowling. Was it something he'd said? He ran back over his words, but he didn't think so. Then it struck him; perhaps she was beating herself up over the umbrella in the way she had over the sack trolley? If she honestly believed she had the monopoly on ideas it could end up feeling like a long old summer. He needed to lighten the moment.

"You'll have to help me choose though. Ruth always says I have terrible taste and we can't bring the library into sartorial disrepute."

Thankfully Ana smiled and followed him into the shop.

Šipan

WEDNESDAY 21ST JUNE

Wrapping her sarong over her bikini, Ana crept from the catamaran, treading as lightly as she could so as not to wake the others. It was barely five o'clock but she felt as though she had hardly slept, the hot sheet twisting around her legs as worry after worry assailed her – some big, some small, some absolutely microscopic in the relative cool of the dawn. She needed to get a grip.

She hopped onto the deserted quayside and slid her feet into her flip-flops before heading away from the village. To her left, the first rays of sunshine were clambering over the dark outcrops of the mountains on the mainland, and slowly, one after the other, the birds in the trees lining the road were filling the air with their song. A new day; their first on Šipan. What would it bring?

That was worry number one. While Koločep had been just about OK in terms of the overall population, Lopud had been a big disappointment. Only two books had been loaned out – both Croatian ones to mothers with young children. She'd honestly expected more from the place, and on and off all night she'd been fretting about whether they'd see anyone at all today. The way things were going, the numbers on her first weekly report to Ivana would look pretty damn thin.

She took the narrow path which forked from the road, luxuriating in the soft carpet of pine needles beneath her feet as she wound her way through the rosemary and rock rose clinging to the slope. The sea glittered below her, inviting and azure, and she hoped she could find the tiny beach she'd spotted as they motored into the bay last night.

Ana rarely took the crystal waters of Dalmatia for granted, but the sea around the Elafiti Islands had a special clarity all its own. Every rock, every fish, shimmered just beneath the water. Gin-clear, Lloyd had called it last night, having run out of superlatives. Gin-clear. Such a peculiarly English phrase, but Ana could not dispute its accuracy.

It was hard not to like Lloyd, despite her initial reservations about having a man on board. After only a few days, it was impossible to see him as the threat to her equilibrium that she'd feared; he was gentle, kind, and certainly respectful. She'd been shocked when he'd told them he was a widower, shocked and saddened, and she hadn't really known what to say. He was too damn nice to have lost his wife so young, and although he'd said he was well over the worst of it now, perhaps it explained the moments he seemed to withdraw into himself. She tried to imagine Tata without Mama, and guessed he would be the same.

Natali was the one who remained an enigma. Oh, she was hard-working enough and knew her job, but she was so comprehensively silent. Did she find Ana and Lloyd too old and boring to bother with? She seemed quite young for twenty-two, but it could be because she looked that way with her elfin face and close-cropped hair. And did it really matter if she was quiet? Well, it did if it meant something wasn't right. They were going to be together all summer, so it was important to have a happy ship as well as an efficient one.

After the library numbers, Natali was worry number two. But was she bigging it up too much? That's what Meri had implied when she'd spoken to her about it. After all, the youngster did have a bit of a stammer, so maybe that made talking hard. It was odd because she'd barely noticed it when she'd interviewed her, but Ana guessed it was one thing pulling out the stops for half an hour and quite another doing it all the time. It would just be nice if she made a bit more of an effort to be sociable.

Should she speak to her about it? Or would that make matters worse? That awful feeling of being out of her depth flooded through her again, Meri's almost instant dismissal of the problem making her feel even worse. Meri was normally right, but this time Ana couldn't quite shake the feeling that she should be doing something. Saying something. But what? She sighed to herself. Perspective, that's what she needed. But with all the other rubbish running around in her head, it was hard. Why were even the simplest of decisions like wading through mud?

Ana reached a place where she could drop from the path onto the triangular patch of shingle. The sun was higher now, the sea shifting and glistening just a few feet away, inviting her in with its siren call. Unknotting her sarong, she weighed it down with her flip-flops, then made her way to the water's edge.

She stopped, letting the coolness run across her ankles,

mesmerised by the ripples around her circling ever outwards. Small fish flicked this way and that, and she watched them for a moment before wading slowly into deeper water, the caress of the waves on her calves, her knees, her thighs. Finally, she dipped her shoulders, surrendering to its embrace with slow arcs of breaststroke, washing the night away.

After a while she stopped and floated on her back, closing her eyes against the burnished golds of the sunrise behind her, willing the sense of oneness with nature to bring her back to herself. The wash and pop of the water in her ears calmed her, but only a little, and soon she began to feel cold so she struck out for the shore.

Emerging from the water, rubbing the salt from her eyes, a man on the beach was absolutely the last thing Ana wanted to see. There was no way out of the encounter; the triangle of shingle was impossibly small, and her flip-flops and sarong were just feet in front of him. He, in his turn, seemed in no hurry to get in, lazily taking off his top and stretching to reveal a tanned, muscular chest covered in a fine fuzz of dark hair.

"*Dobro jutro*," he called as she stood in the lacy edges of the waves, wringing the moisture from her hair. "What's it like today?"

"Refreshing. Peaceful."

His eyebrows arched. "Is that a hint?"

She nodded, retrieving her sarong as he stepped away, and wrapping it around her, aware that in a wet bikini her curvy figure left little to the imagination. "Could be. I haven't had my coffee yet." Had that come over as impossibly rude? She hoped not.

The low sun sparkled in his dark eyes. "Then the advantage is mine. Enjoy your day." He strode past her and within moments she heard a gentle splash. She turned. Strong arms and shoulders propelled him forwards towards the rocks in a smooth rhythm. A very good swimmer, with a body to match. But the main thing was that he'd been perceptive enough to leave her in peace.

Unlike her ex-boyfriend Pajo, who'd called her at some ungodly hour last night. Not that she'd picked up, but she hadn't been able to resist listening to his message telling her his job was bringing him back to Dubrovnik. She mustn't let it get to her; obviously he was going to be looking up old friends. And old friends they were because they'd known each other since childhood and the way their relationship had ended had been as amicable as they come.

Maybe too amicable. Was that why she was feeling so uneasy? Did he have a particular reason for contacting her? Five years after their break-up? Did it have the significance she feared, or was it just a coincidence? *Sranje!* She had enough to worry about without Pajo.

Feeling well and truly grumpy, Ana walked slowly back towards the harbour. If a swim hadn't done the trick, then surely coffee would. She hadn't lied to the man on the beach – that was exactly what she needed. She'd take her mug onto the fly deck to dry off in the warmth of the morning and she'd think about good things, soothed by the view of Suđurad Bay, its houses clustered around the ragged expanse of grass that served as the village square, guarded by the hills which rose on either side and plunged into the water to provide the perfect anchorage. She'd enjoy it all before the others even got up.

Everything was quiet when she boarded *Dida Krila* and a small amount of the calm she'd struggled to find in the water wrapped itself around her troubled soul. Finally, finally, perhaps she could win against the night. She mustn't take her grouchiness out on her crew. It would be unprofessional. And might even give them a hint that she didn't feel fully in control, which was the very last thing she wanted.

Setting the larger *džezva* on the stove, she watched the bubbles rise and fall in the enamel jug as the water began to boil. Spooning coffee into the smaller one, the bitterness tingled the inside of her nose when she poured the boiling water onto the grounds, setting it back on the stove and stirring, stirring, stirring, losing herself in the dark swirling liquid.

Dida Krila wobbled and Ana looked up to see Natali on the transom, Obi in her arms. So much for a peaceful coffee.

"I am s-so sorry," said Natali.

Had her irritation shown on her face? "What for?" Somehow the mild enquiry came out a little too sharply.

"Coffee ... b-breakfast ... it's my job."

Could she not even make herself a drink in her own galley? "Of course it isn't, Natali." The girl's face fell. Oh god, she really wasn't being fair. The last thing she wanted was to make things worse. "We're a small crew. We're a team. It's wonderful you've been making us coffee in the mornings, but it certainly doesn't hurt me to do it for once."

Natali turned away. "I'll feed Obi," she muttered. "Then m-make breakfast."

"There's no rush."

"But she is h-hungry after her walk."

Ana took a mug from the shelf and filled it. There'd be no peace with Natali banging and crashing around. "Oh well. Help yourself from the *džezva*. I'm taking mine back to bed."

Natali nodded, her head still in the cupboard, pretending to look for the dog food, which Ana could see was right in front of her. God, the girl made everything so bloody awkward, even when she seemed as though she was trying to be helpful. And then, to cap it all, she heard Lloyd whistling in his cabin. Bugger the both of them. She just had to hope that coffee and a shower would improve her mood. She needed at least to act like a reasonable human being, even if she didn't feel like one.

Korčula

FRIDAY 23RD JUNE

Why, this morning of all mornings? A dream so real Lloyd had expected to find Jenny's warmth beside him when he woke. He'd been sure it wouldn't happen in his cabin on *Dida Krila*, but now he knew he'd been wrong.

And yet ... and yet ... it had been different, in a way. The yearning for her was the same, but the punch of agony had not come. Perhaps he was beginning to put a little distance between himself and his grief after all. Or perhaps something else, something more pressing, was on his mind.

Ah, here was a feeling he'd come to know rather too well in recent months – guilt. Not the survivor's guilt he'd suffered when the numbness began to fade after Jenny died; this guilt was bitter because it was all his fault. His actions had caused it; he'd earned it, almost. But it was hardly a badge of honour, and what was more, with Korčula quite literally on the horizon, this shiny new guilt was reaching down inside him to find an old, almost forgotten friend.

Bloody Korčula. At least they wouldn't ever be staying on the island overnight. In and out quickly ... just a few hours each week. Thankfully berths in the marina were a precious commodity during the summer months, so last night they had moored off Badija Island, the imposing walls of its former monastery rising as if from the sea, and he'd spent the evening determinedly looking towards it, rather than at Korčula's shoreline behind him.

Now the catamaran was chugging forwards in the morning sunshine, surging inexorably towards the old town, while he sat at the table, his gaze fixed firmly on his mug of tea. He knew he couldn't stay there all day, however much he wanted to. He had a job to do, and that job meant stepping onto the island for the first time in over thirty years. So perhaps the return of his guilt was inevitable, but it was pretty hard to cope with alongside the otherworldly fragility left by the dream. More than anything he wanted to curl back under his duvet and rejoin Jenny in the oblivion of sleep. What he needed to do was to stand, head out onto the deck and look Korčula old town in the eye. Face up to it, move on.

It was only after meeting Jenny that the feelings relating to his time on Korčula had begun to fade. He'd completed his teacher training, found his first job and thrown himself into it, all the while scouring the newspapers for reports of the war in Croatia. But then, just as peace seemed to be on the horizon, he had met Jenny, and slowly but surely he'd realised he could find happiness again.

He'd never told her about Korčula but, by some miracle, loving her, and her loving him, had closed the door on the guilt and pain. He'd been able to move beyond that fateful summer into a new life, and it became almost as though Korčula had happened to someone else. But without Jenny, and stirred up by actually being here, that old life, his young and foolish life, was creeping back. And he'd need to find every last iota of mental strength he could summon to stop it.

God, he was wallowing. Ruth would have something to say about it if she knew. Where was his backbone? It was only a place. A place. He stood abruptly, almost knocking his empty mug to the floor, and stalked onto the deck.

It was a shock to discover they were closer than he had expected, heading straight for the old town, heaped onto its peninsula. Nothing had changed over the years, but it was a UNESCO World Heritage Site, so why would it have? Still that teardrop-shaped hump of land jutting into the sea; still the jumbled, terracotta roofscape cascading down from the slender grey tower of Sveti Marco Cathedral; still the tree-lined esplanade overlooking the water below.

In the morning light, and viewed from the sea, it was even more beautiful than Lloyd remembered. The stones he knew to be grey were washed pink and gold and every shade between as *Dida Krila* rocked towards them, over the wake of a fast-cat ferry. They were so close now that he could see a waiter shaking out tablecloths, the billowing white lifted by the gentlest of breezes, which in turn carried the aroma of rich, meaty *pašticada* towards him.

Was the *pašticada* from then, or now? Seeing the old town again, the memories flooded back from the day Mirjana had first walked him around its circumference, a stolen half-hour between buying his uniform for her father's *konoba* and going back to begin his first shift.

Mirjana's *mama*, Kosana Bilić, insisted on accompanying them to Korčula town. At first Lloyd wondered if it had been to chaperone her daughter, or simply to sign the cheque for his two pairs of black uniform trousers and three white shirts. Already this family was making an investment in him, willing him to stay for the summer, when he himself was far from sure. But Mirjana was so damned lovely it was impossible to pass up the chance to get to know her a little better.

Shopping complete, Kosana took refuge from the heat of the morning in a café, suggesting Mirjana show Lloyd something of the famous old town. Leaving the quaintly old-fashioned outfitters, they strolled through the narrow maze of streets between old town and new. Lloyd soon discovered that most of the useful shops were on this flat strip of land – the grocer, the baker, the electrical store, as well as several places selling clothes.

Mirjana stopped in front of a window with a display of tops in bright highlighter-pen colours, a look of longing in her eyes.

"You like them?" he asked.

"The colours are amazing."

"I think the green would suit you ... or the blue..." He pointed to a crop top with the slogan "Just Do It", and the thought of her voluptuous figure squeezed into it sent his imagination into overdrive. "How about that one?"

Mirjana shook her head. "Oh, no. I'm completely the wrong shape."

"I don't think you're the wrong shape at all—" he blustered, then ground to a halt. He wasn't meant to notice her curves, was he? He was just the new waiter, and it made him sound like some sort of creep. A flush of embarrassment rode up his cheeks, but she laughed. Not at him, but with him. And it felt so good.

Until she snapped them back to reality. "Come on, we have half an hour at the most. Tata needs us back by eleven."

Leaving the maze of backstreets, they ambled past the tiny crescent of beach, then strolled along the quayside beneath the old town walls. In front of the arches which protected the colonnade from the sun, the oleanders were coming into bloom, and above them palm trees swayed in the gentlest of breezes. Higher still, tall, narrow houses rose, packed together on their almost perfectly oval hump of land, golden-grey stone and red roofs topped by the cupola of the cathedral.

Mirjana turned to him. "I know you want to see it all, but today shall we just walk around the outside? Then perhaps we can come back another morning on the bus so I can show you the rest."

"I'd like that."

"So would I." The phrase was simple, but there was such warmth in her dark eyes it seemed they held a message only for him. Which was a frankly ridiculous thought because her next words were a detailed and factual explanation of how the ferry that ran to and from Orebić on the mainland was Korčula's lifeline, but that for most of the year the traffic went both ways, with children from the mainland town attending high school on the island. So he asked about the education system in Croatia, telling her that he wanted to be a teacher himself.

She smiled up at him. "What made you choose that particular career?"

"It was the teachers I had at school. Some of them were

really inspirational, especially for a working-class lad with a single mother. I'd never even have thought about going to university without their input. Never known that I could. So I want to repay that debt and help other children like me."

"And what will you teach?"

"Languages are my thing. I'm not much good at anything else, to be honest. So German, with French as my second subject." He laughed. "I don't think there'll be much call for Croatian … and anyway, I won't learn enough, will I? Won't really experience…"

Mirjana stopped next to the most seaward of the round towers, between the wall that protected the town from the ocean and the old stone houses, one of which was now a bar, even at this early hour pumping disco music from its open doors. "You mean, in just one summer? Assuming you do decide to stay, that is."

Was her question loaded? It was impossible to tell.

"Assuming your father decides he wants me to." He walked on a little way, then stopped. "Are you saying, for just one summer, it isn't worth it?" Two could play at being obscure, but obscurity wasn't what he wanted, and he kicked himself inwardly.

She shrugged. "You will need a little of the language to get by. And I will teach you, but I want something in return."

Trying to act cool, he raised an eyebrow. "A bright blue *baggy* T-shirt?"

"No, of course not. I want you to teach me German."

"Then we have a deal." He held out his hand and she shook it, the warmth of skin on skin stretching up his arm. She held on for a fraction, then dropped his fingers, and started to tell him about Marco Polo's connections with Korčula as they walked under the shade of the Aleppo pines, the waves washing on the rocks below them, slowly heading back towards the coffee shop where her mother was waiting.

But today there'd be no teenage Mirjana sending tingles up his arm and looking so goddam beautiful. No Kesten either, his fellow waiter, with his intense patriotism and swaggering zest for life. Kesten who'd been right after all. But Lloyd couldn't think of those things now. He needed to be positive, focus on the fact that despite the bittersweet memories that had engulfed him, he'd managed to look Korčula in the eye. Now he could go below and organise the books so he was ready to set up the library the moment they moored.

The marina, new since his last visit, was tucked into the flat neck of land on the less touristy side of the old town behind the bus station, and their instruction was to set up just outside its gates. Lloyd stopped in his tracks, taking in the constant to-ing and fro-ing of vehicles and the diesel fumes that choked the air. Was there honestly a worse place for children to come to a library? But what the hell could they do about it?

Looking across the road, he could see that a small park he remembered was still there, although now with a few more benches dotted along its gravel paths and trees which were sufficiently mature to offer a great deal of shade. A pitch beneath them would be perfect. Never mind that it was close to where he and Mirjana used to sit on the grass holding hands, waiting for the bus. Never mind all that. It simply wasn't relevant now.

Ana was noncommittal when he suggested it.

"It isn't where the authorities wanted us so perhaps we shouldn't make a fuss." She bit her lip. "But I do get that where they said isn't great. The pavement's too narrow, and too close to the traffic to be safe for the children, but all the same, I don't really know…" She stopped, shaking her head slowly.

It was a total no-brainer, but it wouldn't do to be sharp with her, just because he was struggling this morning. "Well how about we set up in the park and see if anyone moves us on? My bad if it all goes horribly wrong."

Ana huffed. "Someone to move us on would be one more person than we saw yesterday."

So that was what was eating her. He supposed it had been disappointing when no one at all had visited the library on Mljet, but he'd been too busy worrying about Korčula to think too much about it. He had to stop being so bloody self-absorbed – and sharpish. He was the librarian; it was up to him to work out how to get more families to use it, not wallow around in the past. If it was quiet again, he'd make a list of ideas.

"Today's a new day," he told himself as much as Ana, before marching back through the marina gates to collect the folding table and banner.

He didn't have long to wait for the first customers, a lady he judged to be in her forties with an excited gaggle of half a dozen children, who he'd watched her shepherd from a bus.

"Ah, there you are, under the trees. Excellent idea. Maybe just put the banner on the pavement, so more people will see you." Lloyd more or less pieced together her rapid-fire Croatian, then asked her to speak more slowly. "I will speak in English," she replied. "It is better for the children too. I am Kristina Mikulec and I am their teacher."

"But isn't it the school holidays?" Lloyd asked.

"Of course, but who will bring them to the library if I do not? Their parents are working, so we all came from Žrnovo together." She leant towards Lloyd conspiratorially. "Also I have promised them ice cream when they have chosen their books."

Kristina ushered the children towards the table, then stood back. Lloyd had wondered if she would advise them, but no, she was leaving that to him. He was being observed, albeit in a kindly manner, and when they were ready to leave twenty or so minutes later, she shook his hand.

"I think you'll be very good at this," she told him, "and I have a confession to make. I'm the island co-ordinator for the project. I look forward to seeing you next week."

Lloyd watched the children leave, chattering loudly and heading towards the old town with Kristina in the centre of the group. A co-ordinator who was so motivated she'd actually brought the kids to the library was amazing – a real bonus. He'd have to find out if she had an opposite number on Mljet. But he had little time to consider it, because three teenage girls arrived, two of them too shy to speak in a foreign language and the other practically fluent in German.

After that there was a steady trickle. Mainly older children, but some young mothers with pre-school kids, and all sorts of books were flying from the table, the list scribbled in his notebook lengthening by the hour. Now, at quarter past three, Ana appeared in front of him.

"You wanted some tea bags, didn't you? Natali said there are loads of different ones in the big supermarket at the top of the hill. If you go now you can be back in time to pack up."

"That's brilliant, thank you. I'm down to my last box already and I haven't seen any on the smaller islands."

"You won't. Only where English tourists are expected."

Away from the shady protection of the branches, sweat trickled between Lloyd's shoulder blades as he began to climb the steep pavement. Thank goodness it wasn't far; the sign on the wall of the shopping centre was already peeping over the trees below it. To his right a school lay silent and empty; closed up for the summer, the brightly painted walls of the playground echoing only the rumble of the traffic.

He stopped to catch his breath and gazed at it. Would he ever be able to teach again? Not bloody likely after what he'd done. All right, he'd resigned before anyone had pushed him, but it didn't make much odds; no school worth its salt would employ him with that sort of black mark against his name. So what would he do? What could he do with his future? He was only fifty-sodding-three. Apart from a reason to get up in the mornings, he needed to keep earning until his pension kicked in, but what he'd do once this summer was over, he couldn't imagine.

All he'd ever wanted was to teach; it was woven into the very fabric of who he was, as it had been for Jenny. Their shared passion had drawn them together – the belief that they could make a difference to the children in their care. Even, or perhaps especially, to the ones whom the world seemed to have given up on before their lives had properly begun. Which was why what he had done had been doubly unforgivable; a complete betrayal of everything they'd held dear.

In that terrible moment, another piece of his life with Jenny had fallen away, one of the few he'd had left. A part of himself too – his self-respect, his pride in a job well done. Somehow he needed to get that back, or at least something close to it. This summer was meant to be helping, but right at this moment, standing here, all but drowning in his memories... No, Kristina's words had to count for something. He must be doing OK.

Lloyd shook out his shoulders. Today had been a good day, a busy day – the first really successful one for the library. That had to be something to celebrate, so he'd buy a really nice bottle of wine – perhaps even something fizzy – along with his teabags. They could drink it as they sailed back to Ston for the weekend.

In the lobby of the supermarket his eyes took a moment to adjust to the artificial light, and he was still blinking through his sunglasses when he saw her. He whipped them off, the frame digging into his palm as he gripped them. The woman was some distance away, near the tills. No more than a dark silhouette, but after a moment colour suffused her T-shirt. Bright blue. Highlighter blue.

And he was twenty-one again, standing outside the window of a shop not half a mile from here. Standing next to Mirjana, her hand pressed to the glass. The laughter between them. The fizz of attraction.

A man behind nudged him with his trolley, and he stepped to one side, stuttering an apology, before looking towards the woman again. But it couldn't be... Of course it wasn't. This woman was young, younger than Ruth, even. It was just ... the shape of her face, the turn of her head, something about the careless way she slung her bag over her shoulder... No. How stupid. He must be imagining the likeness.

He was tired. Emotional. Frigging drained of everything. He'd wound himself up to expect a disaster on this goddam island, and this was not – *was not* – it. But come one did, a run-of-the-mill, everyday disaster at that: there were no sodding teabags. Fruit ones, herbal ones, green ones – Earl Grey, even. But no common or garden, plain, ordinary tea. Well, Prosecco it was then. Grabbing a couple of bottles he didn't much feel like opening, he headed for the exit.

Ston

SATURDAY 24TH JUNE

Everyone and everything was still asleep when Ana crept off *Dida Krila* and strolled under the harbourside trees, past the fishing boats and visiting yachts, and the tiny outdoor bar with its padlocked fridges and ashtrays uncleared from last night. Ahead of her, the solid grey towers and walls of Kaštio Fort both guarded Ston and hid its red roofs and honeyed stones from her view, the narrow tracks of the town's ancient walls snaking over the wooded hillside behind it. The fresh silence of the new day sparkled around her, and she took the deepest of breaths. It wouldn't last. It was going to be hot, hot, hot again later.

She unlocked her open-topped jeep and, sweeping the dust from the seat, jumped into it. It would take no more than ten minutes to reach her village on the shore of Malostonski Bay, its clear, calm waters so perfect for mussels and oysters. Farming them had given her family wealth and built the fine, three-storey house on the waterfront they still called home.

Normally Ana loved the freedom that being on board *Dida*

Krila brought her, but right now she needed to get away. If not from her boat, then certainly from her crew. Maybe a bit of distance would help her to properly analyse her growing unease that something wasn't quite right. It was so nebulous at times that she wondered if it was real, but yesterday evening Lloyd had become almost as withdrawn as Natali, so she knew she wasn't imagining it. What the hell was she doing wrong as skipper to make them both so miserable?

Turning off the main road, she wound through the narrow village streets, past modern weekend villas sitting cheek by jowl with smaller houses, the blue of the bay just visible between them. Purple and pink bougainvillea cascaded over garden walls, fluttering in the breeze from her jeep as it passed.

At this early hour she parked easily on the quayside, then she sat for a moment listening to the gentle ripple of sea against stone, mingling with the rhythmic murmur of cicadas. To her right her father's boats were moored in the harbour, the smart wooden *barka* for tourist trips alongside the smaller oyster farming craft. All would go out later; summer was the busiest time of year, and it was constantly in the news how Croatia was booming as a holiday destination.

Ana climbed from the jeep and crossed the parking area to the house, letting herself in through the wrought-iron garden gate at its side. Most of the downstairs was taken up by a workshop and office for the business, but at the back was a terrace and it was here she found her father, looking out over the walled garden as he contemplated the day ahead with a cup of coffee at his side. He was dressed for work in his habitual blue overalls, his thick hair as dark as ever, despite the fact he'd turn sixty next year.

He stood to greet her, enveloping her in a hug that almost

lifted her off her feet. "My darling girl, I was hoping you'd arrive before I have to go."

"I'll come with you, if you like."

He laughed. "I guess even you need your feet on dry land for a while, and anyway, the boat is fully crewed for today. Now, let me fetch more coffee, then we can talk."

Ana sat down and tipped back her head, gazing at the pale blue sky as she listened to his footsteps on the wooden stairs up to the kitchen. Beyond the terrace, her mother's chickens scratched around the shrubs that lined the high garden wall, barred as they were from the vegetable patch to her left, which was overflowing with tomatoes, beans and aubergines. Her parents didn't have to live this way. They could easily buy everything they wanted, but despite their wealth they preferred it, and Ana admired them for doing so.

Her father returned, setting *džezva* and cups on the table between them.

"So, how is your boat of books?"

Ana nodded, picking up her coffee. "It's ... OK."

"Which means that it probably isn't."

Ana shrugged, trying to put him off the scent. "It's been a slow start, but I guess that's to be expected. Except Korčula. That was all right. Pretty good, actually." Which, now she thought of it, made Lloyd's mood last night doubly strange. She checked herself; in the grand scheme of things, it wasn't that long since he'd lost his wife, so maybe she should give him the benefit of the doubt.

"The bigger the island the more children there are. It figures. You're on a hiding to nothing with some of the smaller places."

So did Tata not approve? Or was he just stating a fact?

A fact that he instinctively understood, yet she hadn't considered at all.

"Or you could say," he continued, "that you're providing a service whether anyone uses it or not. After all, with government money nobody expects a return, do they? Once it's been allocated it's there to spend."

That wasn't exactly the case with this project. Not given the reports she had to file and the emphasis on numbers. Numbers of visits to the library, numbers of books loaned out, loans as a proportion of permanent population... It made her head spin, and it was so important. This summer was a pilot, after all, and the funding for future years depended on its success. But she didn't want to disabuse her father – or, more to the point, give him an excuse to ever so casually mention her bringing *Dida Krila* into the family business if it didn't work out. Instead she nodded.

"So, Ana, are you going to tell me what's really bugging you?"

Why did there have to be something wrong? Because he wanted there to be? No, no, she was being so unfair; her *tata* wasn't like that. However, he clearly wasn't going to let this go, and common sense told her she should swallow her pride. Just a little, anyway. He was certainly the right person to talk to about her crew worries – especially since Meri had dismissed them so quickly. He'd been managing people for years.

But how to put this particularly nebulous problem into words? Did it even exist outside her own mind? But she had snapped at Natali again yesterday when all the girl had done wrong was fail to tell Ana she was about to apply new anti-slip coating to the foredeck. She should have been praising her proactivity. As skipper, she was responsible for her crew's happiness, and she was making a very poor job of it.

"Ana?"

"I'm thinking." Start with something she could nail down. Something that might be ... solvable. "It's Natali. She's not very ... well ... communicative."

Tata leant forwards, clutching his coffee cup. "In what way?"

Ana shrugged. "I don't know. It could just be a young-person thing, but she barely contributes when we chat in the evenings or over breakfast."

"And how does that affect the way she does her job?" Typical of him to be practical.

"It doesn't. Not at all. She's one of the best crew I've ever had. She seems to know what needs doing before I even ask her."

"Don't get me wrong, Ana, I really want to help here, but I'm struggling a bit with what the problem actually is."

"So you think I'm being too emotional about this?" They'd had words along these lines before, when she'd been buying *Dida Krila*, and the memory of it still smarted. Especially as the precarious position of her finances meant that in hindsight he might well have had a point.

"I didn't mean that. I'd just like to understand a bit more about it. This youngster's clearly worrying you, so let's talk it through."

He was right of course. She was just being prickly. She'd got up too early, that was all. Needed this coffee and then a shower. She sighed. "I just feel ... responsible. I recruited Natali and I want her to enjoy the summer, not just go through the motions. It'll make for a more efficient ship as well as a happier one."

Tata sipped his coffee. "It isn't just that she's a quiet sort of person?"

"She chats to her dog all the time."

"Maybe she prefers animals to people. I know there are days when I do. Sometimes I even prefer the company of molluscs to the idiots I have to deal with."

So he was comparing her crew to molluscs, was he? Of course he didn't mean that. What was wrong with her this morning? "Yet you do. Deal with them, that is."

"As we all do in the world of work. But you can't please everyone all the time, nor should you try to." Ana shot him a glance. "I know, I know. You think I sound like a broken record, and wanting to make people happy is a really nice thing. However, you can't run a business like that. Even as skipper, that isn't your job. Your crew's happiness is up to them. And only them."

She couldn't stand this line of attack. He just didn't get it. Ana stood, banging her knee on the underside of the table as she did so.

Her *tata* sighed. "And now you're going to switch off entirely, just because I've mentioned your people-pleasing tendencies. I don't know how I can—"

"I'm sorry, Tata. I'm tired and I need a shower. I will think about what you've said, honestly."

He laid his hand gently on her arm. "You can work this Natali business out. With or without my input. I have every faith in you. But first you need to decide what – or whose – the problem really is."

Which meant he thought it was hers. Was it so wrong of her

to want a happy ship? There were only three of them, after all. It wasn't like charter yachts, with guests coming and going. They were stuck with each other, and no one else, until the beginning of September.

She nodded. "Wise as ever."

"Remember, Ana, I have every fai—"

She bent down to kiss him. "I'm sorry I've been grouchy. I'll be fine by the time you come home, I promise." Before he could challenge her again, she ran up the stairs just as fast as she could.

Koločep

MONDAY 26TH JUNE

Natali pushed the tender away from the quayside, waving at Ana before patting down her pockets. Shopping list. Cash. That was all she needed. Obi was already straining her lead towards the crates waiting for the ferry, so it was definitely time to get on with their walk.

As they started across the concrete apron, Obi gave an excited bark of recognition, her tail wagging furiously. The old lady, Baka Valentić, was sitting on the same bench as before, just a few metres away from them.

"Ah Obi, Natali. It's lovely to see you." Baka patted her lap, and Obi leapt onto it, jerking Natali forwards on the end of her lead. "I'm sorry, my dear," Baka continued. "That was a rather silly thing to do. I don't always think. Probably a result of my advancing years."

"It's n-no problem. She's only a small dog after all."

Baka looked puzzled for a moment. "Ah, I see. Small dog, small tug."

"Yes." It seemed rude not to join Baka on the bench,

although she shouldn't chat for too long. Chat! That would be a fine thing. She wanted to, but…

"So how is your library going?"

Natali grimaced. "I think you were r-right and most children would rather play."

"Perhaps it is just early days. The more people see you here, the more they will talk about it, the more they will come… You know how it is on islands."

"Not really. I'm from Dubrovnik."

"And what is it like, living there?"

Natali screwed up her face. She'd never really thought about it before. She had nowhere to compare it with. "Noisy. Too many people. N-not like it is here. These smaller places are very d-different. Calmer. N-nicer, I think."

"And of course on the islands, people talk to you. And you are talking more today."

Was she? She supposed it hadn't felt like too much of a struggle to find the words, but then she didn't feel uncomfortable with Baka like she did some people. Probably because she liked Obi. For her part she'd be more than happy to sit here in silence while the old lady petted the dog, but then she remembered that last time Baka had said she wanted some conversation. Perhaps she was lonely, but wasn't her son…? Inspiration.

"How is your son's visit going?" she asked.

Baka's face was glowing with happiness. "He arrives today. On the next ferry, I hope."

"So he was delayed?" Baka must have been so disappointed.

"It is many, many years since I've seen him. He lives in America, you know. When he left, there was nothing here – no money, you see, after the war, no future. But he promised me that one day he would come back, and now he is."

Of course she'd told Natali this before, but she must be excited about seeing her son again. It was such a shame he'd been held up. Or maybe Baka had got muddled over the dates? She was pretty old, after all. That was the most likely reason, and at least he would be here soon.

Natali stood, lifting Obi onto the floor. "We must go now. Shopping to d-do. I hope you have a wonderful time with him," she said.

Baka leant down to give Obi a final stroke. "Thank you, Natali. I know I will."

Already it was too hot to climb very far up the hill, Obi slowing their progress as she stopped to sniff every bush and wall where another dog had left their mark.

"Fill your paws," Natali told her, figuring it was the dog's walk after all. "It'll take a while yet to unload the vegetables."

The path was lined with houses on either side, properties with generous gardens or groves of citrus around them, shuttered and still in the morning air. No doubt some were weekend or holiday homes, but others bore signs of habitation: washing hanging limply in search of a breeze, or a packet of cigarettes and coffee mug abandoned on a terrace table.

What it must be like to live in a whole house, especially one with space around it, was beyond Natali's imagination. To wake in the morning, not to the sound of traffic or the neighbours upstairs thudding about, but to the hum of cicadas. And then to step outside, watch Obi pad across the grass, sniff the shrubs in her own safe space and without a lead... It would be oh so wonderful, and something about these islands made her believe that maybe even ordinary people could live like that. Not her, obviously. Even Auntie Stela's mantra of positivity couldn't be quite that powerful, but all the same it was a wonderful dream.

Before long, Obi was panting and Natali filled her pop-up bowl with water, watching as she drank noisily.

"It isn't just you," she told her. "I'm thirsty too, and I bet Lloyd is as well. Let's hope there's something chilled in the fridge in the shop." She liked doing little things to make Lloyd smile. He was such a kind man, and it must have been awful for him when his wife died so young.

A path to their right wound down through the trees and they followed its shade until they reached the village square. Reluctantly leaving Obi tied to the lamp-post, Natali scooted into the minimarket's dark interior, blinking furiously as her eyes adjusted. A man with his sleeves rolled almost to his armpits was unpacking fruit and vegetables from cardboard boxes, practically throwing them onto the shelves, and Natali had to dodge an onion as she filled her bag with beans, chard and potatoes.

After peeping outside to check on Obi, who was perfectly happy being fussed by two small children, she dived back in, grabbed two bottles of cola from the fridge and a loaf of bread. Shopping complete, she paid the woman at the till and escaped into the sunlight.

It was as her eyes were adjusting that she noticed the man. Tall and thin with the very palest blond hair, he was wearing a pair of baggy combats, ill-matched with his polo shirt. As Natali watched, he dropped to one knee next to a café table, ostensibly to tie his shoelace, but did his hand flick into the beach bag next to him, then slide into his pocket? She couldn't be sure. Not sure enough to say anything. And how would she find the words, even if she was certain? Who would she tell? The woman with the expensive-looking sunglasses and manicured talons whose beach bag it probably was?

"Not on your life, Obi," Natali whispered. "She looks properly scary."

Oh, she knew saying nothing wasn't right, but she also knew her limitations. Steering clear of trouble was second nature and something her mother had instilled in her from a very young age.

What had she been? Ten or eleven? Working for the summer as a pot washer in the restaurant where her *mama* had been waiting tables. One day she'd noticed something odd: the chef giving meat to a man who she knew had a market stall, and rolls of *kuna* changing hands. She hadn't been so green as to not know what it meant, and that it was wrong, but when she'd told her mother she'd grabbed her by the shoulders so tightly it had really hurt.

"If you say a word to anyone it's you who'll be in trouble. You hear?" And Natali had nodded as Mama had shaken her, just to make sure she really understood.

So trouble was something she was keen to avoid. What if the man she'd just seen – or the woman, happily sipping coffee at the table in front of her – somehow twisted things so Natali herself appeared to be the thief? That would be so beyond awful. She could almost see herself at the police station, Obi taken from her, losing her job... No. No way was she going to interfere.

Much as she didn't want to see where he went or what he did next, typically the man was heading towards the ferry quay too. She couldn't help but watch as he ambled between the café tables, but thankfully he didn't stop again. Hopefully she'd been mistaken. Hurrying Obi along, she overtook him, relieved to get him out of her sight.

At the library table Lloyd was busy chatting to a round-faced woman in a large sunhat, while her teenage daughter picked up one book after another at a glacial pace. Unwilling to interrupt, Natali popped the bottle of cola under the table then headed for the quay.

"That's quite enough excitement for one day, Obi," she said. "Let's get back to the boat."

Korčula

SATURDAY 1ST JULY

As Lloyd swung his feet onto the parquet floor of the sparsely furnished hotel room, just for a moment everything swayed. It must be all those hours spent on the boat; after one night on dry land he was pitching and tossing like nobody's business.

The idea of visiting Lumbarda had been building all week, and a shit week it had been too, starting from the moment that lovely lady's purse had been stolen from right under his nose on Koločep. The number of times he'd run over it in his mind, why on earth he hadn't seen it happen... He'd been so ashamed he'd told Ana about it in the strictest confidence, despite knowing she'd probably have to put it in her weekly report to Ivana.

If his mind had been completely on the job, as it bloody well should have been, he would have been able to stop the theft. But no, he'd been this way and that, worrying about whether Mirjana was still on Korčula. He couldn't let his selfish preoccupation affect his work again, so yesterday morning he'd gone online and booked a cheap, last-minute room in one of the anonymous hotels that fringed Korčula town. He'd told Natali and Ana he'd catch the ferry to the mainland, then take the bus from Orebić to Ston later today. Ana had looked surprised, but it was no one's business but his own what he did with his time off.

If he hadn't needed teabags, if he hadn't seen the young woman in the supermarket, he'd never have been stirred up like this. It wasn't so much that she looked like Mirjana, the resemblance was more in the way she'd moved. It was the really telling traits that screamed close family – things he'd noticed in Ruth all the more since Jenny died, like waving her fork to emphasise a point, scooping up a book left on the bottom step as she raced upstairs.

So was the young woman Mirjana's daughter? And if so, where was her mother? He needed to find out the answer to the second question at least, although what earthly good it would do him, he didn't know. Except he couldn't spend every Friday of the summer looking over his shoulder for the ghosts of his past. He needed to focus on his job.

Having paid for the hotel's buffet breakfast, he figured he might as well eat it, but sitting alone at a table for two in the anonymous dining room filled with chatter and muzak, the old familiar ache for Jenny returned with a vengeance. He didn't think he'd felt this lonely, this alone, since the early days of his bereavement. A solitary rock in a sea of couples and families. The sad old git with his coffee and granola. Except he wasn't old. He shouldn't be on his own. Bitterness rose in his throat, tinged with the sour taste of anger, but he'd learnt his lesson that anger was to be avoided at all costs.

He distracted himself by scrolling through the headlines on

his phone, waiting for the surge of heat to fade. And what was he left with? Guilt. Sodding guilt. All the more destructive for being hidden deep inside. And grief. These days he was even hiding that too, because it was unfair to burden Ana and Natali. After he'd told them, neither had mentioned Jenny again, but on the other hand, why should they? They barely knew him, and had never known her. Why would they care? But feeling he couldn't even say her name in their company was mighty strange. Like he wasn't quite being true to himself.

He was all too aware that two years after the event, no one wanted to be continually reminded of a widower's misery. He even glossed over the worst of it with Ruth, but that didn't mean it wasn't there. Yes, bit by bit it was easing and he was coming to understand that time did heal after all. Except when life threw a massive spanner in the works – a spanner like Mirjana, creeping out of nowhere and grabbing him by the throat.

He'd stood at this bus stop so many times, with Mirjana and with his fellow waiter, Kesten, but right now Lloyd had a feeling of being out of kilter, out of time. Nothing, but nothing, looked the same. Well, maybe the bar opposite was a tiny bit familiar, but that was about it. Back then, Lumbarda's marina had been in its infancy – more of a dream than a reality. Now it was packed with yachts and even one of the small cruise ships that plied Dalmatian waters was moored at the far end of the quay, next to a beach club dotted with, of all things, plywood palm trees.

If it had existed thirty years before, he had no doubt Kesten would have tried to persuade him to go there after work. Kesten had had a strutting confidence and liked a party, but he'd been a good laugh and kind too, always trying to find Lloyd English people to speak to, in case he was missing home.

Sometimes the three of them had gone out on the town on Sunday nights when the *konoba* closed early. Mirjana and Kesten were cousins of some sort, but acted more like brother and sister, teasing each other one minute and going at it hammer and tongs the next, crazy arguments Lloyd's Croatian had scarcely been good enough to follow.

There was one night in particular that he remembered, the hottest night of the year, and Mirjana had looked amazing in the tiniest of mini-skirts that showed off her legs to perfection, and a lemon-coloured top that brought the lights in her almond-coloured hair to life as they strolled along the harbourside to meet Kesten at this very bus stop. Lloyd hadn't been able to keep his hands – or lips – off her, and he remembered having to stop for her to wipe her lip gloss from around his mouth.

Kesten had been leaning against a lamp-post, dressed to the nines in the latest baggy denims and a wildly patterned shirt, undone almost to his navel. Lloyd had teased him about being on the pull, and after muttering something about bloody well having to be, the way he and Mirjana were behaving, he'd laughed and slapped Lloyd on the back. With so much enthusiasm, if Lloyd remembered rightly, it had left quite a bruise.

The Lumbarda Lloyd remembered most, with its curved bay and fishing harbour, was around the headland from where he was standing, its unspoilt beaches, the village itself, tumbling over the hill to Konoba Pecaros. He knew the restaurant still existed; he'd found it on Google Maps one night when sleep had evaded him, the pictures taken by tourists showing it perched on its rough stone wall above the seafront road. Just as it always had been.

But would Mirjana still be there? It was her family's restaurant, so he supposed it was possible. Even her parents could be. They'd be in their seventies now, so not all that old. Goose bumps ran down his back. Her mother in particular would have just as much reason to be angry with him as Mirjana herself. So why the bloody hell was he putting himself through this? In his heart of hearts, he knew it was more than just to stop him being distracted from his job. Was it because, even after all these years, to be able to apologise might give him some closure? Because he needed that closure, because the past was encroaching into his thoughts in such a way it was pushing his grief for Jenny to one side?

He could not, could not, let his memories of Jenny fade. It scared him now, how completely his feelings for Mirjana had been erased in the end. Erased by Jenny and his all-encompassing love for her. A different love, a love that had grown slowly. A love that had matured over the years. A love they'd held above them like an umbrella against life's ills. So, if that was the case, why was what had happened with Mirjana creeping back in this insidious way? Shit, this was complicated. And it needed sorting out.

Lloyd slowly made his way along the marina, trying to look like any other tourist. Maybe he should stop for coffee. But no, if he did, it would have to be at Pecaros, because then he'd have an excuse to ask after the family who'd owned it so many years before. And if they still owned it? He'd cross that bridge if he came to it.

Rounding the headland into the bay where the heart of the old village was, he was surprised he recognised so much.

At first glance, it was like stepping back thirty years: the church with its tower, topped by an elegant colonnade beneath the spire, perched on the hill, the reds of the roofs and the myriad greens of the trees, olives and shrubs forming an unruly patchwork below it. But when he looked closer, most of what had been small stone buildings on the shore were now painted or faced with concrete, and the majority had sprouted extra terraces, or even whole new floors.

Far more cars were parked in front of the houses too, many of them shiny and new. Either the people of Lumbarda had come good from their tourism, or the village had been overtaken by second-home owners. Lloyd fervently hoped it was the former. But what business of his was it anyway? It was a place and a dream he'd abandoned long ago.

It was impossible to miss Konoba Pecaros, its buildings set back slightly on a terrace above the road, even though now it was partly obscured by the three-storey house next door, which he remembered as a single-level fisherman's dwelling with nets hanging outside. So much had changed, how could the restaurant he'd called home for one magical summer be anywhere near the same?

And yet, in most ways it was. Of course, the umbrellas on Pecaros' terrace were new, the shrubs he and Kesten had planted to surround the tables now mature, and a deep pink bougainvillea had colonised one of the sturdy brick pillars supporting the restaurant's gently sloping roof. The shutters on the house behind were plastic rather than wood, and although there was still a hand-painted sign saying "pizza", it was bigger and bolder than Lloyd remembered. But why would everything have been frozen in time, waiting for him to come back? This place may still mean something to him, but the chances were that he himself was forgotten, irrelevant.

He stopped on the quayside to take it all in, knowing he was hidden by the wall of the property next door. Already the sun was blistering hot, but that wasn't the only reason he was dripping with sweat. Dripping, but at the same time icy cold, his feet frozen to the tarmac beneath him. What now? What the hell should he do now? What if he stepped forwards, climbed the stone stairs, and there was Mirjana, clearing the tables? Would he recognise her? But he knew he would ... of course he would. She'd give herself away to him in a moment.

So might she remember him too? And then what would happen? Would she step forwards, say his name? Or pretend she didn't know him, and send someone else to take his order? Or worse, much worse, call him out for what he had done, all those years before?

His stomach clenched dangerously, and he wanted nothing more than to turn and walk away. He flexed his fingers in and out to calm himself. He'd come this far. He had to know. One foot after the other until he reached the bottom of the steps. A moment to draw breath before steadying himself on the wooden rail. He'd count to three ... or maybe to ten ... and then he'd start to climb.

A movement on the terrace above caught his eye. A woman with a shock of dyed red hair, her once round face lined and pinched, her dark eyes boring into him. Mirjana. Despite how changed she was, it could be no one else, and the jolt of recognition was like an electric shock. She was still here after all; he'd found her. Surprise turning to something close to ... what was it? Relief? Elation? Or trepidation?

He gazed back at her, too choked to speak, as time stilled between them. After all these years... He half raised his hand in greeting, but then, with an expression of absolute contempt, she swivelled smartly around and retreated inside.

He had to get away, away from those eyes, full of the loathing his younger self had imagined so many times. But seeing it now, knowing the years had done nothing to blunt it... God, he shouldn't be surprised, but all the same, a tiny piece of him shattered. A tiny piece of hope. Hope he hadn't even recognised he'd been harbouring; hope that after all this time, he could put things right. Hope that had been dashed to pieces on the tarmac beneath his feet.

He was about to turn to walk back the way he'd come when he heard someone calling his name. Not from the restaurant, but from the quayside behind him.

His voice, trapped in his throat, came as though from a distance. Mumbling. Confused. "Oh, hello Kristina."

The teacher who'd brought the children to the library. The only person he even vaguely knew on this goddam island. "I ... I thought you lived in Žrnovo." Even to his own ears it sounded a pretty lame thing to say, but his mouth felt as though it was stuffed with cotton wool. Along with his brain.

She smiled. "No, the children I brought last week do, and yesterday's came from Račišće. I want to make sure they all get a chance."

Lloyd nodded. "Yes. Yes, of course. Of course. I'd forgotten. Well, good for you. Great. I'll see you next week."

It was all he could do to walk, not run, away. He'd made a bloody fool of himself in front of Kristina as well. This morning had been a proper disaster, but at least now he knew.

He would not come back to Lumbarda, and he'd spend every Friday for the rest of the summer praying Mirjana didn't come into Korčula town. If that was his penance, so be it.

Lopud

TUESDAY 4TH JULY

Ana read the message for a second time, but the words remained the same.

Moved into my new apartment. Quite a step up for me – not like my old bachelor pads. You're going to love it! Come and take a look.

Pajo had gone quiet over the last few weeks, and now, five years to the day since they'd split up, this. Given his wording, the timing had to be deliberate. He'd remembered all right. Remembered that stupid, stupid promise. Why had she ever agreed to it?

Because at the time it had felt like an insurance policy, that's why. And even now, perhaps it still was. She put her hand on her stomach; her biological clock was ticking all right.

She and Pajo had known each other forever. Their mothers were friends, and Pajo's father owned the restaurant in Ston where her father sold huge numbers of his oysters. Always a tomboy, Ana had hung out with Pajo and his mates not only through childhood, but into their teenage years. Then Pajo had discovered girls and they'd drifted apart. She'd gone to university and he'd found work in telesales in Split, and before very long he was travelling Croatia as business development manager for a green technology company.

It was when he'd been visiting a customer in Dubrovnik that he'd come across her with Meri outside the jazz café. Knowing it was the closest thing the city had to a gay bar, he'd put two and two together to make about a hundred and fifty, and Ana and Meri had found it amusing not to disabuse him.

The strange thing was, shortly afterwards he'd asked her out. And once he'd got over the jokes – at least, she hoped they were jokes – about wanting to watch her and her girlfriend in bed, they'd rubbed along just fine. They'd had so much in common, mutual interests and friends, and the sex had been off the scale. Their families had been delighted, and after a couple of years there'd been more than just talk of wedding bells in the village – there'd practically been preparations.

Which is what had given Ana such very cold feet. She'd been overwhelmed by guilt, uncertain what to do, and had been mightily relieved when a little while later Pajo had voiced the same misgivings. They were too young to settle down; he wanted to play the field, see the world. He'd been offered a promotion that meant he'd be travelling throughout Europe. They'd got wildly drunk together to celebrate, then in the morning had gone their separate ways.

But not before making the promise. The stupid promise that it now seemed Pajo remembered. The promise that if they were both still single after five years then they'd marry anyway and start a family before they got too old. The problem was, now it came to it, she had no idea how she would feel if Pajo tried to hold her to her word.

Oh, promises could be broken, especially drunken ones, but

was Pajo in fact her best bet if she wanted a family? At least there'd be no false starts, and none of the hassle of a drawn-out courtship. *If* she wanted children, she didn't have time for that. *If*. One small word with very big implications.

She stood and stretched, picking up her coffee cup from the table in *Dida Krila*'s indoor-outdoor salon. Natali was a creature of habit and would want to clean here next, and Ana was really struggling to think what to say to her. Lloyd had become adept at coaxing a few words, but Ana was almost at her wits' end. Yet having begun to watch her closely, she'd seen nothing to indicate that Natali was actually unhappy. Maybe her *tata* was right, and the youngster was an unnaturally quiet person. Maybe Meri was right and it was no big deal. In which case she needed to get over herself.

In many ways, Lopud was the best of their moorings, tucked in the sheltered harbour below the old monastery. The dark green leaves of the trees which shaded the shallow steps to its door at least offered the catamaran's deck some welcome protection from the morning sun. The day was almost completely airless, the flags on the boats around her hanging listless. Surely a storm had to break soon?

Ana hopped from *Dida Krila*'s bow onto the quayside and strolled under the palm trees until she came to the library beneath the enormous holm oak. Lloyd was leaning against the trunk, reading from his Kindle, but frequently glancing at the books set out on the table in front of him. He'd become rather more wary since the purse had been stolen on Koločep, and who could blame him?

"Quiet this morning?" Ana asked.

He looked up at her and nodded. "Worrying, isn't it."

"Oh, I don't know. It's only our third week. Still plenty of time for things to pick up." Ana hoped he wouldn't detect the hollowness of her words, so she delivered them with a broad smile.

He returned to the table, setting his Kindle down. "Perhaps we should try to make it busier, not just leave it to fate."

"How do you mean?"

"If we could discover where the local parents hang out, we could at least do something to remind them of our existence. Word of mouth's beginning to work on Šipan and Koločep, so maybe we just need to kick-start it here and on Mljet."

Ana nodded. It did make sense, and she was kicking herself she hadn't thought of it. As skipper, she should be taking the lead, but she felt so out of her depth. She had no experience of this sort of thing, but she shouldn't be leaving it to Lloyd to state the obvious. On the other hand, he was older and apparently wiser, so could she not learn from him? Or would that destroy her credibility as skipper and project manager? After all, she'd had enough trouble from charter guests who didn't respect her.

Lloyd wasn't like that though. He was genuine, courteous and kind. And more to the point, his idea was a good one and it would be churlish not to swallow her pride and run with it.

"Good call. I'll see what I can find out," she told him, then set off along the promenade towards the long commercial strip of the village, hoping inspiration would strike.

Damn it. Nice as he was, Lloyd was part of her problems too. Something was going on with him, she was sure. Not his grief for his wife, as she had first assumed, but something that had started since he'd been here. Maybe around the time the purse had been stolen, or maybe a little before? Although on the surface he gave every appearance of being just fine, he seemed to retreat a little more inside himself with every passing day, almost as if he were hiding something. Or at the very least, not saying something he wanted to. Perhaps he'd just said it. Perhaps he thought she'd been slow at being proactive to make the library more successful. Well even if she had, she'd damn well put that right. But how?

Ana hopped down onto the narrow beach and eased off her flip-flops, allowing the unfamiliar feel of sand to ooze between her toes. God, it was hot. Hot to the point of burning, so she headed for the shoreline to dip her feet in the water. Nearby, a mother and toddler, both wearing floppy sunhats, were making sand pies, while a baby slept in the shade of a beach umbrella. The scene looked so idyllic, so peaceful, especially compared to the turmoil in her own mind, but was motherhood what she wanted for herself?

No, she mustn't let herself get distracted. Back to the task in hand. How could she find those local parents? Maybe the village had a Facebook group? She whipped out her phone and almost punched the air when she was right, then instantly deflated when she realised the group was private with a string of membership questions she couldn't answer.

Oh, she wished she knew more about this stuff. But then it struck her: Meri did. Meri worked in PR. Surely she'd have an idea or two?

Quickly, she typed, *Can you talk?*

The blue ticks appeared. *Give me five. I'm due a cigarette break.*

But you gave up years ago!

Why should smokers have all the fun ;-)

Ana wandered back towards the promenade, where she sat in the shade of a *konoba* wall, dangling her feet over the sand.

She didn't have long to wait for Meri to call, and she quickly explained Lloyd's idea of trying to reach local parents. "I guess the best way is just to ask around where they hang out, but the trouble is even then, what would we do? We're not here for long enough to talk to them all individually."

"You don't need to. I can help you dream up some eye-catching leaflets or posters, but you do need to know where to put them so people will see them."

"I guess I could head back from the seafront and see if there are any shops or bars tucked away from the tourists. And I'm sure I've seen a chemist's. Local people would have to use that. Maybe they'd help us."

"We make a truly awesome team." Ana could hear the smile in Meri's voice. "You find out whether posters or leaflets would be more useful, and I'll get onto it this evening."

"Meri, you're bloody amazing."

"Oh, I know. Lucky old you that I'm your bestest friend."

Ana was humming to herself as she headed for the pharmacy, her spirits buoyed even further, not only by their promise to hand out leaflets if she could bring some next week, but also having been told the whereabouts of a community hall, which would doubtless do the same. Her next job was to find it. That would be a far better use of her time than beating herself up about her own inadequacies and worrying about how to reply to Pajo. And it should be a whole lot easier too.

Šipan

TUESDAY 4TH JULY

The short sail from Lopud to Šipan had been barely long enough to clear Ana's head, so once the dinner things were tidied away, she rolled her towel under her arm and hopped off the boat. Lloyd was in his cabin calling his daughter, and Natali was giving Obi her last walk of the day, so she hadn't even had to ask them if they'd like to come for a swim. And she wanted to be alone. Needed to be. Just her and the soothing arms of the sea.

The lights from the harbour soon faded, leaving her in total darkness. Although the moon had been full last night, it was only just beginning to ease its way over the hills of the Pelješac, so once she left the road she switched on the torch on her phone, flashing its light along the path ahead to avoid tripping over tree roots or sliding down onto the rocks below.

It was just as well she had to concentrate on where she was putting her feet, because thoughts of Pajo were clamouring in her head. And not in a good way. She had yet to reply to his message, but honestly, it was a total no-brainer. He'd only asked her to visit his apartment. She just needed to type *"Sure, we'll fix something up"*, and that would be that. So why couldn't she?

Ever since she'd watched the young mother on the beach at Lopud, she'd been wondering more and more what it would be like being a mum? Although nothing had actually been said, her parents clearly expected her to have kids; she was their only child and they had a business to pass on. Perhaps if she didn't want to work for them herself, grandchildren might be the solution. But how would children fit with *Dida Krila*? She really didn't think they would. And yet … yet … what if she let this chance of motherhood pass by, then in a year or two decided she wanted it more than anything?

She needed to talk this Pajo situation through with Meri, to see if her friend could help her make some sense of it. Meri was a mother, and despite the fact she absolutely doted on her grown-up son Zac, her undoubtedly biased angle on parenthood would still be useful. To be fair, any angle would be, and Ana had learnt to trust Meri's judgement. Maybe even more than she trusted her own. And anyway, it would be fun to surprise her on Saturday and take her out to dinner at her favourite restaurant to thank her for all she'd done today.

As she'd expected, the beach was deserted, so she slipped off her clothes and tucked them, along with her phone, under her towel. She hesitated for a moment. Did she dare remove her bikini as well? Would anyone come? The cloak of darkness would protect her and the silken embrace of the water over every inch of her body was too alluring to resist.

The contrast with the stultifying night air was blissful, making the small hairs on her arms stand to attention as she immersed her naked body. The tiniest of breezes ruffled her hair as with slow strokes she approached the headland, the easy roll of the sea caressing her as she swam. Water. Her element. Her comfort.

She floated on her back, gazing up at the stars in the distant velvet sky. The moon was higher now, casting its searchlight beam over the waves, and where they kissed the rocks flashes of phosphorescence glowed turquoise-silver, a sight so rare it caught her breath. This was just so bloody perfect and she whispered a thank you to Dida for opening her eyes, and her life, to such joy.

The gentle sparkle and wash in her partially submerged ears was interrupted by the scrunch of footsteps on the beach. Bugger. Bugger, bugger, bugger. Just her luck if a gang of kids was bringing their beer cans and smart speakers down for a party. *Sranje*, she'd need some front to get out of the water if that was the case. But no; thankfully it was one set of footsteps, now drawn to a halt. There was a rustle of clothing, then she half heard, half sensed she was no longer alone in the sea.

She spun over and clung to the nearest rock. Her eyes now well-adjusted to the moonlight, she recognised the man she had spoken to before – from his silhouette at least. Long limbs, broad shoulders, firm buttocks. He was as naked as she was, and for a fleeting moment seemed part of the perfection of the night. A fleeting moment before she saw him stoop, trickle water over his arms and torso, then dip forwards and start to swim.

Ana waited, silent and still by her rock, but the steady rhythm of his strokes told her he was heading towards her. She could, maybe should, alert him to her presence, but any sound at all would shatter the magic of swimming alone in the dark. For both of them. Instead she watched, mesmerised, as the phosphorescence trailed over his arms and legs, highlighting his progress. When he was only metres away he paused and looked towards her. She wanted to somehow tell him not to speak, not to spoil it, but he clearly felt it too, because he put his finger to his lips.

She nodded, then waited until he had passed before making her reluctant way back to the shore. He was a kindred spirit, unashamed of his own nakedness, craving the same silent communion with the water as she felt. It intrigued her, drew her to him in a way she found hard to define. But it was nothing, really. A fleeting moment, that was all, and much as she wanted to prolong it, decency dictated she needed to be dressed and away from the beach while he was still in the water.

Moored off Korčula

THURSDAY 6TH JULY

Used as Natali was to the sea, she'd found it more than a little unsettling when Ana, who was so unflappable, had insisted they leave Mljet early due to reports of storms to the south. But now, tucked into the relative shelter of the islands just outside Korčula's harbour, and with *Dida Krila* doing no more than riding a little over-enthusiastically on her anchor, she wondered what the fuss had been about. She'd certainly seen worse.

Yes, the sky was dark in the direction they'd come from. Yes, the breeze was whistling through the rigging, but Ana had pulled down the thick plastic curtains at the end of the salon to keep the weather out, so they were cosy finishing their supper, and Natali was quite content to listen to the conversation. At least Ana had stopped trying to encourage her to join in. Maybe she finally understood that she couldn't.

Refusing a second glass of wine, Natali stood to clear the plates. A squall of rain pattered against the windows. If it was going to tip down, she needed to encourage Obi onto her little fake grass mat on the deck to do what she needed to do before they both got soaking wet, or worse, before Obi refused to go out at all. She hated the rain.

It took some cajoling and clicking of fingers to get Obi outside, even with no more than a few drops in the air. The moment Obi's drooping tail had cleared the plastic sheets, Ana velcroed them firmly together.

"Sometimes you make me so ashamed," Natali told the dog. "Now get over there and have a pee before it really starts." And start it would; the black clouds hovering over the mainland had grown so huge they had sucked the last of the day out of the sky, with only distant flashes of lightning piercing the gloom.

It was little wonder Obi was reluctant to leave the shelter of the fly deck, and after a few more minutes of fruitless persuasion, Natali picked her up and dumped her on the mat.

Putting her hands on her hips she glared down at her. *"Isprazniti!"* But her command was drowned out by a roar of thunder overhead. As she looked up, lightning split the sky, momentarily blinding her.

She rubbed her eyes furiously, but when she opened them the little green mat was empty. She spun around, but there was no Obi waiting by the closed flaps to be let back in, no Obi huddling in the footwell of the helm station. Where was she?

The Velcro ripped open, the plastic sheet flapping wildly as Lloyd flew out and raced past her to dive into the sea. Then Ana was next to her, screaming to look over the side because the swell was too large for Lloyd to spot Obi from the water.

Natali froze. No, no, this couldn't be happening. Ana dragged her closer to the rail, the rough movement bringing her to her senses, and she threw herself towards the helm station at the stern while Ana took the bow, scouring the dark peaks and troughs for any sign of her dog.

Oh god, she'd drown! She'd drown! If only Natali could swim better, she'd jump in herself to look for Obi. But what if she got into trouble too? Then Lloyd would surely come to her aid, and Obi... Instead, she leant further over *Dida Krila*'s thick, wire guard-rails, almost overbalancing in her desperation, spray foaming upwards to meet her, stinging her eyes and making it so much harder to see.

"There! There, Lloyd, there!" Ana screamed. Natali raced to join her as she pointed frantically to where Lloyd's head was only just keeping above the swell. "About three metres beyond you. She's paddling! You can reach her!"

Lloyd's arms curled through the water, the foam from his kicking legs flashing white in the lightning. He was battling, battling, but closing the gap to where Obi was appearing then disappearing between the waves, at what seemed like the pace of a snail. Oh god, Obi was tiny ... so tiny. The wet fur clinging to her head had shrunk it to nothing. She didn't know how to swim. She'd drown. Obi was going to drown. The thick wire cut into Natali's fingers.

Thunder roared again, right over their heads, and Obi dropped further into the swell. And then, by some miracle, Lloyd was next to her, pulling her to his chest, then flipping onto his back before sculling one armed towards *Dida Krila*.

Ana shouted to Natali over the storm. "I'll drop the ladder, you fetch towels. Loads – for both of them."

When she returned on deck, Lloyd was at the bottom of the steps, handing Obi up to Ana, who took the struggling dog rather unceremoniously by the scruff of her neck. "Don't ever, ever, do that again," she told her, but rather than anger, Natali saw tears in Ana's eyes. It was all that was needed to tip Natali over the edge into uncontrollable sobbing herself.

Oh, this was no good, no good at all. But she couldn't help it. Just couldn't help it. Obi was her world ... her whole world... Her shoulders still heaving, she held out a towel and Ana took it, wrapping the folds around the dog, who was blinking furiously. Then Lloyd was on deck too, breathing heavily and starting to shiver. Lloyd, who had, without even a thought, jumped into the sea to save Obi. Natali pushed past Ana and hugged him.

He hugged her back ferociously. "It's all right, little one, Obi's going to be fine."

"Thank you, oh thank you," she hiccupped, as they remained locked together under the awning, Lloyd's wet clothes soaking into her own. Then she felt, rather than saw, Lloyd's arm reach out and pull Ana and Obi into the embrace, and Natali sobbed all the more because these people were truly amazing and she'd go to the ends of the earth if they asked her to. She clung to them both as tightly as she could. She didn't think she'd ever been hugged like this, and it was exactly what she needed right now.

It was only when Obi began to whimper that they pulled away.

"Now we're all bloody wet." Ana laughed shakily.

"I hope you don't think I acted inappropriately," said Lloyd, stepping back and putting a little distance between them, the guarded expression on his face making Natali sadder than sad. Why on earth would he be thinking that?

"Not as far as I'm concerned," she said firmly.

"Nor me," added Ana, "I think we all needed a hug after that."

Lloyd nodded. "Good, good... It's just ... middle-aged men shouldn't invade young women's personal space like that, but under the circumstances ... and, damn it, I bloody well miss a good hug."

"You can hug me whenever you want," said Natali. Right at this moment she'd do absolutely anything to make him happy. It was a brilliant bonus that she'd enjoyed the hug so much as well.

"Yeah, yeah, me too..." But Ana was staring at the floor. "Look, I'm sorry I'm not, you know, as enthusiastic as you two are about this, but I've had issues in the past... Not that I'm saying you'd cause any, Lloyd – you're the last person, I know that..." She stumbled to a halt. Cool, calm, grown-up Ana was suddenly as vulnerable as Natali herself could be.

"I think," said Lloyd, "we all need to get dry, and have a hot drink. Maybe then we can talk some more."

Ana nodded. "I think we probably need to. All of us." Her eyes met Natali's, and somehow she held her gaze for a moment and nodded.

Much as talking was still scary, something between them felt different. Despite his selfless courage, in the moments after the hug Lloyd had sounded pretty uncertain. He and Ana may be awesomely clever, but now Natali realised they had frailties just as real – and just as hard to articulate – as her own.

"I don't know why I never thought of it before, Obi," she said, as she towelled her down in their cabin. "Maybe because I'm not used to being around clever people, or because I'm not clever myself." She sat on the edge of her bed, cradling the dog to her and marvelling at the revelation. Did everyone find it hard to say things that mattered to them? Ana certainly seemed to have done.

"I mean, Obi, it's not quite the same, because I struggle to say anything very much, but do you know what? I'm going to try. To Lloyd at least, and to Ana if I can, although she's a bit scarier…" But was she? Was she really? All right, she could be a bit sharp at times, but she was the boss – that was her job – but underneath, she'd shown them she was a person too.

By the time they gathered around the salon table half an hour or so later, Natali's adrenalin-induced confidence was draining away. The storm had passed over, leaving a freshness on the breeze that whistled through the windows, which Ana had opened a little to clear the fug. It wasn't exactly cold, but even though Lloyd was bundled up in a jumper he still shivered every now and then.

"Are you all right?" Ana asked him.

He wrapped his hands further around his steaming mug of tea. "Sure. I think in part it's the shock coming out. Everything happened so quickly. But as long as Obi's OK, then all good."

Natali fondled Obi's ears, and the dog looked up adoringly from her lap. "She's going to h-hate water all the more because of it, but I don't think that's too bad a thing."

"It certainly isn't," said Ana. Silence covered the table, the closeness they had felt just a short time before slipping slowly away. Natali could not let that happen. Lloyd had seemed to need it and she got that – he must be missing his wife terribly, after all. But how … what could she say, to make it better?

It was Ana who spoke, sounding very uncertain. "Natali, can I ask you something? It's quite personal, but I need an honest answer."

"Of course." She didn't mean it, but Natali knew she had to do what Ana wanted, however tough it might be. Anything to pull the three of them together again. It felt so important.

Ana took a deep breath. "You don't join in very much when we talk in the evenings, and I'm wondering why."

"Because I don't have anything to say. You're both ... you're so clever, so educated, and me ... I'm nobody."

"Never say that!" Ana blazed. "Of course you're somebody. You're the best damn crew member I've ever worked with, for a start."

Natali's mouth hung open. "But I'm so stupid..."

Lloyd reached out and patted her arm. "You've never struck me as stupid, not once. My guess is someone's been telling you that you are."

"At school ... my stammer ... I was teased ... but it didn't matter because I wasn't very good at anything anyway."

"Academic achievement isn't the be-all and end-all," Lloyd said.

"But you're a teacher!"

"Which is why I get it. Not everyone's suited to sitting in a classroom and passing exams; some of my brightest pupils went on to excel at practical things instead. Like you, Natali. The problem is, the system seems geared to make you ashamed of your skills, rather than proud."

"Lloyd's right," added Ana. "You need to believe in yourself. And I'm sorry if I've been less than patient with you at times. I was worried you were unhappy, and I'm new to being in charge – it's a learning curve for me and I have to admit it's been pretty stressful. Even though I've skippered charter boats, there was always someone back in the office telling me what to do and how to do it. Now I'm on my own."

"This is the happiest I've ever been in a job, and I'm so sorry if you thought otherwise," said Natali. "If I'm quiet it doesn't mean I'm sad. I really wanted to explain that on the very first day but I couldn't find the words. I can never find the bloody words. And when I do, I just stammer all over them."

"Do you realise," said Ana, "that you haven't stammered once this evening? I mean, I wouldn't go as far as to say that I'm glad Obi fell into the water, but at least you're talking. I mean ... we're talking."

"I'm glad we hugged too," said Natali, her voice sounding small. "I liked it."

Lloyd sighed. "I did as well. Jenny, Ruth and I were a very tactile family and I miss it." He looked down. "I miss being able to talk about Jenny too. I should have said, when I told you I'd lost her... I've always spoken about her freely. It's ... comforting, I suppose."

"I think I speak for Natali as well when I say you can hug us any time you want. And talk about Jenny. Of course we'd love to know more about her. I knew something wasn't quite right with you either, Lloyd, and that explains it," said Ana. "God, I'm so useless at this."

"No, you're not," Lloyd replied. "You're just feeling your way. We're all feeling our way. But it will be better now we've been honest. We can kind of help each other along. You said you were on your own, Ana, but really you're not. We're in this together." He stretched his hands across the table and took Natali's in his left, and Ana's in his right. And Natali knew, absolutely knew, that the thing to do was join up the circle. As Obi settled further into her lap, she squeezed Ana's fingers and vowed to herself that she'd do everything she possibly could to make this closeness last all summer long. After all, if she couldn't exactly find the words to tell the others how grateful she was to them, there must be plenty of ways to show them.

Ston

SATURDAY 8TH JULY

"Right," said Ana. "I'll collect the chicken wire from my parents, then we can have a little working party."

Coffee cups, plates and an open jar of jam were strewn across the table. Natali was picking at the last flakes from her croissant and sharing them with Obi, who sat to attention on the banquette beside her.

"I'm sorry Obi's causing all this trouble. *Dida Krila* won't look the same with w-wire mesh all around her."

"She's worth it," said Ana firmly.

"And so are you," added Lloyd, making Natali shrug, but her narrow face was lit by a smile.

Even thirty-six hours had made so much difference. At first Ana had been uncertain, because as they'd unpacked the library on Korčula Lloyd had been unusually quiet, but during the day she'd passed the table several times on errands and when there'd been children around he'd been as engaged as he ever was.

One of her errands had been to buy a decent bottle of

delicious, crisp Grk wine, a speciality of Korčula, some of the very best olives and a block of Pag cheese. She'd so wanted Friday night to be a celebration, because something more important than loaning out hundreds of books had happened this week. After Thursday night, she felt that they understood so much more about each other as people. Now they were a team and for the first time Ana really believed this summer was going to be all right.

She was looking forward to the weekend too. She'd checked with Zac that Meri was free, then booked their surprise dinner for tonight. If she got her skates on they'd have time for a drink or two at the jazz café first, and it would be the icing on the cake to catch up with her other Dubrovnik friends too.

"Permission to come aboard!" Pajo's confident voice rang across the deck.

Of all the—!

It was as if just thinking about him had conjured him up. And, of course, he hadn't waited for her to answer. He was already standing next to the table, his grin reaching all the way to his deep-set brown eyes.

She stood to greet him, brushing crumbs from her shorts. "Pajo. This is a surprise." Trying to keep her frustration from her voice, she turned to the others. "Lloyd, Natali, this is Pajo. We've been friends since we were tiny. Pajo, this is my crew for the summer."

Towering over Pajo's stocky frame, Lloyd stood to shake his hand, and Natali followed his example. What did Pajo want here? Why had he come? To cover her confusion, Ana offered him coffee, then escaped to the galley to make a fresh *džezva* for them all.

The process was soothing, and she tried to close her mind to the fact that Pajo was watching her. Not overtly, but she could see his reflection in the window and it made her flesh prickle. Why, she did not know; there was nothing creepy about Pajo. It was her – just her own feelings – making her uncomfortable around him. He'd done nothing at all. Even turning up uninvited ... that's what old friends did, wasn't it?

She carried the *džezva* and a clean cup through to the salon where Pajo was asking Lloyd about the library. This social chit-chat was fine, but Ana had a busy day ahead and she needed to get on. Perhaps she shouldn't have offered him coffee, made him so comfortable, but what would it have looked like if she hadn't? Rude, that's what. Rude, and a little bit cruel.

All the same, she didn't want to be late getting off to Dubrovnik. If Pajo had gone to the trouble of seeking her out, her need to speak to Meri was all the more urgent. On the other hand, there was safety in numbers. As long as she stayed here with Lloyd and Natali, he couldn't very well ask any unwanted questions.

But as time went by, Ana knew if she didn't move soon her plans for the weekend would be scuppered. Added to which, Natali had relapsed into total silence – not that Pajo was making any effort to include her in the conversation anyway – and she could not let that continue.

She stood and gathered the coffee cups. "It's great to see you, Pajo, but we have a busy morning ahead. I need to get over to Mama and Tata's to collect some wire."

Pajo stretched. "Then I'll walk with you to your car. There's something I want to ask you."

Cornered. Absolutely cornered. Surely, surely, this wasn't the big question? But, of course, it wouldn't be – not out of the blue like this. More likely it was to set a date for going to see his apartment, which could easily be put off. What the hell was she panicking about? She scooped up her keys and hopped from the transom onto the quayside, where she turned to him.

"OK, Pajo. Spit it out."

He fell into step beside her. "That's not a very nice turn of phrase. Especially when I'm asking you to a party. The old gang from school are having a get-together and it would be great if you were there too. I ran into Janko and he said they haven't seen you for ages. It's his birthday."

Relief ran through her. This was no big deal. She'd more than likely be working when the time came anyway. "Sure, no problem."

Pajo's smile dimpled his chin beneath his carefully cultivated designer stubble, stirring an unwelcome memory of how attractive he could be. Unwelcome? If it was that unwelcome, why was she even considering...? But if children were what she wanted, they might as well have a handsome father. And one who was also her friend.

He was speaking again. "That's brilliant. I'll pick you up at two. Here or at your parents' place?"

"It's today?" Oh no. Really oh no. Why, oh why, hadn't she asked him when the party was? Her head was all over the damned place.

"When did you think? I said it's Janko's birthday."

He had as well. And she'd agreed to go – just this minute. She couldn't change her mind and let him down. It might have been different if Meri had known she was coming, but even so, she'd have been between a rock and a very hard place. *Sranje* and *sranje* again.

"Here, then," she said feebly, and he reached to kiss her cheek.

"Don't forget to bring your swim stuff. Janko's dad is letting him have the *barka* for the afternoon."

So they'd be stuck together for the duration. There'd be no leaving early, no escape. Except into a crowd of people she'd known since childhood, and for that small mercy Ana was mightily thankful.

Ana eyed Janko's father's traditional wooden *barka* critically. Sure, it was a beautiful craft, but how he could spare it – and both his sons – on a Saturday afternoon in July was beyond her. Her *tata's* boats would be rammed with tourists by now, all eager for a glass of local wine and a taster of oysters.

Pajo jumped on board near the small kitchen-cum-engine-house at the stern, and Ana followed. They made their way forwards under the canvas awning, greeting friends as they went. There were back-slaps and hugs all around before the motors spluttered into life, and they found a space towards the bow end of one of the wooden benches that lined the deck.

She immediately understood why Pajo had invited her; everyone else was part of a couple, and most had children too. In fact, the boat was swarming with them, and now it was ready to get underway they were either charging from one end to the other or leaning precariously over the wooden rails. And shouting. Lots of shouting. Ana could barely hear herself think.

She watched as Janko cast off the mooring ropes and his brother thrust the engines into reverse, the clear water foaming against the quay. On the other side of Malostonski Bay, the wooded hillsides rose into the bluest of skies. In different circumstances, preferably at *Dida Krila*'s helm, the afternoon would have been perfect.

Now she felt trapped, and mad at herself for agreeing to do this. It would take them the best part of half an hour to reach the deserted island where they were planning to swim and cook a barbecue, so when Pajo handed her a bottle of beer she took it. Hopefully it would improve her mood.

"This is nice, isn't it?" he said, stretching his arm along the rail behind her.

She nodded. "It'll be good to catch up with everyone once we get there."

"In the meantime, we can catch up with each other. I can't wait to hear all your news."

Ana looked around. The twenty or so other adults were all either talking or trying to corral their children, effectively leaving her and Pajo quite alone. OK, conversation it was.

"Tell me about this new apartment of yours."

"Oh no. I want you to come and see it for yourself. But it's big, you know. Plenty big enough for—"

She cut across him. "I will. Honestly. I'd like to. It's just so hard when we're both travelling. I take it you're still on the road for work?"

"Oh yes. I was in Venice last week for a conference." He started to tell her all about it, his voice rising and falling with the level of noise from the children. Did they ever shut up? Did Pajo? Luckily all she was required to do was sip her beer, and nod.

The journey seemed to take forever, but after helping to unload the boat, Ana stripped off and plunged into the crystal-clear water for a swim. She needed time to herself to get into the right headspace, so she struck out past a small headland into a secluded cove. There she rested against a partially submerged boulder, kicking her legs lazily, and letting the sun's rays release the knots from her shoulders. The roughness of the rock on her skin reminded her of the night on Šipan when the stranger had joined her in the water, and their shared, silent communion with the elements. Pajo's laugh rose from somewhere behind her. A little of that silence would be good right now.

Sranje! She needed to get over herself. It was nobody's fault but her own that she hadn't explained to Pajo she'd misunderstood the party was today, and that she already had plans. She was the fool, all right, so she needed to quit being miserable and make the best of it.

Back on the island's narrow pebble beach, she wrapped her sarong around her, then joined two other girlfriends from her schooldays in setting out salads, bread and pastries on the plastic table which had been carried from the boat. They topped up each other's wine freely as they worked, chatting all the time, mostly praising their children and moaning about their husbands.

"What it is to be single!" Ana laughed.

"So you're not back with Pajo? We did wonder, seeing you together."

"No. He just thought I might like to come along."

"Do you think you'll ever settle down?" Renata asked.

Tanja snorted. "Not if she's got any sense. You've grown, somehow, Ana, since you got that boat of yours. Not trying to run around keeping everyone else happy anymore. God, I envy you your freedom."

Renata rolled her eyes. "What's Spiro done now?"

"You mean apart from coming home *razvalio* last night and waking the kids?"

"You should be used to that by now, my friend. At least it's only on Fridays."

"But every Friday? What if I wanted to go out?"

Renata shrugged. "Then go on a Thursday."

Tanja put her hands on her hips. "Whose side are you on? Show some solidarity, woman. It's horrible! He gets all loud and clumsy ... not to mention randy, and totally incapable of following through. Then the bedroom stinks of beery farts in the morning."

Ana shuddered. "That does sound disgusting."

Tanja folded her arms. "Stay single."

"No, but honestly," said Renata, "I don't know how I would have got through my mum dying without Luka. He's my absolute rock. To know someone loves me as unconditionally as she did ... it's made all the difference. Knowing he's there, whatever happens. And yes, of course we row. Of course he can be a pain in the arse, but I guess I can as well."

"All right, Mrs Loved Up." But Tanja was laughing and sloshing more wine into their glasses. "Spiro owes me. My turn to get pissed and he can look after the kids."

So amongst married women, the jury was split. How on earth was she expected to make any sense of it? And even supposing your marriage was good, like Renata's, you were still tied to the other person, had to consider their wishes. And children multiplied that tenfold. Ana watched them now, playing on the beach, half a dozen of them running in and out of the water, and two little girls on the edge of the scrub collecting pine cones.

Their serious searching, interspersed with giggling and whispering, was certainly cute and she found herself smiling. But that was all. Nothing she might regard as a tug of maternal feeling. Then why did she think she might want kids? Oh, there were reasons, of course there were: the look in her mother's eyes when she held her friends' grandchildren, for one; and that fear of her biological clock ticking away; and of leaving it too late. Or was her reluctance more to do with feeling completely inadequate when it came to shouldering parental responsibility? Seeing a family as a tie, and not the joy it should be.

She didn't have much experience of responsibility, full stop. Her jobs throughout her twenties had been interesting and varied, but she'd never stayed long enough in any of them to get a promotion or forge a career. It hadn't mattered. Not until the great wake-up call almost five years ago, when Dida was dying and she'd had to make the biggest decision of all.

The biggest until now. And much as she wouldn't change buying *Dida Krila* for the world, she did have to acknowledge that in practical terms it hadn't been her finest hour. She hadn't thought it through, not really, and now she was teetering on the brink financially, reliant on a project that wasn't going too well. She couldn't make the same mistake over the husband and children thing, that was for sure. The implications would be even more disastrous. At least with *Dida Krila* she had a get-out. If she joined the family business, she may lose her freedom, but she'd keep her boat.

She glanced over to where Pajo was chatting to Janko. He saw her and waved, his face lighting up. If she did decide she wanted a family, then he was definitely her best shot. And if his behaviour was anything to go by, he was keen on the idea.

And she liked him – she did. When she wasn't being so narky with everybody. They'd always been good mates. She knew his faults. Maybe he could be a bit overbearing and arrogant, but only when he was showing off. There were worse faults in a man, that was for sure.

Same family background, same friends. No unpleasant surprises. She slapped down the little voice telling her there'd be no surprises at all. With a bit of effort on both sides, she and Pajo could make it work, she knew they could. As a means to an end, at least. In many ways it made perfect sense, so until she'd made up her mind one way or the other, she'd better stop being such a sourpuss and be sociable. Enjoy the rest of the day.

Picking up her wine glass, she wandered over to join him.

Koločep

SUNDAY 9TH JULY

Natali nudged the tender into a gap in the rocks on the seaward side of the ferry quay. Boy, there were a lot of boats in the harbour today, most likely because it was the weekend, and she'd almost given up before she'd noticed this spot. But Obi needed her walk, and she'd told the others she would do it while Ana took Lloyd to swim in the famous Blue Cave on the other side of the island while there weren't too many tourists about. Good luck with that one, given how rammed Donje Čelo was.

A squat red-roofed villa dominated the nearby shore, and she wondered for a moment if she'd moored in a private area, but neither of the women sunbathing on the concrete platform in front of the house so much as noticed her. She looped the rope around an outcrop, then, tucking Obi under her arm, scrambled over the uneven surface and onto the quay.

"Well, if it isn't Natali and Obi." Baka. But what was she doing here, sitting on the same bench, wearing her usual sun hat and floral dress? Where was her son?

"Hello Baka." There must be something else she could say, especially as Obi was straining in her arms to reach her new friend. The answer was obvious. "H-how is your son's visit?"

Baka smiled up at her. "He will come today. The six o'clock ferry."

No! He hadn't let her down again, surely? Yet here she was, almost half an hour early, waiting for his boat. Natali had a sudden image of Baka sitting here every day since last Monday waiting for him, and the thought made her angry and sad all at the same time. But it wasn't her business to comment. Not even if she could work out what to say.

"I've made *soparnik* for supper," Baka continued. "You can't get good food like that in America. In his letters he said it was all hamburgers."

"Does he write t-to you often?"

"My, you're better at conversation this week."

"I'm t-trying."

"You're doing very well. Now, come and sit next to me for a while. If you have time, of course."

Natali sat down, and a delighted Obi, freed from her arms, leapt at Baka, jumping up to lick her face.

"Oh, I am sorry."

"Don't be. It's a long time since I've been kissed so enthusiastically."

"Your other s-son. Does he not visit? You said he lives in Split."

"Yes, he visits when time allows, but running a restaurant means he is so busy. Especially in the summer. Mateo is a dutiful boy, steady like his father was, but not affectionate like my Valentin. He will hug me, while Mateo makes sure my cupboards are well stocked. They show their love in different ways. What about your family, Natali?"

What about it? What could she say? Perhaps Baka would not like her if she admitted she and her mother weren't close, especially because it was probably her fault. She'd been such a disappointment to her, and she probably should never have been born. After all, she'd been told so many times she'd ruined her mother's life. But having been asked about her family, Natali could not exactly lie.

"You do have family?" Baka asked gently.

"Yes, I have Obi. That's where her name comes from: *obitelj*."

"No mother, no father?"

"My father was a tourist from Sweden. My m-mother..." Natali frowned. "We are n-not ... that is to say..."

"Sometimes family relationships are not easy," Baka said. "My granddaughters, I gave them everything, but now they are teenagers they do not visit me. I expect I am too old, too boring. And Valentin, well, he is so far away. But I have good friends around me and after all, Natali, we can *choose* our friends, can't we?"

Natali nodded. She wasn't very good at friends either, although Auntie Stela's daughter was just two years older than her and had always been kind. Obi was friend and family, but now she was wondering if that was enough. After Thursday night she would go to the ends of the earth for Lloyd, but was that friendship? Could it be, when they were so very different in every way? And Ana, much as she admired her and was coming to like her, when all was said and done, Ana was her employer, not her friend. Were friends important? Baka obviously thought so.

Baka was looking at her curiously but Natali really didn't want any more questions she'd struggle to answer, so she said, "Tell me about your friends, Baka."

"The friends I had when I was your age? Well, let me see. Things were very different on the island then. We were poor. No tourists, just fishing, and some of the men going to work on the port at Gruž or at sea. We didn't worry much about school, either. The priest held classes in the church so we learnt to read and write, but not much else. But reading ... I loved to read, Natali, but there were so few books. I wish we'd had your library.

"Then we had a new priest, a younger one, and he had a wonderful book of fairy stories and he let me borrow it. Oh, the world it opened up...! Dragons, witches, underwater kingdoms. Yes, that was my favourite. *Fisherman Plunk*. Do you know it?"

Baka really was rambling on. Maybe she was nervous about her son arriving on the ferry. Or not arriving. Maybe it was just because she was old. But Natali felt comfortable sitting next to her and for once she was in no hurry. Especially as Obi had settled with her head on Baka's lap.

"I don't know the story," she told her. "What's it about?"

"Eventually I came to realise it's about the power of women. But that's getting ahead of myself. Like all fairy tales it happened a long time ago, but I like to think, not very far from here. There was a fisherman called Plunk, and he was a very disgruntled sort of fellow, fed up with his simple life and greedy for great riches. So he decided he would not fish for three days to conjure up a spell.

"Well, it worked, and on the third day, the Sea King's daughter, the Dawn Maiden, rose from the waters in her silver boat and granted him a wish. He told her he had no joy in his world, and she promised that when he went home he would find all he needed.

"When Plunk got back to his shack he found a poor orphan girl waiting for him, and she offered to be his wife. At first he was not sure, because he'd been expecting gold, but he did not want to turn away his luck so he agreed. And do you know what? This girl was a marvellous storyteller, and every night her tales took him to places he could never imagine and filled him with joy."

Baka paused. "You see, Natali, it is also a story about stories, and those are very special, don't you think?"

"I'm n-not much of a reader."

Baka rested her hand briefly on Natali's arm. "Then you should be, because as well as joy, you can find comfort and love within the pages of a book. Friendship too. Anyway, back to Plunk and his wife. As time went on, they had a child, Winpiece, and the stories got even better, but Plunk was still waiting for his gold, and in the end became angry with his wife and made her go out and search for the Sea King's castle and the Dawn Maiden so he could ask her what had happened to it."

"What a horrible bully!"

Baka nodded. "Exactly that. Well, the poor girl fell asleep on the beach, so exhausted was she by her searching, and when she woke Winpiece was gone. Her grief was a terrible thing. It struck her dumb, and she went home and remained silent.

"So things were even worse for that miserable old fool Plunk, but again he tried his spell of not fishing, and the Dawn Maiden rose from the sea and granted him one more wish, so he asked her to show him the way to the Sea King's castle. The next new moon, he followed her instructions, through all the trials and tribulations that keep mere mortals out, and reached it.

"Well, of course it was a wonderful place, and filled Plunk with so much delight that he became as though he was quite young again, laughing and turning cartwheels, which pleased the Sea King, who made him a sort of court jester. And, laughing loudest at his antics was a little baby, who Plunk recognised as Winpiece, his very own son."

Natali was so entranced by the story that the blast of the ferry made her jump. Baka laughed. "Well, my dear, if you want to find out the ending, you'll have to read it. I am sure it's in one of those library books of yours. Anyway, you will appreciate the marvellous descriptions of the Sea King's castle all the more in the hands of a skilled storyteller."

Natali stood, lifting Obi down from Baka's lap. "Thank you," she beamed. "I'll ask Lloyd. I really want to know."

Baka stood a little stiffly, and leant on her stick. "Now, I must meet the boat."

"Of course you must," said Natali. "This is a very important day."

But would it be? Natali was curious to see what this errant son was like, assuming he did actually turn up this time, so when she had walked a little way along the steeply sloping path to the upper part of the village, she stopped in the shade of an overhanging oleander and watched. Just a few people got off the ferry, battling through the throng of tourists and day trippers waiting to get on. And as the crowd cleared, she saw Baka, standing quite alone.

Natali's throat was thick with tears. Should she go to her?

What was her son playing at, stringing his mother along like this? She was sure his sensible brother in Split would have something to say about it. But as she watched, one of the men loading newly arrived crates of beer onto a trailer stopped and spoke to Baka, clamping a hand on her shoulder.

"It's OK, Obi," she said. "Baka has her friends around her, and I mean, it's not as if we belong here." Giving a very gentle tug on the dog's lead, she carried on up the hill.

While Ana was cooking supper and Lloyd was talking to Ruth, Natali crept into the cabin where the books were kept. She gazed around at the neat stacks of boxes, each one carefully labelled. Even if she found the right one, would she be allowed to take it? Of course she would have to ask Lloyd first.

Along one side of the bed were the books for small children in Croatian, but although the shiny covers were beautiful she couldn't find any fairy tales. They were mainly modern stories about animals. And families. Families, of course. She remembered that now – one of the reasons she hadn't liked reading at school.

Obviously, the German and Italian books were no good to her, although perhaps some of the English ones might be. But the fairy tales were from her own country. Would they have been translated? She opened a box marked "young adult fantasy" and peeped inside.

The cover of the paperback on top looked amazing: a young woman dressed completely in black rode a purple dragon through a sky the colour of the sea on the calmest day. Who was this girl? What a life she must have! Natali couldn't remember books looking so exciting. It wasn't what she was searching for, but when she flipped it over she was staggered to find that the heroine had been born with only one arm so had been rejected by her family. How cool was that? Well, not for the girl, obviously, but the fact that the story was about a less than perfect person…

"Looking for something to read?" Natali jumped at the sound of Lloyd's voice. "It's fine, you know. You can. Just as long as you tell me which books you take."

"I was really looking for a fairy tale about a fisherman someone started to tell me, but … but … I would like to try this, if I can." Why on earth had she said that? She didn't want to start it and let Lloyd down by not finishing. "It's so long though, since I've read a whole book…" Like, ever. She wasn't clever enough for books, surely? But both Ana and Lloyd had said she wasn't stupid, and even though the idea was taking some getting used to, she really wanted to believe it. Perhaps finishing a book – a book in English, at that – would prove it one way or the other.

"Why not just give it a go? If it's not for you then you can pick something else. And if you come across words you don't understand, just ask me. Or maybe you can read English better than you feel you can speak it?"

Natali nodded, gazing at the book and gripping it more tightly.

"I do understand," Lloyd continued. "Talking in a foreign language needs a lot of confidence. I find it tough speaking Croatian, but I'm old enough and ugly enough not to care what anyone thinks."

She looked up at him. "How do you get like that?"

He frowned. "I guess … it comes with age. But when I say

'anyone', what I mean is strangers, people I don't know that well. I think we always mind what people we care about think." Natali was shocked to see so much pain in his eyes. He cleared his throat. "What was the fairy tale you were looking for? Perhaps I can help."

"It was about a fisherman called Plunk who was greedy and mean to his wife."

"I don't know it, but I'll see if I can track it down, if you like."

"Yes, please."

"OK, but right now I could murder a beer, and supper smells amazing. Let's go up."

Korčula

FRIDAY 14TH JULY

Ana sat in front of her laptop at the chart table in the corner of the galley, chewing her thumbnail. Not that there was much left of it. Her weekly reports to Ivana had that effect on her. She'd filled in the numbers relating to the books – a pretty scary row of red minuses against the targets – but what about the words? She had no words to explain it at all, and she was completely relying on Korčula to pull the overall total into the black.

Mljet had been a complete blank again, and she'd been almost as fed up as Lloyd had seemed on the sail here last night. Which was a shame, because Lopud had been an absolute triumph. Not only had Meri's leaflets generated half a dozen new customers, but Lloyd had had the bright idea of offering to visit the community centre after the library closed to read to the children. It was fair to say the manager, Filip, had bitten off her hand when she'd mentioned it, and it was all arranged for next Tuesday. If it went well, Lloyd was determined to root out similar opportunities on the other islands. But perhaps she wouldn't mention that to Ivana yet. Just in case it didn't work out.

Ana spun her seat left and right, gazing beyond the marina quay as a yellow taxi boat made its way towards Badija. She was no further on with unravelling her own problems either, and last Saturday had left her feeling totally confused. At one point she'd believed she was asking herself at least some of the right questions, but after she'd joined Pajo they'd had such a laugh, even helping Spiro to organise beach games for the children. In fact, she couldn't believe how much she'd enjoyed it. Maybe it had been the amount of wine that she'd drunk – more than enough to make everything a little rosy.

In the warm light of day – and the small hours of the night – she'd realised very quickly that rosy was not what she needed. And to make matters worse, another weekend would go by without her seeing Meri, who was heading off on a girls' trip to Zagreb. She so wanted to talk to her friend face to face about Pajo, but she was rapidly running out of options.

"Ana! Ana?" a woman's voice called, and she peeped out of the window to see Kristina, Korčula's library co-ordinator, on the marina quay.

She stood and walked through the salon to meet her. "I'm here. Come aboard."

Kristina stepped rather gingerly onto the transom, grabbing the rail as *Dida Krila* swayed.

"It's all right," said Ana. "She's very stable, but if you're not comfortable we can sit here." She indicated the nearest banquette.

"Thank you." Kristina dropped onto the seat. "It's crazy, being an island girl, but I've never been good on boats."

"Can I offer you coffee? Or a cold drink, perhaps?"

"No. Sit down for a moment, I need to talk to you about something."

By the look on Kristina's face, this was serious. Was the island withdrawing its funding? That would be a disaster. An absolute frigging disaster.

Ana's mouth went dry. "OK."

"It's about Lloyd. Someone's accused him of being a thief."

"A thief!" Her jaw literally dropped open. Lloyd? No way. Absolutely no way.

"Yes. I have to say I was surprised too. It was why I didn't bring any children last week. I needed to think this through. But the person is adamant, and reliable. And then of course…"

"Who is this person?" Ana folded her arms.

"She owns a restaurant in Lumbarda."

"That's ridiculous. When could Lloyd have gone to Lumbarda? We can't moor here until ten and we have to leave by four." But then … but then … he had stayed over one Friday night… *Jeben ti!* No, think, Ana, think. There had to be a reasonable explanation, there just had to be. Maybe he'd gone there and forgotten to pay his bill? That would explain it. She pulled herself back to what Kristina was saying.

"It's admirable of you to want to protect your team, but you and I both know he could have, because I bumped into him there the Saturday before last. And I have to say he was behaving most oddly. However, it transpires the theft was years ago, which was why I was so unsure about saying anything, but then I went to a meeting with Ivana and the stolen purse from Koločep came up."

The purse. The frigging purse. But Lloyd had been distraught. For days. But then, that very weekend, he'd gone to

Lumbarda. Ana's heart plummeted. Was there some sort of link? She cleared her throat.

"Did you tell Ivana your suspicions?"

"No. There was a whole room full of people. We were discussing many projects, not just this one, so it would not have been appropriate. I thought the best thing was to come to you."

"So let me get this straight. This woman in Lumbarda is saying he stole something from her restaurant the other Saturday?" Surely he couldn't have done? Lloyd? It made no sense at all.

"No, I told you. It was when he was on Korčula before. Thirty years ago."

So what did thirty years ago have to do with anything now? Ana began to fold her arms then stopped. Lloyd had been to Korčula before? Why had he never said? Of course, there could be one very good reason why he hadn't. The heat of the day pressed down on her, making her spine prickle with sweat and her stomach churn. She needed time to process this, but Natali had only gone to the marine supplies store so she wouldn't be away for much longer. Then Lloyd would come back and...

She stood abruptly. "Thank you so much for telling me. It's something I needed to know."

"What will you do? We can't have a thief running the library."

"And we can't call someone a thief without evidence."

Kristina sighed. "I know, but I'm in a difficult position, and if it hadn't been for the purse as well... Perhaps it might be easier to focus on proving whether or not he took that than on something that happened years ago."

Proof? But how could it be proved? "OK, Kristina, you had time to think this through, and now I need some. Would you mind giving me your number? Then we can talk next week."

Numbers exchanged, Ana helped Kristina off the boat and watched her walk briskly along the quay. Behind her the old town rose, brightly coloured trip-boats bobbing in the harbour, but to Ana it was all a blur. What the hell was she expected to do now?

She returned to the galley, crouching to stroke Obi's head when she lifted it from her basket. Could it be true? Could Lloyd have stolen something thirty years ago? And if so, did it matter so very much now? After all this time, the woman could easily have been mistaken. But the purse... Kristina was right. It put an entirely different perspective on things. As did the fact he'd never even mentioned that he'd been to Croatia before, let alone this island. That he'd lied was the most damning evidence of all.

Ana picked up her phone, then put it down again. She had to speak to Ivana. She felt so disloyal, though. Everything she'd known about Lloyd up until the moment Kristina set foot on the boat had been good. But why hadn't he told them the truth about coming to Korčula before? *Sranje*, she didn't want this hanging over her all weekend. She had more than enough to think about. She would pass it up the line to Ivana before the woman sneaked off early and be done with it. She picked up her phone again.

"Hi, Ana, you've just caught me." She'd been right about that at least. "What can I do for you?" At least Ivana wasn't wasting time on social pleasantries.

"Kristina came to see me. She says someone's accused Lloyd of being a thief."

"What?"

"Apparently it was thirty years ago, but I thought you should know what's being said."

"You're right. These sorts of rumours don't help anyone and we're a public body. We need to be whiter than white. What's your gut feel about the guy, Ana?"

"I would have said ... I mean, I've had no issues with him at all. He's been brilliant, in fact. But of course he was there when that purse was stolen on Koločep. I know it's a small thing, and he seemed devastated by it at the time..."

"If he'd come to us with an unblemished record, I might have agreed with you."

Ana went cold. "He didn't?"

"No. He resigned from his teaching job under a bit of a cloud, but his references were impeccable, and when I phoned his former boss she told me it had been an absolute one-off and there were mitigating circumstances. He'd been working in the school for more than twenty years without even half a black mark against his name. But all the same, these one-offs add up."

"So did he steal something from the school?"

"No, nothing like that. He assaulted a pupil."

"He did what?" Ana screamed down the phone, shock and rage bringing the bitter taste of bile to her throat. "You employed someone with a record of assault, for a live-aboard job with two women, without even telling me?"

"He does not have a record, as you put it, or we would never have taken him on. Don't exaggerate, Ana. Do you not think I checked with the British police as well as his previous employer? There were no charges, nothing at all, and he was the best candidate by far. None of the others even came close.

But that's not the point. You need to investigate this theft. Find out what happened."

This was so not in her job description. She was about to tell Ivana that, when Obi jumped up and rushed towards the transom, wagging her tail for all she was worth. Natali was back.

"Have a good weekend, Ivana." The words stuck in Ana's throat, but she forced them out in as civil a tone as she could manage. Her phone skittered from the chart table and spun across the floor, her hands shaking almost too much to pick it up. Lloyd, a thief? A man capable of assault? It went against everything she thought she knew about him. But so did the fact he'd never said he'd been to Korčula before. How the hell could she have got him so frigging wrong? The nausea that had been threatening exploded through her and she only just made it to the sink in time.

Natali's tentative hand was on her shoulder. "Are you all r-right?"

It should be frigging obvious that she wasn't. But Ana couldn't take this out on Natali; it was none of her doing. She was a victim too, if only she knew it. "No, not really," she managed to whisper.

"You should go and lie down," Natali told her. "I'll clean up here."

"We ... we need to be on the move in an hour."

"Well if you're too sick, we can't, and that's the end of it. But ... but if you can just pilot us out of the harbour, Lloyd and I can sail her home. I've done it before. Not on *Dida Krila* of course, but other b-boats, and I've helped you…"

Ana raised her head, leaning heavily on her hands, the

joints of her fingers white where she gripped the side of the sink. "I know you can do it. Thank you." It was a godsend. Natali was a godsend. Because, more than anything, it meant she would barely have to face Lloyd tonight. Ana had no idea how on god's earth she would manage that.

Ston

SATURDAY 15TH JULY

The soft light of early evening was so different in Ston to London, Lloyd thought, and he luxuriated in its quiet calm as he and Natali strolled past the high grey walls of Kaštio Fort then along the canal that led to the harbour. After walking Obi, they'd stopped in town for a beer, and, pretty sure that Natali hadn't had that many treats in her young life, Lloyd had bought them both the most delicious, plump, juicy burger, so they didn't even have to worry about cooking.

They paused at the humpback footbridge, leaning on its curved chrome rails while Obi sniffed around, the wide inlet in front of them a grey-blue mirror. Just visible between the folds of the hills, the road to Dubrovnik spanned the inlet on spindly, concrete legs. Lloyd had been more than pleased to see it last night as they'd sailed the last few kilometres in almost complete darkness. Although Natali had skippered well, it had worried them both that Ana was sick in her cabin, and he'd been relieved this morning when she'd disappeared early to spend the weekend with her parents to recuperate.

"I wonder how Ana's feeling now?" he mused.

"Hopefully the bug will go as quickly as it came. I mean, she didn't even get to the loo; when I came back she was throwing up in the sink, poor thing. And I think she had a fever too, because when I took her some water before I went to bed she insisted I lock my cabin. Something about thieves being around."

"At least she was well enough to drive this morning. Some rest in a proper bed will do her good." They walked on, past the shack that served as both harbour office and bar, the flat expanse of the salt pans to their right glistening in the pale evening sunlight. "Anyway, Natali, I've got a surprise for you. I found your *Fisherman Plunk* story on the internet. I'll lend you my iPad so you can read it while I phone Ruth."

She looked up at him and grinned. "Thanks, Lloyd, that's great. If I see the lady again on Monday it will be wonderful to tell her I know the ending. And I think by later this week you will need to help me to choose a new book. The dragon one is ace."

"I was flicking through the fantasy stories when we were on Mljet, so I do have a few ideas."

"Fantasy is a good name for them. You do escape to a make-believe world. Not that I have anything I need to escape from for the moment, but it's still fun to imagine." Which made Lloyd wonder just how tough Natali's life could be.

They drew level with *Dida Krila*, Lloyd fishing in his pocket for the keys. Natali grabbed his arm.

"The door ... it's open – just a little b-bit. I know we locked it."

"We did." Sweat prickled his palms. They had definitely left the boat secure.

"D-do you think Ana was right about the thieves? Maybe her f-friend at the harbour office messaged her or something."

OK, however nervy he felt, this was up to him. If nothing else, he needed to keep Natali safe.

"You wait here," he told her, "just in case they're still on board. If you hear me yelling or anything, run to the bar for help."

"Should we g-get someone first?"

He shook his head. "It's probably fine. If they were watching us leave then they're long gone by now." He sounded so convincing he almost believed it himself.

Lloyd slipped off his deck shoes and stepped gingerly onto the very centre of the transom, trying to balance his weight so he rocked the boat as little as possible. If someone was here who shouldn't be, he didn't want to alert them to his presence. He needed to surprise them; at least that way they wouldn't be lying in wait to surprise him.

Outside the galley he stopped and listened. Shit. Movement. Something like rustling, and it was coming from his hull. Should he go on? Or go back for help? But he couldn't risk them getting away, not with any of his stuff. He had so many pictures of Jenny on his iPad he couldn't bear to think of it in a stranger's hands. They were precious and they were his. He balled his hands into fists, then released them, massaging his fingers.

He crept down the steps, alert for every sound. His cabin door was shut and he knew he'd left it open for the air to circulate. Someone was in there. He looked around the cramped passageway. Nothing he could use as a weapon. He was on his own.

Inside the cabin, he heard a cupboard door close and his

holdall scraping across the floor. It galvanised him into action. No thieving little shit was going to take his things, his personal things. No frigging way. In a single movement he flew down the hallway and flung the door wide.

"Ana!" The word choked from him as he clung to the handle.

She was kneeling on the floor, rummaging through the fleeces and wet weather gear he'd left in his bag. He blinked. Surely this couldn't be happening? It was so surreal he almost wanted to laugh, but it wasn't funny in the least. If he'd had more to drink, he might even think he was imagining it.

"Ana?" She stood slowly, her eyes meeting his. Eyes that were steely and cold. "What are you doing?"

"Searching your cabin. As skipper, I have the right—"

"You have no such right! Not without asking me first. What the hell are you playing at?" Disbelief was turning to anger. How could she do this? Why would she want to? The hairs on the back of Lloyd's neck stood on end, his body stiff with fury. This was … beyond. *Way* beyond. The flush of anger ran up from his chest and he had the strangest sensation of growing, of filling the doorway…

No. Stop. Take control. This couldn't happen again.

"Explain." He spat out the word. He didn't trust himself to say any more.

Ana put her hands on her hips. "You're the one who has some explaining to do. Where did you put it?"

"Put what?"

"The purse."

"What purse?"

"The one you stole from that woman on Koločep."

"The one I what?" Lloyd was literally open-mouthed.

"You don't deny it?"

"Because it's too frigging ridiculous to even consider. Why the hell would you think that?"

"Because you have form, that's why. Form you didn't tell us about. Theft, assault… What else are you hiding, Lloyd Richards?" Ana was yelling now, her face puffy and red. Lloyd gripped the handle tighter, the metal digging into his fingers. So she knew… She knew… Oh god, this would change everything. Time stilled. Ana's face zoned in and out of focus, the moment of silence stretching. Stretching until…

He turned and fled, barely noticing Natali at the far end of the passageway, then stumbling up the steps, through the salon. Feet shoved into shoes, then running, running, and sobbing with shame. Because it was all he could do.

Trying to contain her tangled emotions, Ana followed Lloyd into the hallway, but to her amazement Natali was blocking it, her arms gripped tightly around Obi and shaking with fury.

"What the hell have you done?"

"Me?"

"Accusing Lloyd of those things. How could you? He's the kindest, bravest, most honest man I've ever met, and if you can't see that then I don't know where you've been this last month."

Never mind where she'd been, where had this Natali? To see her like this was a revelation. Ana had to explain herself. Fast.

"Kristina came to see me on Friday afternoon. She said Lloyd had been accused of theft."

"And you believed her? Just like that?"

A whimpering Obi still in her arms, Natali clambered up the steps into the galley, Ana trailing behind. "Will you at least let me explain?"

"You listen to me first. I heard you say something about a stolen purse on Koločep. When was that? The second time we visited? It wasn't Lloyd. It was a pickpocket. I saw it happen."

"You saw a purse stolen from the library and you said nothing?" This was all she frigging well needed and exhaustion shot through her.

Natali faltered, her eyes momentarily downcast. "No, n-not from there. I don't know anything about that. It was in the square. He was so clever, so quick, that at first I wasn't sure. But he went off towards the ferry quay so he would have passed the library."

It did sound credible, more than credible. It wasn't only Ana's legs that were shaking, it felt like the whole boat. The whole planet. Whyever had she even embarked on this stupid venture? She'd spent all day wondering what to do, even changing her mind a dozen times about whether or not she should disturb Meri's weekend, before finally deciding against it. She'd worked herself up into such a state that when Lloyd and Natali had sent her a selfie from one of the bars in town she'd leapt into her jeep and put her crazy half-plan to search Lloyd's cabin into action.

It hadn't been only Kristina's words, it had been Ivana's. The fact that Lloyd had assaulted someone... He clearly wasn't as honest or straightforward as Natali believed. And he'd never told them he'd been to Korčula before. But was it really for her to blurt all this out now? Without even asking Lloyd for the truth?

Jeben ti! That's what she should have done – talk to him. Not creep around behind his back in the most awful way, just because she was frightened that what she needed to say would upset him. She'd done that anyway now. And some. She'd split the whole bloody library apart. Ruined it for everyone. All she wanted to do was put her head in her hands and howl, but with Natali glaring at her that wasn't an option. In fact, there was only one course of action she could possibly take.

"I need to find Lloyd," she said.

"You most certainly do."

But where would he have gone? There were only two choices: back towards Ston, or down the lane along the inlet towards the village of Broce. She had a hunch it might be the latter; he'd been so steaming angry. But would he want to walk it off on his own, or drink it off in town? This was no time for pride, so Ana ran to the harbour shack and asked the barman if he'd seen him pass.

Her gut feel was right; Lloyd hadn't headed into town. If she walked fast, she might just catch up with him, but her reserves of energy were at a low ebb after throwing up the evening before and not eating much today. She needed to take it steady or she might not make it at all, and this was far too important to screw up again.

It took her the best part of half an hour to reach the split in the road just before Broce. Which way would Lloyd have gone? She had to take a chance he'd have stayed by the water. Dusk was beginning to fall, the long shadows of a ruined house on the inlet reaching across the road. Traditional music drifted from a nearby terrace, but otherwise all was quiet, still. If she remembered rightly, there was a *konoba* just a little further on, near the tiny harbour.

If nothing else, she needed a drink of water. Perhaps Lloyd had too.

She spotted him sitting at a table close to the quay, a glass in front of him. Not water, but whisky or brandy by the look of it. She'd never known him to drink spirits before. Natali's voice came back to her. What the hell had she done?

"Lloyd?" He turned to look up at her, his eyes red rimmed and deeply lined.

Sranje! She couldn't bear that her stupid, stupid actions had caused so much pain. She hated to cause anyone pain. Why hadn't she just kept her mouth shut?

"I am just so sorry. I need to apologise … to explain…"

He gestured to the seat opposite him and she pulled it out, its wooden legs scraping on the concrete surface.

They sat in silence, looking at each other without their eyes actually meeting. It was up to her to speak, but as she was shaping the words in her head Lloyd said quietly but firmly, "I am not a thief."

"I know. I know that now. Natali said she saw a pickpocket operating that day on Koločep."

"OK." More silence. Ana was gasping for some water, but it was impossible to call the waiter at such a critical moment.

"I'm sorry, I'm sorry. I do believe you. Honestly."

Finally he nodded. "Well if that's the case, what I'm struggling with is why you suddenly thought I had stolen the purse. Or have you had your suspicions all along? You've hidden it very well if you have."

"No! Of course not. It was Friday. Only Friday. Kristina came to tell me someone was accusing you of theft. Before. When you were on Korčula before. Not that you ever said you'd been there." She battled to keep the frustration out of her voice. If he'd been completely honest, she'd never have doubted him. Perhaps there was fault on both sides. But all the same...

Lloyd picked up his glass, the last rays of the sun highlighting the liquid as he swirled it around. He looked at her. "You don't have a drink. Wait..." He leant towards the waiter who was clearing the next table. "*Oprostite...*"

"*Sto biste?*"

"Another whisky for me, please. Ana?"

"Red wine ... and a jug of water. Thank you."

While they waited Lloyd said nothing, just turned his tumbler around and around in his hand as he gazed at the view over her shoulder. Would he admit to being on Korčula before, or would he not? He might just say it was none of her business. The strip lights on the terrace had taken over from the dregs of the day, throwing his strong features into sharp relief. A grey tinge to his skin made him look defeated, old.

It wasn't until their drinks arrived that he spoke again. "I didn't say I'd been to Korčula before because it was painful."

"You don't have to..." *Sranje*. She didn't mean it. She needed to know.

"I do. I came here in '91. I meant to travel around, but instead I got a job in a *konoba*, fell in love with the owner's daughter ... and she fell for me. But then the war came and ... anyway..."

His hand was shaking as he put down his glass. She wanted to put hers over it in comfort, but she didn't quite dare. This still all felt too raw. "It's none of my business."

"Not before, maybe, but now it seems it is. I couldn't keep looking over my shoulder every Friday, Ana, I couldn't. I knew that after the first week. So the day I stayed on, I went to find her. To see if she was still there, really. And the moment she saw me... God, if looks could kill I'd have been six foot under Lumbarda quayside. I was just pulling myself together to walk away when Kristina came along. She lives in the village. Maybe Mirjana asked her about me. But I swear, I absolutely swear, I stole nothing. Not then. Not now. There must be some misunderstanding. Maybe Kristina got it wrong?"

He sounded so pathetically hopeful that Ana nodded. She needed to summon up the courage to tell him Kristina had seemed convinced, but the only words that came out were, "I believe you."

And she did. Lloyd may be hiding things about his past, but his denial of any theft had been so complete. And anyway, whatever he'd done as a young man shouldn't be impacting his life now. Or impacting the library. It just wasn't fair. The library affected all of them, not just Lloyd. She needed it, Natali needed it ... and she had to admit that Lloyd was the one driving it forwards.

Despite her strong desire to weep, Ana knew she had to take control of her ragged emotions. Already her head was fuzzy with the wine, and that wouldn't do. She needed to be sharp, sharp. Well, as sharp as she possibly could be. She flagged the waiter, asking for bread with cold meats and cheese, but when it came he brought another round of drinks as well.

Lloyd cleared his throat, his voice stiff and formal. "I hope, Ana, we can rebuild at least some of the trust between us. It will be a long and difficult summer otherwise. If you want me to stay, that is?"

"Of course I want you to." Without any one of them the project would fail, and she needed it to succeed so badly. But to rebuild their trust completely ... that required an answer to something else. Would Lloyd be prepared to give it? It was as if he had read her mind.

"The supposed theft isn't the only issue, is it? You know ... you mentioned ... although Ivana promised she wouldn't say..."

"I had to tell her about the theft allegations, so it came out. She said ... you'd ... assaulted someone." She picked up her glass and put it down again. "Do you mind if I ask what happened?"

Lloyd sighed. "It was a pupil, Ana. I was in a position of trust, and that made it worse. Beyond worse." He ran his hand over the top of his head. "And I do mind telling you what I did. I mind terribly." He took another gulp of whisky. "But I will. I slammed him against the classroom wall."

He'd done what? Ana stared at Lloyd, unable to help herself. How could this apparently kind and gentle man have done such a thing? And, given he had, how come Ivana had thought it was all right to employ him? Even without her head spinning with wine, this wouldn't make anything close to sense. And how should she react? *Sranje* and *sranje* again. Trust was a hell of a long way off right now.

She took a deep breath. "That's not the Lloyd I've come to know." At least that was the truth.

"It's kind of you to say so, but it is me. It will always be part of me, and I'll never forgive myself. And you did believe I could do such a thing, because you told Natali to lock her cabin door. There's no point denying it, just to be nice, or we'll never put this right. We'll circle around it, pretending it didn't happen, and I won't work or live like that." For the first time, there was real resolve in his voice.

Ana sighed. "OK, you're right. I did want to try to make you feel better, but that doesn't mean I lied. Believe me when I say I'm struggling to imagine you hurting anyone, let alone a child." He raised his eyebrows. "Oh come on, Lloyd, give me a break. I'm way, way out of my depth. I just sail boats."

Lloyd nodded slowly. "I get that. You're young, and even the most experienced of managers... Well, anyway, I'm so very sorry you're having to deal with this shit. But we do need to be honest with each other, and honesty sometimes hurts. I'm going to tell you exactly what happened in that classroom, then you can decide if you want me to stay. There's no need to be kind – you have to do what's best for you and Natali. For the library. My feelings don't come into it."

The *pršut*, which would normally taste so delicious, sat heavy and greasy in her stomach. She washed it down with another mouthful of wine, then nodded.

"It was a class of fifteen and sixteen-year-olds, most of them with some sort of behavioural difficulties which made learning a challenge. I didn't usually teach them. Someone was off sick so I offered to fill in. It was the sort of work my Jenny loved and did all the time, and I suppose it made me feel closer to her. Especially as, well, this sounds silly, but ... it was the anniversary of our first date, and these anniversaries really sting, so I thought doing something positive might take me out of myself.

"We taught in the same school, always had. She filled my life, Ana, everywhere. So of course these kids knew her. And this lad, this lad ... he started to say the most awful things about her. Really awful." He paused, looking to the darkening sky as though for inspiration. "I knew ... I knew he had problems, I knew all that. But I lost it with him. Saw red.

Literally. The next thing I knew I was slamming him against the wall, telling him to shut the fuck up. It was only the classroom assistant pulling me away that stopped me... I'm not sure I wouldn't have killed him otherwise. But it brought me to my senses, and I went straight to the head's office and resigned.

"She was more than good about it. Said that instead I should go to my doctor and get signed off with stress, that there would have to be an investigation but she was sure she could make it right because of the circumstances, and because the lad had always been trouble. Then when I was ready, I could come back. But the thing is, Ana, it wasn't right. It was totally and completely wrong. I abused the position of trust the school put me in." He stared at the table. "Jenny would have been so ashamed."

"I think Jenny would have understood."

He looked up. "That's what Ruth said. And everyone told me not to throw away my career. But I already had. The moment I touched him." He released his tumbler from his grip, massaging his fingers. "So now I'm here. For some reason they accepted me, and it's been a lifeline, to be honest."

God, what he'd been through, on top of his grief, and now to have accusations of theft levelled at him too. Ana could barely imagine how he might feel, but one thing she did know was that she had to support him through this. However it had looked at first, Lloyd was the good man she had always believed him to be, and relief flooded through her.

Finally, she did reach out and place her hand over his. "Ivana said your references were impeccable."

"She gave me a chance. I want to repay that."

"Is that why you're so passionate about making the library work?"

"In part. But mainly because I understand how good it could be for those kids." A ghost of a smile appeared on his face. "And I love working with them. I've really missed it." He paused. "Also because I think, deep inside, I have a point to prove to myself. I need to be part of something good and useful. It breaks my heart I can never go back to teaching, and I really need the library to be a success."

"So do I. And the best way to achieve it is to continue to work together." Ana raised her glass. "Let's drink to that and say no more about it."

They chinked across the table. They'd both made mistakes so surely they could move beyond them and put things right, despite the fact they'd probably both have goddam awful hangovers tomorrow. Despite the fact she had no idea how to sort this out with Ivana. But that was for another day. Even seeing Lloyd half smiling was all she wanted right now. That and to finish the bread and cheese, then stumble back along the path to bed.

Ston

SUNDAY 16TH JULY

Lloyd switched the shower to cold and angled the jets onto his face, if jets was the word for them. Oh, they were more than adequate to wash with, especially for an onboard bathroom, but as for blasting away the hangover from hell – no chance. Hopefully Ana wasn't feeling quite this bad. At least she'd kept off the whisky, but his one objective when he'd arrived at that bar had been to get drunk as quickly as possible.

Pulling his towel from the back of the door, he rubbed his hair vigorously. Which did sod all for his headache. What he needed was to get dressed and get up to that galley and drink about a gallon of water. Right at this moment, he didn't think anything else would work. Then as soon as he could stomach it, food. A bacon butty would be perfect, but in Croatia bacon was different.

He lowered himself gingerly onto the banquette. Croatian bacon. The morning Mirjana's father had offered him the job. He'd been in the *konoba* the night before for supper and he'd seen her then: her beautiful smile set in her round, dimpled face; her perfect, almond-shaped eyes; her luscious figure. He'd never have dared speak to her, but then he'd overheard some German lads planning to leave without paying, so he'd tipped her off.

And the next morning she'd been on the beach, waiting for him after his swim, inviting him to breakfast. Bacon and eggs. Except the bacon had been raw. Of course, now *panceta* was fairly commonplace, but back then in England everyone thought that pork had to be cooked to within an inch of its life or it would poison you. Mirjana had noticed him pushing it around his plate and when he'd explained, her father had whisked it away and grilled it, leaving them alone at the table, him completely tongue-tied in front of this beautiful girl. Then, when Zoran came back, he'd offered Lloyd a job for the summer, and of course he'd accepted.

It should have been such a happy memory, thirty-odd years on. First love and all that. But the way it had ended ... and now it seemed it hadn't ended at all. Not for Mirjana. He still couldn't get his head around why she'd lied to Kristina about him; it didn't fit with anything he knew about her. Yes, at the time she'd had every right to be disappointed in him – angry even. And she had had a quick temper – he'd witnessed some absolutely blazing rows between her and Kesten – but he'd never known her to hold a grudge, or be anything other than completely honest.

People changed, or maybe life changed people. Lloyd hung the towel back on the door, and started to dress, his head thudding every time he moved. So he sat down again, T-shirt balled between his hands.

He didn't think he'd ever been actively hated before. Last

night, in the whisky-induced haze and relief that Ana had finally believed him and wasn't going to sack him, he'd managed to push the thought to one side. Now it was circling around like a particularly nasty black crow, stabbing him every so often with its beak. To engender the sort of malice that made someone spread such awful lies thirty years later…? It didn't bear thinking about.

And he wasn't going to think about it. Never mind that it was actually making him shake, he had something more pressing to do, and not just drink his body weight in water. Ana may be happy to let him stay, but Natali had to be too. And she needed to know the whole truth first.

He found her sitting at the table, checking carefully along the length of one of the safety harnesses before ticking it off on her weekly maintenance list. She jumped up when she saw him, Obi skittering to the floor before charging in his direction, tail wagging manically.

"I boiled the kettle," Natali said. "I thought you would need tea quite badly this morning."

He crouched down carefully, trying to stop his brain from knocking too hard against his skull, and tousled Obi between her ears. "I was in a state, wasn't I?"

"You both were. I haven't even seen Ana yet. B-but I was so very glad you're friends again. What she said to you … what she did … it was awful."

"And you need to understand why she did it, so sit back down." He straightened, feeling closer to seventy than fifty-three as his knees cracked. "I'll get some water. I can't face tea just yet. I only have a few bags left from the ones I brought with me and I need to make sure I enjoy them."

He ran the water until it was cool over his fingers, then

filled a pint glass, forcing himself to drink half of it before topping it up and returning outside. Natali looked up at him expectantly, but her face was so trusting that somehow he couldn't bring himself to sit next to her, so he propped himself against the galley door.

"First, you need to know that I'm not a thief. But I did do something bad – very bad – which is why I'm not a teacher anymore." He took another gulp of water. "I'm afraid I ... I lost my temper and attacked a pupil."

"They must have done something terrible to make you do that."

Oh, the child's faith in him. He could have hugged her there and then, but she needed to know it all. So he repeated everything he'd said to Ana last night, while she listened, never taking her eyes from his face.

When he finished she folded her arms. "Sounds like that boy was a nasty piece of work. We had plenty like him at my school. Girls too."

Lloyd shook his head. "Not bad, troubled. In and out of care, foster homes, never having a proper family ... needed medication he didn't always take... I let him down so badly. Let everyone down."

Natali stood and walked towards him, enveloping him in a hug, her thin arms squeezing so hard he thought his ribs might crack. "He let himself down. He should never have said bad things about your wife. I bet he did it deliberately to hurt you." She looked up at him. "People can be cruel, Lloyd."

He hugged her back a little awkwardly because the glass was still in his hand. "You know that from experience, don't you?"

"Yes. At school it was h-horrible. I'd have cheered if a teacher had thumped one of those bullies."

"But you're OK now?" he asked her. "Things are OK in your life now?"

She smiled. "Of course. I have Obi and I have a wonderful job with lovely people. And anyway, my Auntie Stela always tells me it's best to be positive, because all manner of good things can happen if you are. She says it's karma." Natali stepped away from him. "I can hear Ana moving around. I should put the coffee on."

It was only a few minutes later that Ana appeared in the galley, greeted by Obi's excited barks. She ran her hand over the top of her hair, which was already escaping from its scrunchie.

"Obi, I love you, but please shut up."

Natali crouched down, holding the dog's little face between her hands. "You. No barkies. Ana and Lloyd are feeling ... delicate."

Ana looked at Lloyd and rolled her eyes. "You too?"

He raised his water glass in her direction. "God, yes."

"A quiet morning, then." Ana said.

"Shall I take Obi for another walk?" Natali offered. "Once I've made the coffee, of course."

"Coffee? You are an angel." Ana popped some pills from a blister pack. "I need it to wash these down. Want some, Lloyd? Or have you already taken something?"

It was tempting, but no. Lloyd moved to the tap and refilled his glass. "I'm sticking to the hard stuff. At least until I'm up to eating."

Ana groaned. "Don't even mention food."

As Natali busied herself with the *džezva*, Lloyd took himself outside, perching against the cabin roof in the shade of the fly deck. The faintest of breezes ruffled his T-shirt as the air found its way between the hills that enclosed the long inlet connecting Ston to the sea. The water was a glassy blue and the boughs of the trees on the opposite bank swayed gently. A fishing boat puttered past, its wake spreading fantails behind it.

Something Natali had said was bothering him. He supposed it was good in a way, that her auntie's mantra helped her to stay positive, and right now he could certainly use some of that, but for him it didn't ring true. He and Jenny had always believed in shaping their own destinies, making plans, taking action, and they'd brought Ruth up to be the same, not waiting for some nebulous cosmic force to do it for you. But if that nebulous force was the only tool you had…

"I'm going to see Ivana this week to see if I can put this right." He hadn't even noticed Ana was beside him until she spoke.

"What will you tell her?"

"That the woman on Korčula is lying and Natali saw a pickpocket on Koločep the day the purse went missing."

Lloyd frowned. "Doesn't that put Natali in rather a bad light? That she didn't tell anyone?"

Ana groaned. "Oh god, I'm so rubbish at this. I thought I had finally got over myself enough to do something, rather than just feel horribly responsible yet utterly useless. Why can't I just make one frigging good decision?"

"You make good decisions all the time, Ana. They come so naturally, you don't even notice. Like your call to close early at Mljet the day of the storm. Like knowing the best line to take *Dida Krila* in different conditions."

"I mean the important ones."

"Those are important. The most important. They keep us safe."

"You're trying to make me feel better, aren't you?"

They were shoulder to shoulder and he gave her a squeeze. "I'm telling it how it is, that's all. Like I said last night, as far as running a project's concerned you're on a learning curve, and it's entirely my fault you've been thrown in at the deep end. But I can help, you know. Offer some advice if you need it? To try to make amends."

She squeezed him back. "Yes, please." She paused. "I ... I made a decision once, a big one, and although in my gut it was right, if I'd thought about it more..." She trailed off.

After a few moments he asked, "Do you want to share?"

She shook her head. "Not right now. To be honest, I still can't be a hundred per cent sure if I was right or wrong, so let's stick to what we can change, huh?"

Ana was right. Look forwards, not back. "Sounds like a plan," he told her.

Koločep

MONDAY 17TH JULY

Natali helped Lloyd to load the last of the boxes onto the sack trolley, then balanced the pop-up banner on top. The ferry heading towards Dubrovnik was expected any moment, and she watched as he forged his way through a group of holidaymakers surrounded by luggage. Closer to hand, two men were unloading empty beer crates from a tractor-trailer.

She wound Obi's lead more tightly around her hand. "We'd better get out of the way."

One of the men stopped as she walked past. "*Oprostite*, you're the girl who chats to Baka. Natali, is it?"

Astonished he knew her name, she nodded. "Y-yes."

"I need to talk to you."

"Is Baka all right?"

"Yes, yes." He stopped, rubbing the stubble on his chin. "Well, yes and no."

Had her son not coming upset her so badly that she was ill? Had she had a fall?

But the man's smile was encouraging. "Don't worry. There's just something you need to understand now that you're becoming friendly. She said only yesterday how much she was looking forward to seeing you."

"I ... I like talking to her too."

"That's good. Very good." He frowned. "And you mustn't let what I'm about to say change that. Valentin, the son she waits for, he died almost fifteen years ago."

Had she heard him right? That didn't make sense at all. "Then w-w-why...?"

"She's getting a bit forgetful. Probably has some sort of dementia, truth be told. She manages very well in most ways, and when she doesn't, the village helps out. But a few years ago she started meeting the ferries, expecting Valentin to come. You see, he was on his way to visit from America when he had a heart attack."

"That's so sad for her." To her surprise, Natali felt choked by tears. To wait every day, to be disappointed every day, to go home alone... How awful must that be?

"Oh, you are a sweet child. Baka was right. But perhaps it isn't all sad, you know. Sad, of course, that Valentin died before he could come home, and certainly Baka and her late husband suffered very much at the time. But now she doesn't suffer, because she thinks he's on his way. She has hope. And waiting for him gets her out of the house and she talks to people. And she cooks a proper meal each day, which she might not do otherwise."

Natali nodded. It was so much to take in, and way beyond her experience. "S-so everyone pretends he is still alive?"

"I suppose so, yes, because if we told her he wasn't it

would hurt her most terribly. Every time anyone said anything it would be like he had died all over again, because she doesn't remember."

"My friend, Lloyd, he lost his wife two years ago and it still makes him sad."

The man nodded. "And there is nothing as bad as a parent losing a child. Nothing. The bonds are so strong. Anyway, I must get on. Thanks for understanding, Natali. If you want to know anything else, please do ask me. My name's Dorijan and I'm always here." He bent to pat Obi, sending her tail into a frenzy of wagging, before returning to his work.

Slowly, Natali walked away from the quay. The upward path was still shaded, and unwilling to go past Lloyd while she was trying to make sense of what she'd been told, Natali took it. Poor Baka, to lose her son when he was finally on his way to visit her. It was just the most awful time for it to happen, when she'd doubtless been full of excitement to see him. And now she was getting old, her mind was playing tricks and taking her back to those last moments of happiness when she knew he was alive.

What made it doubly strange was that in other ways she didn't seem forgetful at all. She remembered Obi's name, and Natali's, and knew when to expect them, and even what they'd talked about before. It was almost as though Baka was living in two separate times at once, and she just couldn't grasp how that might be.

"But I don't have to, do I?" she murmured to Obi. At least she wouldn't be angry with Valentin anymore. And of course it wouldn't change how she was with Baka. Why should it? No one was perfect, after all.

"Natali! Natali!" Baka's voice sounded behind her and she turned, her greeting drowned out by Obi's excited yips.

Baka was waving from outside a modest stone house surrounded by citrus trees, their tops just visible over the bougainvillea-covered wall. Of course, the slope was so steep above the village that the height of the trees made perfect sense. Either the house was built up, or went down to a second floor that Natali couldn't see from the path.

Baka closed the wooden gate leading from a terrace lined with pots of herbs, and waited on the path. Obi was so excited she all but scrambled along in front of Natali, her claws clicking on the asphalt.

"Are you on your way to meet the ferry?" Natali asked, as Baka bent to pet Obi.

"Yes. Valentin's coming back from America today. Isn't it wonderful? And what's more, I've made some *medenjaci*. With Marin's honey. You know, he has the stall next to the library."

Natali nodded. "I do."

"Don't worry, young lady, I've baked enough for you as well. Here." She straightened, pulling a paper bag from her handbag. "I have them ready. I know you come on a Monday."

"Baka, that's so k-kind of you, thank you." Natali's voice felt scratchy. No one had ever baked anything for her before.

"It is my pleasure. You need feeding up. But now I must go, or I'll be late."

"I'll come with you. I have something to tell you." Natali fell into step beside Baka, whose walk was really quite spritely for one so elderly. "My friend Lloyd found the *Fisherman Plunk* story. It's wonderful, isn't it, what his wife goes through to get their baby back. She faces every challenge so bravely – some of them were properly scary."

"It is wonderful, and also understandable. There is nothing a mother won't do for a child, is there?"

Natali changed her shrug to a nod just in time. There was very little her mother would actually do for her, but it was the hand life had dealt her, and that was that. At least she'd had Auntie Stela's wise words to guide her and she'd been right – good things did happen if you stayed positive, and this summer was turning out to be absolutely the best.

She and Baka parted company at the bottom of the path, just as the ferry was nosing its way onto the quay, the rumble of its engines filling the bay. How would Baka feel when she realised her son wasn't on it? Was the sorrow new to her every day, every time? Natali shook her head. It was completely beyond her comprehension. She popped one of the little round *medenjaci* into her mouth. She'd never had one before and the flavour was exquisite, the soft dough melting into honey and a spice she couldn't quite recognise on her tongue. It was so very delicious that it made her a little tearful that Baka would never again share her wonderful baking with her son.

So typical her phone would ring when her hands were plunged into the galley sink, washing chard. Natali's phone never rang. It was most likely a nuisance call, but all the same she wiped her hands and checked.

The word *Mama* filled the little screen, but she had taken too long to answer and the call went to voicemail. Just as well. She couldn't think what her mother might want, but at least this way she would have time to consider her answer. And finish preparing the chard.

A few minutes later the phone rang again, but Natali let it go to voicemail. Honestly, did Mama think she sat around waiting for her to call? She was working. And if she'd phoned while they were mooring or tacking or something else important, she wouldn't have been able to answer anyway.

She looked at the clock on the galley wall. It was only quarter past three, so now would be a good time to see what her mother wanted, before Lloyd packed up the library and they prepared to leave. She dried her hands thoroughly, put the chard in the fridge, then leant against the work surface. Ana was in her cabin, so at least she had some privacy.

Sranje! Her *mama* was sobbing in the message. She should have picked up. "He's left me," she wailed. "Dario's gone back to Italy. He … he promised he'd take me, but he told me this morning he'd changed his mind. Oh, Natali, my heart is broken. I'm too old … no one will ever love me again. Please call me, *draga*. Please."

Natali toyed with the phone in her hand. It was not the first time Mama had remembered her existence the moment she broke up with someone. Not the first time she'd said her heart was broken and she'd never recover. Normally all that her mother required was for Natali to turn up on her doorstep and hold her hand, nodding and providing a tissue every so often, then somehow cobbling together a meal from the limited contents of the fridge while her mother got drunk. Oh, and phoning whoever her *mama* happened to be working for at the time to tell them she was ill. And repeat, two or maybe three times a week, if necessary, until Mama pulled herself together and went back to her job – or found a new one if they'd sacked her.

In the past Natali had done all this, if not willingly, but

because she could. In fact, when the guy before Dario had bailed it had worked out quite well because she'd been sofa surfing, unable to find anywhere cheap enough to rent, and she'd actually moved back home. Until her *mama* had got fed up with her being there all the time, and had started to shout at Obi, which had very much not been all right. But by then it had been November, and she'd found a bedsit above a restaurant that had closed for the winter. They hadn't minded her having Obi because they thought a dog would keep down the rats. As if! Obi would run a mile if she saw one.

But now it just wasn't possible to drop by whenever her mother needed her. All the same, it felt pretty cruel to make Mama fend entirely for herself, and sort of awkward, because last time Natali had taken advantage of the situation, so perhaps she owed her mother. At least a call or two. Sort of dropping by, via phone.

"That was a big sigh." Ana's head appeared at the top of the steps as she began to climb to the galley.

"I've h-had a message from my mother. She's split with her boyfriend and it sounds like she's in a bit of a mess." Natali sucked her lip. "She'll want me to go home, but of course I can't."

"Home's Dubrovnik?"

Natali nodded.

"Then you can," said Ana, shrugging.

"Well, perhaps at the weekend. Take the bus from Ston..." But that wouldn't be soon enough – or probably good enough – for her *mama*. Nothing ever was.

"No, come with me tomorrow. I've fixed up to see Ivana so I'm getting the early ferry, then back in the afternoon."

"But won't one of us need to help Lloyd?"

"It's Lopud. It's an easy set-up. I'm sure he can manage." Ana put her hand on Natali's shoulder. "It's family after all. He'll understand."

Dubrovnik

TUESDAY 18TH JULY

Were the county offices actually designed to make people feel small? Standing outside the tall iron gates, a severe white pillar on either side, Ana seriously considered it. Even the row of neatly trimmed cypresses looked forbidding. Especially as her trousers were sticking to her legs after the bus ride from the harbour and her hair was all over the place. As usual.

Ivana was waiting and she'd best get this over with. At least she had something to look forward to afterwards. She was meeting Meri for lunch so she'd finally be able to talk to her about Pajo and the whole knotty motherhood question. And it was not a moment too soon; he'd messaged her again yesterday to fix up a date for dinner at his new apartment.

This was so not the time to let her mind wander. She needed to get herself across that courtyard and through those impressive double doors, and she needed to be honest with Ivana. And calm. That's what she and Lloyd had agreed.

Honest. And calm. Calm, calm, calm. If she said it enough, she might just feel it.

Even though Ana was bang on time, Ivana kept her waiting before finally showing her through to the small room where they'd met before. Ana sat down at the table while Ivana filled plastic cups of water from the cooler, then placed herself opposite. Last time she'd sat next to her. Should she read something into that?

"So, Ana, what have you found out?" No preamble. No niceties.

Big deep breath. "I've spoken to Lloyd and he has categorically denied stealing anything."

Ivana tutted. "I wouldn't expect anything different. He's not exactly going to confess, is he?"

Ana was tempted to say that Ivana didn't know Lloyd, but held her tongue. Biting back wasn't going to help anybody. She needed to stick to the facts.

"First, I think we can discount his involvement in the theft of the purse from the library, as Natali tells me there was a pickpocket operating on Koločep that day. Apparently another purse was taken at a café in the village square that morning."

"Apparently?"

Was Ivana going to question her every statement? Was that how the land lay? Ana felt her hackles rise. "Natali was nearby when it happened."

"And it couldn't have been Lloyd?"

"No. He definitely, *definitely*, didn't leave the library."

Ivana sat back. "Well, that's something. It's my judgement on the line here too, Ana, my reputation. But at least I'm in a position to put things right if we've made a mistake. And I'm willing to."

Was she implying that Ana wasn't? And what did she mean, "her judgement *too*"? Ana wasn't making any judgements; she was just saying how it was. "I can only tell you what I know." She tried to smile pleasantly, but it was hard through gritted teeth.

"And by now you should know everything," Ivana snapped.

Ana ignored her comment and carried on with what she'd been about to say.

"As far as the historical accusations are concerned, Lloyd has no idea why the woman would make such claims. He freely admits he had a relationship with her when he was a student working on Korčula, but that was more than thirty years ago, and he's adamant he stole nothing."

"According to Kristina, the woman is adamant he did."

"Can she substantiate the accusations? It's a very long time ago."

"You were the one Kristina came to, Ana. Did you not ask her?"

Sranje. Ana folded her arms. "I was far too shocked. And it was coming up to three o'clock. I needed to phone you."

"Our office hours are eight to four, as well you know."

Oh, that really took the biscuit. The bloody woman had actually told her she'd been on her way out of the door. It was just as well Ivana gave Ana no time to speak.

"Have you spoken to Kristina since?"

"No."

"Then you have not come to me with the full information. I am hardly going to accept Lloyd's denial when there's the question of the assault in the background."

That really was a step too far. "It didn't bother you when you appointed him. For a live-aboard job with two women."

"No, you're wrong. It did bother me, until I satisfied myself it was a one-off. However, now I'm not at all sure Lloyd's the person we believed him to be. And as I said, Ana, if a mistake was made, I will put it right."

There could be no misreading the threat in her words. Furious as she was with Ivana's whole attitude, Ana needed to stay focussed and say her piece.

"As his headmistress explained to you, the assault was a one-off. Lloyd told me why it happened. He'd not long lost his wife and one of the older pupils, a known troublemaker, said the most awful things about her…"

"And Lloyd attacked him? Doesn't say much for his mental stability, does it?"

Every time Ana opened her mouth, Ivana took it the wrong way. Talk about screwing this up. The most important meeting of her life and the woman was running rings around her. She needed – *needed* – to save Lloyd's job. The library wouldn't work even half as well without him. And it had to work, to secure her own future as well as his.

Ivana was speaking again. "I suppose, if the library was as successful as we'd hoped, this might be less of an issue. But we need it to perform on Korčula in particular, because it's the biggest island. Their contribution makes the project far more viable, and if no one there is using it, they may well be unwilling to continue with their share of the funding. And we need it, especially given how you've managed to achieve absolutely nothing on Mljet, which quite frankly borders on incompetent."

Oh, no. Ivana wasn't blaming her for that as well. It was so not fair. "And it couldn't just be because you decided to put the library in the wrong place? Mljet is almost forty kilometres long, and we're stuck at one end of it, right in the tourist zone and nowhere near most of the population."

"It's no good getting defensive. It's not as though you've made a better suggestion."

Sranje and *sranje* again. She was not prepared for this. "I didn't know I could," she said.

"Of course you can. You're *responsible* for the project, Ana. Do you know what that means?"

But Ivana had to sign off everything. The woman's attitude beggared belief, but ripping into her was not the answer. "I'll research it on Thursday." What else could she say?

"Now that I've mentioned it's a problem. You and Lloyd aren't exactly being proactive, are you? Is this some sort of extended holiday for you both? On government money?"

"No!" Angry tears smarted in Ana's eyes but she wouldn't give Ivana the satisfaction. She calmed herself by speaking slowly and deliberately. "We are doing things. Lloyd, in particular, has loads of ideas. Like the story time session at the community hall on Lopud tonight. Believe me, Ivana, we want to make this work as much as you do. More so, probably."

"And Korčula? If you can't stop the rumours and get people back to the library, there's little point in doing anything on the smaller islands. If the numbers don't add up, Ana..."

Backed into the same bloody corner where they'd started. What could she say? "I'll talk to Kristina."

"Good." Ivana stood, and when Ana followed she found her legs were shaking. "Thank you for coming in," said Ivana. Ana knew she should think up some polite response but it was beyond her, so she nodded, then trailed after her towards the front door.

Arriving early at the pizzeria where she was meeting Meri for lunch, Ana ordered a large glass of wine before she'd even sat down. God, she needed it after that. She'd gone in there to defend her crew and the project, and instead she'd been ripped to shreds. And to make matters worse, she'd almost lost it with her boss. She'd needed to get her on side, not completely alienate her. What a goddam mess.

She'd made so many bad decisions over the last few days it was no wonder she couldn't trust her own judgement. More than once, she'd put the entire project in jeopardy because she couldn't think things through and come to a reasonable conclusion. She should have spoken to Lloyd, not ransacked his cabin. She'd only avoided disaster because of his fundamentally good nature. Then this morning with Ivana…

Ana pulled herself up short. There was no point beating herself up about it again and again. She had to focus on herself or she'd waste her time with Meri moaning about Ivana, not talking about her future. Right now, she needed to set out the whole knotty question in her mind, so she could explain it properly.

She sat back and wrapped her fingers around her wine glass. There were so many choices, but they really boiled down to one thing: should she continue to fight for *Dida Krila*, as her grandfather would have wanted, or retreat into the safety of the family business, maybe even alongside marriage and children, as no doubt her parents expected?

That was the nub of it, but as for which bit came first, which was most important... It had to be parenthood, right? That was a lifelong commitment. Lifelong. And full-on too, for the early years at least. No taking off on *Dida Krila* whenever the mood took her, and even just the thought made her feel sick inside. But wasn't being a mother what every woman was meant to want? What if she'd struggled to find fulfilment when she was younger because she'd been ignoring the obvious?

"I'm sorry, I'm sorry."

Ana looked up, blinking, moments before Meri threw herself onto the chair opposite. "For what?"

"I'm late, but I've just had the most frigging awful morning. The worst ever. Honestly." Her eyes looked bloodshot and watery, her purple mascara smudged. She hadn't been crying, had she? In all the years she'd known her, Ana had never seen Meri cry.

She put her hand on her arm. "What's happened?"

"It's Zac. Well, Zac and Tomi. A few weeks ago Zac found him doing lines at a party."

"Cocaine? No!"

"Yes. And you know what he said to him? That everyone does it, so it's not a problem. And when Zac tried to argue he told him to fuck off and leave him alone."

"So they've split up?"

Meri shook her head. "I wish they had. But Zac's crazy about the guy. He's been saying for months he's the real deal, and they've been so happy together up until now. Well, after the party Tomi apologised and everything seemed OK, so Zac didn't mention it to me. Except now he's found out it's a regular thing and it seems he's been hiding it from Zac for quite a while. He turned up at home at seven this morning, absolutely distraught."

"So what's he going to do?"

"That's the hard part. The hardest part for me, that is. He wants to stay. To try to convince Tomi this isn't OK and he needs to stop. But what if he won't listen?" Her voice dropped to a whisper. "What if Tomi kicks off and gets violent? Or talks Zac into doing a line and he gets hooked too?"

"Oh, Meri. I don't know what to say." And she didn't. She really didn't. This was so outside any of her experience, but it ripped her apart to see her friend like this. "If there's anything, anything at all I can do…"

"I know, Ana. I know you're here for me, and it's such a relief because there's no one else I can share this with. I'm just so frigging glad we decided to meet in this place. If we'd gone to the jazz café there'd most likely be someone there we know, or someone who knows Zac and Tomi, and I need to keep this under wraps. God, it's such a mess." She tried to smile. "I'm such a mess. But here you are – my Ana, my rock. Calm as anything. Thank god for wonderful you."

Ana squeezed Meri's warm arm. "You talk, I'll listen. Maybe we can even work something out." She waved at the waiter. "But first, wine. And let's order some food."

"I'm not sure I can eat." Meri gave a little shrug.

"But you're going to. OK?" Ana glanced at the menu. "We'll share a *capra* pizza, yes? With extra artichokes and a large side salad."

Meri sat back. "Since when did you get so bossy?"

Ana considered. It wasn't like her, that was for sure. Yet taking charge felt like the right thing to do under the circumstances. She wanted to take the weight off Meri by becoming the one who made the decisions, even if they were only simple ones.

"Because right now, bossy is what you need me to be. How are you going to be there for Zac if you aren't looking after yourself?"

Meri fiddled with her fork, finally looking up. "You're right, I know."

"Well, that's my role in all this. I know nothing about drugs, I know nothing about children, but I can and will be your self-care conscience. I can nag you from anywhere in Dalmatia, you know." Her voice softened. "And listen to you. And prop you up. I'm here for you, *draga*, come hell or high water. You know that."

For the first time Meri smiled. Sort of. "And aren't I the lucky one to have you as my friend."

Coming out of the supermarket on Gruž harbour some hours later, Ana swung the bag containing her purchases in her hand. At least something had gone frigging well right today. Finally. She tried to be thankful for small mercies. Right at this moment, it felt highly unlikely she'd see any big ones.

Poor, poor Meri. Ana's heart was physically aching for her. Zac was her everything, her beginning and end. Walking down the hill to the port, Ana had found herself thinking about that bond a lot. At first it had seemed like a depth of feeling she could barely begin to comprehend, but then she'd thought about her own parents. How much they loved her – and she them. Which had been no bloody use at all because it had flung her back into that whole wretched circle of not wanting to let them down. They only had her. Didn't she have to give them grandchildren, to carry on the family business and name?

Natali was waiting at the bottom of the ferry gangplank, a skinny blonde figure in a swirl of holidaymakers carrying backpacks and suitcases. Her shoulders were hunched, and Obi sat almost on top of her feet, leaning into her shins. The dog jumped up when she saw Ana, and let out a single bark, her tail wagging frantically, while Natali tried to smile.

"Come on," said Ana, leading her onto the boat. "We'll sit in the café. It'll be quieter and cooler in there."

Most of the passengers were tourists who would doubtless stay outside, but the view held no new pleasures for Ana, certainly not today. She chose a table near the ancient air-conditioning unit and while Natali settled Obi underneath it, went to the counter for two colas. On impulse she added a couple of bars of chocolate. Lord knows, they could both do with a treat.

"How was your mum?" Ana asked as she sat down.

Natali screwed up her face. "Not g-good. In bed, crying. But that is normal after a break-up."

"Has she had a lot of relationships?"

"Loads. I think she f-falls in love easily. She is happy for a while, but then she pays."

Ana nodded. She couldn't imagine growing up in such a household, and that was probably why Natali and her mother weren't close. With all these men in and out of her life, she probably hadn't had a lot of time for her daughter. It was a completely different shade of motherhood to add to the confusing kaleidoscope in her head.

Natali broke off a piece of her chocolate. "I t-tried to help her feel better. Made her coffee, brushed her hair. Went out to the shops so she has something in the fridge, even though she says she isn't h-hungry." For the first time she smiled. "I was hungry though. This is great."

"Shall I get you something more if you haven't eaten? A cake, a sandwich?"

"No. This is good. Really good. Lots of sugar." Natali looked down at the table again. "The thing is, Ana, she wants me to g-go home. She can't pay the rent without me, so she'll lose her apartment. Sometimes when she's like this, she even loses her job because she's so unreliable."

Had she heard right? If she had then the library project was well and truly crumbling around her. God, imagine having to tell Ivana they needed a new crew member... But no, this was about Natali first and foremost.

"And do you want to go?" she asked her gently.

"No, no. I love my job. I want to stay with you and Lloyd."

It was all she could do not to sigh as relief rushed through her. "Well that's all right then."

Natali looked down at the table, and began to tear the chocolate wrapper into tiny, neat shreds.

"Oh. So it's not all right."

"It's d-difficult. If I went, and if she goes back to work, we could manage, as long as I get a job cleaning or pot-washing or something. And Obi and I ... we'd have somewhere to live, maybe even until January or February."

"Why until then?"

"These things ... it's hard to explain, but there's a p-pattern. She will be very sad for a while, then more normal again. Putting on make-up, doing her hair, going out. Then she meets someone new. Then she starts saying it's awkward with m-me at home." Natali shrugged. "You know how it is."

"No, Natali, I don't. It sounds to me as though she's using you." Maybe she shouldn't have said it, but it was the truth. God, some people! Some mothers.

"I know, I know. And I wouldn't even be c-considering it except…"

"Except what?"

Natali couldn't look at Ana, and her words were muffled. "She said she'd k-kill herself if I don't go. And she hasn't said that for years."

Honest to god, that took the biscuit. Ana bit her tongue to stop herself blurting the words out loud. She had no idea which was worse: that a mother would put that kind of pressure on her daughter, or that she'd done it before, presumably when Natali was no more than a teenager. Oh, there were layers and layers here. She'd never imagined Natali's upbringing had been so very awful, and it was something of a miracle she'd turned out as well as she had.

But what could Ana say? What could she do? Every fibre of her being wanted to help Natali, to take charge of the situation as she'd instinctively done with Meri, but this felt entirely different, and without Lloyd's wisdom and experience to guide her, she barely knew where to begin.

"Tell me about the last time she threatened to do this."

Natali shrugged. "Oh, like I said, it was ages ago. It used to be every time she had a b-break-up, and when I was little it terrified me that she'd do it and I'd be left on my own."

"I bet it did. It would terrify any child and frankly it's cruel. Did you talk to anyone about it?"

Natali nodded. "One of my aunties. They're just my mum's friends, not relations, but Auntie Stela has always been extra good to me. So I told her, because I didn't know what to do. Mama was furious."

"And are she and your mother still friends?"

"Oh, yes." Natali paused. "You think I should talk to her?"

"I think she'd have an angle. I mean, for what it's worth, your mother's threatened suicide before and hasn't done it, which means it's probably no more than a cry for help. But I don't know your mother."

"Thanks, Ana. I'll talk to Auntie Stela. That's a great idea." She screwed the shredded chocolate wrapper into a ball in her fist. "I'm so s-sorry. I haven't even asked about your meeting with Ivana."

Ana put on what she hoped was a reassuring smile. "I'll tell you and Lloyd about it over supper. Now, look what I managed to find in the supermarket…"

Lopud

TUESDAY 18TH JULY

Checking the map on his phone, Lloyd left the promenade and cut through the public gardens. He wished he had the time to explore them; the cool shade under the trees was beguiling, and between their trunks he could glimpse a fascinating array of statues and columns, but he couldn't afford to be late.

Thank goodness Ana and Natali had come back on the four o'clock ferry. Filip, the manager of the community centre, had dropped by to see him this morning to suggest Lloyd took the library books with him for story time – which was a great idea – but by the end of a long, hot day he'd needed to freshen up, and there hadn't been time for both.

So Ana had taken over, and shooed him back to the boat. When he'd asked how her meeting with Ivana had gone, she'd rolled her eyes and said something about an arse-kicking session, but she hadn't seemed too worried, so perhaps she'd somehow managed to smooth things over. It'd be a bloody miracle if she had, but he couldn't waste any more time worrying about it now.

It was going to be daunting enough reading three short stories to under-fives in a language he was far from confident with, but he'd checked some of the trickier pronunciations with the girls last night so he was as ready as he would ever be. As long as it increased footfall to the library, he didn't care if he made a fool of himself. He just didn't want to have a negative effect on this island as well. As it was, the thought of returning to Korčula on Friday was filling him with absolute dread.

He found the community hall in the far corner of the park. It was a squat, concrete building, with a plaque dated May 1963 next to its open front doors. No wonder it looked as though it had seen better days, but a buzz of voices drifted from inside, punctuated by children shrieking happily. It was clearly well used and well loved.

Ana was behind the library table in the foyer, and to Lloyd's surprise it was surrounded by teenagers. Filip emerged from the mêlée to meet him.

"Lloyd, *dobrodošli*. There's table tennis club in the main hall, and they're taking an interest in the books, which is what I hoped would happen."

"That's great. Thank you so much, Filip."

"No, thank *you*. Your story time is a good addition to our programme and as we have no budget for events it's hard to provide different things."

Lloyd indicated the room to his left where the noise of children playing had gone up several decibels. "I take it a few have turned up."

Filip beamed. "Oh, yes. Seven in all. Come and meet them."

Once Filip had introduced Lloyd to the parents, he clapped his hands and told the children to sit down. The wooden floor was scattered with large, brightly coloured cushions and as they settled, Lloyd slid onto one too.

"You can have a chair, you know." Filip told him, but Lloyd shook his head.

"It's easier to make eye contact down here." He smiled confidently, but as Filip explained what was to happen, the inside of his mouth went dry. He had so little experience with the smallest of children; nothing to draw on at all. Apart from one spell during his teacher training, he'd always worked with teenagers – he knew nothing about infants.

But he did. He really did. He was a father, damn it. He'd read to Ruth until she was almost eleven, books they'd cherished together, so of course he knew how to do this. Clearing his throat, he began the first story, each word becoming easier than the last. Seven sets of eyes were glued to him; a teddy bear clutched tightly, a thumb rammed into the tiniest rosebud mouth. His heart soared. It was going to be all right.

Even once he'd finished it was a while before he and Ana could dismantle the library, as most of the parents wanted to borrow something – as had a few of the table tennis players, which more than doubled their numbers for the day. But finally, as the books went back into their boxes, Filip shook Lloyd's hand.

"I think we can say that was a big success," he told him. "Is there any chance you'd consider doing it again?"

"I don't see why not. It fits with our sailing schedule and I really enjoyed it. The children I used to teach were older – I didn't realise how much fun the little ones could be."

Ana grinned. "You were a natural with them, Lloyd. The way you did all the different voices for the characters."

"There is something else," Filip went on. "I don't suppose you would consider relocating the library here?"

"Here?" The possibilities were running through Lloyd's mind.

"Yes. You would get far more footfall of local people, and I'm always looking for new things to add to our programme."

It would be an absolute godsend, not least because it was cooler inside. But the decision wasn't Lloyd's alone.

"Ana? What do you think?"

A moment of uncertainty flashed across her eyes, but then she said, "It's your call, Lloyd. If you think it will be better, then we'll do it."

Lloyd turned back to Filip. "Let's say we'll try it for the next two weeks and see what happens."

Filip slapped him on the back. "Fantastic. I'll put up some posters. See you next Tuesday then."

They were halfway back to the boat when it dawned on Lloyd that Ana was unusually talkative, but had said nothing more about her trip to Dubrovnik. In fact, she was going on and on about how Natali had been planning to take Obi for a walk, then go to the minimarket to find something quick for supper, maybe something to barbecue on deck once they reached Šipan; then about a man they passed, who'd set out a tablecloth to one side of the path and was selling cheap plastic toys; and about the trip boat that looked like a pirate ship which had just arrived in the harbour.

He stopped, leaning on the sack trolley. "Ana, it's OK. If you don't want to tell me what happened with Ivana right now, if you need time to process it first, then I'm fine with that." He wasn't, of course, but he couldn't bear to see her like this, scrabbling for the next sentence, when normally a companionable silence would do.

She looked up at him. "Thanks, Lloyd. Over supper. I'll tell you and Natali together. But rest assured, she fully accepts you didn't steal that purse." Which presumably meant it was about all Ivana had accepted, and the thought was a thump to his solar plexus, bringing him tumbling down from the high of the community centre. Shit. Shit, shit, shit.

They walked on to the harbour, the soft rays of early evening sunshine making the monastery and its church tower glow golden grey above them. This was a pretty, pretty little place, but would he be back here next week? Was that why Ana had hesitated over Filip's offer?

As they began to unload the boxes, Lloyd felt truly sick inside. They were beginning to achieve so much with the library; reaching out to children of all ages with the books, talking to the older ones so they could practise their languages. They were doing so well on three of the five islands, and he couldn't bear to let all this go; to walk away, with the job only half done. And that was without even considering the personal cost of being forced to go home with yet another failure behind him.

He carefully stacked each and every box, trying to put off his return to the galley for as long as he dared. Of course he was being a coward, but he really didn't know how he'd face the conversation he knew was coming. What he would say, how he'd react, when Ana told him Ivana had said he had to go.

One thing was for sure, he couldn't pretend to be sorting the books forever. When he finally shut the cabin door behind him, he was astonished to hear giggling from the galley, which was about the last thing he'd expected. What the hell was going on? He'd been about to call out that he was going to phone Ruth, but curiosity got the better of him and he climbed the steps.

Ana could barely contain her excitement as she thrust a plastic bag into his hands. "We have a surprise for you," she said, grinning from ear to ear.

He looked inside. Teabags. Two large boxes of English Breakfast teabags. He dropped them on the floor and hugged the girls to him as though his very life depended on it.

"You two are bloody amazing. You have so much shit of your own to think about at the moment, and you remembered my teabags. That's so..." His voice cracked. As they clung together, it felt like they were an island, a tiny island, buffeted by the sea. But one island, all the same. Whatever Ana had to tell them, they were in this together.

Šipan

WEDNESDAY 19TH JULY

It never ceased to amaze Ana that whatever else was going on, Lloyd was always able to smile and laugh with the children – really, properly, belly laugh by the sound of it. As she approached, she could see that his face was no longer grey beneath his tan, but glowing with what looked very much like happiness.

"Ana!" he called, "come and meet Marta and Mila. Their mum's sent some of her gorgeous *kroštule* again."

"Except," said the girl with her hair in a ponytail, "there are not as many as there should be, because our dog found them when they were cooling. Wow, Mama was cross."

Her sister mimed running and finger wagging with lively enthusiasm, and Ana remembered Lloyd telling her that Marta was deaf and adored reading because it took her into worlds created simply from words she could see on the page. It only went to show how important the library was, and the thought sent Ana's heart plummeting.

After leaving Lloyd a fresh bottle of water and his

lunchtime sandwich, Ana continued to wander through the village. Children played on the town beach behind the harbour, splashing each other noisily, and music drifted lazily from the bar nearest the water. The only shop on the grassy square was the minimarket, and although she could have bought wine there, she was after something more local.

The narrow inland streets felt forgotten, the only living creature a cat sunning itself on a doorstep. She thought she remembered a wine shop, but when she reached it, it was closed. Very closed, given the dust gathering on the bottles in the window. Just beyond, some enterprising soul had set out a wooden sign. *"Wine tasting 500 metres. Buy direct from the vineyard."* It wasn't far, so it was definitely worth a punt. And if she could taste before she bought, so much the better. You could never be sure with these small producers.

The wine was a displacement activity. She knew it was. She hoped that by walking away from *Dida Krila* she might be able to forget herself, just a little. It was a completely new feeling, one that left her mouth dry with angst, but somehow her problems had become tied up with the boat... No, that wasn't right. It was just at the moment that it was hard to think of life onboard without remembering the gloom that had wrapped around them last night, both from Natali's situation and from her own abject failure to deal with Ivana.

Not that she'd admitted exactly how badly she'd stuffed up the meeting. It had been hard enough to break it to Lloyd that she hadn't been able to clear his name. That he hadn't been believed. To be fair, he'd been pretty sanguine about it and told her she needed to do whatever she needed to do. But from the look of him first thing this morning, he hadn't slept very much either.

Everything about yesterday had knocked sideways her fragile confidence in her ability to do this job. Of course, when she'd woken in the night she'd thought of a hundred better ways she could have dealt with Ivana. Things she could have and should have said. Things that would have certainly improved the outcome for Lloyd. The same with Natali, really. She'd looked to Ana for guidance about her mother and the cupboard had been pretty much bare.

At least she'd been able to help Meri, but she knew Meri so well she'd instinctively known what her friend needed. She needed Ana to be the strong one for a while; to be her rock, when it was so very often the other way around. She'd called her first thing this morning, listened while she sobbed over Zac going home to find Tomi high as a kite, then later called again to check that she'd actually eaten something before leaving for work. Meri had sworn at her then, but she'd had an almost laugh in her voice when she'd done it.

Already the houses lining the footpath were thinning out. To her right was a high stone wall, and on the left the ground fell away into a small, dry valley, a couple of villas nestling near the bottom, one surrounded by hives. The still air was filled with the smell of charcoal, herbs, and meat cooking, so typical of *peka*, and sure enough a small *konoba* came into view, deserted now, but if the delicious aromas were anything to go by it would be buzzing by nightfall.

A little way beyond the *konoba*'s rickety tables the path became a road, and at the bottom of a track angling back on itself was another sign for the tastings, "Winery Rašica". She smiled at the use of English – eminently sensible if you wanted to attract the tourists.

Turning past a small plot of vines, Ana found herself

walking between olive trees, some so old their thick trunks were twisted and gnarled into rope-like patterns beneath the whispering leaves. To her right, an impressive vegetable garden was set out in front of a characterful old farmhouse, green-shuttered outbuildings making up the lowest floor beneath its stone-balustraded terrace.

She was almost in front of it when a man wearing a checked shirt and denim cut offs emerged, blinking in the sunlight. She knew him immediately. The guy from the beach. What were the chances? But he wouldn't recognise her, surely?

"Had your coffee today?" he asked, dark eyes twinkling.

Oh, so he remembered her all right. And as a grumpy old cow, rather than a fellow moonlight bather. Just her bloody luck.

"You have a mighty good memory," she replied, with her best cheerful smile. "And yes, for the record, I have."

He nodded. "Even so, I'll refrain from corny comments about not being sure it was you with your clothes on."

Oh, so he'd noticed her underwear on the beach that night, had he? She had to call him out. "To be fair, I wasn't entirely sure I recognised *you*. Clothed, I mean."

"Perhaps I'm not as memorable." But he was. And there was a spark about him that Ana found infectious, despite knowing it was probably just a prelude to his sales patter. He didn't disappoint.

"Right. I guess you're after some wine? Would you like to try it first?" Straight down to business.

"Please. I'm looking for something good."

"Oh, I'm good. And the wine's even better."

How could she not respond? She would look so churlish if

she didn't, and anyway, she found that she wanted to. This harmless banter was making her feel better already.

"So are you sweet or dry?"

He didn't laugh, didn't blush, just looked her straight in the eye. He understood the game, all right.

"Well-balanced. I hope. Taste and see, then you can decide. What to buy, I mean. I assume you are interested in buying?" A very slight arch of his eyebrows.

"I need a few bottles to restock the catamaran."

"You charter? Is that why you're back on the island?" His tone was different now – interested, friendly. Maybe she'd exhausted his supply of one-liners.

She shook her head. "We're running a children's library over the holidays. Mainly books in English and German as part of the county's literacy programme, and Wednesday is Šipan day."

"Then I must bring my daughter when she comes back next week. She's a great reader and a book in English would be a good challenge." He started into the outbuilding, and Ana followed. "Divorced dad, you see. Co-parenting though. I'm lucky."

The room he led her into was windowless and smelt a little musty. Racks of bottles lined the walls, all neatly labelled, and a barrel stood next to an old-fashioned oak dresser whose shelves were filled with glasses, wine stoppers and stacks of small plates.

Corkscrew in hand, he looked over his shoulder. "I should probably introduce myself. I'm Luko Rašica, but most people call me Raš."

"Ana Meštrović. Nobody calls me Meš."

"I'm not that brave, so Ana it will have to be. Now, what

would you like to try? Personally, I think the reds are better, and anyway, I don't have much rosé left."

"I like a pragmatic man. Guess it'll be the reds." Chatting to him was as easy as he was on the eye. He wasn't conventionally good-looking. His face was too angular, his nose a little bent, but there was something about him all the same – sparkle, an inner confidence – that was making her fizz with attraction. There was no point trying to rationalise the feeling. This was nothing but a very welcome slice out of time, so she'd better give in and enjoy it.

"OK. Our wines are a little different to the norm. Since taking over from my father, I've been replacing the local vines with more internationally recognised varieties like cabernet and merlot. They grow very well here and, just as importantly, foreign tourists recognise them on the labels."

"Where are your vines? I only saw a few rows by the gate."

"Those are for show, mainly. Most of them are in the island's central valley. It's the perfect microclimate. But honestly, I can get very boring about soil and grapes, so let's just taste."

Raš uncorked a bottle and poured them half a glass each, walking into the shaft of sunlight from the door and swirling his around. Ana did the same, then lifted the wine to her nose to inhale the aromas.

"Wow! That's almost like chocolate."

"It's the merlot. Try it."

Ana took a sip and an explosion of fruit hit her mouth. "That's good," she said.

"Only good? I was hoping for exceptional at the very least."

"I'm no wine buff."

"Would you like to learn?"

"Do lessons cost extra?"

"Well, let me see ... it's Wednesday, and that's when I give free classes, but only for women of impeccable taste."

"Looks like I lucked out. Unless calling your merlot *good* rather than *exceptional* disqualifies me?"

He laughed. "Oh no. That tells me you have potential, but still a great deal to learn."

It was almost an hour later when Ana strolled back to the village, the carrier bags in her hands chinking as wine and olive oil bottles rubbed together. Yes, she'd spent a fair bit of money – Raš was a consummate salesman – but she'd enjoyed his company too; listening to his tales of a year spent in California learning about wine-making, and about the eco-house he'd built for himself in the olive grove when he returned. And, of course, trying to spot the differences between his merlot, cabernet and *plavac mali* wines.

It had been just what she needed and she couldn't help but feel a little bereft now she was returning to the real world. But Raš's company had certainly buoyed her up, and when she smiled at a passing tourist she knew it came from deep inside. Perhaps it wouldn't last, but maybe enough of it had seeped into her soul to enable her to cope just a tiny bit better with Natali and her bloody mother, with Ivana's bitching, and her own sorry inability to defend Lloyd. And if all else failed, they had plenty of excellent wine to drown their sorrows.

∽

Ana heard the clink of glasses even before Lloyd appeared on the fly deck, where she was messaging Meri to ask what she was having for supper. Barely a breeze reached into Suđurađ Bay to ruffle her hair, the air sticky around them.

"Natali's phoning her auntie so I thought I'd give her some space." He waved a wine bottle in her direction. "And I didn't think you'd bought this to look at."

Ana took the glasses, while he pulled a corkscrew from his shorts pocket. "Natali's mother ... it's such a bloody mess," she said.

Lloyd nodded, easing himself onto the other end of the banquette. "I don't think I'd realised quite how difficult her childhood must have been. To be bullied at school, and to have that kind of instability at home as well…"

"All the same, I'm afraid she'll go home now. And what if she didn't, and her mother really did end it all? She'd feel guilty for ever and a day."

"Which is most likely why her mother said it. Natali's beginning to get a new confidence, and her mum may have sensed that. We don't know, but maybe Natali even told her she wouldn't go back. So of course she used her trump card."

"You think it was that deliberate?"

Lloyd shook his head. "Probably some and some – instinct taking over, to get what she wants."

"I'm so out of my depth here. On the ferry back to Lopud I was terrified of saying the wrong thing, of making Natali jump to the wrong decision."

"Whatever that decision might be. One thing's for sure, we can't make it for her, but we can certainly talk it through with her, help her to consider all the options. I'm not sure it's something she's used to doing. Not sure she's had too many choices before now, to be fair."

"She said if she went back she'd have somewhere to live

until after Christmas. I'd never really thought, you know, whether she actually has a home. How terrible is that?"

Lloyd sighed. "Not to mention having to go from low-paid job to low-paid job, and I don't expect rent is especially cheap around Dubrovnik. It's such a shame that Obi means Natali can't get work doing what she's really good at."

"And she is bloody good at it. She's a lovely kid, too. I don't want to lose her, Lloyd." Tears pricked the back of Ana's eyes and she took a swig of wine.

"Me neither, but it's her life." He laughed. "That's what I'm always saying to Ruth: don't worry about me, you have your own life."

"Lloyd, however have you coped?"

"I don't know. Except I had to. Much as I wanted to at times, I couldn't die with Jenny." He looked out across the rippling water. "It's better now I'm here though. I hoped it might be, and in spite of everything, that part ... it really is."

Although that was good, in so many ways it was the last thing Ana wanted to hear. It underlined her abject failure to secure Lloyd's job. The job that was helping him to heal. This was awful, awful.

"I've let you down too." Her voice came out as little more than a whisper.

Lloyd slid along the banquette and put a hand on her shoulder. "No, you haven't."

"I have. I should have just told Ivana that without you there's no library and been done with it."

"That sounds like rather a high-risk strategy."

"Oh god, so that would have been wrong too! See what I mean? And this project is so important to us all – you for your recovery after losing Jenny, Natali for a stable home, and for me ... well, for me..."

"What does it mean to you, Ana?"

She clutched her glass tighter. "Financially, it underpins my whole future. But it's more than that. I needed this summer as thinking time because I still don't know what shape that future might take."

"How do you mean?"

"Oh, in lots of ways." Ana was cross and frustrated with herself for even mentioning it, but she felt she owed it to Lloyd to explain. "I suppose ... I suppose ... at the heart of the matter is whether or not I want children. I'm thirty-five, Lloyd. I need to make up my mind and all I do is dither this way and that."

"Listen, Ana, kids are a really big deal. The biggest, and not a decision to be taken lightly. That said, Jenny and I aren't a great example because she fell pregnant within months of us marrying and that was certainly sooner than we'd planned. Turned out it was the best thing that happened to us, but it's not for everyone. Just think of Natali's mum. From where I'm sitting, parenthood doesn't seem to be her thing at all, and from what I've seen, the world would be a better place if every child was really wanted."

Ana was relieved he'd given her a reason to turn the conversation away from her own troubles. She already felt like she'd overshared. "And right now, Natali should be our priority," she said firmly.

He nodded. "Of course. But beyond that, going forwards – and assuming Natali stays – we all need to pull together even harder. Talking to you has made me realise that each of our futures is uncertain after the first of September. You have your big decisions to make, I have no job to go home to, and nothing I want to do except teach, which for obvious reasons is closed to me. But at least we have homes, unlike Natali. Suicide threats aside, no wonder it's tempting to go back to her mother."

Ana tried to smile. "So we're all in the same boat. Metaphorically as well as literally."

She was rewarded when Lloyd laughed. "So we need to keep afloat as long as possible, while we work out what to do for the best." He counted on his fingers. "Let's get the Natali situation sorted first, then we can analyse how to improve the library's performance in each location, because my personal situation aside, that's what should persuade Ivana to keep things going."

"I wish I had your clarity, Lloyd."

"It's not clarity, it's … experience."

He hesitated for a moment, as though he was about to say more, but they heard a scramble of paws and claws on the steps, and Obi appeared, Natali close behind her.

"How did you get on?" Lloyd asked.

Natali sat down on the other banquette, Obi leaping up to curl next to her. "Auntie Stela's going to see Mama." She screwed up her face. "She remembers how upset I used to get when she, you know, said that thing when I was younger. Auntie Stela said she would t-try to work out if she really means it."

"That sounds like a start," said Lloyd.

"Yes." Natali looked down, stroking Obi's head.

"You know how much we value you, Natali." Ana hoped she'd already made that clear, but it didn't hurt to actually say it.

"You are very kind."

"No, it's the truth. We make a good team."

Natali nodded, again without looking up. "I know that, really I do, and I want us to stay together more than anything. B-but ... what you said yesterday... Ivana n-not being happy about ... things." There was a silence.

"Go on," Lloyd prompted her.

"I don't want to leave. I really, really don't. But if I tell Mama that and she's angry, or if she can't pay the rent on her f-flat like she says and she loses it, then if this week or next the library has to stop, Obi and I will have nowhere to go."

"Natali," said Lloyd, "do you mind me asking what you plan to do in September?"

Natali shrugged. "I don't have any p-plans. I know now perhaps that was a b-bit stupid, but I was so pleased to get a live-aboard job that I couldn't bring myself to think beyond it. But I'll have money left over at the end so—" She ground to a halt.

"Oh, Natali, this must be so hard for you," said Ana.

"So you thought that by the end of the summer you'd have enough money to find somewhere to rent?" Lloyd asked.

Natali looked up at him. "Maybe not that much, but something. And being b-back on a boat, I thought it might be easier to get another job on a boat, but then there's Obi and I can't leave Obi." She was fighting tears, and Lloyd moved over to wrap an arm around her shoulder.

"There are day boats..." Ana mused. It was a shame her parents didn't need anyone, but all their employees were long-standing, friends almost. On the other hand, if she did put *Dida Krila* into their business, she would need crew. Oh god, another complication she didn't know how to deal with.

"The way I see it," said Lloyd, "there are a few factors

affecting your decision, Natali. The first is your mother's mental health, and then there's whether the library will continue or not. Now, we can't do anything about the first, but we can the second. Ana and I were talking about that before you came up. We need a plan for each island."

Lloyd was so damn good at this. Ana wouldn't mind betting he already knew exactly what they should do, but it suddenly came to her how crucial it was that each of them make a contribution. If only to underline to Natali how important she was. "OK," she said, "we'll have a brainstorm. I'll jot down each and every idea on my phone, then we can pick out the good ones."

"What, me too?" Natali asked.

"Of course you too," said Ana. "We'll need to pull together to make this work so let's start as we mean to go on."

"Right," said Lloyd, "let's go."

They all looked at each other, and Ana could see something close to panic in Natali's eyes. It was up to her to take the lead, just like she'd done with Meri yesterday.

"Mljet. My gut feel is we're in the wrong village. Apart from the people who work in the cafés and bars, the only ones who even walk past the library are tourists. So I'm going to ask around and see if I can find out how to contact the head of the school."

"Now we're at the community centre in Lopud," said Lloyd, "I'll ask Filip what their other activities are, on the days we aren't there, then write a note to each of the leaders about the library."

Natali was petting Obi, studying the dog's back as though she'd never seen it before.

"OK," said Ana. "I'll phone the transport company and ask if we can put some leaflets on the buses on Šipan."

Natali looked up. "M-maybe on Korčula too?"

"Good idea," said Lloyd. "There's a bookshop in Korčula town as well, so perhaps…"

"Why would they help?" asked Ana, then bit her tongue. "Sorry. We're not meant to discuss the ideas, are we?"

"No, we're not. Or really decide who's going to do what, but let's keep going. Maybe we can hang a sign around Obi's neck."

"That's silly," said Natali.

"But silly's OK."

"Really?" her eyes were wide.

"Silly as you like."

"We could hang a sign around *your* neck, Lloyd." Natali giggled.

"And I could walk up and down, ringing a bell, before the library opens."

Out of nowhere, they were all laughing. Obi jumped onto the floor, bounding between them and barking madly. If nothing else, their cares had been forgotten for the briefest of moments and Ana basked in the glow of it all. They were working together. Properly together. She had to believe they could win.

Korčula

FRIDAY 21ST JULY

Lloyd shook the water from his hair as he breached the surface, then inhaled deeply, sending the fresh saltiness into his lungs as the morning sun skimmed the red-orange roofs of the former monastery on Badija island, making them glow. He trod water, fiddling with Jenny's engagement ring on its chain around his neck, his movement sending ripples sparkling across the smooth surface of the sea.

It brought to mind those first few mornings when he'd camped on the beach in Lumbarda all those years ago; the peacefulness of the sun rising above the majestic slopes of the Pelješac, the freshness of the water against his skin. And there, one day, waiting for him on the beach, had been Mirjana. The cause of so much joy then, and so many problems now.

Today they returned to Korčula and he had the same kind of sinking feeling he'd experienced before each and every one of Jenny's appointments with her consultant – knowing in his heart of hearts it was going to be bad, but all the same praying that perhaps, perhaps, there'd be a ray of hope somewhere.

And then he felt guilty comparing them, because today wasn't life or death. Except, perhaps, for the library's future. And his own.

Today Ana was meeting Kristina. It was all very well him being positive in front of the others, but he knew the score: if Mirjana's damaging rumours couldn't be scotched, then the most important part of the library couldn't carry on if he was involved. Quite simply, to salvage the summer for the others, he'd have to go home.

It would be a bitter pill to swallow, especially now they had so many ideas to improve the library's performance. The hour or so they'd spent on Wednesday night had been inspirational as well as hilarious, and even drawing an absolute blank on Mljet yet again had only dampened their mood a little. Because now they had a plan to deal with it.

Ana had spent most of yesterday talking to local people, and then on her phone, and had finally tracked down both the head of the elementary school and the manager of the cultural centre on Mljet, both of which were in the largest village, a good half-hour's drive from Pomena where they moored. The upshot was that she was going to meet them next week to see if there was a better place to site the library. So that was all hopeful. Now he had to face bloody Korčula again.

Lloyd ducked his head underwater in a futile attempt to give himself some clarity. But perhaps clarity wasn't the issue here. Perhaps it was guilt. Guilt about the girl he'd left in a war zone more than thirty years before. If he'd been wondering how differently her life would have turned out if he'd been a little more perceptive and a whole lot braver, then the chances were she would have done too. So it was something of a no-brainer that she'd never forgiven him. *That* he understood. But to lie about him? That was something else.

If only they had not ignored the gathering clouds of war so completely, then everything might have turned out differently. But was he fooling himself about even that?

"There'll be a war, nothing's more certain," Kesten said as he and Mirjana wiped down the tables after a busy night's service. Lloyd himself was in the kitchen washing up, but he could still hear most of what they were saying.

"You're exaggerating. Bigging it up because you want to impress us all with your talk of joining the army. It's nothing but a few skirmishes," Mirjana replied crossly.

"This business at Kijevo is more than a skirmish, as you call it. The bloody Yugoslav army's siding with the Serbs, and far more openly this time. They're meant to be keeping the peace, but they made everyone leave the village just because they're Croats. And the village is in Croatia – on *our* side of the border, not theirs."

"But that's the point, everything that's happening is on the borders. Tata said there's bound to be friction until things settle."

Lloyd heard the familiar scrape and tap as she tipped a chair against a table.

"With respect to your father, he hasn't spoken to the guys manning the artillery base at Raznjic. They drink in the village most nights, so of course I've been talking to them, and they told me they've been put on high alert."

Mirjana sighed. "To do what, exactly, if they have so much time to drink?"

"Well, they can't go into details, can they? I'm just a civilian. But not for much longer. The Croatian army needs every man it can get, and by next week, I'll be one of them."

Kesten was always full of bluster and puff, but this time it sounded to Lloyd as if he meant it. To be fair, the army was probably a more exciting prospect than waiting tables all his life, and there couldn't possibly be a war in modern-day Europe. The UN or someone would bang a few heads together and that would be that.

There was the scrape of another chair, then Mirjana asked, "So you would fight these men you drink with?"

"No, because they are planning to do the same. Their sergeant's a Serb, but they'll get rid of him and become a Croatian unit. Weapons and all. Most of them are from Dalmatia anyway, and they're loyal to our new country."

"But that's ridiculous. It sounds as though the army's going to be fighting itself. Why would you want to get involved?"

"Pah! Don't tell me you'll miss me, not now you've got your fancy English boyfriend. But he'll go too – sooner than I will, probably. Foreigners always run at the first sign of trouble."

Lloyd was about to call out from the kitchen to defend himself, but Mirjana jumped in.

"Lloyd won't run. He's going home soon anyway, as you well know. But he's coming back. He promised me. At Christmas."

"Don't be a bloody naïve little fool," Kesten hissed furiously. "We'll be at war well before Christmas. When he leaves, you'll never see him again, so you'd better damn well get used to the idea. If he really wanted you, he'd have asked you to go with him."

"And how do you know he hasn't?"

"Because you'd be shouting it from the rooftops if he had, and packing your bags. And you won't even have me to run to once he's gone, because I'll be away fighting. For your freedom."

Within moments Mirjana appeared behind Lloyd, clasping her hands around his waist and resting her head on his back. "Don't listen to him. I'm not. He's an idiot, and we have our plans."

Later, they lay together after making love on the gallery of the old olive press – their secret place at the edge of the village. The warm smoothness of her cheek rested on his chest and his arms wrapped around her shoulders, suddenly she asked him if he was going to tell her what was wrong.

Half smiling at her perception, he sighed. "It is obvious?"

"Only to me, and only here."

"I get that. It's like … it's like … when we're alone like this we truly feel the pulse of each other."

"And normally we beat in time. But tonight, I don't know, you're a little out of sync. Is it because of what Kesten said? Or President Tuđman's ultimatum to the Serbs? I'll understand if you think you should go home before the week runs out."

"I don't." He tried to keep the uncertainty out of his voice. "But your mother does. And she thinks I should take you with me."

Mirjana shot into a sitting position. "She thinks what?"

He levered himself up too. "Please don't tell her you know. She asked me not to say anything, to make it seem like the idea came from me. I feel so much better now I've told you though. I'd hate there to be any secrets between us."

She paused for a moment before asking, "What did you say to her?"

"That I'd think about it." He was so ashamed that he could barely look at Mirjana. "I got the impression that really disappointed her. I told her it would be hard to find somewhere for you to stay, but she said that they had found me somewhere, and that if I really loved you I'd find a way. Is that what you think too?"

"No. I can't go with you, Lloyd, because of something Mama doesn't know I know." It was her turn to look away. "I should have told you, but Tata swore me to secrecy. Mama's ill. She needs heart surgery, and there's no way I can leave before she has it. It's why our original plan of you coming back at Christmas suited me so well."

"Mirjana, I'm so sorry. And you've carried the weight of this all along." He hugged her to him. "If there's anything, *anything*, I can do to help ... and I swear, I won't leave until the last possible minute."

"I love you, Lloyd Richards. You are one amazing man and I wouldn't change a thing between us." She wriggled just free enough to kiss him. "Every day we have is precious, so we need to make the most of them, not worry about the future. That will take care of itself."

"God, Mirjana, you're so wonderful, so wise." And he pulled her back onto the blanket, and began to trace a slow, sensuous curve around her breast with his index finger, all the while dropping butterfly kisses across her face. She was right. Now was what was important. Now they were making the memories that would see them through the months of separation.

He'd never shared with anyone what had happened during those last days. Not even his mother when he'd first got home from Croatia – he'd lied and told her their relationship had just fizzled out. The agony he'd carried inside him had been bad enough without opening the wound to her concerned questioning. And of course, by the time he met Jenny some years later, well, he'd wanted to forget, been ready to forget, and he'd wanted to believe he could be a better man when he loved again.

But now he knew he had to talk about what had happened. He had to admit what an insensitive coward he'd been, because it was unfair to expect Ana to defend his corner with Kristina unless she knew the whole truth. Mirjana had clearly spoken to the woman, so it would be more than easy for Ana to be wrong-footed, and he didn't want that to happen, especially with her confidence at such a low ebb. Anyway, now he was confronted by lies, wasn't the truth the only option?

His mind made up, Lloyd struck out through the water towards *Dida Krila* with renewed purpose. He'd tell Ana, and Natali too, over breakfast. All right, he'd go down a peg or two – or maybe even three – in their estimation, but it was definitely time to come clean.

He showered as quickly as he could, then as soon as he sat down at the table he plunged right in.

"Ana, before you talk to Kristina today, you need to know exactly what happened between Mirjana and me in 1991."

She looked at him over the rim of her coffee mug, her eyes troubled. "OK," she said in that slow way she did when she was uncertain.

Natali sprung up. "Should I go? Clear the table, or—"

"No. I don't want any secrets between us. Mirjana may be hell-bent on damaging the library by spreading lies about something I didn't do, but she does have genuine reason to dislike me and I want you both to understand why."

Natali sank back down and instinctively reached across the table to take his hand. The child was one in a million; Ruth would adore her, and his heart was suddenly filled with longing that one day they would meet.

"As I told Ana, I came to Korčula in 1991, and to cut a long story short, I was offered a job waiting tables at a *konoba* in Lumbarda. Mirjana was the owner's daughter, and she was part of the reason I accepted. She was lovely… Over the first couple of weeks, I realised I was falling for her big time and I knew I couldn't stay if she wasn't interested in me, so I screwed up all my courage and told her. Luckily she felt the same."

"That's so romantic," Natali murmured, "just like in the new book I'm reading."

Lloyd nodded. "I suppose it was. Well, yes, of course it was. So we started going out. Her father was pretty laid back about it – I'd always got on well with him – but for most of the time I was there, her mother was less than keen. She wasn't well, although she kept it a secret. Mirjana told me she had heart problems and was waiting for surgery, so I guess she had a lot to contend with without her daughter falling for a foreigner.

"And I did understand her concerns, although she never

voiced them directly to me. A guy who worked with us, Kesten, he was some sort of distant cousin of Mirjana's, and initially he was worried about her getting hurt too, although over the summer he became a pretty good friend to me as well. But within just a few weeks, Mirjana and I were head over heels, and talking about a future. Or at least, whether one might be possible.

"I suppose if I'd been really romantic, Natali, I'd have taken her back to England with me there and then. But for a start, I'd convinced myself it wasn't practical – I was beginning my teacher training in the October and would be living in university accommodation. And Mirjana said no way would she leave the island anyway, not until her mother had her operation. She needed to be there to help her. So we agreed I'd come back over at Christmas, and maybe at Easter too, and we'd make some decisions then."

"That all sounds very reasonable," said Ana.

"Yes, it was. But this was the summer of '91 and increasingly there was talk of war. Croatia was such a new country. Mirjana's father thought it would be against their interests to fight and I suppose I just wanted to believe him. Maybe I needed to, or maybe it was love making me blind. I should have understood where the skirmishes along the border would lead, especially with the Yugoslav forces siding against Croatia. Kesten warned us again and again what was going on, but I didn't take it seriously, even when he said he was joining the army himself."

Lloyd paused and took a sip of his tea. Yes, this was painful to share, but as he rambled on and the thoughts and memories resurfaced, he recognised a spark of catharsis in it too. A spark he needed to focus on to keep him talking.

"When the conflict began to spread, Mirjana's father told me I should think about going home, and despite having been against the relationship all along, all of a sudden her mother took me to one side and told me I should take Mirjana with me. But Mirjana was adamant she wouldn't leave. At least, I thought she was, but I wonder if, given what's happened now, perhaps I was wrong. Maybe Mirjana came to believe that her mother was right when she said if I left her in a war zone then I didn't love her enough.

"That last morning was crazy. Her father woke me before five and took me into Korčula town to queue for my ferry ticket. He promised he'd bring Mirjana later so we could say goodbye, but it never happened. Kesten came instead. Somehow he found me on the quay in the midst of all the bedlam, and he had a message from Mirjana, saying that I'd hurt her so badly by leaving her behind that she never wanted to see or hear from me again."

Natali squeezed his hand. "Lloyd, that's so sad."

Ana was frowning. "I just don't get it. She said—"

"She did say she wouldn't come, but when we made our plans, we were completely oblivious to the threat of war. And I'd told her it wasn't practical while I was still a student, and maybe she thought, deep inside, that I didn't really want her to. So perhaps when she changed her mind she felt she couldn't tell me." He shrugged. "As the war took hold, I realised I should have done everything I could to get her to safety. Who knows what she endured because I didn't get her out? And if I've never properly forgiven myself, it's little wonder she hasn't forgiven me either."

Ana shook her head again. "All the same, it sounds more like a tragic misunderstanding than—"

He cut across her. "It is what it is. But now you know the truth, you can tell Kristina as much or as little as you need to." He stood up. He'd said enough. His eyes were smarting and his mouth felt dry as dust. "I need to clean my teeth. It's probably time we were heading off anyway."

It was half past three when Lloyd watched two teenage boys approach the library, more or less his first customers of the afternoon. One, who was carrying a book underneath his arm, he had seen a few times before, but the other was a newcomer.

"*Dobar dan*, Vlatko," he called. "How did you enjoy *Lovelace & Babbage*?"

The boy set the book down on the table. "It was wicked," he said in English.

Lloyd laughed. "You're extending your vocabulary, I see."

"Yes. This is my friend Mislav. We met some English girls on the beach. Their dad kept saying 'wicked' and I kind of liked it."

"Yes, it is a good word, but if you want to impress those young ladies with your command of their language, I suggest you get up to date." He searched on his phone. "Here's a list of current slang I can airdrop if you like. It's constantly changing and very different to my day. I mean, 'tight' used to be that someone was mean with their money. Now it means they're cool."

Mislav nudged his friend. "You were right, this guy is ... tight." The boys burst out laughing.

As Lloyd helped them choose their books, he saw Ana cross the park from the direction of the old town. A gentle breeze stirred the palm trees above his head, but his hands felt clammy and he wiped them on his trousers.

At this distance he could read nothing in Ana's face. Neither had she waved in his direction, yet he knew damn well she had seen him looking at her. Her hands were screwed into the pockets of her shorts, her shoulders hunched, as she waited for the lads to leave before approaching.

"Do I still have a job?" No point in beating around the bush.

"Kristina says she'll talk to Mirjana."

"And that's it?"

Ana's lips formed a thin line. "For the moment. She said she needs both sides of the story."

"So how much did you have to tell her?"

"That you'd had a relationship that ended in misunderstanding. A misunderstanding that was probably painful for you both. I didn't see the need to elaborate."

Lloyd nodded. "So, 'for the moment' we carry on."

"They were Kristina's words, not mine." Ana snapped.

"Sorry."

She nodded, hands still buried deep in her pockets. "How's it been?"

"Quiet. Bloody quiet."

"Come on then, let's pack up. I've had enough of this place today."

He nodded. Despite the banter with the boys, he couldn't disagree.

Dubrovnik

SATURDAY 22ND JULY

Natali waited for Auntie Stela at the corner of the street. The stuffy heat rose from the waters of the harbour, trickling between the low-rise blocks and making her armpits prickle. Stifling, drab and grey. That just about summed up this part of Mokošica. Even the morning sun inching around Mount Srđ did nothing to improve it, the air thick with fumes from the cars and the noise of their engines. Why on earth was Mama so desperate to keep her apartment here? It was horrible. But of course, her *mama* had never seen the islands. She probably wouldn't much like them if she did.

Natali shifted from foot to foot. This was not going to be good. For a fleeting moment she wished she had brought Obi with her, but it would have been silly to annoy her mother before they'd even started. Or more importantly, make Obi suffer the hour-long bus journey each way in this heat when she could have a lovely walk along the inlet with Lloyd instead. The sooner she could get on the return bus herself, the better.

She heard Auntie Stela's heels clicking on the pavement before she rounded the corner. Beneath the swinging hems of her linen trousers, glittery raspberry-coloured toenails peeped from her sandals, and there was more than a hint of pink in her spiky blonde hair. Her lipstick was the same bright coral as her rip-off Gucci bag, leaving Natali in no doubt that she was all glammed up ready for battle.

"There you are, Nat," she greeted her cheerily. "Couldn't face going into the lion's den alone?"

"I d-didn't fancy being chewed up."

Auntie Stela grinned at her attempt at a joke. "Or being wept over. Your *mama*'s not at her best, poor love, but she still shouldn't expect you to come running when she clicks her fingers."

Natali trailed after her up the narrow stairs to the second floor, where Auntie Stela hammered on the door. Natali wrinkled her nose; the air on the landing was dusty and stale, the paint on the walls grubby and cracked. Why had she barely noticed these things before? Yet in truth, she'd hardly visited in recent years. She'd never been invited.

When her *mama* inched open the door, she was wearing a crumpled nylon housecoat, although Natali noticed she had bothered with eyeliner and mascara. The uncharitable thought that it would give a better effect if she cried – no, *when* she cried – crossed Natali's mind, but she tried to quash it as Mama put her arms briefly around her.

"You've come. Oh, you did come." She stepped back, looking her up and down. "Where is your suitcase?"

"Natali isn't staying," said Auntie Stela firmly. "Not at the moment, anyway. There are things we need to talk about first."

Mama grabbed Auntie Stela's hand. "But I need her. I need

company ... someone to look after me... I can't cope on my own."

"You could if you pulled your finger out. Look at this place! It's a tip."

"What's the point in keeping it nice now Dario's gone?"

"For yourself. For your own self-respect. And as I said on Thursday, you're well rid of the lying bastard."

"Don't w-worry, Mama. I'll c-clean up."

Mama clutched her arm. "Thank you, *draga*. I knew you'd understand."

"Only enough so we can have a cup of coffee without catching something," said Auntie Stela firmly. "Then we're going to talk."

Her mother huffed, and sat down on the sofa, which Natali noticed was covered with biscuit crumbs.

"So you ate the *tortica* I bought you?" she asked.

"When you feel too wretched to cook, they're easy."

"Lina, get a grip," said Auntie Stela crossly. "You live off microwave meals anyway. It's a miracle Natali knows how to make proper food."

"She doesn't cook it for me," her mother retorted.

"She does for me because I give her a roof over her head when she needs it," Auntie Stela snapped back.

"I'm giving her a roof now." But whatever her *mama* said, Natali did not need that roof. Not at the moment, anyway.

Silence. Natali waited half in and half out of the arch to the kitchen. Dirty cups and glasses covered every surface – not that there was much space anyway because the room was so tiny. It was smaller than the galley on *Dida Krila*. And it smelt of greasy drains, making her stomach heave. Oh god, she couldn't live here, she really couldn't.

"Mama, I c-can't. I—"

"More likely you won't. Whatever it is you're trying to tell me." For a moment her mother sounded annoyed, but then a deep sob escaped her. "I'm so low, darling, so very low. Who knows what I might—"

"You can cut that out, for a start," said Auntie Stela. "You've cried wolf too often for anyone to believe you really would kill yourself, so stop taunting Natali with it."

"But ... but I'll be out on the street. I can't pay the rent on my own." Mama's head sank into her hands. This was the real threat, and Natali knew it. She understood all too well what it was like to be homeless; how damn frightening not to be completely sure where you'd be sleeping. She really didn't think her mother could cope with that. Natali looked pleadingly in Auntie Stela's direction, but she said nothing, just gave her a vague nod. This was what they'd agreed; Auntie Stela would back Natali up, but when it came to the crunch, she needed to tell her mother herself. Mama would keep on and on at her otherwise; wear her down; lean on her for as long as she needed to, then throw her out again. Natali had to break the cycle. She owed herself better than that.

The thought was a strange one; not entirely alien, but almost as though it had been growing inside her and she'd only just recognised it. She didn't want to be in the company of a woman who gave every impression of not really liking her, who treated her as a drudge. If she agreed to it, she'd be as stupid as Mama had always told her she was. And she wasn't. She knew that now. Thanks to Ana and Lloyd. Why give up the friendship and comfort of living and working with them any sooner than she had to? She was happy on *Dida Krila*, and so was Obi.

Slowly Natali returned to the sofa and took her mother's hand.

"Think about it, Mama. If I came to live with you, I would have to give up my job. The only work I could get in the city would not be so well paid, and then there's the question of Obi…"

"You care more about that dog than you do me."

Natali could not deny it, so it was best to avoid the subject and offer an olive branch instead. "If you like, I could come to see you on Saturdays?"

"But I need you, darling, I need you." Tears glistened in Mama's eyes, and Natali did not doubt she meant what she was saying. Mama had never been good at living alone. But Natali had never been enough for her either. If she had been, then perhaps a whole lot of things would be different.

"Well," she said, "m-my job ends at the b-beginning of September so maybe then."

"And in the meantime you will help with the rent?"

Oh god, what could she say now? She was cornered on this one. No way out.

"Don't be ridiculous, Lina." Auntie Stela folded her arms.

"Why is it ridiculous? She said her job is well paid, she's living aboard so she won't be spending any money, and it's not like she has a social life or any friends. I brought her up, Stela, fed her, clothed her—"

"Left her alone for hours, subjected her to a string of your boyfriends. *Jeben ti*, Lina, I've been more of a mother to the girl than you have."

Natali looked down at the wooden floor. There were crumbs there too. Biscuits and crisps. Scratches as well, where the furniture had been moved. Months, if not years, of grime in the gaps between the boards.

"Natali? Natali?" her mother shook her arm.

She couldn't look up. "I ... I want to h-help you, Mama, but I have my own life to live."

"Not even a little bit of money every month? I wouldn't need much to keep this place."

"I ... I..."

Auntie Stela stood. "If it's only a little bit of money that you need, then you can get yourself bloody dressed and go back to the restaurant. And with that useless *šupak* Dario gone, you won't have to come home bowing and scraping to him, so you can ask for extra hours."

"You're a heartless bitch, Stela," Mama moaned.

"Then that's you and me both. Come on, Natali, we're going. Your mother needs to get ready for work."

Natali tried to stand but her mother gripped her arm even tighter. "So you side with her over me?"

Auntie Stela's eyes met Natali's. Slowly she pulled her arm away, massaging the red marks left by her mother's fingers. Red marks she remembered, as though from a long time ago. She took a step away from the sofa. "No, Mama. I'm not siding with anyone. I'm doing this for myself."

"*Odjebite!* The pair of you! I never want to see you again."

As her mother sobbed hysterically, Natali gathered her bag and followed Auntie Stela out of the flat. She felt curiously light-headed and had to stop at the top of the stairs.

"She doesn't mean it, you know."

Natali nodded. "I've heard it so many times before."

Her auntie gave her a quick kiss on the forehead. "You're a

good girl, Nat, you know that?" Natali nodded. "Right. Well, I think we've earned a cheeky lunchtime cocktail, don't you? And I reckon you're buying."

Natali's smile felt wobbly, and if nothing else she badly needed to sit down. "I reckon I am."

Ston

SATURDAY 22ND JULY

As the heat of the day pressed down on Lloyd, the silence in the catamaran weighed heavily around him. He was so rarely on board alone, but with Natali in Dubrovnik and Ana having gone to see her parents, the emptiness was almost unbearable. Even Obi lay motionless in her basket, limbs akimbo as she slept.

He'd taken her for her walk early, along the inlet towards Broce, but not nearly that far. There was little shade on the path and it had been no time before she'd started panting, so they'd returned to *Dida Krila* and after a long, cool drink of water, Lloyd had set about making chicken curry for dinner tonight, figuring the longer the spices had to mingle, the better.

Now, as he sat in the salon, clutching his empty mug of tea, he had no idea at all what to do with the rest of the day. Truth be told, he was too tired from his sleepless nights to even think about it, so perhaps he should try to catch up. Lie down at least. He doubted he had the energy for anything else.

As he edged around the table, Obi opened one eye and

rolled over, before staggering to her feet and shaking out her soft fur.

"Sorry," he murmured, reaching down to scratch the top of her head, "I didn't mean to wake you." The poor animal probably hoped he was going to take her to wherever Natali was, but she skittered after him happily enough as he descended to his cabin, curling up on the corner of his bed.

Lloyd closed the curtains to dim the light sparkling on the surface of the water and stretched out on his back. On the shelf to his right was his photo of Jenny, and he picked it up, gazing into her eyes. All last night it had felt strange that Ana and Natali knew something about him that Jenny hadn't; something that had been so important once, and now was again. For totally different reasons.

But by the time he'd met Jenny, Mirjana hadn't mattered, had she? Except that perhaps she had. Because she had shaped him; shaped how his new relationship had progressed. Slowly, cautiously, sometimes feeling he'd been several steps behind, because he'd had to be sure that Jenny wouldn't disappear as well, before he'd finally committed.

"Did I hurt you, the way I was with you at first?" he asked her. Impossible to know now. Far too late. But in the long term, they couldn't have been closer, happier, more in love. And Mirjana hadn't felt like a secret because he'd blocked her from his mind.

He traced Jenny's cheek, glassy in its frame. "Perhaps I should have told you." A thought occurred to him, and he frowned. "Perhaps I'll tell you now. There was someone before you; someone I loved, but I think in a very different way. We were so young, you see, too wrapped up in ourselves to notice what was happening around us, like the fact that her country was on the brink of war."

He sighed. "This is why I never wanted to go to Croatia on holiday. Not even when you found that bargain cruise. Which is pretty ironic, really, given where I am and what I'm doing now." He faltered, What the hell was the point? "Oh, Jen," he whispered, "can you even hear any of this?"

Tears stung his eyes. He knew she couldn't hear, and yet he needed to tell her so badly. He never would be able to, not really, and his whole being ached with the heaviness of the thought. But perhaps... He remembered her saying once that if she lost the battle then she would always live on in his and Ruth's hearts. He hadn't wanted to listen at the time, but now he realised it was true. A tiny piece of her would be with him always. Even when he was ready to move on, her soul would be walking quietly alongside his.

Was he moving on now? Doing things she would never know about, making friends she would never meet. Almost without him realising it, the process was well underway. But to step completely into the future? So many times, he'd wondered if the tangle of memories and guilt had been stopping him healing, and perhaps he'd been right. So even though Jenny couldn't hear him, it was time to tell her everything.

With a definite purpose, Lloyd plumped his pillows under his head, then propped up Jenny's photo on his chest. "Buckle up, beautiful," he told her. "This is the whole sorry story from beginning to end."

Koločep

MONDAY 24TH JULY

Natali handed Lloyd the ice-cold bottle of water she'd bought at the minimarket and he pressed it against his forehead.

"It's so damned hot today," he said. "Not even a breeze."

"It's making everyone grumpy too," she replied. "Especially the woman in the shop. She really snapped at me when I asked if the veg had come in yet, so I guess it hasn't."

Lloyd shrugged. "I'm sure there's a tin of tomatoes on the boat."

Natali nodded. It wasn't the same, but she knew he had more important things to worry about than his supper. Like what that lying cow Mirjana might say to Kristina for a start. But all the same, when she'd come back on Saturday afternoon she'd noticed the tiniest of changes in Lloyd, although it was hard to pinpoint exactly why or what it was.

She carried on along the path towards the quay and the rocks beyond, where she'd moored *Dida Krila*'s tender. The late-morning ferry had left a while ago and the next wasn't due until early afternoon, so she was as surprised as Obi was delighted to see Baka on her bench.

"I thought you would have gone home to get out of the sun," Natali said.

"I'm waiting for a ride." Baka indicated one of the lawnmower tractor-trailers. "My friend brought me all these peppers from her garden – they've ripened so early. I'm going to make *ajvar* relish but I can't manage these bags as well as my stick."

"That sounds lovely. If you don't want to wait, I'll carry them up for you."

"Would you? *Ajvar* takes so long, by the time the peppers have roasted then cooled. I really need to get on so it's ready before Valentin arrives."

"Of course." Natali wound Obi's lead around her palm and took a carrier in each hand. They weren't heavy, but they were certainly bulging, and her mouth began to water at the thought of the delicious relish Baka was planning to cook.

"I've never made *ajvar*," she told her.

"Then you shall help me, and in return I will give you a jar."

Natali hesitated. "I'd like to, but I must make sure Ana doesn't need the tender. Or there's no urgent work for me to do." But *ajvar* would be the perfect accompaniment to the *ćevapi* she had planned for supper, so she wouldn't mind betting that Ana wouldn't be hard to persuade.

From the path, Baka's house appeared to be a simple single-storey stone building with neat white shutters, but its position on the steep hillside meant there would be a cellar, or even more rooms, carved into the bank beneath the part she could see. Below and around it was a sizeable citrus grove, but Natali couldn't tell if the trees were oranges or lemons. There was so much about the islands she didn't know, although increasingly she yearned to find out.

Baka pushed open the door and Natali followed her inside.

"You don't lock it?" she asked.

"Why would I do that? Everyone here is honest."

Natali shook her head. "I saw a pickpocket in the village only a few weeks ago."

"Pah! They're too lazy to climb up the hill."

She followed Baka through a living room that was cool behind closed shutters. As her eyes adjusted, she could make out a sofa and two easy chairs, with old-fashioned lace protecting the arms and decorating the backs of the seats. A dark wood sideboard dominated one wall, its top covered with photographs, some black and white, some colour, but no doubt all family members. Looking at them made Natali realise there wasn't a single picture of her in her mother's apartment.

Even if there had been one before Saturday, it wouldn't be there now, Natali could guarantee it. Mama would be cross for days – maybe even weeks – but Natali couldn't help that. Everyone – Auntie Stela, Ana, Lloyd – had said she'd done the right thing, the best thing, and in her heart of hearts she knew it too. Her mother would come around, and in the meantime, well, it wasn't as if she generally heard from her from one month to the next anyway. You couldn't miss what you didn't have. And right now she had the prospect of cooking with Baka for the next couple of hours and that promised to be so much fun.

As Natali put the bags of peppers on the scrubbed wooden kitchen table, Baka flung the shutters wide and sunlight poured in, making every surface sparkle. A plethora of mismatched pottery jugs, mugs, and plates filled the double row of shelves which lined the walls, and on the windowsill was a pretty glass vase of white and yellow daisies.

"Right," said Baka, tying an apron over her dress, "once the vegetables are roasting we will make some coffee, but for now I would like you to pick two aubergines. The biggest ones. Through that door are the stairs to the lower floor, and you will find the plants just in front of the house."

Obi trotted happily after Natali, down the wooden steps and into a wide corridor lined on one side with shuttered windows. On the other were the open doors of three rooms, and Natali couldn't resist peeping into them. The middle one was a rather quaint bathroom with an antiquated shower over a curved bathtub, and the others were generously sized bedrooms. Natali felt a pang when she saw the made-up bed and jug of daisies in the one closest to the stairs. How often would Baka refresh the flowers ready for her son who would never come home?

And yet she understood what Dorijan had said about it being no bad thing if it saved Baka from the agony of knowing Valentin had gone forever. Natali couldn't begin to understand the workings of the human mind, far less how Baka felt or what she thought at the end of every day when she came home alone, but it was not hers to question. Was she, in fact, doing something not dissimilar herself, by refusing to look beyond the summer?

The thought had begun to take root in her mind when Auntie Stela had given her a hug as they said goodbye on Saturday and told her to stay positive, that something would come up because it always had before. But quite a few of the somethings had been less than ideal, and the thought of going back to cleaning or pot-washing filled her with dread. It was so unrewarding, but with her school certificates being such poor grades, what else could she do?

She stopped with her hand on the door handle. There must be something. Surely there was something. If she'd learnt anything about herself this summer, it was that she wasn't half as stupid as she'd thought she was. Look at all those books she was reading, for a start. All those new words. And in English too! If she could do that, then could she do something to actually shape her life after September, like the people in the stories did, rather than leave herself at the mercy of Auntie Stela's karma?

But that was not for now. Baka would be waiting for the aubergines, so she opened the door and went outside, Obi following half a pace behind. As Natali looked around, the little terrier sniffed the air then zoomed off between the trees. Natali only hoped the walls were in good repair so she couldn't get out, but Obi's excitement as she ran, and sniffed, and ran again, all the while wagging her tail, was palpable, and filled Natali's heart with a huge ball of joy.

Back in the kitchen, Baka had halved the peppers and put them in a large, enamel dish. Natali washed the aubergines under the tap and cut them into large chunks as Baka directed, then everything went into the oven.

"We roast them until they're almost black," Baka said. "It gives the smoky flavour we need. So now I will make coffee and you can crush the garlic. Lots of garlic. It's how my Valentin likes it."

They worked in companionable silence, Obi following Baka around hopefully.

"She likes it here," Baka said.

"She loved the garden. Ran everywhere. She isn't often off her lead."

"Then shall we take our coffee outside? As long as you carry the tray. I made some *savijača od višanja* this morning. My wrists still ache from working that pastry but the cherries are wonderful at the moment." She leant towards Natali. "I'm sure Valentin won't mind if we have a couple of slices."

"Do you make everything from scratch?"

"What else would I do? Made with love is the best."

Natali nodded. "I like to cook too, but I don't know many recipes."

"Your mother did not teach you?"

"My mother cannot cook at all. Everything in the microwave. I learnt from the television when I had no work."

Baka tutted. "No wonder you are so thin." She loaded an extra slice of the strudel onto the plate. "Never mind. Now you'll be able to make *ajvar* and perhaps, if there is time another day, when Valentin is out seeing his friends, I can teach you more recipes."

From nowhere, Natali's eyes filled with tears. "I'd really, really like that."

Baka rested a sun-spotted hand over hers. "So would I."

Šipan

WEDNESDAY 26TH JULY

Ana reached out and touched her phone. Six o'clock. She'd actually slept – eventually. No thanks to Pajo, phoning at about eleven last night to ask her to supper on Saturday.

She'd had no reason, no reason at all, to refuse his invitation. He'd left her absolutely no wiggle room, and once she had finally agreed she'd been left in no doubt what they'd be talking about either. His promises to make it a night to remember, one fit to mark the start of a new chapter, had kept her awake into the smallest hours, without coming anywhere near a conclusion.

She settled back into her pillows. In the light of day, common sense told her the fact she seemed to be incapable of telling Pajo honestly why she kept putting him off should be raising all sorts of alarm bells. As should the uncomfortable realisation that she couldn't quite get that winemaker, Raš, out of her head. If she could talk to Meri about it, she was sure her friend would have an angle. She'd probably ask how Ana could even be considering sharing her life with someone she couldn't fully open up to, especially when she found she was so intrigued by another man.

But what Pajo was offering wasn't a conventional relationship; it was a marriage of convenience. Quite literally. A way for them both to make their parents happy, and to start a family of her own. If only she could be absolutely sure that she didn't want children, then she could tell Pajo no. At least there'd be a reason, not an excuse. She'd searched and searched her heart for the answer most of the night, leaving her feeling like a limp and ragged mess. This way and that, that way and this, and she was sick of it.

She needed the answer, not only for herself but for Pajo too. If she didn't want this, then she needed to tell him, so he could move on as well. If it wasn't so damn early she might even be able to screw up the courage to phone him right now and come clean about her uncertainties, but within minutes her resolve had drained away, like water trickling through her fingers. She remembered Lloyd's words about honesty sometimes hurting, and she didn't want to hurt Pajo. But if she couldn't make him happy either... *Sranje!* Round and round in circles again.

Whatever she decided, surely it was better to tell him to his face, which made Saturday a rather scary deadline, on top of all the other scary things this week – like worrying about what Mirjana might tell Kristina and like meeting the head of the school on Mljet. Ana needed a clear head all right, and for that she needed a swim. But first her morning message to Meri to find out if she'd slept at all was way overdue.

Even after her broken night, Ana was more than pleased to see Raš on the beach. Standing in the shadows of the trees around the path, she watched him pull his top over his head. His muscular shoulders were completely in proportion to his body, not overdone in the gym, but presumably a natural result of his work. He was absolutely gorg— But no. No way should she treat him as a sex object. She'd hate it if the boot was on the other foot.

What would be nice this morning was his company, to take her away from her thoughts. She almost called for him to wait for her, but instead of heading into the water he stared out to sea with his arms wrapped tightly around his chest. Something made her hold back, waiting for him to move, but he didn't.

When she slithered down the bank he turned, the ghost of a smile on his face.

"You looked thoughtful," she said. "I didn't know if I should disturb you."

"It's a public beach."

"Yes, but…"

"And you are a tactful woman who can read body language very well. It's nothing really, except it is something. My daughter chose not to come this week because one of her friends is having a party."

"How old is she?"

"Nine going on nineteen."

"Then parties are important. I guess she knows her *tata* will always be there."

"But I'm not, am I?"

"You said you co-parent?"

"We do, and generally very well. We even go on family holidays, spend Christmas together and all that. But she is with her mother more during term time because of school, so holidays are precious." He shrugged. "At least the school is better in Dubrovnik. The one on Šipan is so small. According to her mother, everything on Šipan is small. Too small."

"If you don't think I'm prying, is that why you split up?"

Again, he looked out across the water towards Lopud. "I should have known it was a risk. Jelka is a city girl, and she said she could settle here, but I think the reality didn't live up to the dream of island life. I don't mean to put all the blame on her because it wasn't like that. She couldn't stay, and I couldn't leave. My land, my vines ... in the end they were more important than my wife and child." He turned, shaking his head. "So now you will think I'm a bastard. Well, it's the truth."

"If your ex said she could live here, then presumably she knew the score."

"I don't think she properly understood what it's like though, especially in winter when everything is closed. And, of course, the stakes were much, much higher once Manda was born." He sighed. "This land, *my* land, it's in my blood, like it actually flows through my veins. I could no more turn my back on it than... It's my purpose, Ana, the reason I was put on this earth." He paused. "I guess that sounds a bit crazy, and I'm sorry to burden you. You're too good a listener, I guess."

It didn't sound crazy. In fact, it sounded more than familiar. What Raš felt about his land, what he *knew*, was exactly what the sea was for her. No one, not even her *dida*, had put it so perfectly. Or so honestly. But Raš had also pointed out that it came at a terrible cost when you had a family. If honesty sometimes hurt, perhaps being true to yourself did as well.

She needed to reply, although the words, when they came,

sounded husky. "It's the same for me with the sea." She stopped and met his eyes. "Sometimes, if I can't get out on the water, I feel as though something inside me will shrivel and die. I could never be happy without being able to take off on *Dida Krila* whenever I want." There. She'd said it. But she had a family too; a family she would hurt almost as badly as Raš had hurt his if she followed this through.

But at least she'd realised before she started another one. Realised with a start that the truth she had voiced with such clarity to Raš meant the answer to the children question was definitely no.

He interrupted her thoughts. "*Dida Krila*?"

"My catamaran. My grandad was the same. All his life. The sea was his gift to me."

"I've seen her in the harbour and she's a stunner. It's great that you're keeping his memory alive in such a special way."

The tears that had been threatening most of the night welled into Ana's eyes. Regret? Relief? She turned away and began to unwind her sarong.

"Talking of the sea, time to get in, I reckon, don't you?"

"Yes, but Ana, first … I don't suppose you'd like to have dinner with me? Not next week because Manda will be here, and we don't date when…" He flushed. "Actually, we've agreed not to date at all at the moment. It's complicated, but I'd love to spend more time with you. As a friend?"

"As a friend is good. Perfect, in fact." But was it really? Or was she just saying it to please him? Raš in his bathing shorts certainly pushed all the right buttons in her body, but if friendship was all that was on offer, she'd take it. She already knew she was looking forward to dinner with Raš far more than supper with Pajo. Which didn't just tell her something; it screamed it. But she still owed it to Pajo to explain to his face that she couldn't keep their promise.

~

Back in her cabin, Ana stood in front of the mirror and tried the words out.

"I am not going to have children." She watched her mouth as it shaped them, waiting for a reaction to kick in. Nothing. All she felt was relief.

She tried again. "I will never have children." No strong emotions at all.

"Mama and Tata will never be grandparents." Now that stung. She bit her lip, her brow furrowing. But the feeling was for them, not for herself.

What had Lloyd said? Something about every child being really wanted? And she had to face it: hers would not be. She couldn't play god with someone's life like that. She thought about Natali, and everything she'd gone through, because neither of her parents wanted her.

She pulled her hair into its scrunchie then stepped away from the mirror to make her bed. Around her, *Dida Krila* creaked and rocked on her mooring, and she could hear Natali setting the table for breakfast in the salon above. The smell of coffee mingled with the vague undertone of diesel. This time tomorrow they'd be on the water, heading for Mljet, the open sea around them, salt in her hair, and already she was craving it. She simply could not give it up.

Every so often during the morning as she pottered around the boat, Ana found herself testing her decision. The thing that surprised her most was that it hardly felt like a decision at all, just something she had always known, which had floated to the surface. She knew it was right and that she had to tell Pajo, but how the hell she would explain it to her parents, she could not imagine.

She had almost forgotten that Kristina was meeting Mirjana until her email arrived. It was short and to the point: the woman would not change her story. As far as she was concerned, Lloyd was a thief. Ana thumped the chart table in frustration. That told her nothing she didn't already know. What had Lloyd supposedly stolen? Why had no one challenged him at the time? Did Kristina even know? When Ana tried to call her, her phone went straight to voicemail. Kristina was clearly avoiding her, so what was the point of leaving a message?

She powered down her laptop and made her way along the harbour to where Lloyd had set up the library next to the ferry ticket cabin. He was chatting to a couple of teenage boys with beach towels under their arms, so Ana hung back, idly watching a young couple on a table in front of the *konoba*, trying to feed their toddler some pasta. Everywhere, everywhere, were parents and children. But now it mattered so much less.

Once the boys had moved away, she approached the table. There were a good few gaps in the collection of books, which was a positive sign.

"Going well?" she asked.

Lloyd nodded. "Best day here yet, I think."

"That's good, because I don't have the greatest news for you. I've had an email from Kristina, and Mirjana is sticking to her story."

"So what happens now?"

Ana shook her head. "She didn't say."

Lloyd walked away from the table into the shade of the cabin that served as the ferry ticket office, and Ana followed. "Do you know what's pissing me off most about this?" she said. "That there's no substance to her accusations. I mean, obviously you didn't steal anything, but what were you meant to have taken, and when? How on earth can you even begin to defend yourself if you don't know?"

"There's only one way, and I probably should have done it before now. I need to talk to Mirjana, whether she wants to or not. I'll stay over on Friday night again, then get the ferry and bus back to Ston afterwards."

"You'll do no such thing. We'll all stay over. I'll phone the marina at Lumbarda now to see if we can get a berth."

"You don't have to do that."

Ana silenced him with a glare. "But I want to. And I know Natali will too. We're in this together, remember."

It was going to be an awkward conversation with Pajo, even to do no more than put him off for a week or so, but she was sure she'd made the right call. Not only did she want to support Lloyd, but given her decision, she needed the library to succeed more than ever.

Korčula

SATURDAY 29TH JULY

"Right, I'm off." Lloyd hoped he sounded more confident than he felt.

Ana and Natali looked up from the chart table where they were discussing the best route for the long sail back to Koločep tomorrow.

"Are you sure you don't want me to come?" Ana asked.

"We've already been through this and, grateful as I am, this is down to me," he snapped. "Sorry ... sorry..."

"I understand," said Ana, and Natali gave him the biggest possible hug.

Despite his nerves, Lloyd had been surprised that this morning at least a tiny slice of the inner calm he'd achieved since telling Jenny about Mirjana last Saturday had stayed with him. Admittedly, it was buried pretty deep inside, but it was there all the same, and had been the only thing that had made yesterday in Korčula town bearable. As he walked along the marina, he clung to it for all he was worth.

It was only just after nine and the sole person he passed

was a jogger, the tinny sound issuing from her headphones cutting the birdsong with an unnatural rhythm. Would there even be anyone at the *konoba* yet? But unless things had changed so very much, on a busy summer Saturday there'd be plenty of preparation work to do, and anyway, the family had always lived in the apartment above.

What was the shape of that family now? If he was right and the woman he'd seen in the supermarket was Mirjana's daughter, there would most likely be a husband – one who would no doubt take his wife's side, and perhaps who was stirring the trouble. Maybe there were more children, even an aged parent or two. Mirjana's father had always been good to him, so perhaps, if he was still around... Perhaps even Kesten, although Lloyd did rather hope that his old friend hadn't spent his life waiting tables. Maybe he'd even stayed in the army that he'd been so keen to join.

Already Lloyd was standing at the bottom of the steps to Konoba Pecaros. If he hesitated too long, wiping the sweat from his palms onto his chinos yet again, he might never climb them, so he propelled himself upwards and into the restaurant.

What hit him first was the old familiar smell: faint whiffs of charred wood from the pizza oven and the hint of stale wine overlaid with fresh coffee. Rich tomato sauce on the stove. As he looked around, he realised the tables were in much the same places as before, but the ceiling had been boarded out so there was no longer any rustling rattan above his head. Next to the bar hummed a vast glass-fronted fridge, filled to the brim with bottles and cans of beer and soft drinks.

Someone was whistling in the kitchen so he followed the sound, pushing on the door. The curly-haired man chopping peppers looked up, and said in Croatian, "We're not open yet. Not for another hour or so."

The thickness in Lloyd's throat made replying all but impossible, but he swallowed it down. "I'm looking for Mirjana."

"Oh, OK." The man yelled towards the stairs. "Boss, someone to see you!" Before she could ask who it was, Lloyd retreated to the restaurant.

He heard footsteps above. Not light like a girl's, but solid, businesslike. The girl he'd known so well had become a woman he didn't know at all. He knew nothing about her, except that she was the type who held grudges. And acted on them.

"Oh, so it's you." Mirjana's hand rested on the door jamb. Her dark eyes were hard as coals, the lines beneath them etched deep, her mouth thinner than he remembered.

"We need to talk."

"Do we? You may want to, but I have nothing to say."

Despite her nonchalant tone and raised eyebrow, she was gripping the wood tightly. Perhaps this wasn't easy for her either. Perhaps she was feeling less confident than she sounded.

"Then could I perhaps ask for a few minutes of your time to listen?"

She gave a brief nod. At least she hadn't turned and walked away.

"Thank you. I'll get straight to the point. I need to know what you think I stole. I need to clear this up if I possibly can, because—"

"What I think you stole?" She mimicked his bad Croatian accent cruelly, and a flicker of anger stirred inside him.

"There's no need for that," he told her crossly. "Let's at least be civil with each other."

"Civil? Civil? After what you did, you lying bastard! All summer you took us in. Playing at being so nice, making me think—"

"Playing?" The heat was rising under the collar of his polo shirt, a trickle of sweat running down his back. He mustn't lose it, he mustn't. One more try. If not for himself, for Ana and Natali.

"You played us all. You're nothing but a conman!" Mirjana yelled. "And me, just an innocent nineteen-year-old, sucked in by your lies. You sure had your fun with me, didn't you? I bet you were laughing behind our backs the whole time, even when you were screwing me."

How could she believe that? "Mirjana, no! That wasn't how it was at all. It was real, all of it, at least for me."

"Like fuck it was."

A tidal wave of anger washed over him. "Well it was until you sent Kesten to do your dirty work. And still I loved you. I grieved..." He flung his arms in the air. "Oh, what's the point?"

Mirjana took three steps towards him. "The point is, you stole my mother's jewellery. The point is, you dared to come back. The point is, I want you off this island. Permanently."

"Your mother's jewellery?"

"Every last piece of it, as well you know." Mirjana moved even closer, wagging her finger. "It killed her. What you did bloody killed her. And when she died, all I had to remember her by was the sodding earring you dropped on your bedroom floor." The finger became a fist, raised in his direction.

"Mirjana, no!"

"Mirjana, no." She mimicked him again. "Is that all you have to say for yourself?"

His breath was ragged as he inhaled deeply. "Just one more thing, one very important thing. I stole nothing. Nothing at all."

He turned away so sharply he felt dizzy for a moment and reached for the back of a chair for support. His fingers groped the air as the sea in front of him blurred. But no, he would not show weakness. Would not show this stranger anything. It was all he could do not to stumble down the steps, her eyes surely boring into his back as he slowly walked away.

He stopped when he came to a bench and sat down, taking one deep breath after another. He could still feel the blood pumping through the veins in his neck, his head thudding in time. He clenched his fists and unclenched them again and again, then sat back and closed his eyes, listening to the wash of the waves on the rocks below, feeling the sun relax his muscles one by one.

His first thought when he opened his eyes again was the irony of choosing this spot. He'd chosen it before, long before there was a seat here. Chosen it as the place to tell Mirjana that he was falling for her and if she didn't feel the same then he'd be leaving. Which had led to it being the place they'd first kissed, with the soft navy hues of the night around them, the waves caressing the rocks at their feet.

It hadn't been his first kiss, not by a long chalk, but it had felt as though it was. It was the first time he'd put his lips against a girl's and it had meant something more than curious exploration, or vague attraction, or downright lust. It was as if they had been communicating at a deeper level, opening doors within their hearts and minds, places where only each other could go.

And it had felt that way all summer, as if there'd been a web of magic tying them together and keeping everyone else out. The slightest glance or touch between them had meant so much. Oh, it sounded ridiculous now, but at the time it had been gloriously real. Until it had become devastatingly so. Until he'd misread her so badly. Until she'd decided not to come to the harbour. Until she'd shattered his swollen heart into the tiniest of pieces.

Lloyd stretched his legs in front of him and steepled his fingers between his knees. A bee buzzed through the wild rosemary on the bank, distracting him from his line of thought. Up until now, he'd struggled to believe that the responsibility had been anything other than his alone, but seeing Mirjana so hard-faced, so intransigent, he began to wonder. It had taken two to make them; had it taken two to break them as well? She'd been so young, with no hint of the woman he'd met this morning. The knocks that had shaped this bitter and angry Mirjana had undoubtedly come afterwards. Had they even started the day he left? What had driven her decision to send Kesten to the harbour? Her mother, persuading her to salvage some pride and stay at home, telling her once again that in going alone, he didn't love her enough? Or that underneath it all she had truly expected him to take her to England and to safety, and his total misreading of her had been a betrayal of everything they'd had.

Same old, same old, same old. Round and round. But why lie about him now? Because revenge was best served cold? Because she simply couldn't bear the thought of him on the same island as her? She'd said she wanted him gone, but to brand him a thief was a pretty extreme way to go about it. But it was also a sure-fire way of losing him his job. And after all this time, how could he disprove her accusations? Who would believe a foreigner against a respected local businesswoman?

Which meant the dangerous rumours would not stop. Which meant the library's reputation would continue to be compromised. That couldn't be allowed to happen because of a lie, but what the hell could he do about it?

Lloyd stood, unwinding his long body and raising his fingers skywards. Until he had at least an idea of how best to move forwards, there was no way he could go back to the boat. The girls probably thought he was happily chatting to Mirjana, instead of heading towards Bilin Žal Beach in total turmoil.

If he left Croatia there would be no librarian for the final weeks of the summer, and, therefore, no library. If he stayed there'd be no library on Korčula, where a great deal of the funding came from. So no library. Or maybe, *some* library, just less of one. Was that the answer? To work for four days and expect someone else to pick up the slack? Or was that running away?

But they were beginning to achieve so much good. Even their new site on Mljet had proved promising. He needed to cling to that thought, because it might just keep him from drowning in his own misery. The teenagers he now looked forward to chatting to every week, extending their language skills by talking about their books; the little ones on Lopud who were comfortable enough to use him as a human climbing frame as soon as he sat on the floor; the twin sisters on Šipan who came on the bus and always brought a bag of their mother's homemade *kroštule* for him.

But it was more than that, much more. The bonds of

friendship and support they'd built on *Dida Krila*; the way Natali was beginning to blossom; Ana's rapidly improving leadership skills, even if she didn't recognise them herself; the role he knew he was playing in both these things, and how that was helping him too. Even if what he'd done in the past had put the library at risk, the fact he'd turned into a man who could be a father figure to Natali and a mentor to Ana ought to be a source of great pride. And now he thought about it, it was.

The list of good things was growing, making him feel stronger with every step. Even his grief for Jenny felt more manageable – an ache rather than agony. More happy memories than bad. It was good, better than just good; it was actually some sort of miracle. And he wasn't going to give up on it all without one hell of a fight. Even if the only weapon he had was to protest his innocence again and again.

Was he strong enough now to face Ana and Natali and tell them what had happened? He reckoned so. But what he could not do was walk back past the *konoba*. There were two other possible routes, but retracing his steps to the harbour then threading his way through the backstreets would take him too close. The other was along Bilin Žal Beach, and over the hill, past a place that had been more than special to Mirjana and him.

The pain of the past should be easier to face than what had happened today.

~

They were on the beach as usual, that Sunday evening, the kisses they shared as the sun set behind them leaving him burning for more. She was voluptuous, beautiful, irresistible.

Except he had to resist, because he was that little bit older than her, and would be leaving at the end of the summer.

As dusk settled over the beach, and the group of campers staying at the far end began to play their guitars, Mirjana stood and reached for Lloyd's hand.

"Come with me. I have a surprise for you."

"What is it?"

"It's a surprise, you idiot." But as she pulled him close, she caressed the front of his shorts, her intentions suddenly crystal clear.

But was she sure? "Mirjana..."

"Shh."

Taking his hand, she led him across the beach, the fine shingle crunching beneath their feet. They went just a few steps up the road, and through the open gate of the olive grove, where they slipped between the silent trees and stopped in front of a low stone building.

"What is this place?" he asked.

"An olive press. Nobody uses it at this time of year. Nobody comes here."

The door creaked as she opened it, sending a roosting bird fluttering from a nearby branch. He jumped and she laughed at him, before telling him to wait at the bottom of a ladder leaning against what looked like a gallery above. As his eyes adjusted to the darkness, he could make out the press, which filled the centre of the floor, its huge, round grinding stones and wooden levers worn smooth by generations of hands and covered by a thin film of dust. Clearly, no one came here. They would be completely alone.

He could hear her moving above him: a rustle of fabric, a click of a lighter, then shadows dancing from what he assumed were candles. Undoubtedly, she was going all out to make this romantic, so he'd better live up to her expectations.

Eventually she called him and he climbed, his heart thudding in his chest, so much so that he gasped when he reached the top, not from exertion, but from the sight of Mirjana's naked body stretched out on a blanket, surrounded by flickering tealights.

"You're even more beautiful than I dreamt you would be," he whispered. "And believe me, I've dreamt of little else for weeks."

He pulled his T-shirt over his head then pushed his shorts to the ground and stepped out of them. He slid next to her, nestling so close that they seemed to touch at every point. Skin on skin. A blissful, lingering electric shock ran through him – ran through them both, he was sure – and she tilted her head to kiss him.

Wrapping an arm over Mirjana's shoulder, he slowly, slowly, slid it down her spine, goosebumps rising under his exploring fingers. He needed her like he'd needed no girl he'd slept with before. But she had to want it too.

"Mirjana, you're sure? Really sure?"

"Yes, I am. But Lloyd, you should know, I haven't done this before. There hasn't been anyone I've wanted to…"

It was time, more than time, to tell her the feelings he'd been too scared to voice before now.

"Then I am honoured you want me to be the first man to make love to you. And I promise you, it will be making love, because I do love you. Very much."

Tears sparkled in her eyes as she looked up at him. "You're not just saying that, are you?" she gulped, "because I love you too and I couldn't bear it if…"

"Of course I'm not. I'd never lie about something so important. I've been trying to find the right moment, but I worried I'd be coming on too strong. But here, now, it's absolutely right to tell you. And to show you."

∼

How could so much love have turned to such hate? The thought dragged Lloyd back down to the depths. It may be time to face the girls, but to face the old olive press? That would be a step too far.

He'd have to head back past the harbour instead.

∼

Natali fingered the edge of the banquette as Ana scooped her wine glass from the floor of the fly deck. "We have an early start for Koločep tomorrow so I'm off to bed," she said.

Lloyd nodded, unclasping his hands from behind his head. "Me too."

He seemed better after a good meal and a few drinks, thank goodness, more like his positive self. When he'd come back from the village this morning and told them Mirjana had refused to listen to a single word he'd said, Natali thought he'd looked so fragile that for a moment she'd almost been afraid to hug him in case he broke into a million pieces. And when she did and looked up, there'd been tears in his eyes.

After telling them what had happened, he'd gone to his cabin to call Ruth, but hadn't emerged for hours. Ana had gone to the beach for a swim, but Natali had stayed, reading her book, although it had been very hard to concentrate.

And through her lack of concentration, a plan had formed. She'd promised herself she'd do everything she could to keep this wonderful crew together, and now was the time to act.

She stood, the dog jumping from her lap. "I just need to walk Obi, then I'll t-turn in as well."

The narrow floating walkway between the boats wobbled as she stepped onto it. On either side, yachts of all shapes and sizes rocked gently, but none were so smart and well-loved as *Dida Krila*. On one or two of them, groups of people sat in the cockpits, eating, drinking or chatting, but most were quiet and Natali supposed the occupants had either gone out for the evening or, like she was meant to be doing, having an early night.

"You're a good excuse, Obi." The little dog's tail wagged enthusiastically, as though she knew exactly what Natali had planned and was excited by it. Which was more than Natali was. This was frankly very scary, but do it she would because she'd do anything – anything – to help Lloyd. "He saved your life, remember," she murmured, but already they had reached the quayside and Obi had found an extremely interesting bin to sniff.

"Later." Natali said firmly, and set off past the beach club in the direction of the old village. Obi dragged behind, so she scooped her into her arms. "We need to get this done," she whispered as she fondled the dog's silky ears.

It was even harder to be brave standing outside a busy *konoba* on a Saturday night. Would this Mirjana even agree to see her? Maybe she should wait until closing time. Natali's legs shook as she stood at the bottom of the steps. It was so full of people up there, talking, laughing, eating; having a good time. She buried her face in Obi's soft fur.

The concrete steps would catapult her into the middle of all those customers, and that in itself was terrifying, so perhaps there was another entrance? Somewhere she could creep in around the back and ask one of the staff if she could see Mirjana. The *konoba* had a terrace, festooned with different coloured lights, so maybe she'd try up there.

A girl she guessed was just a year or two older than her, and wearing a white T-shirt with *Pecaros* emblazoned across it, ran down the steps.

"Is your dog all right?" she asked. "Only, you're carrying it, and you look a bit worried."

"N-no, she's f-fine. Just sometimes she c-can be obstinate."

"Oh, I see." The girl reached forwards and stroked the top of Obi's head. "But she's so cute!"

Natali nodded. "Her n-name's Obi."

"Hello Obi. Now, are you guys looking for some supper?"

This was the moment. The ideal moment. "No. I'm l-looking for Mirjana."

"Mama?" The girl looked surprised.

"I know you're b-busy and it's not a good time, but we're s-sailing early tomorrow and…"

"Mama's not working tonight. Can I help at all?"

Oh no. Natali hadn't even imagined Mirjana wouldn't be at the *konoba*, and to her intense shame she found tears pooling in her eyes. "I d-don't think so. It's about my f-friend. He … he…" But what else could she say?

"The man who came this morning?" The girl's voice was sharp. "The one who stole my grandmother's jewellery?"

"But he didn't. I swear he didn't. H-he couldn't have."

The girl folded her arms. "Listen, I've grown up with that story since I was little." She stopped, frowning. "Neither of us was even born when it happened. How can you be so sure?"

"Because I know Lloyd. He saved Obi's life. He's the k-kindest man, the t-truest friend."

"So he's sent you here to upset Mama all over again?"

"No! In f-fact if he knew, he'd be really cross. But I wanted to try to explain to your mother. It's s-so important she stops spreading l-lies about him."

The girl folded her arms across her chest. "But they're not lies." Despite her words, Natali could sense her discomfort.

"I s-suppose, like you said, it was before we were born, and you believe your *mama* and I believe Lloyd. But it's not just Lloyd she's affecting," Natali rushed on. "It's Ana, and me, and a whole load of children spread over five islands."

The girl's eyebrows tilted a little above her deep brown eyes. "I don't understand."

"We run a library. For local children to have books to read in the summer. Here, perhaps you have something like that already, but on the smaller islands there is nothing. And Lloyd reads to the little ones too in some places, talks to others in English or German. And it's Ana's boat, and me ... well, I really, really need a job where Obi can come too and that's hard to find..." Oh, she was explaining this so badly.

"But this is nothing to do with Mama."

"It is. It actually is. There's a lady called Kristina. She's in charge of the library on Korčula and your *mama* told her Lloyd was a thief and ever since then she's stopped bringing children and wants him gone, which I do understand. If she thinks he's dishonest, I totally g-get it. But he's not. He knew nothing about the jewellery until today. I promise you, he didn't. Oh, please, you have to believe me."

The girl nodded slowly. "I do believe you. I just don't think I buy what Lloyd's been telling you. I think you've been spun a lie as well."

Natali set Obi down on the road. "He's a good man. And I know bad when I see it, you can certainly trust me on that one." There was nothing more to be said. Nothing at all. "We must be going. Early st-start tomorrow. We only stayed so Lloyd could talk to your mother and it's a long sail to Koločep."

She started to walk away, but the girl called after her, asking her name.

"It's Natali. Why?"

She pulled a phone from her pocket. "And what's your number? I'll try to talk to Mama about this, but it mightn't be easy to find the right time. Your friend coming here this morning has really rattled her. It's given her one of her headaches, and she hasn't had one of those since Tata died."

"Thank you. Thank you so much."

"I'm Krasna, by the way. And I think you're so brave, Natali, coming here." She laughed. "But then, you don't know Mama like I do."

Sailing from Korčula to Koločep

SUNDAY 30TH JULY

They'd slipped from Lumbarda's quayside before six, and even now, with the eastern tip of Korčula sliding away behind them, the sun was only just topping the hills of the Pelješac, a cool breeze filling *Dida Krila*'s sails. It was a moment of calm, the sole sound the water washing gently against the hulls. Ana relished it, completely alone on the fly deck, but with the comfort of knowing her friends were somewhere below.

Not that any of them had been particularly cheerful this morning, but that was understandable. The outcome of Lloyd's attempt to talk to Mirjana hung over them all, and there'd been none of their usual banter as they readied the catamaran to sail. But Ana knew a day on the water would go a long way to restoring her equilibrium, and she hoped it would for the others too.

She looked at her phone, scrolling through the string of short messages that had accumulated between her and Raš over the last few days. It had started when she'd used the email on his website to make sure he had her number to fix their dinner date, and he'd sent her a photograph of a vine, asking her to guess which grape it was. She'd had a feeling it was *plavac mali*, which was also grown on the shores of Malostonski Bay, and after a quick internet search to confirm it she had replied, earning herself five gold stars from Raš's Private Wine Academy, as he called it.

Lloyd's damp head appeared at the top of the steps, and he carried a mug in each hand.

"Coffee for you, tea for me," he said. "Then I might feel halfway human."

"Did you sleep?"

"Not much. You know those thoughts you get at two in the morning? Well, one of them took hold." He looked at her sideways. "Ana, be honest with me, should I resign? I want to do what's best for the library."

She hadn't expected this. But why not? It was Lloyd all over to put the library first. "You have to do what's right for you too, but there's no need to rush into a decision. When I looked at my emails before I turned in last night, I noticed I'd received an out-of-office message from Ivana in response to my weekly report. She's on holiday next week, and I'm hopping mad she didn't tell me, but all the same it buys us some breathing space. Once she's back, she'll be running out of time to recruit anyone else. And there's no way on god's earth she'd find anyone as good as you anyway."

He smiled. "I have to say I'm relieved. Yesterday, after I saw Mirjana, well, obviously I was really low. But after a while, I realised her attitude made me want to fight harder than ever for the library to succeed. The trouble is, there's sod all I can do on Korčula because there's no way to clear my name."

"Well, let's forget Korčula, shall we? Focus on the other islands."

"But Korčula contributes so much of the money. What if they don't commit to funding next year because of all this?"

Ana shrugged, as if it didn't matter. "Let's leave next year to look after itself, shall we?" she said, a little too carelessly.

"Have you made any decisions about your own future?"

She shrugged again. "A few." She so didn't want this conversation now. She wanted today to be about relaxing and dreaming up a suitably gorgeous photo of the sea to send with a quiz question for Raš.

Lloyd took a sip of his tea. "I may be talking out of turn, but is there a reason you doubt your decision-making ability so much?" Clearly, he wasn't going to let this go. Just when she didn't need him reminding her of her father.

"My track record this summer ought to be enough." She laughed, trying to lighten the mood.

"Why? From where I'm sitting it's the same as most people's: a little bit wrong, but mainly right. Like deciding to speak to the head teacher on Mljet about siting the library somewhere else. That was a great idea; I never expected to lend out eight books on our first day at Sobra. It makes me wonder why you lack so much confidence in that respect."

"I guess ... I guess I haven't had all that much practice. I've never had a job with any responsibility, not until now. I spent my twenties having fun, living in the city, moving from one place to another working in tourism, but never actually making a career of any of them. Five day a week work so my weekends were free to go sailing with Dida."

"So sailing has always been your passion?"

"Totally." Like she'd admitted to Raš, she needed to be on

the water, needed times like these to set her equilibrium right. She couldn't give it up, and yet if the library failed she still might have to. But there was no way she was going to say it and add to Lloyd's woes. If he was going to fight even harder, then she would too. But not today. Tomorrow would be soon enough.

Ana looked around, judging the wind and the distance. She needed another way to head off his questions. "I'm going to tack in a minute. Where's Natali?"

"Cleaning the fridge as though her life depends on it. Want me to help?"

"Please. Can you take the headsail?" It would get him down the steps and out of her hair.

Once he was in position, Ana leaned over the rail and yelled, "Ready to tack?" Lloyd's thumb shot up in acknowledgement, and the sail billowed over her head as she steadied the boom with one hand and turned the wheel with the other, the spray licking *Dida Krila*'s hulls and sparkling in the sunlight. It was beautiful, magical, and she felt as though her *dida* really was beside her. She missed him so keenly at moments like this, yet all the same she knew she was only here because of him, and she was so damned grateful.

Next Saturday was Victory Day, when her parents always held a party in his honour. It had been so special to him. More so than Christmas, more than his birthday, even, and he'd relished sharing it with both family and friends. This year, Ana wanted her friends to be there too – Lloyd, Natali, and Meri, if she could make it. Meri could certainly do with some fun; the stressful summer she was having made Ana's pale into insignificance. Zac and Tomi were still up and down, although over the last few days Meri had said she'd been given reason to hope.

Never mind that Pajo would most likely be at the party too, but she'd have to face him at some point and tell him she couldn't keep their promise. Since she'd postponed their dinner, he'd been ghosting her, totally ghosting her. The only reason she was sure he'd seen her message was the tell-tale little blue ticks on the app. He was sulking, she knew. It wouldn't be the first time and it was nothing she couldn't handle.

But Pajo wasn't the real problem. Not anymore. Not now she knew in her heart that motherhood wasn't for her. But telling her parents still played heavily on her mind. Maybe if she offered to put *Dida Krila* into their business it might soften the blow. Could she even do that? The way things were looking, she might very well have to.

Koločep

MONDAY 31ST JULY

Natali helped Lloyd load the last of the boxes of books onto the sack trolley, then Ana handed her Obi's lead.

"I'll try not to be too long," she told her, winding it through her fingers. "Just give her a walk, then buy the bread. There's nothing else?"

Ana shook her head. "No, that's it."

Natali unlooped the catamaran's rope from the squat, metal stanchion and threw it to Ana, just at the moment the ferry nosed around the headland. She wouldn't have much time to talk to Baka now, which was bad news because she wanted to. She had to tell someone what she'd done on Saturday, because the more she thought about it, the more uneasy she'd become. Baka was so wise that Natali knew she'd say if she'd made a big mistake she needed to somehow try to put right. But when she looked, Baka was nowhere to be seen.

"That's odd, Obi," she murmured as they walked towards her usual bench. The dog sniffed around, seemingly as puzzled as Natali. She glanced towards the uphill path, hoping to see Baka hurrying down it, but there was no one in sight.

"Worrying, isn't it?" It was Dorijan, the man she'd spoken to before, and Natali nodded. "She met the early boat," he continued. "I'll go and check on her once I've finished unloading, but it might be a while."

"I'll go now," said Natali. "I've been to her house before."

He smiled at her. "I know. She's been telling everyone what a wonderful time you had making *ajvar* together."

Natali all but ran up the steep hill, dragging Obi behind her. For once the little dog scrambled along undistracted, as though she, too, sensed that something was wrong.

Reaching Baka's terrace, Natali hammered on the door, but there was no answer. She pushed it, relieved it was unlocked as usual.

"Baka! Baka! It's Natali." The air hung heavy in the living room as silence surrounded her. Not a murmur. Not a movement.

Holding desperately onto a faint hope that Baka might be in the garden and had lost track of time, she rushed through to the kitchen, then ran down the stairs. She'd almost reached the halfway point when she saw Baka's ankles and feet sticking out from Valentin's bedroom.

Oh god! Oh god! Please let her be all right.

Natali catapulted herself down the last few steps, Obi tumbling beside her, and knelt next to Baka on the floor.

She opened her eyes and stared at Natali, but her face looked strange, contorted almost. "Flowers... Valentin's flowers..." she whispered but the words were indistinct and Natali knew straight away she'd most likely had a stroke.

Scrabbling for her phone, she dialled 112. She counted the

rings. One, two, three. Only three, but it felt like it took them forever to answer, then questions, so many questions: could Baka speak, could she raise her arms, while all the time Natali was screaming inside for them to send someone. But they had, the voice on the other end assured her. The emergency boat was on its way.

Half an hour. At least half an hour. Even with Natali's rather basic first aid, she knew that time could be crucial. Was there a doctor on the island? And someone to wait for the boat on the quay and bring them straight here? But how could she leave Baka to find out? She couldn't, she absolutely couldn't.

"Help's coming," she said, taking hold of Baka's hand, spotted and wrinkled in her own smooth one. At least Baka was able to squeeze back, and that gave Natali hope.

"Can't get up... Valentin, where is he?"

"H-he's on his way, I expect."

"No, he's here. I made him coffee. He's smoking as usual ... naughty boy."

The hairs on the back of Natali's neck stood on end. Had Baka really seen her son? Had he somehow come for her? Was she ready to go with him? Never, ever religious, involuntarily Natali crossed herself, while Obi snuggled closer to Baka, resting her head on her hip.

"Dear little thing..." Baka murmured. "Dear dog..."

Her words were increasingly indistinct. "Shh now," Natali said. "Don't try to talk. Just rest until help gets here."

Baka nodded and closed her eyes, her grip loosening a little on Natali's hand. Had she said the right thing? Or was it better to keep her alert and talking? Oh god, she didn't know. Perhaps she should yell for help? But down here at the bottom of the house, who would hear her?

A bee buzzed against the window, desperate to escape, but that and Baka's breathing were the only sounds. Natali hung her head.

Oh please, please, don't let me have screwed up again.

Saturday night had been bad enough, not knowing if she'd done more harm than good, but this was a matter of life or death and if Baka died, and trying to get more immediate help would have saved her, she'd blame her stupidity forever.

A man's voice called from the kitchen above. Dorijan.

"Down here," Natali yelled. "I think she's had a stroke. I've called 112."

Baka's eyes shot open. "Valentin?" Footsteps thundered down the stairs. "No … no…" She closed them again.

"She thinks Valentin's here," Natali whispered.

"*Sranje!* That's bad."

"But she can grip my hand so that's good. Is there anyone who can help? A doctor, maybe?"

He shook his head. "The clinic's not open this morning."

Baka gripped Natali's hand. "Tell him … tell him … he must find Val…" she slurred.

The man crouched down. "You know who I am, Baka?"

"Find him … find him for me…"

He touched her lightly on the shoulder then stood. "Don't worry, I will. I'll go down to the quayside to wait. And I'll call Mateo." The last words were for Natali's benefit, she knew, and she nodded to show she understood. She hadn't even thought of Baka's other son. The living one.

Once again, silence filled the air. Even the bee was still, or had found a way out, and Baka's breath was shallow. Every instinct in Natali's body told her to try to keep the old woman with her.

"Shall I tell you a story?" Baka attempted to nod, but it was more of an awkward twisting of her head. "How about *Fisherman Plunk*? We both like that one."

More footsteps above. Two paramedics, a woman and a man, and Natali scooped up a whimpering Obi and leapt out of their way as they ran down the stairs, leaving them space to kneel next to Baka. She retreated to the hall, eyes brimming with tears.

Please, oh please, let them save her.

Then there was a familiar aftershave, a warmth next to her. "Your friend from the harbour told me what's happened. Marin's minding the library."

"Lloyd, Lloyd, w-what if I've made things worse? W-what if I should have d-done something different? W-what if she dies?" Natali was shaking and her teeth chattering so much it was hard to force the words out.

Lloyd enveloped her in his arms. "You called the paramedics. You stayed with Baka and made her comfortable. Of course you've done the right thing. You always do."

Natali buried her head in Lloyd's chest and howled.

Lopud

TUESDAY 1ST AUGUST

Propping a note saying he would be back at half past four against a pile of books on the library table, Lloyd called to Filip that he was going for some fresh air. His days at the community centre were long because of reading to the children, but they were so very rewarding. This morning he'd had a lengthy and complicated conversation in German with two older teenagers studying languages at the high school in Dubrovnik, and just an hour ago a university student who was working in one of the restaurants for the summer had asked him a question about Shakespeare. Now that had really stretched him.

Here, in a space where everyone congregated anyway, it was easier to get to know local people. Filip had explained that there was a small elementary school on Lopud, but with so few children that two teachers taught everyone, with ages mixed together. Very often the kids left at fifteen, or went to a vocational school away from the island. Whichever route they chose, many ended up working in tourism where language skills were important.

This insight had made Lloyd even more passionate about making the library the very best it could be. It was one thing being told about the Croatian education system, but quite another seeing the results of it first-hand. And despite how it sounded, from what he could tell, the results were generally good. It just felt strange to think that children could leave school so young, like Natali had. He had an inkling that with a longer education she'd have far more options in life. The same went for these kids too.

But Filip had also told him there was a new system giving adults the opportunity to catch up on some of the schooling they'd missed. It was only in its second year, and normally the participants had to pay, but if Natali was interested it could be just the thing to broaden her career prospects. Lloyd had ascertained that distance learning was possible, and Filip had said he thought there were plans for students' work experience to count towards their grades as well. Once Natali was over the shock of what had happened to Baka, he'd need to sit down and talk to her about it.

Lloyd had been relieved that when Ana had dropped by with his lunchtime sandwich, she'd told him Natali had had a call from Baka's son, saying his mother was doing well in hospital and thanking her for her prompt action. It was too soon to know how good Baka's recovery would be in the long term, but she was certainly well enough for Natali to visit if she wanted to.

Lloyd was delighted that Natali had made such a good connection with the old lady. The youngster clearly didn't have many friends, and in just a few weeks the crew of *Dida Krila* would go their separate ways. He knew Ana was trying to find work for Natali close to her in Ston, so far without luck, and he worried about how she would fare as winter approached, because as things stood she had no job and no home after the beginning of September.

The park was all but empty at this time of day, the view down the broad central walkway to the sea overhung with vibrant pink bougainvillea, the pillared pots on either side of the steps to the promenade framing Šipan opposite in a picture-perfect postcard of the Elafiti islands. Down every path was some interesting piece of stonework – a rustic arch set with seashells, an intricately carved column with animals and birds highlighted by the sunlight slanting through the palms and Aleppo pines above.

Whoever designed this garden had surely had peace in mind. Jenny would have loved it, and in his heart Lloyd was telling her all about it. His fruitless discussion with Mirjana behind him, and Ivana away from her desk for a week, some of the weight had been lifted, giving him the mental space to return to dealing with his grief. Except now that grief seemed to be subtly different. Had telling Jenny about Mirjana really been as cathartic as it had felt at the time?

He'd only loved two women in his life: his young, all-consuming passion for Mirjana, then the solid, deep wonder of finding his soulmate in Jenny. That description made his feelings for Jenny sound rather unexciting, which wasn't fair, or true. His relationship with his wife had been everything in every season. A lifetime partnership, ended far too early, which he could now look back on with intense gratitude. Nobody could touch that, or take it away, and whatever happened it would always comfort him.

It didn't mean there weren't still moments when he missed her so keenly he could weep, but they were fewer and further between. He was actually beginning to heal. He felt ready to move on with his life. He still didn't know where the hell it would take him, but perhaps that came next, provided the long shadow of the theft accusations didn't follow him home as well. But surely, surely, Ivana couldn't put something in a reference without an iota of proof.

In five weeks' time he'd be back in London. Maybe he could talk to his old headteacher. If she thought it might be possible, one idea was to ease himself back into the profession with some supply work – provided anyone would have him. A very big *provided* indeed. But with Jenny gone, he had to try. He had to try to return to the profession they'd both loved. The way he'd behaved towards that child had been terribly, terribly wrong, and it always would be, but it had been an aberration. He understood that now. Understood that grief was a kind of madness; that his guilt about what he'd done shouldn't be allowed to change who he was.

Lloyd looked at his watch. He needed to get back to the community hall and prepare for story time. The children would be waiting, and he'd spent the quieter moments of his week rewriting *Little Red Riding Hood* in Croatian. They were going to love it.

Dubrovnik

WEDNESDAY 2ND AUGUST

Walking off the ferry without Obi, Natali felt as though she was missing an arm, and it unnerved her almost as much as the fact that Baka's son had said he'd meet her to drive her to the hospital. In one way she was grateful: it was a forty-minute walk up the hill to Lapad, and not only was it incredibly hot, it would also give her so little time with Baka before she had to start back to catch the return ferry to Šipan.

On the other hand, she had absolutely no idea how to fill the minutes in the car with this stranger. She could only hope he'd do all the talking, but he would, at the very least, require answers. And how would she find him in the first place? How was she supposed to remember what he looked like from the photos in Baka's living room? This was beyond awful.

At the bottom of the gangplank, she stepped to one side to scan the quay, the hum of the ferry's engines subsiding behind her. There, near a scrappy hedge a few metres away, was a man in a crisp navy polo shirt holding a piece of paper with her name on. Hidden by the crowd, she stood for just long enough to take him in. He was a bit younger than Lloyd, she reckoned, but his head was almost bald, although he boasted a neatly trimmed beard. And he wasn't smiling. But who would be, with their mother so ill in hospital?

Natali edged sideways out of the throng. For Baka, she could do this.

"Hello Mr Valentić. I'm N-Natali." Damn. She'd almost got through that without stuttering too.

He held out his hand, which was cool to the touch. "Call me Mateo, please. I am sure my mother would wish it."

"How is she?"

"I will tell you in the car. I am afraid I parked rather precariously so I'm anxious to get back before there are too many blowing horns."

Natali followed him from the quay and down the tree-lined street. Cars and buses crawled along as usual, belching fumes into the stifling afternoon. Mateo led her to a navy-blue SUV and held the passenger door open for her to climb in.

As soon as he had negotiated the vehicle away from the kerb and into the crawling traffic, he thanked her again for how quickly she'd acted on Monday.

"The medics say she'd be in a much worse position if no one had found her for hours."

"I knew something wasn't right as soon as she d-didn't meet the ferry, but it wasn't only me. I was j-just the one who was free to go to look for her."

"It has always been a comfort to me that she has the community around her. Especially with her mind beginning to go."

"I think..." No, perhaps it wasn't for her to say.

"Go on," he prompted, glancing at her with dark eyes which suddenly looked so like Baka's.

Natali shook her head. "You're her son. You know her b-better than I do."

"You have seen her more often these last weeks, though." He sighed. "It is just too busy in the restaurant this time of year for me to get away, although of course now this has happened I regret it."

"Her memory ... it is only V-Valentin. Otherwise she seems fine to me. We were cooking together last week and she knew perfectly well what to do. No need for recipes."

"I'm afraid that might be different going forwards. Following the stroke, she's very ... confused, shall we say. She thinks I'm still courting my wife, and we've been married for twenty years and have two daughters. She might not know you at all, Natali. You need to be ready for that."

"Thank you for warning me." Natali wound her hands together in her lap. "But that is not a big problem. I am fond of your mother, but I have not known her for long, so I s-suppose it is to be expected." Being instantly forgettable was part and parcel of her life, and generally it was a very good thing. But right at this moment, it didn't feel that way.

"She thinks a lot of you too. She talks about you and your dog when we speak on the phone. I have to admit that I was a little concerned about your intentions, but your actions on Monday ... and now that we've met I can see you have an honest face. In the restaurant trade you learn to spot crooked people very quickly."

"If you are worried, I have good references."

For the first time he laughed, and it was a warmer sound than Natali had expected. "I am not trying to employ you."

There was silence while he negotiated the junction at the end of the harbour. "And I have no wish to offend you, either."

"You haven't. This must be a very stressful time."

"It will mean changes. Big ones. Even if Mama recovers well, I can't see her being able to return to that house, so she will need to come and live with me in Split. The girls will have to share a bedroom, and they won't like it, but it is what it is. They need to learn about family duty."

"B-but will your mother want to l-leave Koločep? Meeting the ferries..." Natali trailed to a halt. Valentin had been this man's brother. The loss of him must have left a gap in his life too.

"We will all need to make adjustments."

They had reached the hospital car park, so Natali jumped out and looked around her. She had never come here before – had never needed to, thank goodness – and she had no idea what to expect. The layers of white concrete glowed in the sun between lines of black windows, but the landscape around the building was softened by trees. Once he had locked the car, Natali followed Mateo up a shaded path to an entrance with a café to one side, its bright umbrellas lending a dash of cheer to this frightening place.

It was blessedly cool inside and they walked down corridor after corridor then up two flights of stairs before arriving at a ward.

Mateo stopped. "Ready?"

Natali nodded.

"Then here we go."

She followed him across the room, then through the curtains which surrounded Baka's bed. She stopped, unable to bring herself to move any closer. Seeing Baka attached to so many bleeping and buzzing machines, with wires and plastic tubes everywhere, was horrible and her mouth went dry. Perhaps Mateo was right; Baka wouldn't recognise her, and even though she'd tried to sound brave in the car, how that would feel if it happened she didn't quite know.

But this wasn't about her, it was about Baka. Natali stood up straighter.

Hold that thought, stay positive, and everything would be fine.

At least Baka's eyes were closed and her face, although still a little twisted on one side, looked peaceful.

"Mama." Mateo spoke gently. "Mama, Natali's here to see you."

After a few moments, Baka opened her eyes, the right one drooping a little. She focused on Natali then shook her head from side to side, trying to form a word, which sounded a little like *"Obitelj"*.

"No, Mama, Natali's not family, she's a friend."

"My d-dog's called Obi," Natali told him. "She must have remembered what it's short for." A huge lump filled her throat, but she swallowed it back down. This was so not the moment.

Mateo nodded. "That's promising. Come, sit next to her." He moved the plastic chair at the side of the bed so it was facing his mother, and Natali slid onto it.

"So, Baka," she said, "Obi's not here because she had to stay on the boat. She isn't allowed in the hospital."

Baka moved her lips, and Natali thought the word trying to escape was "hospital". Actually, if you listened and watched closely, her speech wasn't all that difficult to make out, and clearly Mateo had realised this too.

"Yes, you're in hospital, Mama. After your stroke."

Baka swallowed, gathering the next word carefully. "Valentin?"

When Mateo said nothing, Natali spoke. "You don't need to worry about him. When he arrives, the men on the harbour will tell him where you are, I'm sure of it."

"You ... make *soparnik*?"

Unsure exactly what Baka meant, Natali patted her hand. "You need to rest and get well, not worry about other people. Everything will be fine."

Glancing across at Mateo she knew it was probably the most awful lie, but what else could she say?

Šipan

WEDNESDAY 2ND AUGUST

Ana called down the stairs to Lloyd as he stashed the last of the books.

"Fancy a walk? It'll distract Obi until Natali's ferry gets in." The dog had spent all afternoon sitting on the transom, staring in the direction of the short concrete quay a couple of hundred metres away. She knew where her mistress had gone all right, and for a moment Ana wondered if she could even be persuaded to leave the boat.

But with her lead attached to her collar, Obi shook out her ears and didn't object when Ana picked her up to carry her onto the harbourside. After a baleful glance towards the empty space where no doubt she thought the ferry should be, she turned and trotted after them.

"So tell me about Victory Day," Lloyd said.

"I guess for a lot of families it isn't a big deal. It's in the middle of the tourist season and most people around here are too busy to treat it as a proper holiday, but it always meant so much to Grandad that we've carried on celebrating it. As well as marking victory in the Homeland War, it's also the official day to remember Croatian Defenders. My grandfather was a defender, and he lost some of his friends in the conflict.

"In the morning he'd always watch the memorial service at Knin on the television on his own, then he'd come to our house and Mama would cook a special lunch for all the family. Over the years it grew into quite the party, with neighbours and friends invited too, so when Dida died we decided to carry on in his memory."

"It must be a very special day for you."

"It is. He was my inspiration in so many ways."

They had reached the point where the path split away from the road, so Ana went ahead, the sea rippling turquoise and silver below them through the pines. Obi slowed, sniffing around the patches of wild rosemary, her movement releasing their pungent aroma into the still summer air.

Ana looked over her shoulder at Lloyd, who was walking behind her on the narrow track. "My friend Meri will be joining us for the party. She'll be staying on the boat."

"I guess you'll be needing me to stack the book boxes better. The way things are in the spare cabin, she'll struggle to get to the bed."

"If it's too much trouble she can always share with me."

"Won't that be rather cramped?"

"Wouldn't be the first time we've bunked up after a party. At least she doesn't snore."

Ana had her fingers crossed that Meri would actually be there. Zac and Tomi were talking about going to Tomi's family in Zadar for the holiday weekend and if that happened – which was a big if, given how up and down things were with

Tomi's coke habit – getting away herself would give Meri some much needed downtime.

Reaching the small beach and led by Obi, they scrambled down the bank, dislodging dust and pebbles as they went. Raš hadn't been here this morning when she'd come swimming, but with his daughter staying she hadn't really expected it. Since Manda had arrived, his messages had become nightly, rather than daily, and the tone had subtly changed – less banter about grapes, more personal messages sharing tiny snippets of his day and asking about hers. But what did it mean? If, in fact, it meant anything at all.

Lloyd interrupted her thoughts. "It will be good to meet Meri at last."

"She's a very special person, the most important in my life after my parents. We clicked from the moment we met, years ago. We're there for each other, but we don't cramp each other's style. However close we are, I understand completely that her son comes first, just like she understands how much I need my freedom."

"That's an interesting phrase to use."

"In what way?"

"That you *need* your freedom. Not that you like it, or you want it, but that you need it. Is that the key to those big decisions Ana Meštrović? To what you want from life?"

Freedom? Freedom to do … what, exactly? To spend as much time as she wanted on *Dida Krila*? To not be tied down? Ana released Obi from her lead to run around the enclosed space, kicked off her flip-flops and walked to the water's edge, allowing the gentle waves to kiss her toes. Lloyd did not follow, and she was grateful. Freedom was important, but so was doing the right thing to make those you loved happy. Raš had told her about the terrible cost to his family of his choices, and it weighed heavily on her shoulders that she could so very easily hurt hers. Her rejection of motherhood would be bad enough, but if she rejected the business as well... Would that feel like a rejection of Mama and Tata themselves?

When she'd gone home when Dida fell ill, she'd had every intention of settling down to work in the oyster business, and her parents had been so damned happy. But when Dida had died and left her his money, instead of really giving the business a proper go, she'd bought the catamaran and that had changed everything. It had given her that precious freedom, the freedom of the seas that her grandfather had craved until his very last days.

But her father had quickly worked out a way that *Dida Krila* could be part of the business. He clearly thought her boat was a temporary aberration, no more than a hiccup in his plans. But he was wrong. Freedom was everything. All she wanted. She checked herself; no, it was what she *needed*. Lloyd was right.

She closed her eyes and took a deep, shuddering breath. Didn't her parents deserve something from her too? Didn't she owe them another try, to reward their patience, and all the financial support they'd given her when Dida was ill? And to maybe compensate them a little because they would never be grandparents? She thought of Raš, and his sorrow over how he'd let his daughter down. She would struggle to live with that sort of guilt if she shattered her family's dreams. But what about her own?

With a start she noticed the ferry had appeared from nowhere and was approaching the headland. Calling to Obi, she stuffed her feet into her flip-flops, then linked her arm through Lloyd's.

"We'd best go meet Natali. If we're not there when the ferry comes in, this little scrap will never forgive us."

Even before Ana actually saw Natali emerge from the dark hold of the ferry, Obi let out a series of sharp barks and dashed forwards, almost choking on her lead. Ana scooped her up out of harm's way as the cars began to move off, filling the air with their fumes. But still the little dog wriggled and fussed and yelped as though Natali had abandoned her for a fortnight rather than a couple of hours.

"Shh..." Ana told her, burying her face in her fur. "She won't be a minute." And sure enough, seconds later Natali was beside them, ruffling Obi's ears as the dog tried to leap from Ana's arms.

"I've never seen her so excited," Ana said, laughing and handing her over.

"She's missed me as much as I've missed her. Has she been good?"

"Up until now."

Lloyd led them from the quay. "How was Baka?" he asked.

Natali screwed up her face. "It's hard to tell. She was asleep most of the time. Her son says she's confused when she wakes, but she didn't seem too bad to me. He thought she wouldn't know me, but she must have done because she asked about Obi."

Lloyd laughed. "Everyone's favourite dog."

"Do they think she'll make a full recovery?"

"It's early days, but they want to move her to a rehab facility as soon as they can. Her face looks droopy on one side and her speech is a bit slurred, although you can understand her if you concentrate. But Mateo told me her left arm is almost completely useless at the moment."

"I suppose it could have been worse," Ana said.

Natali nodded, but she didn't look convinced.

"What is it?" Lloyd asked, putting an arm around her shoulder.

"Mateo wants her to live with him in Split, but I don't think she'll want to go because of Valentin. Even in the hospital she's asking for him."

"If her rehab goes well, perhaps he'll change his mind."

"He was very decided. I think he's that sort of man. He knows what's best. Or at least, he believes he does. I realise it's not my business, but I don't want her to be unhappy."

Lloyd gave her a squeeze. "Of course you don't, but it's far too soon to worry about it. Rehab after a stroke can be a long old road."

"I don't want you to be unhappy either, Lloyd." Natali said it quietly, but in a tone of voice that made Ana falter, then fall into step beside them. She glanced across at Natali, who looked deeply troubled. What on earth had happened?

"And why would you think I was? There's a beer with my name on it in the fridge and *šporki makaruli* for supper."

They had almost reached *Dida Krila* and Natali stopped, taking a visible breath before she spoke. "Last Saturday night I tried to see Mirjana, to tell her what a good man you are and to persuade her to back off. But she wasn't there and I spoke to her daughter instead, and now Krasna wants to meet me on Friday."

"Why didn't you say?" Ana was incredulous. For Natali to head off alone, to meet an absolute stranger, spoke volumes about how much her confidence had grown. At least some good had come out of this whole wretched mess.

"After I'd done it I thought ... m-maybe it was the wrong thing, but I was just so desperate to keep us all together, for the l-library. Then we were sailing all day, then Baka got ill, then I thought nothing would come of it, so it might not matter..." Natali's features puckered as she frowned.

"Except now it does," said Ana.

Lloyd looked thoughtful for a moment, then he said. "Come on, cheer up. I messed up so completely when I tried to talk to Mirjana that you can't have made things worse." But when Ana looked at him, she couldn't tell what he was really thinking. And from where she was standing, worse was entirely possible. But so was better.

At least Natali had made a decision and done something about it.

It was well beyond time she took a leaf from her book.

Korčula

FRIDAY 4TH AUGUST

"Well here we are, Obi. Let's hope Krasna isn't too long."

The wonderful aromas of bread, tangy, melted cheese and rich, sweet custards drifted over them from the nearby bakery, and Natali knew Obi would be straining at her leash to get closer if it weren't for the crush of people around them. It was another sweltering day, and the harbour was busy with the diminutive cruise ships that made their way up and down the islands on a weekly basis, disgorging their human cargo in a sweaty mass of visitors eager to see the beautiful old town and sample its cafés and restaurants.

A tour group swirled around them and Obi pushed herself into Natali's ankles. She was about to bend down to pick her up when she saw Krasna emerge from the estate agent on the corner.

"Sorry to keep you waiting. I saw you from the window, but I am not allowed to start my lunch until half past. Shall we go to the *pekara*? They know to serve me quickly and we can sit in the back, away from the tourists."

"You work in the estate agent's?" That would explain the smart white sleeveless blouse and navy skirt. Even having changed into clean shorts and a polo shirt, Natali felt properly scruffy beside her. She could barely imagine what it would be like to dress up for work; her jobs were normally so grubby that she wore her oldest clothes.

"I only help in the *konoba* in an emergency. My mother always encouraged me to do better for myself, not to be reliant on tourists."

"Do you still live there?"

"No. With my boyfriend." She twisted a small diamond engagement ring Natali hadn't noticed before. "We're getting married next year."

"Congratulations." It seemed like the right thing to say.

At the bakery counter they ordered flaky spirals of *burek*, stuffed with spinach and cheese, taking them through to a tiny back room Natali hadn't realised was there.

"It's only for the locals," Krasna explained. "Somewhere we can have our lunch."

"I expect it's d-difficult in the summer."

Krasna shrugged. "A small price to pay for the visitors we so badly need. Now, is Obi allowed a bit of my pastry?"

Natali grinned. "Only a tiny piece. It's not good for her, and it's best to wait until we have almost finished eating, or she will pester you for more." She leant under the table to pat Obi's head. "Now you, lie still under there."

Krasna picked up her *burek*, then put it down. "I wanted to explain about Mama. I told her you had tried to find her on

Saturday, and what you said about Lloyd." Krasna sighed. "She hasn't put it into words, but I think she's finding this extra hard because she's only just getting over losing my father."

"I'm so sorry." This time Natali's response was heartfelt.

"Thank you. It's been more than a year. He had pancreatic cancer but we didn't know. Just for a month before the end and it was brutal. It's only really since Easter that she's coming back into herself – talking about him more normally, going out with her friends … then your Lloyd turns up out of nowhere. It must have been such a shock."

"Lloyd's wife died of cancer too. He wouldn't be here otherwise. And he has a grown-up daughter."

"Don't tell me, she's an estate agent!"

"No. She works for a company helping people to find jobs. They're very close. He talks to her every night."

"I think, when you lose a parent, you do become closer to the other one." Krasna fed Obi a scrap of pastry under the table, and Natali felt her tail thump against her leg. "What about your family, Natali?"

Nice as Krasna seemed, Natali didn't really want to explain. "That's Obi," she grinned. "And you've just made her a very happy dog."

Krasna nodded. "Can I ask you…? I mean, can you do me a favour? Me and Mama, that is."

Natali took a gulp of her cola. This was it. "Go on."

"Mama has a question for Lloyd, something he said that doesn't make sense to her."

Well, at least she didn't expect Natali to try to persuade Lloyd to leave Korčula for good. "What is it?"

"It was about Mama sending someone called Kesten with a message, but she didn't. I can tell it's bothering her."

This was so not the moment to play messenger herself. They didn't have time. Ivana would be back from her holiday on Monday. "P-perhaps you would like to ask Lloyd?"

Krasna traced a *burek* crumb across the table, then looked up at her. "Yes. I think I would."

They walked together past the tourist office and the Marco Polo shop, dodging into the road to avoid the crowds of people, Obi firmly in Natali's arms.

"How do you stand this?" she asked.

"You get used to it, and it's only for a few months."

They turned into a side street that was far too narrow for cars and filled with useful shops rather than ones selling T-shirts or souvenirs. It was quiet enough for them to walk side by side, but they did not speak again. Krasna was no doubt caught up in her own thoughts, and Natali was thinking about Krasna.

Well, not Krasna, specifically, but her life. Her round-the-year job, her smart clothes, her plans to marry and settle down. She'd said that her mother had always encouraged her to do better for herself, which presumably meant she'd stayed on at school and got qualifications – the exact opposite to Natali's *mama* who'd wanted her earning as soon as possible. But now, this summer, Natali had experienced that kind of encouragement from Lloyd and Ana. Was it too late to make something of her life as well?

Lloyd was sitting on a bench close to the library table, Kindle in hand. But he wasn't reading; he was gazing out over the marina. Natali had told him what time she was meeting Krasna, and it was bound to be distracting him. How would he feel meeting Mirjana's daughter himself? What was she about to put him through? But no, this was the right thing to do. This time she was sure of it.

As they neared the table he looked up, then stood.

"Lloyd, this is Krasna," Natali said, rather limply.

He held out his hand and shook hers. "Pleased to meet you. I saw you in the supermarket up the road a few weeks ago. You're very like your mother."

"Some people might say so."

There was an awkward silence. Natali realised it was up to her to fill it. "K-Krasna came with a question from Mirjana, and I thought it was best she asked you herself."

Lloyd stuffed his hands into his trouser pockets. "Fire away."

"Something you said to Mama last Saturday didn't make sense to her. Something about sending Kesten with a message."

Lloyd frowned. "Well she did." He paused. "But I think the best thing I can do is tell you what happened that morning. You have to remember, it was chaos. People expected war to break out any minute, and there'd already been fighting to the north of Split. Your grandfather was adamant I leave. Your grandmother had already told me she wanted me to take Mirjana with me, but your *mama* and I had discussed it and decided it wasn't the right thing to do. Or at least, I thought we had.

"Anyway, the next morning her dad woke me before five, because someone had told him I needed to be in the ferry ticket queue early. Your mother was still asleep, but he promised me he'd bring her into town later to say goodbye.

"By the time I left the ferry office there were crowds everywhere. Around the bank, the shops ... I'd never seen anything like it, and I just hoped Mirjana and I would find each other. I waited for ages on the steps to the old town gate where we always met, but eventually I knew I needed to get to the quayside. I kept looking out for her, but it was our friend Kesten who found me, and he said Mirjana had sent him."

Lloyd's shoulders had drooped as he talked, and instead of looking at Krasna and Natali, he was gazing out over the busy road at the trip boats bobbing on the quay beyond. Natali wanted nothing more than to give him a great big cuddle. He looked so isolated, so alone.

"It's silly, really," he continued. "I've hardly spoken of this before. At the time, and for years afterwards, it was the worst moment of my life and I'm not exaggerating. It knocked me for six, because Kesten told me she couldn't bear to see me because I didn't love her enough to take her to England, and that she never wanted to hear from me again. I was stunned. Even now I can barely remember anything about the journey home from Croatia."

"But you said Mama didn't want to go."

"Which was why it was a bolt from the blue. We'd talked so often about a future together, and how it might work. We'd even made plans that she'd join me the next summer, once I'd finished my teacher training. Of course, that was before the war. Kesten had warned us often enough that the conflict was coming, but we didn't want to listen. We were too wrapped up in each other, and in our dreams.

"I've asked myself a million times what made Mirjana change her mind. Maybe she listened to her mother after all. To be honest, Kosana never really took to me, so maybe she wanted to turn her daughter against me when I wouldn't take her to safety. But the truth is, I shouldn't have left without

Mirjana. I should have moved mountains to get her to London. I should have turned back at the quay and gone to fetch her. But I didn't."

After a long silence, finally Krasna nodded. "Thank you for being so honest with me. I will try to explain to Mama."

Lloyd smiled wryly. "Honest? Was that a slip of the tongue, or did you mean it?"

"I mean it. I don't think you're the conman Mama believes you to be. The way you spoke ... it must have been painful. But I need to think this through. I've grown up with the story of the Englishman who stole the jewellery, and now..." She shrugged. "If you'll excuse me, I need to be back at work." She turned on her heel and walked away briskly, leaving Lloyd and Natali staring after her.

"So Mirjana didn't make up those accusations to get rid of me." Lloyd leant heavily back against the table. "I assumed..."

"I wonder what really happened. If we could find out..."

He shook his head, frowning. It would be wonderful if they could, but it was completely impossible. "Natali, no. It was all so long ago. I guess, maybe, with war coming there were dishonest people who wanted valuables they could trade if the currency collapsed. It literally could have been anyone. People were in and out of the *konoba* all day."

"I suppose you're right. You could tell Kristina your theory though. It might make a difference."

"Or it might sound like an excuse."

Natali tucked her arm into his and gave it a squeeze. "Anyway, I thought you were very brave, telling that sad, sad story again."

"Yes, but we both had our happy endings with other

people. Or at least, I assume Mirjana did, because of her daughter."

"I think so. Krasna told me her father died last year though. Cancer, like your Jenny."

"It takes too many, too soon." His voice carried an infinite sadness, but she couldn't see his face because he'd broken away from her to stretch his fingers upwards towards the trees. He clasped them together, then dropped them.

"Right. I need to rearrange those books for the fourteenth time, to see if it attracts any custom. See you later." He bent down and patted Obi. "You too, little one. Be good."

As Natali crossed the road and walked through the bus station, she still felt uneasy. Krasna may have believed him, but what would Mirjana make of Lloyd's story? She'd write it off as even more lies, probably. And just where would that leave them? All she could do was cross her fingers firmly behind her back and hope that something might change for the better.

Ston

SATURDAY 5TH AUGUST

Deep in thought, Lloyd laid the blue and white striped shirt on his bed. He hadn't worn it for years, but he remembered the day they'd bought it as if it were yesterday. He and Jenny had been going to a neighbour's barbecue and the weather had turned unseasonably hot, so they'd popped up to the West End to find her a sundress and she'd insisted he have something new too.

He could see her now in Marks & Spencer in Marble Arch, holding the halter-neck maxi dress in front of her and twirling this way and that. "Am I too old for this?" she'd asked him, and he'd replied that she'd never be too old. Oh, how those casual words had come back to haunt him over the months and years that followed, as treatment after treatment failed to curb the cancer spreading through her. After she'd died, that bloody dress had been first in the bag for the charity shop.

Now he was beginning to accept that he had been granted a privilege she'd been denied: the chance to grow older and to grasp that life with both hands. Perhaps he wasn't quite ready to grasp it, but he felt capable of putting a tentative finger on its pulse. So yes, he was looking forward to Ana's parents' Victory Day party, and yes, he was going to wear the shirt. He'd even send a selfie to Ruth once he'd put it on.

Of course, that didn't mean his problems – no, *their* problems – had magically disappeared, but last night on the journey from Korčula they'd decided to make a big effort to put them to one side this evening. On Monday, Ivana would be back at her desk, and when Ana sent her weekly report tomorrow, he'd ask her to suggest that they found a replacement librarian for the last few Fridays on Korčula. Although it felt like admitting to something he hadn't done, this was no time for pride. It was the only practical solution. Figures were on the up for every other island so he just had to trust that Ivana wouldn't throw her toys out of the cot and sack him.

He couldn't allow himself to hope that Krasna believing his story would in any way persuade Mirjana. She'd always known her own mind – to the point of obstinacy at times. It was an essential part of who she was. As a young man he'd accepted it, perhaps glossed over it, and he certainly hadn't felt the full force of it until now. But he also recognised that given Krasna's remark about growing up with the story, she'd believed him to be a thief of the worst order for more than thirty years; the idea would be pretty much ingrained by now. But what had really happened to the jewellery? It was pointless trying to speculate, but it gave him a small degree of comfort that Mirjana hadn't made the story up out of vindictiveness.

Around him, *Dida Krila* was quiet. Meri had arrived an hour or so before, and he'd left her and Ana talking on deck, while Natali walked Obi into town for supplies. Tomorrow she was taking the bus to Dubrovnik to visit Baka in hospital, and Lloyd was nervous about what she might find. But that was another worry to set aside. He looked at his watch. Time to shower, shave, then put on that shirt and send Ruth that selfie before they set off for the party.

Somewhere between attacking the enormous buffet, toasting the Croatian Defenders with local wine from the barrel, and the music starting, the party had moved from the Meštrović's garden to the quayside in front of the house. The food had proved irresistible: long boards of cured meat, cheeses, olives, gherkins, almonds and grapes, served with the freshest of bread, and, of course, there'd been huge bowls of steaming *musule na buzaru*, mussels fresh from the bay, cooked simply in white wine, olive oil and garlic.

Now Lloyd was feeling the effects of his overindulgence and needed a walk. The sun had not long dropped behind the Pelješac's spine of hills, and the red, blue and white lamps strung around the terrace glowed in the warm, still air. Moths flitted between them, and a particularly confident chicken strutted beneath the table, looking for scraps.

After glancing around to check that Natali was still happily chatting about recipes with Ana's mum, Tereza, Lloyd made his way down the side of the house. Someone had set up an impromptu bar on the waterside, and surprisingly loud music pumped from a smart speaker balanced at one end of it. Ana and Meri were dancing with a group of other young women, while the men stood around clutching their drinks. Lloyd smiled wryly; some things didn't change, no matter where you were in the world.

Soon after they'd arrived, Ana's father Antun had taken him down to the quay to point out the oyster beds in Malostonski Bay, promising that one weekend he'd take him out in the boat to witness some of the process. Lloyd had been surprised at the size of this long, narrow sea enclosed in the arms of mountains on either side, its conditions perfect for the shellfish that gave the area its wealth.

He strolled to the end of the extended breakwater, smart wooden trip boats creaking quietly as they jostled with their more workaday fibreglass counterparts in the tiniest of swells. Further along the bay, a cluster of lights glowed as the muted pearls and greys of dusk deepened into silky blue. Above the Croatian mainland proper, as he thought of it, the moon rose in an enormous silver-white ball. Even with the music thudding behind him it was all so perfect.

He and Mirjana had walked home from the old olive press on many a night, the moon in all its phases glittering above those self-same hills – hills with a war bubbling and brewing beyond them, a war he'd ignored despite all Kesten's warnings, until it was almost too late.

The end had come quicker than he and Mirjana had ever imagined. They should have taken more notice when Kesten told them he was joining the army, but just a few days later they heard on the radio that the Croatian military had taken a number of Yugoslav barracks, including the one at Ploče, just the other side of the Pelješac peninsula on the mainland. Suddenly there had been no doubt in anyone's mind that this was more than skirmishing over borders; it was the prelude to war.

That night there were no tourists in the restaurant, only locals anxiously discussing what might happen next. Already the shop shelves in town were emptying of essentials – tinned food, candles, paraffin, medication. Who knew what would happen and what would be needed? Young men far less gung ho than Kesten were pledging to defend their homes and their country.

It wasn't even eight o'clock when Mirjana's father, Zoran, abruptly announced they would be closing early, and without even properly tidying up, bustled Mirjana and Lloyd upstairs to the apartment, where Kosana had prepared a supper of *burek* with sliced tomatoes and olives, and hard-boiled eggs. As they sat at the table, Zoran opened a bottle of Pošip wine, the good stuff, and poured them each a glass.

"Because it is the last time we will eat together," he explained. Lloyd went cold at his words. "*Moj sin*, it is no longer right for you to remain here. Tonight you must pack up your belongings and tomorrow you must leave."

Lloyd was almost too choked to speak. Zoran had called him his son. He gripped Mirjana's hand tightly.

"So soon?" His voice felt scratchy.

"Yes." Zoran sounded firm. "Already life is turning on its head. Who knows what will happen to ferries and flights. At least if you go now you can get to Dubrovnik, and even if there are no planes to England you can take a boat to Bari where you will be safe."

Mirjana pushed her plate away. "I'm sorry, Mama, I just can't..."

"Me neither," Lloyd added. Everything seemed to be in

freefall. How could they eat and drink as though nothing was wrong?

"But you must," Zoran urged. "If only so we break bread together one last time, and raise a toast to meeting again."

Lloyd picked up his wine and Mirjana followed suit. As four glasses clinked in the centre of the table, Lloyd cleared his throat. "Thank you. Thank you for being a family to me. I will come back – as soon as I can. I promise."

They stayed a little longer, then Zoran shooed the two of them outside, claiming fresh air would do them good. But the reality was that he understood they would need to say their private goodbyes.

In silence, they passed the fishing boats, then headed along the rock path towards Bilin Žal beach. The night had an otherworldly quality to it – the moon streaking the water as the tiniest of waves lapped the shore. It was a shred of continuity to cling to, when everything else was so out of kilter. Tomorrow they would be saying goodbye, and the war made it uncertain for how long.

"Now it's come to it, I wish … I wish I'd tried harder to find a way for you to come with me. I can't bear the thought of you staying, especially if there's going to be a war."

Mirjana clamped her arms around him, burying her face in his chest. "But it cannot be, we know that. You saw how pale Mama was tonight. Even if it was practical for me to go with you…"

Now, having refused to see it all summer, Lloyd had no doubt they were sleepwalking into agony. There was only one way to get through this, one way to make the pain even remotely bearable. They had to believe in their future.

He lifted her face, and together they looked back across the bay. "The mountains, the sea ... they will not change. And it will be the same moon we see. And *I* will not change, Mirjana. I will come back. And all the time I'm away, I'll love you."

"And I you," she whispered.

In the gallery above the old olive press they lay in each other's arms, but did not make love. They just held on in the velvet darkness until the church clock chimed midnight, when they walked silently home.

Lloyd sighed. The same moon was above him now, shimmering in the water in time with the pump of music. But everything else... Still, it was too late to dwell on it. It was what it was, and he should get back to the party, if for no other reason than he needed a glass of water. He was scanning the bar when someone grabbed him from behind, pulling him into the mass of dancers. Ana. It had to be. Her face was glowing with happiness and exertion. Then he noticed Meri pushing through the crowd, dragging Natali behind her.

"Got them both!" she said, laughing breathlessly. "You have to dance to this one – it's Ana's favourite." Lloyd knew the song too; it took him back to happier times before Jenny fell ill, and an outdoor George Ezra concert they'd been to with Ruth. The rain may have poured down, but they'd had the most amazing evening. Memories were everywhere today, and he was learning to keep the good ones and shake off the bad. By the time the chorus came around he was yelling "shotgun" with the best of them.

Ana wrapped the four of them together into a tight group, arms around each other's shoulders. Even Natali looked less self-conscious now, and Lloyd felt friendship and love course through their embrace. These young women were nothing short of amazing, each in their own way, and he was the luckiest man on earth to have met them.

They danced together for two or three songs until the music slowed, then Lloyd and Natali stepped away, heading for the bar to renew his quest for a drink. Looking behind him he could see that amongst the couples wrapped up in each other, Ana and Meri were holding each other's hands while they swayed drunkenly to the music.

"Now d'you see why I had to dump her?" He recognised that voice and turned to see Pajo a few feet ahead of him in the middle of a knot of men, his words slurred and more than loud enough to cut through the music. "Just look at Ana with that woman. *Odvratno ponašanje!* Did I ever tell you I saw them together in a gay bar? I should have known then, shouldn't I?"

Lloyd stopped in shock at what he had heard, and Natali barrelled into his back. He wasn't going to let that homophobic little shit get away with this. But he wasn't as quick as Ana's father, who pushed his way into the heart of the group.

"Got a problem with my daughter, Glavas? Doesn't look as though you have a problem with my hospitality." He eyed the brimming wine glass in Pajo's hand.

"I didn't—" Pajo started, but Antun held up his hand.

"Oh yes you did. You shot your mouth off, as per usual, but now you'll listen to me. It was a very good day my daughter left you. Just look at what she's achieved since: her own boat, her own flourishing business, an independent way of life that makes her happier than you ever would have done. She's her own woman now. A pioneer. An example for others to follow where she leads and I, for one, am extremely proud of her."

Beside him, Natali began to clap and Lloyd joined in. Antun turned to them. "Knowing Ana as you do, naturally you agree."

"Best boss I've ever had," Lloyd said.

"And me," Natali added.

"Long may it remain so. I don't want anyone tying my Ana down. Certainly not anyone so"—he stared at Pajo with a look of disdain on his face—"mediocre. I want her to continue to fly."

Pajo was studying his shoes as though they were the most interesting things in the world, and a few of the men around him nodded, while others looked away. Ana's father clapped his hand on the shoulder of the nearest one.

"Enjoy the rest of the party, lads, but maybe one of you ought to take Pajo home before he gets into any more trouble."

Ston

SUNDAY 6TH AUGUST

Ana held her mug in both hands, then sipped her coffee, bitter and strong. Oh, this was bliss, absolute bliss. Obi was curled up on the banquette next to her, having settled quite readily once she understood Natali was leaving without her. A cooling breeze drifted across the deck. Best of all, Meri was sitting at the end of the table, tearing at her breakfast croissant with her long fingers.

"So what's with you and Pajo?" her friend asked. "He turned up to the party late, then didn't come near you."

Ana shrugged. "Probably my fault. I cancelled dinner with him last weekend. He didn't even reply to my message."

"What a child!" Meri rolled her eyes.

"Well, there was a little bit more to it than that, but I haven't wanted to bother you with it, what with everything going on with Zac."

"Stupid girl," Meri said, but softly. "I've always got bandwidth for you, whatever else is happening in my life."

"Yes, but it didn't seem fair to burden you."

"Ana, cut that out. How can I burden you, as you put it, if you won't bend my ear when you need to? We're better than that."

"I know we are. But I could see you were struggling, so…"

"You decided to struggle as well, all the while propping me up with your messages and calls. For which I am mightily grateful, by the way. I don't think I'd have got through these last few weeks without you, and I'm still completely exhausted by it all. But now Tomi's parents have offered to pay for rehab I'm hoping he can turn a corner, and I'm very proud of Zac for standing by him."

Ana found it hard to envisage what could ever make Meri not proud of her son, but all the same she murmured, "And so you should be."

"That's as maybe, Ana Meštrović, but actually we were talking about you. And Pajo. What's the deal? Even since you split you've always been such good mates."

"The split is the problem. Or rather, what we promised each other at the time. Except I seem to have made that problem go away. Which is a good thing." She frowned. "I just don't like the bad feeling."

"You never do, that's your problem. But go on, spit it out."

"OK, in a nutshell. When we broke up, we agreed that if we were both single in five years we'd get back together and start a family."

"A family? You've never even mentioned wanting kids in all the years I've known you."

"Haven't I?" Ana tried to sound vague, even though she was pretty sure it was true. "Well, anyway, that time is up. At first I couldn't even be certain Pajo remembered, but then he kept messaging me that he'd bought an apartment in

Dubrovnik and he wanted me to see it. And the hints got bigger and bigger, and I kept making excuses, although I knew I couldn't put it off indefinitely... Anyway, I agreed to go last weekend, but then Lloyd needed my support so I bailed."

"So, Pajo behaving like a sulky toddler notwithstanding, do I sense there's more than you just wanting to play nice behind this?" Meri's lips were set in a firm line.

"I didn't want him to call me out on our promise."

"You could have just said no."

"Except ... I wasn't entirely sure I wanted to."

"You still love him?" Meri's eyebrows shot into her purple-streaked fringe.

"No, of course not."

"Then I don't understand. Well, to an extent I do. I know you, Ana, and I know you bend over backwards to make other people happy, but to marry someone you don't love? Are you out of your mind?"

In one furious sentence, Meri had distilled all Ana's rambling thoughts over half the summer into one crystal-clear point. But there was still something she needed to know in order to understand.

"It seemed to me that Pajo was my best chance of having children."

Meri's hand covered hers. "And you want them?"

"That was the problem. I didn't know. I think I was more scared of closing the option down than anything, but the more I thought about it, the more doubts I had. I looked at Natali's miserable childhood as an unwanted kid, and then I talked to Lloyd, and he said every child has the right to be properly welcomed into the world and loved..."

"Did I hear my name?" Lloyd appeared in the galley

behind Meri, who swivelled to glare at him. He stepped back. "Oh, bad timing. OK. If I can just make a cuppa, I'll leave you to it."

"No, you don't have to go."

"Ana, are you just saying that?" asked Meri sharply. "Are you people-pleasing again?"

Ouch. That hurt. Meri had never used those awful words before. "I don't people-please," she retorted. "I'm my own woman."

"That's as may be," said Meri, "but you're a double-sided coin, if ever I've known one. Lloyd?"

"I think everyone is multi-faceted."

Meri tossed her head. "Very diplomatic. But what I mean is this: Ana is certainly an independent woman who values her freedom, and I love her for it. She's never happier than when she's on this bloody boat. However, I also have a hunch that what was behind this ridiculous notion of settling down with Pajo was other people's expectations. Your parents in particular." She fixed Ana with a hard stare. "Am I right?"

Ana could do nothing but nod. She'd wanted this conversation with Meri, but never in a million years had she expected her friend's reaction to be so harsh. The trouble was, she was undoubtedly speaking the truth and although Ana knew it, it made her squirm like a two-year-old inside.

"I suppose it was a car crash waiting to happen," Meri continued. "Your parents instilling that sense of duty and loyalty into you on the one hand, and your *dida* showing you freedom with the other. Then giving you the means to achieve it. I think he was the one who knew you better, my love."

Lloyd joined them at the table. "Ana's parents know her too. And they're proud of her and what she's doing."

The last thing Ana needed right now was a platitude, and she expected better from Lloyd, so she told him so.

He held up his hands in surrender. "It isn't. It really isn't. Last night Pajo was bad-mouthing you to his mates and your father waded in all guns blazing. He was magnificent." Lloyd smiled. "Now let me see if I can remember some of the things he said ... that you're a pioneer, a role model, an independent woman who achieves so much... And of course he said he's very proud of you. And that you're happier now than you ever were with Pajo."

Ana folded her arms. "It's one thing defending me in front of—"

"Ana. No." Meri's voice was sharp. "Listen to what the man's telling you. *Believe* what Antun said. And believe me when I say that, as parents, all your folks will ever want is for you to be happy."

A pioneer. Independent. Ana closed her eyes. If only, if only, Lloyd was right and her father really meant those words. But something didn't ring true.

"Then what about their massive hints about me going into the family business?" she asked.

"Well I don't know about that," said Meri. "You'll have to talk to them. And I suggest you do it soon. Today, even."

Lloyd sounded thoughtful. "Maybe they just want you to know that if you need it, the option's there. A sort of safety net now you've given up chartering, so your financial future isn't so uncertain."

"No. It isn't like that. When Dida was ill I needed to come home, so I started to work for them, said I'd give it a go, and they were so happy. But as his health deteriorated I spent more time with him and less in the office, and then of course he left me the money and I bailed completely. Without so much as a thank you or a second thought. Except during Covid when they propped me up again. I really do owe them."

"From what Antun was saying last night, I don't think they see it like that at all," said Lloyd. "Are you sure you're not tying yourself in knots trying to meet an expectation that isn't really there?"

"Exactly." Meri thumped the table, sending croissant crumbs jumping. "Anyway, Ana needs to do what's best for herself, not anyone else. Now get in that jeep of yours and head over there."

Slowly Ana shook her head. "Which would just be pleasing you. I need time to process this, then time to have that important conversation with Mama and Tata when we won't be rushed. Today we need to be away by noon so we're on Koločep by the time Natali's ferry gets in."

Meri took her hand. "But you'll do it next weekend? Promise me, Ana. I reckon once you've really found out where they stand, a few more things will fall into place."

Ana wound her fingers through Meri's. "There's one thing I will be telling them, one thing I have decided: motherhood isn't for me." She shrugged. "It must be right, because I made up my mind almost two weeks ago, and don't feel remotely frightened or sad saying it out loud, just relieved."

"Well done you." Meri leant across and kissed Ana on the cheek. "That's a massive step."

"Probably the biggest decision," said Lloyd. "Start as you mean to go on, Ana." He stood and stretched. "Right. I need a proper breakfast so I'm going to cook some eggs. Anyone else hungry?"

As Lloyd disappeared into the galley, it would have been

the perfect moment to mention Raš, but somehow Ana wanted to hug the secret of him to herself a little longer. She wanted that dinner date, but beyond that, it was hard to see... If he just wanted friendship, well, that wasn't enough for her, despite what she'd told him. Being tied into a traditional relationship wasn't for her either. Nor for Raš. So there was, at least, common ground. She just had to find a middle way that would work for them both, because with every message they exchanged, that 'both' became increasingly real.

Dubrovnik

SUNDAY 6TH AUGUST

Natali shuffled uncomfortably on the plastic hospital chair and set her book on her lap. It was a great story about a young girl set at some time in the future who had to decide whether to risk death or take a drug that would ruin her life, but right at this moment she wasn't doing it justice. She glanced at Baka, who was still asleep – had been asleep since Natali arrived. She looked so peaceful that Natali didn't want to wake her, even though the nurse had said it was OK.

Now it was August, the problem of what would happen in September was looming large in Natali's mind. She and Obi had had a brief stay of execution, because in the fortnight after the library project finished Ana had taken on a private charter for two Danish couples who were relatives of a local olive grower, and she'd asked if Natali would stay on to crew for her. But after that? Natali just had to hope that another charter would come up. But it would only be for a few more weeks at best, because Ana had told her she liked to get *Dida Krila* tucked safely into her permanent berth in Ston by mid-October, before the weather became unreliable.

She had wondered about asking Ana if she could live on the catamaran in return for doing the winter maintenance, but it didn't feel right. She knew how much Ana valued the freedom the boat gave her, so what if there were some bright, calm days when she wanted to take her out? If Natali and Obi were actually living on *Dida Krila*, they'd be bound to compromise that, and she'd hate anything to sour their friendship.

One thing was certain: Natali needed some sort of plan. It wasn't fair on Obi to spend her life hoping and praying that suitable work might just turn up. Actually, it wasn't fair on her either. She was beginning to understand that she might be worth better. That she had skills. Skills that were transferable into year-round work, like Krasna. But no actual qualifications. Was she clever enough to at least try the adult education programme Lloyd had told her about? There was bound to be reading and writing involved, which kind of scared her, but the way she was devouring whole books... And Lloyd had told her in no uncertain terms that reading would improve her writing too.

"Natali ... should have ... woken me." Baka's voice sounded stronger than it had on Wednesday, and Natali smiled.

"You need to rest. And I have all afternoon."

"Not working?"

"It's Sunday. I'll get the six-fifteen ferry to meet the others."

"You'll look for Valentin?" The long fingers of Baka's good hand smoothed the sheet under them.

"Of course I will. If I see him at Gruž before we board I'll send him straight here." Oh, it felt terrible lying like this, but if it saved Baka the grief of knowing…

"You should marry him, you know."

"Marry who?"

"Valentin, of course. Good man … will make you laugh … always laughing…"

"But he doesn't know me, Baka. He might not like me."

"He does. Always did. He told me."

Who on earth did Baka think she was? And yet only minutes ago Baka had known her name. This felt like a whole new level of confusion, sending Natali's brain into free fall. She needed to pull herself together. Fast.

"But does he like dogs, Baka?"

"Dear little Obi."

So that was all right. Baka did know who she was, and she felt weak with relief. Not for herself so much, but for Baka's state of mind. Maybe it was just an extension of what had apparently been happening for years, this fantasy world where Valentin was still alive.

"When he comes … someone must cook for him." Baka murmured.

"Only until you're better, Baka. No one cooks like you."

"I do?"

Oh god. Had Mateo been right after all and his mother's mind was badly affected by the stroke? And if she couldn't cook, which was so deeply ingrained into her very being, what else had she forgotten how to do? How on earth would she be able to look after herself? Please, please, let it be because Baka was still a little sleepy, she thought.

Before she told anyone about this development, Natali decided to see if she could tease any kitchen memories from her. She had to be certain of what she was saying, because it could affect both Baka's rehab and her future.

"We went to a party last night," she said slowly.

Baka nodded eagerly. "Tell me."

"It was for Victory Day. There was dancing and everything, and Obi ate far too many scraps, but Lloyd promised to take her for a long walk this morning. The food was wonderful though. The *sir i vrnhje* dip especially, so I asked the hostess for her recipe, and she said she put a little tarragon into it. From her garden. Do you grow tarragon, Baka?"

Baka frowned. "Aubergines ... tomatoes..." She gripped Natali's hand. "Natali, they need water. Will you do it?"

Relief surged through Natali. At least Baka remembered her garden. "Of course, but I expect your neighbours are looking after things." She paused. "What do you put in your *sir i vrnhje*?"

Baka shook her head. "I ... I don't know." A deep sadness was etched into the old woman's face. Did she sense that something important was lost? Did she know there were things she couldn't remember?

Footsteps tapped across the linoleum floor, and the curtain rings rattled as a tall woman of about Ana's age wearing a white coat appeared.

"Ah, good," she said. "Are you family? We're moving Mrs Valentić to our rehab unit tomorrow, but there are things she needs. Clothes and the like."

"Natali ... my son's fiancée."

Natali wanted the chair to swallow her up. She had to put this right, but how could she in front of Baka? She looked pleadingly at the medic.

"Fiancée? But your daughter-in-law came on Thursday."

"My other son. Valentin."

"Oh, I see." She raised her eyebrows in Natali's direction, who gave the tiniest of shrugs in return. Thank goodness the woman knew enough about Baka to understand. Mateo must have told her.

"I am going to the h-house," Natali said, "to water the plants. Perhaps I could…?"

"Perfect. Come with me to the desk and I'll give you a list."

Natali touched Baka's hand. "I won't be long."

She followed the woman to the nurses' station in the corridor outside. "So who exactly are you?" she asked.

"Just a f-friend. But I'm fond of her and I want to help, although I'm sure her neighbours have everything in hand. It's a wonderful c-community."

The woman smiled. "I'm sure it is."

"She'll miss it if Mateo makes her move to Split. Will the rehab help her to remember how to do things?"

"That I can't tell you, because we don't really know how bad her memory was before the stroke."

"It was fine," said Natali firmly. "Apart from Valentin, that is. Only a couple of weeks ago she was teaching me how to cook…" Tears flooded her eyes and she rubbed at them furiously with the back of her hand.

"Now come on, none of that," said the medic kindly. "You're here to cheer Mrs Valentić up. Now go through this list with her and see if she can tell you where to find everything in her house. It will be a good test."

∽

When Baka fell asleep for the third time, Natali crept from the hospital ward. It was a shame there wasn't an earlier ferry; if she could get to Koločep sooner she could pack Baka's bag this evening, rather than take too long out of the working day tomorrow. She already felt guilty about needing more time off, in part because she knew Ana wouldn't say no and it felt like taking advantage, which was the very last thing she wanted to do.

To Natali's relief, Baka had done quite well with the list, remembering where most things were. She'd also told her that the woman next door had a key to the house, so perhaps she would help her to find everything else. There were so many things Baka still remembered perfectly. Was that cause for hope she might be able to go home after all?

Natali walked slowly down the hill through Lapad, past houses which were almost all holiday lets or small hotels. In the gaps between the buildings, she could see the silvery expanse of Gruž harbour ahead, the small boats owned by locals crammed into its blunt end, bordering the narrow park that edged the promenade. She could grab a bottle of cola and some chocolate then sit there with her book, or she could really spoil herself and splash out on coffee and cake at Rhea Silvia. It would be cool and shaded under its awning and she was sure she could make it last the hour or so she'd have to wait. Plus it was quite a smart place so she was unlikely to bump into anyone she knew – anyone who might tell her mother she'd come to Dubrovnik without visiting her.

She felt guilty about that, but it couldn't be helped. Her mother might even be working, because Auntie Stela had taken her to the hairdresser to cheer her up, then practically dragged her back to the restaurant to restart her shifts. Natali could never have done that, because her *mama* simply wouldn't have gone. It was better for both of them that Natali had stayed out of the way.

Good old Auntie Stela and her mantra of positivity. It had helped make the toughest times of her life bearable, but now there was the smallest of voices inside her questioning whether positivity alone was enough. When Lloyd had told her about the adult education course, he'd said it was a great way to start taking her future into her own hands, which was exciting. But also properly scary, given how rubbish she'd been at school.

She knew from the books she was reading that change only came in the characters' lives when they made it happen themselves. Could she do the same? A steady, year-round job would make all the difference, but it kept coming back to the same thing: better qualifications. Even if she was capable of studying, she'd need money to pay for the course and somewhere to live so she could do it. But in that case, she'd be working all hours to pay the rent, so how would she find the time? However much the idea appealed, the practicalities were stacked against her.

Sod it. She'd treat herself to an iced coffee and a slice of Rhea Silvia's delicious chocolate cake. At this hour on a Sunday afternoon, most of the tables stood empty under the café's generous awning. It was a peaceful time between lunch and the cocktails the place was famous for. Natali sank into a low, cushioned chair next to a potted palm and studied the menu. It wasn't cheap, but she was here now. Her stomach had been telling her for some time that it needed sustenance, but first she'd better let Ana know what she'd committed to with Baka.

When Natali pulled out her phone she found a message

from Krasna. A strange one. Could she ask Lloyd which ferry he'd taken when he'd left Korčula? Ferry? Then Natali realised. She meant all those years ago, before the war. How on earth was he going to remember that? And why was it important? But from what she'd seen of Krasna so far, it would be. She typed a quick reply, saying she was in Dubrovnik and would ask him later, then realised a waitress was hovering over her. Order first, text Ana next, then try to chill for an hour with her book until the ferry came in.

Mljet

THURSDAY 10TH AUGUST

Ana typed a few words into her laptop then stopped. The noise from the quayside was a distraction, but right at this moment anything would be. She didn't know which was worse: the clatter and clang of the small ship unloading next to them or the thud of music from the nearby bar, which was the only building on this part of the waterfront that didn't look as though it was falling apart.

She swung the seat in front of the chart table around, then stood and stretched. The small port of Sobra had better views, that was for sure. The deep, sheltered bay was surrounded by wooded slopes, but at this end of the harbour a road had been gouged out of the hillside, leaving a scar of yellow rock amongst the green. Beneath it was a rag-tag collection of buildings, some in pristine condition and others with crumbling walls and gaping windows. It was a far cry from the wild beauty of the nature reserve at the other end of the island where they had been mooring, that was for sure.

But this rather ordinary village was definitely the right

place to be. Local people lived and worked here. It was the island's only all-year-round ferry port, so they passed through it and came here to shop. More to the point, these people had children who were using the library. They would have been all summer if the county education department had bothered to get the location right, which was something she'd be stressing in her report to sodding Ivana. As long as she could think of a way to do it tactfully.

The wretched woman had pounced almost as soon as she'd come back from her holiday. Ana had reluctantly gone with Lloyd's suggestion that he would effectively resign from Korčula and Ivana's response had been predictable, heavily implying that it was an admission of guilt. Ana had been caught off-guard while she was loading updates to her navigation software, but curbing her instinct to bite back sharply, she'd managed to tell Ivana quite calmly that she believed Lloyd had the library's best interests at heart.

Now she had to make sure that was evident in her report, and she certainly had plenty to say. For a start, Lloyd had added another hour to his working day on Lopud, this time before the library opened, for a coffee and English conversation session with not only the older teenagers but a smattering of adults too. And today, the head of the elementary school on Mljet had asked if he could run some sessions for his pupils once term started – more than a few if he could find the budget. Of course, Lloyd would be back in England by then, but it didn't hurt for Ivana to know how impressed the headteacher was with him.

If nothing else, the boost to Lloyd's confidence had been timely. Tomorrow could well turn out to be the most important day in the library's summer. He was going to need every last iota of everything he could muster. So would she. She was nervous as hell – mainly for Lloyd, but also for how the day would affect the library's viability beyond this year, which in turn would affect the conversation she needed to have with her parents on Saturday.

Stretching again, Ana went outside and climbed the steps to the fly deck, where Natali was mending a tear in the mainsail.

"What do you make of Mirjana asking to see Lloyd?"

She looked up from the fiddly task of smoothing flat the patch of adhesive-backed sailcloth.

"I'm more hopeful since Kristina offered to run the library."

"You think they're connected? I kind of assumed Ivana had twisted her arm."

"It's possible, but the timing made me wonder. Krasna messaged me first thing yesterday, didn't she? Then within a couple of hours Kristina called you. If Ivana had put pressure on her, I reckon it would have been sooner."

Ana lowered herself onto the edge of the banquette. "It's a nice theory and I so want to believe it. This morning Lloyd looked as though he hadn't slept at all."

With a final press on the fabric, Natali stepped away and sat down. "So would it help if I told him I think it's a good thing, or would that just build up his hopes? I mean, what I'm thinking is that something he said to Krasna last week has thrown up doubts in Mirjana's mind."

"Why would Mirjana suddenly decide to believe even just one thing Lloyd said when she's spent all summer calling him a thief and a liar?"

"Krasna believed Lloyd. Maybe Mirjana listened to her

because she's her daughter. I mean, at least she wants to talk to him."

"I hope you're right, but I just think we need to be ready to pick up even more pieces. I offered to go with him, but he refused. And it feels like … oh, I don't know … that you and I have our own problems to deal with right now too. I just hope we can support him enough." God, she sounded so negative. She patted Natali's hand. "Sorry. Look, I'll leave you to it. I need to do as much as I can of my report before tomorrow. Just in case."

"We're stronger together, Ana." Natali's voice drifted after her down the steps. Maybe she was right… No, she should be right, but Ana wasn't feeling it at the moment.

Back at the chart table, she tried to apply herself to her report once more, but every single word needed dragging from the deepest recesses of her brain. It wasn't even the noise from the quay, it was the clatter and clang inside her head as well. How could she write something positive, when it was the last thing she felt? The library's future was on a knife edge. Tomorrow was everything.

But no, no. It wasn't. Really it wasn't. Apart from Korčula, every island was doing well. She needed to buck up her ideas. She needed to channel some of that bliss from Sunday morning and the joy of dancing together from Saturday night; Natali's positivity from just a few minutes ago. Were they stronger together? They damn well were. Furiously deleting most of what she'd written so far, she started again. This time, she recorded all the good stuff, telling it how it was. Within fifteen minutes, the only blank paragraph was Korčula.

With the report out of the way, it felt as though a weight had been lifted from Ana's shoulders, but now she was on a roll it was exactly the right time to gather her thoughts to talk to her parents on Saturday. She just had to work out what she was going to say – what was important, and what was not. There'd be no backing out, because provided Zac and Tomi were all right, Meri had invited herself to join them again on the sail to Koločep on Sunday. Obviously she'd expect a blow by blow account of what had happened.

Ana winced. It wouldn't come to blows, she knew that, but how on earth was she going to refuse her parents everything that had ever been important to them? It felt almost as though it was a rejection of them as people, but that was as far as it possibly could be from the truth. She loved them so much, and they loved her. How could she even be thinking of disappointing them like this?

Yet how could she not? It was her life, and she only had one shot at it. She couldn't live for them, however much she loved them. Maybe that was what she'd say. But even so, to tell them she would not be running the oyster business that had been in the family for so many generations felt too big, too final. If only she could trust herself to get the decision right.

Dida Krila. That's what it came down to. Both now and, she realised as she looked around the galley, after Dida had died. Something that had felt so right at the time, could still end up going disastrously wrong.

With the clarity of hindsight, she could see that she'd decided to buy the boat on a whim, in the throes of her grief for her grandfather. Oh, she'd tried to be sensible as well; her father had helped her with the financial forecasts, she'd done her research, signed up to a charter business that, Covid notwithstanding, had delivered on its promises of income. But what she'd never even considered was the work itself – dealing with the public, being nice to them all the time, putting up with their unreasonable demands. And her inability to do so had driven a coach and horses through her business plan, putting everything at risk.

Her inability. Nobody else's. But on the upside, chartering had been making her unhappy so she'd stopped it. The idea of being with Pajo had been the same, so she'd put an end to that too. Clumsily, unfortunately, but she had done it. Maybe she hadn't done either particularly well, but she had made decisions that were right for her, and now she realised that was something she should be proud of.

All the same, there was still a significant chance the library pilot project would be judged unsuccessful, then where would she be next year? Could she still lose her boat? Not as long as she had the safety net of putting *Dida Krila* into her parents' business, but she couldn't keep relying on them for handouts. Maybe the time had come to properly embrace the freedom she talked so much about needing, to forge a career from it, a life. She needed to regard the last few years as a massive learning curve. And if she was that strong, independent woman her father was apparently so proud of, perhaps she could even do it. Without a safety net.

She ran her hand along the smooth edge of the table in front of her. Inhaled the faint smell of diesel and coffee, mixed with the warm salt breeze; felt the gentle rock of the swell below her. Looking out of the window, the view, however humble, was new today and would change tomorrow. As would the colours of the sea, the winds and tides, the shapes of the clouds in the sky.

These, and more, were Dida's gifts and she could never be without them. It sounded nebulous, even a little crazy – exactly what Raš had said about his land and his vines. But the sea was in her blood, like it had been in Dida's, and there was nothing she could do about it, even if she wanted to. She needed, yes needed, to come and go, if not exactly as she pleased, but to be free to sail her own ship through life's choppy waters.

Raš. That was another matter she could take into her own hands. Even though when she'd popped in to buy some wine yesterday, he'd told her his daughter was staying for an extra week, she wanted this sorted too. Everything was lining up so she could make a fresh, clean start.

She'd been confused by how short he'd been with her at the winery, almost as though he couldn't wait to get her off the premises, but as soon as Manda had gone to bed, he'd messaged to apologise, opening up about how tough he was finding it to mix fatherhood with his personal life at the moment.

When you say personal life, you mean me, she'd replied.

A pause. *Guilty as charged. Don't know why. It's doing my head in a bit.*

Do you want to step back a little?

I'd miss our chats if I did. I'm probably overthinking it.

Probably. How are those grapes ripening?

His answer had been another thing that had made her determined to get a date in the diary, because the harvest was likely to start before the end of the month. Defying their recent convention of evening messaging she typed:

How about dinner the Tuesday after Manda goes back? To work out whether or not it's a date.

Not expecting a reply any time soon, she put her mobile down on the table next to her. Taking a knife from the drawer, she set about peeling and chopping potatoes for the *gregada* she was cooking for tonight. She'd bought some red bream from one of the fishing boats this morning, but the stew would need hours on the hob for the flavours to mingle.

Her phone buzzed and she turned it over, reading the notification on the screen.

"You've got yourself a d..." A *d*? What sort of *d*? She opened the app to read the last word.

You've got yourself a deal ;-)

Shaking her head, Ana started to laugh.

Korčula

FRIDAY 11TH AUGUST

The water was like glass as *Dida Krila*'s tender slipped over it, the putter of its motor breaking the silence of the morning. Around Lloyd, the tiny islands were somnolent behind closed shutters and all was still, except for a mother and child on the shaded beach on Vrnik who were no doubt making the most of the cool of the day. As he followed the curve of the shore, ahead of him lay Lumbarda, red roofs peeping from the tree-lined headland and the sun glinting from the narrow steeple that topped the church tower.

Slowing the engine, he nudged the tender between the fishing boats on the old village harbour before slinging the rope over a metal stanchion and mooring along the bay from Konoba Pecaros. This was it. No turning back. But there never had been, not from the moment Natali had told him about Krasna's message. Pretending the energy of a much younger man, he jumped up onto the quayside then walked briskly towards his fate.

Pecaros was quiet at such an early hour, and Mirjana must

have heard him climb the concrete steps because the kitchen door opened the moment he stepped into the restaurant.

Her smile was fleeting. "Good morning, Lloyd. Thank you for coming. It will be easier to talk in the apartment, I think."

His brief glimpse of the *konoba*'s kitchen as they walked through revealed that a great deal of updating had been done, although the basic layout was much the same. Stainless steel had replaced old wood, and the pizza ovens were twice the size, but none of this should surprise him. It had been so many years.

He followed Mirjana up the stairs and into the apartment, where she waved him through to the lounge.

"Take a seat," she told him, "and I will bring coffee."

Despite the instruction, he couldn't settle. Instead, he prowled between the orange-brown sofa and matching chairs. Under an ornate mirror was a small table covered with framed photographs, and he stopped to look at them. There was one of Krasna and a handsome young man with curly hair, which he assumed to have been taken quite recently; one of Krasna as a child of about nine or ten, standing between Mirjana and a portly man with laugh lines and little in the way of hair. Her husband? Yes. Tucked at the back was a wedding photograph, which included Mirjana's father but not her mother.

Hearing the clatter of cups from the kitchen, he made a dive for the sofa. In front of him the coffee table boasted a small peace lily in a terracotta pot. He hoped it was a sign. On the floor nearby stood a cardboard box, and his breath caught in his throat when he saw the photo on top: Mirjana, Kesten and himself in their *konoba* uniforms of white shirts and black trousers, arms linked in front of the bar. He'd never seen it, but he recalled it being taken. It showed Mirjana as he remembered her: round face, big smile, dancing eyes. Not the same woman at all as the one in the pictures under the mirror.

She came in carrying a tray full of what was surely her best crockery, capped with a blue and white china coffee pot and a plate brimming with homemade spiced *paprenjaci* biscuits.

"I hope you still like them," she said. "I used my father's recipe."

"Thank you. Thank you for remembering."

"It is by way of an apology. I have caused you so much trouble by telling Kristina you were a thief, but I honestly believed it."

"Believed?" He leaned forwards.

"Yes. Now I have discovered the truth." She picked up the photograph from the top of the box. "It was Kesten, *u klinac* Kesten. I know one shouldn't speak ill of the dead, but—"

"He's dead?"

"Years ago. In the war. But that comes later. It's part of the story. But god, I'm so angry, Lloyd. Even more angry than I ever was at you, and I didn't think that was possible."

Lloyd could barely grasp what this grim-faced Mirjana was saying. That Kesten would steal from his own family, and that he was dead. "But why would he do that?"

"For the same reason he lied to me about you the morning you left. He told me you'd taken an earlier ferry. I never sent him with a message, Lloyd, and I can only imagine what he told you I said." Lloyd rocked back in his seat. Kesten had lied to Mirjana. Lied to them both. Set them against each other. He passed his hand over his face.

"I have the strangest feeling ... like everything I thought I knew about that day is unravelling."

Mirjana rolled her eyes, and a glimpse of the girl she'd once been caught in the top of his chest. She laughed, but it sounded hollow. "Tell me about it. These last few days ... everything unravelled for me too. It is a very good word to use. That morning he ruined both our lives, Lloyd, and I'm so fucking angry. Thirty years later ... and still it makes me—" She took a deep breath. "But I need to explain. Coffee?" Suddenly she was back in polite hostess mode, but if that was her way of dealing with this, then fine. He didn't even know how to feel himself.

"It was Saturday, Victory Day, and I walked up to the church. Oh, you know I am not religious, but I do it every year, just to stand by the flag for a few moments and place a bunch of rosemary beneath it to remember Kesten. And I suppose, because Krasna had met you and had told me your story, I was thinking most especially of that last morning as I walked back home. But something didn't fit and it bugged me."

"Ah, the time of my ferry."

"Exactly. What you told Krasna sounded so precise and I began to wonder why you would bend the truth in that way. You know, to make it sound as though you'd waited for me. But then I realised that if you had left earlier, as Kesten told me, how would you have known that I hadn't been waiting for you on the steps as we'd agreed? And if I had, it would have exposed what you said as a lie, so why would you have mentioned it?

"You see, that day, Kesten came to the *konoba* quite early. I was devastated you'd gone, but Tata had promised to take me into town to say goodbye so we were hurrying through the prep. Not that we expected many customers, but still there were jobs to be done..." She paused, gazing at a spot on the wall above Lloyd's left shoulder. "Then Kesten arrived, and said that he'd seen you get on an earlier ferry with some other English people so I'd be wasting my time going into town."

"But why? Why would he say that?" Lloyd was aghast.

"Because he was in love with me. Only, that bit comes later."

Lloyd had worked with Kesten all summer, drank with him, joked with him. So how come he'd never guessed? Was it that self-absorption again? Had he and Mirjana been too wrapped up in each other to see what was under their noses?

"So he came into town instead of you to lie to me as well? To tell me you never wanted to see me again because I wouldn't take you to England with me? Oh god, Mirjana, why didn't I see through it? I should have known you'd never—"

She twisted her fingers together, white patches appearing where the tips dug into the backs of her hands. "It's the same for me. Exactly the same. My lack of faith… It's been eating away at me these last few days. I didn't even stand up for you when we discovered Mama's jewellery had gone."

"But why did he need to take that as well?"

"To make us believe how bad you were. To make sure I'd hate you. He confessed it all in a letter to me. If your Croatian's still up to it, you can read it for yourself."

"So if he put it in a letter, why accuse me now?" None of this was making sense. Was it the coffee zinging around his head? He reached for another biscuit to try to mop up some of the caffeine.

"Because I didn't read it. Not many weeks after you left, Kesten went away to the war. He wrote to me, telling me he loved me. Of course I didn't want to know. I'd never felt that way about him, not in all the years I'd known him, and besides, I was so hurt by you that there was no way I wanted another man in my life. So I replied, as a friend, asking him not to mention it again.

"But he persisted, and after two more letters I did not open any more. I had this grand idea, you see, this big dramatic gesture, that when the war was over I would hand them back to him still all sealed up and tell him to piss off in no uncertain terms. Except he was killed, and then I couldn't bring myself to throw them away so I hid them in a box." She smiled weakly. "You have no idea how long it took me to find them. All that crap I didn't throw out after Tata died, all stacked up in the old chicken shed."

"W-what happened to your mother?"

"She never got the surgery she needed, so she had a heart attack. She didn't even make it to Christmas. And I added that to the score against you, blaming it on the shock of what you'd done, and then I got angry, and love turned to hate." She handed him the letter and stood. "I need to talk to my chef. I'll do that while you read it."

The stillness settled around him, the bands of sunlight from the half-open shutters slanting across the room. The paper was cheap, and Kesten's writing cramped, but Lloyd recognised it from countless restaurant orders scribbled out that summer. Despite everything he'd learnt this morning, he still felt sad for the life so brutally snuffed out.

It was all there. Not that Lloyd could understand every word, but he knew enough to get the gist. to understand that it was a confession because Mirjana's mother was dead and Kesten wanted to return her jewellery.

It had always been Kesten's plan to drive a wedge between them when Lloyd went home, but when he visited the next day he'd realised Mirjana was grieving, not angry, and he knew he hadn't done enough. So he'd sneaked upstairs and emptied Kosana's jewellery box, leaving a single earring in Lloyd's old room for the family to find.

Lloyd knew he probably should feel angrier, but instead a strange emptiness filled him as he contemplated a spinning vision of his life unfolding quite differently from a certain point. What was that film he'd taken Jenny to see when she was on maternity leave? *Sliding Doors*? But he'd had a good life. It had taken him a hell of a long time to get over Mirjana and the guilt he'd felt about leaving her behind, but eventually he'd been able to move on. As long as Jenny had been by his side. As long as the past had stayed in its place.

But it hadn't. And now that past had become his present too. As Mirjana came back into the room he was reading the last paragraphs of the letter, including Kesten's description of where he'd hidden the jewellery in the drains at the barracks near Lumbarda where he'd initially been stationed.

"You understood?" Mirjana asked and Lloyd nodded. She sat down heavily opposite. "Those wasted years, all those wasted years." As she shook her head, a tear splashed onto her blouse, and instinctively he reached across and took both her hands.

"No, not wasted. We had different lives. Not the life we planned together, and, of course, I regret that, but we found our way to happiness all the same."

"You were happy with your wife? Krasna said she died ... like my Milo. He was older than me, but still I did not expect him to leave me so soon. He was a good man, a good father."

And a good husband? But Lloyd did not ask. "Yes, I was very happy with Jenny," he said, "and we have a daughter too. Ruth. She's twenty-five."

Mirjana looked at her hands in his. "I think ... I think you have been changed by this less than me, and I cannot decide if that makes me angry or glad."

"Why would it make you angry?"

"Because I have become a hard and bitter woman, Lloyd. I see the worst in people and not the best. And now, to top it all off, I mistrust my own judgement."

"You have no reason to do so. Kesten wove such a compelling web, and you'd known him all your life. He was family too, if I remember. Some sort of cousin?" She nodded. "Then why would you not believe him?"

"I just... Oh, what does it matter what I feel? I have caused you great harm, and no doubt worry, this summer, but I have already told Kristina I was wrong and that you are innocent. Now that you know the truth, she'll be able to tell your boss in Dubrovnik too. You should have been angry with me, Lloyd, but you have been kind. You always were kind, like my father. It was one of the things I most loved about you."

"Well I knew it couldn't have been my good looks," he joked.

She pulled her hands free and gave his a gentle tap with her index finger. "Oh you, fishing for compliments. You are still quite handsome, I suppose. For your age."

"And you..."

She wagged her finger. "Don't say it, Lloyd. You were meant to laugh."

"I know that. But I do want you to know that I can still see the girl I knew inside the woman."

"Then you must be looking too hard." She stood and brushed down her skirt. "Now, I have work to do. But will you perhaps come back tonight? With your colleagues from the library? Dinner will be on the house and the pizzas are better than ever. Milo was half-Italian and he made quite a few changes."

"Not tonight. We need to be back in Ston. But maybe next week? If you give me your number I'll call you." He typed it into his phone as she dictated it, leaning over his shoulder. As he closed the app she looked at his screensaver.

"Is that Ruth? With your wife?"

"Yes, a few years ago now. Before Jenny got ill."

"A happy memory, then."

"Yes. And more than anything, we must treasure those."

She nodded. "They are life's jewels, not necklaces and earrings. I think Mama was wrong about that, but some of the pieces she lost were her mother's too. When she died, I missed not having those because they were a link to her. We buried her with her wedding ring so all I have is that one earring Kesten left for us to find."

Lloyd felt the chain around his neck where Jenny's engagement ring hung, hidden and close to his heart. It was so much a part of him now that he usually forgot it was there, but he knew he'd be devastated if he lost it.

He followed Mirjana to the stairs, but halfway down he stopped. "What happened to the old barracks?"

She shrugged. "A few of the buildings have been repurposed but mainly it's derelict. The tunnels are a bit of an attraction for adventure seekers. They say the views are terrific from up there. Why?"

"It's a crazy thought, but could your mother's jewellery still be where Kesten hid it?"

"I doubt it. It's a long time ago, remember. And people exploring places like that tend to have a good poke around."

"But worth a look? I'd be glad to go with you. Next weekend maybe?"

"Let's see if I can get cover for the *konoba* before we start making plans. If nothing else, we could take a picnic."

Lloyd nodded. "I'd like that."

"Me too." And as the girl who'd been Mirjana all those years before smiled shyly, the tiniest of tremors ran through him. Relief? Or something altogether unexpected?

Ston

SATURDAY 12TH AUGUST

Ana crept along the passageway and peeped around Lloyd's cabin door. He was fast asleep and snoring gently, his long arm flung towards the photo of Jenny on his bedside shelf. It was no surprise that he was exhausted so, mug of tea still in hand, she returned the way she had come. Yesterday had been some roller coaster for him – for all of them really, given he'd more or less collapsed in the galley after telling them his name was clear.

Scared out of her wits, Ana had grabbed his arm and steered him onto a banquette, but it had turned out the stupid, sleep-deprived man hadn't eaten more than a biscuit or two, so Natali had rushed around making his favourite fried egg sandwich and a large mug of tea and slowly his colour had returned as he'd shared the extraordinary story.

"It's like in a book," Natali had whispered, her eyes like saucers. Very different to Ana's own reaction – an expletive-ridden barrel of vitriol for Kesten – but Lloyd had shaken his head.

"He must have gone through hell that summer, seeing Mirjana and me so much in love." So she'd told him he was a frigging saint and flounced off, but he'd laughed, and as soon as he'd finished his lunch, had gone to join Kristina in the library.

Having reassured herself that Lloyd was all right, Ana could put off her visit to her parents no longer. To stop herself backing out, she'd called her mother yesterday afternoon to ask if they could set aside time before lunch to talk about her future. There'd been a short silence before her *mama* had agreed, but what did that silence mean? Was she overthinking it?

The drive through the vineyards to the village had never felt so long, and it had little to do with the summer traffic, some of which was threading its way through the narrow streets to join her father's trip boats. The little harbour was packed with cars so she parked the jeep across the double doors of the workshop, then walked slowly up the shaded path towards the terrace. There was no turning back now. She just had to remember that whatever was said, nothing could break the bonds of love between her and her parents. This summer she'd come to realise that was a blessing rather than a god-given right. She knew how lucky she was.

Her mother and father were sitting at the table under the vine, which was lush with leaves and hung with dusky dessert grapes, full and almost ripe. One of her father's greatest pleasures was plucking one straight from the bunch and popping it into his mouth, and she felt more than a little tug at her heartstrings as she recalled him lifting her up when she was tiny so she could do the same.

She kissed her parents then sat at the end of the table as her mother poured from the jug of iced lemonade between them, asking how her week had gone.

"Very good. Very good indeed. Lloyd's name has been cleared," she said, and told them the outline of what had happened the day before. "I only hope we can make up sufficient ground to persuade the powers that be that the pilot's a success. But if how busy the library was yesterday is anything to go by, that shouldn't be a problem."

"So you'd do it again?" her father asked.

"Yes. Without a doubt. My share of the government grant covers my repayments on *Dida Krila* for the year, and more, so it rather underpins my future."

"The future you want to talk about?" asked Mama. It wasn't any of the openings that Ana had rehearsed, but it was as good a start as any, and it had happened all by itself. So much for her constant fretting about the right way to begin the conversation.

"I wanted to spend time this summer making some decisions, but as it happens I've barely had a moment to think. But nevertheless ... Tata, Mama, I'm so grateful for everything you've done for me these last few years, and the fact that you've always wanted to welcome me into the business, but ... it isn't for me."

"So what will you do?" her mother asked, but Tata hushed her.

"Ana, please understand. We never intended to put pressure on you to join us and I really hope you didn't see it that way. We just wanted to make it clear that it was an option, something you could come back to at any time if things didn't work out elsewhere." He shrugged. "A safety net, I suppose."

Could that be right? He'd used exactly the same words as

Lloyd. Lloyd who was a father himself. She fingered the glass in her hand. She'd need to think this one through properly later, but for now the most important thing was to keep the conversation moving forwards. "You really don't mind?"

"In practical terms, I'm hoping you won't drop off the radar completely. It's good to have you around to help catch up with the paperwork over the winter – you know what a mess I make of it. But again, if you decide you want a clean break then I could always employ someone. It wouldn't be the end of the world."

"Of course I'll help out when you need me, it's just … I don't think I'll ever want the responsibility of running things. I know it sounds pathetic, and perhaps I should have grown out of it by now, but I don't want to be tied down."

"I understand," said her mother. "Probably more than you realise. You want to be on the water, and in that way you are so like my father. How he ever stayed around long enough to have two children I'll never know." She laughed. "We barely saw him, but you … you were his little soulmate, so I suppose, in my heart of hearts, I always knew…"

"You're not disappointed?"

Mama looked a little unsure, but her father burst out, "Of course not! We're so damned proud of you, Ana, of everything you've achieved, of how independent you are. You've always worried that you can't make decisions, but as a matter of fact you've made some really tough ones, because you've never taken the easy way out of anything. Most of the village girls would have married Pajo, had a brood of children, and done bits and bobs for the business. But no, you're different, you've followed your own dreams, and that's really rather wonderful."

Instead of looking regretful, Tata's eyes were shining with pride. She glanced across at her mother, who nodded.

"All we want is for you to be happy."

"I want to make you happy too," Ana replied, "and it was hard to come to terms with the fact that my choices probably weren't the ones you'd have made for me…"

"No!" Her father slapped his palm on the table. "It's *your* life, Ana. *Your* happiness. We make our own." He reached for his wife's hand.

Ana closed her eyes. "Even without grandchildren?"

"Even that. The family name might continue with the business after my days or it might not. Legacy is not so important. In fact, it's not important at all. It's how you live your life while you're on this earth that matters. That's how you should be remembered."

Oh my god, they were so bloody wonderful, making it this easy for her. Parenting was such a tough job – too tough for her – and they were absolutely ace at it. "Thank you. I mean, that sounds inadequate but I'm just so damned grateful to have the best parents in the world."

Her father winked. "I don't know about that, but perhaps now you know you can stop pleasing us, you'll stop trying to please other people too."

"I'm trying. Really I am."

"So tell us," asked Mama, "what are your plans?"

"In truth, they're a little up in the air. I suppose I'm still searching, in a way. But if the library runs for the next few years, and if I can continue to charter for people I actually like … and there are other opportunities I'm learning about. There's a very swanky holiday let on Lopud whose guests sometimes want a day trip on a boat and they've asked if I'm interested. They can't be the only place, either. There's that boutique hotel on Šipan, for a start."

"So not one, but a number of different income streams? I think that will suit you down to the ground, Ana. And if money's tight, well—"

"No, Tata. I appreciate the offer, but I'll live off what I earn. Anyway, it's not as though you charge me rent for my room here."

"You make enough money and I might!"

"Our own daughter? Over my dead body!"

Laughter filled the terrace, bathing Ana in its warmth. Everything had been so easy that now she was wondering why she'd been worrying about it for so long. But in so many ways she was a different person to the one who'd helped Lloyd to load the books onto the boat back in Dubrovnik those few short weeks ago. A more confident one, despite the cock-ups along the way.

Boy, it had been some learning curve. A learning curve that was just the beginning.

And that made her fizz with excitement.

Sailing from Ston to Koločep

SUNDAY 13TH AUGUST

Dida Krila's motor puttered gently beneath them as they passed smoothly down the long channel that led from Ston to the sea, the gentlest of breezes finding its way through the galley windows, which Lloyd had opened wide. In a drunken moment last Saturday, he'd rashly promised Meri an English Sunday roast, but it was far too hot for that. She'd have to make do with chicken salad instead.

Already the delicious aroma of herbs, lemon and roasting chicken was seeping through the oven door. He'd stopped counting the number of times he'd had to send Obi back to her basket, and not because she was looking for Natali, who had gone to visit Baka. She seemed to be under his feet wherever he turned, her big brown eyes peeping out from under her floppy canine fringe, the epitome of cupboard-loving cuteness. He'd never owned a dog in his life, but perhaps when he went home he might get one.

When he went home, or ... *if* he went home. Well, of course he'd go back to London to see Ruth, and he absolutely could not wait. But after that? Possibilities were opening up for him, which was something he couldn't have imagined would happen a little over forty-eight hours ago. Mirjana discovering the truth had changed, well, everything.

He pulled a plump, sweet onion from the vegetable basket and, having sloughed off its skin, began to slice it for the salad. Even the smallest thing seemed so much easier now, but it did feel a little strange not having the dead weight of Mirjana's accusations on his shoulders. It was as though his world had spun through a hundred and eighty degrees and left him feeling rather disorientated.

On Friday afternoon he'd been on such a high, and while he'd been chatting to Kristina in the scant gaps between library visitors, had told her about the part-time language teaching post the headmaster on Mljet had talked about. To his surprise, she'd asked if he was going to take it, but he'd told her it was only half a job, if that. And if she could find him the other half? She'd gone on to explain that there were plenty of opportunities on Korčula, not least because Dubrovnik University was moving some of its courses to the island.

It was certainly food for thought, but he needed to get his head around it first, then talk to Ruth. Being based partly on Korčula would probably bring him into Mirjana's orbit, and whether that was a good thing he had no idea. Even if he hadn't imagined the tiniest of sparks was still there, it was highly unlikely she'd feel the same. But this wasn't about her. It was about him and what he wanted. And more than anything, that was to get back into a classroom and teach – something that was being offered to him here in Croatia, and would at the very least prove difficult, if not impossible, back at home.

With the salad complete, the potatoes on the hob, and the chicken cooling, he clicked his fingers to Obi, then pulled some beers from the fridge before making his way up to the fly deck.

"Lunch won't be long," he told the girls, "but there's time for a drink first." He turned to Meri. "Not a traditional British roast, I'm afraid – it's far too hot."

She pursed her lips. "You disappoint me. But men normally do."

"Then I apologise, on behalf of us all." He swept a low bow, almost overbalancing.

"Don't spill those beers," said Ana.

"No chance of that." He handed them around. "Cheers."

They chinked bottles together, and Lloyd sank down next to Meri.

"We were just talking about Ana's future," she said. "What do you reckon the library's chances are now that your little local difficulty on Korčula has been sorted?"

"Better. We were run off our feet on Friday afternoon." He swigged his beer. "I think the local organiser felt a bit guilty about the whole thing, although she has no reason to, so she pulled out all the stops to get the kids there. And once people have books, they'll need to bring them back. And hopefully they'll borrow more. Then, if we can persuade Ivana that the whole summer on Korčula would have been like that, we're laughing."

"And if she doesn't throw me off the contract…" said Ana glumly.

"Whyever would she? As far as she's concerned, I was the problem, not you."

"Yes, but I haven't handled it very well with her at times and I really don't think she likes me."

"Pah!" said Meri. "She doesn't like anyone. She's known for it. But she does like to be associated with something really successful."

They'd come to the end of the channel, and Ana turned her face into the breeze, assessing it. "We could sail," she said. "Lloyd? Up for it?"

"After lunch maybe? The potatoes will only be another few minutes and then we can eat."

They took in the vista that was opening out in front of them, the only sounds the low murmur of the engine and the wind dancing through the wires. Here the sea was almost a circular lake, enclosed on one side by the parched hills of the mainland, and on the other by fingers and dots of islands, some so tiny they were little more than rocks. A couple of yachts scudded across the blue, and ahead of them Lloyd could see a small cruise ship pass the northwestern tip of Šipan and turn into Slano Bay. All was peaceful, all was calm. What a place this would be to live.

"So what happens to you, come September?" Meri asked, almost as though she could read his mind.

"First thing will be to go home and see my daughter. After that, I don't know. I had thought of maybe trying to see if I could get work as a supply teacher, you know, filling in when people are sick, but there are so many hoops I'd have to jump through." He stared into the distance. "But I'm also beginning to wonder if it might be possible to come back to Croatia."

"Lloyd! That would be incredible," said Ana. "What would you do? Take that job on Mljet?"

"Yes. I mentioned it to Kristina yesterday and she thinks there might be opportunities on Korčula too. Language teaching, conversation classes, maybe even some private tutoring. But I need to find out what Ruth thinks about the idea first. Plus, there's the question of how workable it would be in practical terms as there's no direct ferry between Mljet and Korčula in the winter."

"That's easy. Keep a car at Prapatno. The ferry from there to Sobra runs all year, as does the Orebić to Korčula one." Ana grinned. "You could even live in Ston, nice and close to me. There are plenty of empty holiday apartments out of season."

Lloyd looked thoughtful. "In which case, I might be able to provide a base for Natali if she needs one. I really hope she decides to study to improve her qualifications, and that way I'd be around to help."

"She is a worry."

"How come?" Meri asked, so Ana explained that it was hard for Natali to find accommodation and anything other than the lowest paid work with Obi in tow.

"Does she have to keep the dog?"

"*Sranje*, yes. That dog's her family. Her mother sounds like a manipulative bitch, and her father disappeared years ago. I'm keeping her on for a while once the library finishes, but it's only for a matter of weeks. I've got a charter she can help with, then she can stay aboard and do some maintenance." Ana sighed. "After that, I don't know. I just don't know."

"You're trying to make plans for her," Meri said, "but maybe she has plans for herself. That's typical of you, Ana. Just when you're free of one set of ties you find another."

Ana glowered at Meri, but Lloyd stepped in. "Meri's right. The best we can do is to keep talking to Natali about this, let her know we're here for her, and that she doesn't have to leave everything to her Auntie Stela's karma." He stood and stretched. "Right. I need to rescue those potatoes before they boil dry. Meri, if you don't mind, I'll need a hand to bring everything up."

She followed him down the steps, stopping at the bottom. "Lloyd?"

"Yes?"

"I'm glad you're thinking about staying. Ana will miss you if you go."

"And I'll miss her. And Natali. I've only known them a couple of months and yet…"

"You know what they say about friendships forged in fire?" Lloyd shook his head. "That they're as strong as the ones that have weathered the test of time."

Lloyd felt his eyes mist up. "I hope so, Meri, I really do."

Dubrovnik

WEDNESDAY 16TH AUGUST

Mateo Valentić's wife was waiting for Natali on the shaded terrace of Rhea Silvia, just as they'd arranged. It was all very odd. Not only had she taken Natali's number from her husband's phone without him knowing, she'd then sworn Natali to secrecy. What on earth could she want? Chances were it wouldn't be good news, and although Natali wasn't one to lose sleep over anything, it was making her uneasy.

If she had caught the earliest ferry from Šipan, goodness knows what time Dina Valentić had set out from Split. No wonder she already had an empty espresso cup next to her, and the remains of a croissant. If those crumbs were to find their way under the table, no doubt they'd make Obi a very happy dog. Perhaps Natali would even treat herself to one, but with only a few weeks of the season left, and no real plan for what would happen after September, she was becoming increasingly conscious of money.

After gathering her breath under the trees outside the restaurant, Natali stepped towards the table.

"Mrs Valentić?" She recognised her from the pale green linen dress topped with a set of chunky wooden beads she had said she would be wearing. But looking beyond the elegant outfit, Natali could see how nervous she was from the way she repeatedly wiped her palms on the paper serviette.

She held out her hand, and Natali took it. "Dina, please. Thank you so much for coming." The words rushed out. "I'd rather not only Mateo, but Baka too, know nothing about this."

"If that is important to you, then of c-course."

"It is, it is. I don't like going behind anyone's back, but until I know if you can help I'd rather keep this between us." Dina sat down, as did Natali.

"You know I'll do anything I can to help Baka."

"Including making sure she gets the future she wants, and not the one Mateo's currently insisting she has?" Ah, so that was what this was about. Natali fervently hoped she didn't expect her to try to persuade Mateo what was best for his mother, because she was sure she couldn't do it.

A waitress was already hovering. "Coffee?" asked Dina. "Something to eat? This is my treat."

"Thank you. A *bijela kava* for me please, and a croissant." As the woman had so far ignored Obi, at least Natali would have her own crumbs to give her.

"So you don't want Baka to come and live with you?" she asked.

Dina looked down at her plate, then back at Natali. "Please don't misunderstand me. I know my duty. If Baka wanted to come then I would not be saying this, but as it stands, her being in Split would only make everyone miserable. Even Mateo. He's just too blind to see it."

"So what do you want me to do?"

"I did wonder … you know … if there was any chance at all that you might want to be Baka's live-in carer? We'd pay you, of course."

This was so, so not what Natali had expected and it sent her mind into a whirl. She reached down and fondled Obi's ears. "You know that's n-not what I do? I crew yachts. I'm a mechanic."

Dina's face fell. "Oh, so there's no chance at all? Baka talks about you a lot. She's obviously fond of you."

Natali was fond of Baka too, and if this might be a way of her returning to the home she loved, then perhaps she shouldn't dismiss it out of hand. She should at least think about it. She kept telling Ana and Lloyd how much she wanted Baka to be happy, so she wouldn't be much of a friend if she didn't.

"I didn't say I wouldn't consider it … for the winter at least. My work is seasonal, after all."

"I wouldn't ask for myself, or if I didn't think it was the right thing for my mother-in-law, but if she comes to Split it's going to affect my daughters so badly, especially the younger one. You see, they're going to have to share a room, and my eldest is seventeen, and, well, quite noisy – always playing music, on video calls with her friends. But the little one, she's dyslexic so she has to work really hard for school and needs quiet to do that. It's her future… She's set the bar high for herself. She wants to be a pharmacist. There will be such terrible arguments."

"That does sound tough," said Natali. She surreptitiously dropped a piece of pastry on the floor for Obi, and tousled her soft ears. Yes, she got what Dina was saying about her daughter, but this was her future too, and it dawned on her that she might need peace and quiet to study as well.

"So it isn't a definite no?" Dina persisted.

Two images clashed in Natali's mind so violently it was all she could do not to put her hands to her ears: one of sitting in Baka's garden in the sunshine, eating homemade cake while Obi ran free; the other of days spent cooking for Valentin, waiting for Valentin, freezing herself into Baka's past for years and years and years, while her own life passed her by.

Dina was looking at her. She had to say something.

"The trouble is," she replied slowly, "that the commitment is open-ended. Because I'm so fond of Baka I would find it hard to let her down if it didn't work out. Or simply if the time came for me to go back to my normal job. I mean, if, by the end of her rehab, we know she'll only need help for a few months and then she'll be fine on her own, I'll do it gladly."

"Or perhaps if it was only for a few months because she will not be fine," said Dina with a sigh.

"What do you mean?" It didn't sound like a casual comment. Natali could feel her heart beating faster.

"Mateo will be even more angry with me if I tell you because he doesn't want it spread all around the island, but it isn't fair to ask you to make this decision without knowing."

Yet Natali was pretty sure Dina wouldn't have said anything unless she thought she had to. This was a mother protecting her cubs and Natali felt an unwelcome stab of jealousy. But it was a fleeting thought. She was better than that.

"So?" she asked.

"When they did the brain scan to assess the stroke damage, they found a number of smallish tumours. Too many to operate on, unfortunately."

Natali's hand went to her mouth. This was awful, awful. Poor Baka. This on top of everything.

"How did she take the news?" she whispered.

"She's forgotten about it. Or chosen to forget. Mateo was with her when they told her and she definitely understood, but later when they tried to introduce her to someone from the palliative care team she told them they'd got the wrong person because she'd had a stroke and would soon be going home."

"Perhaps it's like with Valentin and it's good she's forgotten, because what she doesn't know can't hurt her."

"You understand her so well," said Dina. "That's what makes you the perfect person to look after her."

And if Natali did agree, and if Mateo could be persuaded, it got Dina very neatly off the hook. But all the same, if it was best for Baka, how could Natali not even consider making her last weeks and months happy?

"Do they know how long?"

"It's a guess, but they told Mateo six months to a year."

Natali reached for Obi's comforting warmth beneath the table. Everything Dina had said was tumbling and turning around her brain. She needed time to absorb it all. Time to get a handle on her emotions. She didn't want to be bursting into tears the moment she saw Baka.

"I'll consider it. That's all I can say."

"Thank you." Dina stood, fishing in her handbag for her purse and car keys. "I'll settle the bill then we'd better go and see her, hadn't we?"

"Yes, but I'll walk. That way we'll spread out our visits, and she might think it strange if we arrived together."

"Very well. I can only stay for half an hour anyway. It's a long drive back."

Natali nodded and watched Dina retreat inside the café to pay. "Come on, Obi," she said. "I can think of a route through at least two parks and you're going to love that." Not as much as she loved the citrus grove around Baka's house. She had no doubt Obi would adore living on Koločep, with the unimagined freedoms it would bring her, and that was a pretty significant factor in Natali's decision.

But could she even be a carer? To someone she was fond of, yet someone she knew was dying. It was all very well to want to make Baka's last few months the happiest possible time, but how sad would it be to go through that? She'd need to dig pretty deep to do it, but she had a feeling she could. Thank goodness it wasn't a decision she needed to make alone. She had Ana and Lloyd to help her. And she knew for certain that they had her best interests at heart.

The stroke rehab unit looked for all the world like a small hotel built into the edge of the hospital grounds, with views over Velika i Mala Petka Park. The wide path running up to its smoked glass doors was bordered with neat rose bushes and on most of the windows floral curtains peeped from matching loops. It was certainly a lovely environment for Baka to regain her strength, and Natali clung to the thought. She couldn't allow herself to think about those tumours. Like Baka herself, for the next couple of hours she had to pretend they didn't exist.

Taking a deep breath, she went into the comfortably furnished reception area. The only thing which gave it away as a medical establishment was the woman behind the desk wearing a white uniform.

She jumped up to greet Natali. "Oh, are you the new animal therapist? What a sweet little dog. Our residents will love him."

"Her. She's called Obi. But I'm not the therapist. In fact, I didn't even know that was a thing. I'm here to visit Mrs Valentić."

"And you are?"

"Natali. Natali Putica."

"Ah, the one she says is going to marry her late son."

Oh. That was not so good. "She d-did mention it one time when I saw her in the hospital."

"I think you might find the idea's rather taken hold. Do you mind?"

Did she? It was nothing to her really, and if it made Baka happy…

"I can easily go along with it. Everyone on the island pretends he's alive so she doesn't grieve for him all over again. It's not a problem."

The woman nodded. "It is very kind of you to collude with such a fantasy when you become an important part of it. You don't have a jealous boyfriend?"

"No, it's just me and Obi, so really it makes no difference."

The receptionist led Natali outside and pointed out where Baka was sitting next to an umbrellaed table at the far end of the terrace which ran along the front of the day room. Was it

Natali's imagination, or did her face look more normal? Certainly one eye was still rather slanted, but her mouth...

On spotting Baka, Obi let out a sharp bark and scrabbled towards her, almost choking on her lead. Baka, who'd been gazing out over the trees, turned and smiled. No, her mouth wasn't quite right yet, but Natali was sure it was improved.

"Obi! Natali!" she called. Her voice was certainly stronger too. "How wonderful to have visitors at last." Oh. This was not so good. Dina must have only just left.

Natali gave up the battle to hold Obi's lead, and she raced to jump onto Baka's lap, trailing it behind her. "She's so pleased to see you," Natali said, bending to kiss the old lady's cheek.

"And I'm pleased to see you both." She ruffled Obi's ears. "So how are you, little family? Have you been a good dog for your *mama*?"

Natali laughed. "In the main. But on Lopud yesterday she tried to chase one of the *konoba* cats. There was a lot of hissing and spitting, so I don't think she'll do it again. The cat was almost as big as she is."

Baka looked down fondly. "Plucky little soul." Some of her words were still indistinct, but that was no big deal. Not in the grand scheme of things.

"I watered your vegetables on Monday and everything in the house seems fine."

"Ready for Valentin then. You will bring him as soon as he comes, won't you?" Baka frowned. "Why hasn't he come? Mateo has."

Natali thought for a moment, uncertain what to say. "Well, I suppose America is much further away than Split."

"You are right, of course. You're a patient girl, Natali, to wait for him. All these years…"

What could she say? The receptionist was right; it was one thing to go along with it, but it felt like another to … what was the word she'd used? Collude? Perhaps it was a little weird, but even so it was flattering that Baka's delusions included her as part of her family. Flattering and heart-wrenching at the same time. No one had actually wanted her in their family before. Oh god, she had to change the subject before she dissolved into tears.

"How is your arm?"

"Useless. I don't know why they're wasting my time with physio."

"Because it needs to be better for you to go home."

"But you and Valentin will look after me." She nodded, almost as if to herself. So had Dina got the idea of asking her to care for her from Baka? Did she want it too?

"But … but…" Natali searched for inspiration. "You will still need to cook. He loves your cooking best of all."

"I … I don't remember."

Natali squeezed Baka's hand. "You will." She almost added, *"and I'll help you"* but much as she wanted to, it sounded far too close to a commitment.

It would be madness, utter madness, to do that without a great deal of thought. And anyway, whatever Dina said, Mateo was against it, and for the first time she was grateful for his intransigence. It bought her time, if nothing else. She looked down at Baka's liver-spotted hand in hers. Although she hardly knew this woman, she'd shown her nothing but friendship and understanding. She knew how much Baka wanted to return home to Koločep, and Natali really wanted to help. To thank her, as much as anything. In the same sort of way she'd do anything for Ana and Lloyd. But surely, surely caring for Baka would take too big a slice out of her own life? Just at the time she needed to grasp her future by the scruff of the neck as well.

Korčula

SATURDAY 19TH AUGUST

Lloyd checked his rucksack for water and torches, then flipping his sunglasses firmly over his eyes pulled *Dida Krila* forwards on her mooring rope and stepped onto Lumbarda quay. Bloody *rakija*. He'd forgotten how potent it was, and how essential it was to the Croatian idea of hospitality. It had always flowed freely at Konoba Pecaros and last night had been no exception.

Only Natali was unscathed this morning, because she'd had the good sense to refuse a second glass, saying she didn't like the taste. Ana was yet to do more than crawl into the galley for a coffee, which she'd taken straight back to bed, and he was in no fit state for an adventure, despite the two large mugs of tea and fried egg sandwich he'd struggled to force down.

It had been a wonderful night though, full of laughter and fun. Krasna and her fiancé had joined them at their table, and it had been a joy seeing Natali and Krasna get on so well. Sadly,

Mirjana had only managed to sit with them between frantic bouts of activity behind the bar. It was August and the place had been heaving, so the reality was that they'd hardly seen her, but today he and Mirjana would be alone.

Memories of his twenty-one-year-old self fluttered close to the surface: the instant attraction he'd felt when he'd seen her emerge from the kitchen carrying his plate of fish and potatoes, the only meal on the menu he'd been able to afford; the slow realisation of what it might mean when her father offered him a job for the summer; the torture of not knowing if she felt the same. Was that why his palms were sweating now? Or was it down to this bloody hangover?

Mirjana was waiting for him in the alleyway next to the restaurant where she kept her car.

"How are you this morning?" she called. "The *rakija*, it was good?"

He laughed. "The *rakija* was bloody evil, as I suspect you well know."

A smile dimpled her cheeks. "Nobody forced you to drink it."

"True enough. But thank you again for a wonderful evening. We all had such a great time and the pizzas were the best I've had in Croatia."

"Of course. Milo's legacy. But come, we need to get going. It's already warm and I am not sure the tunnel entrances will be easy to find."

They headed out of the village, where Mirjana turned left towards the eastern end of the island. Their route took them through vineyards famous for the island's Grk and Pošip wines, which at this time of year were hanging with almost ripe grapes. Mirjana told him how most of the winemakers had become attractions in themselves, offering tastings and tours.

"I could never have dreamt we would have this scale of tourism on Korčula," she said. "We're an important destination now, but it's taken a while."

Despite the gentle thudding behind his eyes, Lloyd thought it was time to grasp the nettle. "The war must have made things hard," he said.

Mirjana nodded. "In so many ways. But now, all is good."

They fell silent as the road took a sharp bend away from the coast and climbed between overhanging trees. Through the trunks, Lloyd glimpsed olive groves on either side and wondered if Mirjana too was remembering their hideaway above the old olive press. He doubted it; she would see olives every day. They were only a novelty for him.

Their lives were not only different to their youthful dreams, but they were different to each other's. Yes, they both had grown-up daughters, had both lost their lifelong partners to cancer, but there the similarities ended. He'd gone back to London, followed his childhood ambition of teaching, lived in a nice terraced house with a bustling city around him. And he'd travelled – just on holidays, but at least he'd seen something of the world, while Mirjana had remained here, right where she'd always been, doing what had always been expected of her instead of spreading her wings as she'd wanted. No wonder she'd been angry when she'd first seen him on the island, then when she'd found out what Kesten had done.

Eventually they passed a squat, concrete building, ruined now, but which had clearly once been the barracks' guardhouse. Beyond it a rusted metal gate the width of the road hung open and Lloyd caught a glimpse of a no entry sign stuck to it. The wire fences in various stages of disrepair that threaded between the scrubby bushes and trunks of the Aleppo pines only reinforced his increasing doubts about whether they should be here at all.

The road forked in two, and shortly afterwards it became too narrow to continue. Mirjana reversed the car into a sandy layby near where the track split, and turned off the engine, the sound of cicadas immediately filling the air.

"Right," she said. "We need to figure out where we are. I asked around during the week, and my friend Ivica remembered delivering fish here with his father when the barracks were operational. He said we need to keep the main buildings behind us, then we'd be on the right path to the old gun battery on the headland. Typical of Kesten to assume I'd know how to find the entrance." She rolled her eyes.

"At least the info I picked up online suggested that once we reach the battery we'll be pretty close, and I tracked down a YouTube video from a couple of years ago that gives at least a bit of an idea of what it looks like. But the people who filmed it wandered around for ages before actually finding the tunnels."

"It's too hot for that," said Mirjana firmly, opening the car door. "Come on, let's get on with it."

Lloyd drained his first bottle of water and left it in the footwell, putting Mirjana's in its place in his rucksack. Thankfully the liquid was beginning to do its work and his headache was receding, but the day still had a slightly otherworldly quality to it. Whether it was the last of his hangover, the heat, or something entirely different, he couldn't work out.

Mirjana sprayed herself liberally with insect repellent then handed the cannister to him. "You're still a magnet for them, I suppose?"

"Not so much. I'm probably a bit more leathery and not as sweet these days. But nevertheless..." He sprayed himself too, then handed it back to her. "Better safe than sorry. Thank you."

They set off, keeping to the left of a low pile of rubble that had presumably once been a useful part of the barracks. A larger white building still stood, daubed with graffiti, its doors and windows agape like so many open mouths screaming, and it was all Lloyd could do not to shudder.

"Before he was posted to the mainland, Kesten asked me several times to come up here," Mirjana said, "but I never would. To be honest, I didn't go anywhere in those months after you left, just worked and slept. Or rather, I tried to."

"I'm sorry."

She rounded on him. "You can't be sorry, because it's not your fault. I thought at least we'd established that."

"Yes, but for the longest time I felt so guilty about leaving you here. I watched the war from a distance, especially those first few months when Dubrovnik was under siege. I should have taken you with me, Mirjana, however impractical it was. I should have taken you to safety, but I didn't."

"And I wouldn't have gone. I could never have left with my mother so ill, so you're off the hook for that one too."

Lloyd nodded. She'd exonerated him completely, but it would take more than her words to completely erase the guilt. Had guilt become a habit? Not during his life with Jenny, when he'd been happy and content; he'd had no need for it then. But when he'd attacked that lad... God yes, the guilt had come back, and since he'd been in Croatia, it had managed to entwine itself with the regrets from his past, not to mention his fears of not being able to grieve properly for Jenny while he was in its clutches.

How come it was so easy to see that now? Guilt was such a pointless, pointless emotion – as if you could change the past. Learn from it, sure, then look to the future. He stopped in the middle of the track. The future. Might it prove to be a different shape entirely?

"What is it?" Mirjana asked.

"Nothing, nothing. A twinge in my leg."

She rolled her eyes. "A young lad like you? But maybe your leg has a point. We're not the kids we used to be, and I'm wondering whether coming here at all was a crazy idea."

Lloyd resumed walking beside her. "Of course it's crazy, and quite frankly this place is creeping me out, but I think if we don't try to find your mother's jewellery we'll always wonder. And once we reach the right starting point, Kesten's instructions seem straight forward enough."

Mirjana nodded. The chirp of the cicadas surrounded them, accompanied by the distant wash of the sea against the rocks. From their position on the path, it sparkled below them on three sides, a pair of white-sailed yachts the only moving points in the expanse of shimmering silver-blue.

"I've been thinking about Kesten a great deal this week," said Mirjana, "despite not wanting to. I'm so angry with him. As angry as I was with you at the time, perhaps even more so, because he was family to Mama after all, and I hate him all the more because of that. I know what you said last Friday, but please tell me you've come around to feeling at least a little the same."

"I think ... hatred is too strong a word for me. I don't think I've ever actually hated anyone, although I hated

Jenny's cancer all right." He grimaced. "But I guess the best part of thirty years of teaching taught me nothing if not tolerance."

"So you did become a teacher?"

"Yes."

She turned her head to look up at him. "Then why are you working in a library?"

"I made a stupid mistake and I had to resign." He told her exactly what had happened, and why.

To his surprise, she laughed. "I must say, I am very relieved you are not perfect. That would make you extremely hard to like."

"Far, far from it. Although I do recall you used to think I was." He winked.

"Another imperfection. A middle-aged man who winks." But her eyes were sparkling in just the way he remembered.

"So for the record, is winking good or bad?"

"Work it out for yourself. You were always the clever one."

He snorted. "And what about you? Running a hugely successful business? Isn't that clever?"

"It was what I was brought up to do. Perhaps, whatever might have happened between us, it would always have been that way. I've thought about those might-have-beens so much this last week, but we can't possibly know. For a start, we wouldn't have seen each other for years because of the war. Even without Kesten's scheming, we can't be sure it would have worked out, can we?" An almost pleading tone belied her laughter, and Lloyd put his hand on her arm.

"No, we can't. We can't second guess anything because it didn't happen. All we have is where we are now." A moment of stillness surrounded them, and Lloyd's head began to thump again, in time with the blood pumping noisily through his heart. Mirjana blinked first.

"And where we are now is very close to the top of a cliff," she said, "so we'd better watch our step. Look, there's the old battery, so what's next?"

Lloyd pulled his phone from his pocket. "I put the co-ordinates into Google Maps, so let's see." He angled the screen towards her and away from the sun. "We need to keep the battery to our right, but it looks as though the path shelves very steeply, so be careful." He was about to offer her his hand, but she set off ahead of him, the gravel and grit beneath their feet soon giving way to lumps of slippery shale punctuated with rocks and small, scrubby bushes of pine and wild thyme, releasing their fragrance as they passed.

Mirjana came to an abrupt halt where the path petered out into a steeply slanted slab of rock with the sea hundreds of feet below.

"Over there to our right. There's some sort of structure. Or at least, what's left of one. I wonder if that's where the entrance is?"

They edged along the treeline until they were above a curved wall, built to surround an oval-shaped platform. A couple of metres below them, half-hidden by the cliff-face, was what looked like the entrance to a tunnel, but it would be quite an ask to clamber down over the mass of broken rocks and boulders to reach it.

"I'm sure it's the place in the video, but do you think you can make it?" Lloyd asked.

"We've come this far."

"We need to be sure we can get back up again. This might be the only viable entrance."

Twisting her head around, Mirjana looked him up and down. "You look pretty well muscled to me, and although I'm not exactly built for this, I've got strong arms from years of kneading pizza dough."

Lloyd nodded. Mirjana was certainly even more curvy than she'd been before, but given how she'd coped so far her fitness wasn't in doubt. Nor her courage, as she half climbed, half slid down the slope in front of them, gripping a trailing bush for support before jumping into the concrete-lined pit at the bottom.

Within minutes they were both in front of the entrance. Lloyd took off his rucksack then reached inside for the torches. Beneath an arched ceiling, man-made steps led down into the cliff, the walls on either side stained with rust almost as far as they could see. Mirjana pulled Kesten's letter from her pocket.

"And so, we begin," she said. "First fork, turn left."

At the bottom of the mortar-lined staircase the neat walls gave way to rough-hewn rock and the steps to a grit-covered floor. It was little more than a cave, Lloyd thought, a cave burrowed out for humans. Underground. Clandestine. A deep sorrow rolled through him. What had the men who'd lived and worked here seen when they'd gone to war? What had they had to do? No wonder the place was making him feel so uncomfortable.

The wash of the sea faded behind them, leaving only the steady scrunch of their feet. Lloyd followed the round beam of his torch, fixed firmly on the tunnel ahead, but behind him Mirjana was flicking hers from walls to ceiling and back. Not much further in were signs of former habitation and the walls became smooth again, and tinged with green. The air smelt heavy and stale, and Lloyd shivered, goosebumps appearing on his arms.

"There's a jumper in my rucksack," he said, then asked Mirjana if she wanted it.

"No. I think I can see the fork ahead. This shouldn't take much longer." She shuddered. "It's horrible down here, really horrible."

"You can go back, if you like."

"Not likely. We're in this together."

As they neared the fork, a breath of slightly fresher air teased them, and at the end of the path to their right Lloyd could just make out a small circle of light. "At least there's another way out," he said. "That makes me a bit happier."

"Unless it leads to a vertical cliff-face."

"I'm loving your optimism."

"Sarcasm. Another fault. Good." At least she was still joking. There was a rustle of paper as she read the next instruction. "Third door on the right is the shower room."

Lloyd moved forwards again, counting the blank holes in the walls. No doors remained and there was little inside the concrete-lined rooms either, only the remains of a broken metal bunk bed in one. The place had been stripped and he began to lose heart. The people who'd done this would surely have found the jewellery.

The third room was no different, except three round holes in the floor gaped at them, surrounded by a scatter of broken ceramic tiles. He stopped at the door, aware of Mirjana's warmth next to him.

"This is it. The moment of truth. Which one did he say?"

"The middle one."

Wishing he'd at least brought a glove of some sort, Lloyd

crouched on the floor while Mirjana held the torch over him. He knew that any last dregs of water would be long gone, but he didn't like to think what sort of wildlife might have taken up residence in the drainage system. At the very best a spider, at worst a rat or a snake. But hopefully his groping fingers would meet nothing that was actually capable of movement.

In fact, they met nothing except gritty dust as he reached downwards, so he knelt on the floor to lean closer to the hole. Still nothing, so he lay flat on his stomach. "Let's hope my arms are longer than Kesten's," he muttered.

"I'm sure they are." Mirjana's voice came from close beside him. "You were so much taller. Miserable little bastard that he was." She sounded so venomous she'd probably give any stray snake lurking in a corner a run for its money.

He braced himself and plunged his arm back down into the hole. At least now he'd reached the bottom and yes, he was sure there was something, some sort of plasticky fabric, tucked into a groove just behind where the vertical and horizontal pipes met.

"There's something here," he told Mirjana. It was stuck fast and he tugged it gently. What if it ripped? But even if it did, it wouldn't be impossible to pick up one by one the small pieces of jewellery he hoped were inside. Just painstaking and time consuming. And the chill of the concrete beneath him was already seeping into his bones.

He wriggled his fingers more firmly around the bag, grazing them in the process, but now he had just enough purchase to work it free. The fabric held, and he closed his fist around it, hauling himself to his knees as he pulled it up the drain.

Sitting back on his aching calves, he opened his hand.

Mirjana's torch like a spotlight illuminating a man's sponge bag with a drawstring top, grubby beyond belief, but which looked as though at one time it had been striped. As she took it from him, she brushed his arm.

"You're freezing!" she said. "Get up this minute. We'll look at this when we're back in the sun."

"What if it's the wrong one?"

"Oh very funny. You are such an idiot, Lloyd."

"There's no fool like an old fool. Isn't that what they say?"

Mirjana looked around. "I don't see anyone old."

"Two adventurers in the prime of life." Lloyd jumped to his feet, dusting off his trousers.

"Come on then, Indiana Jones, let's get out of here."

It was only when they reached their picnic spot at Raznjic Point that Mirjana asked Lloyd for the sponge bag. The almost circular outcrop formed the far eastern tip of Korčula, and with the hills on the mainland barely visible through the heat haze, it felt as though they were at the end of the world. From a little way off came the cries and screeches of tourists enjoying a cliff-jumping adventure, but otherwise they were completely alone.

Thankfully they were protected from the ferocity of the midday sun by a small copse, and Mirjana spread out the rug she had brought at the edge of the trees.

"I've made my own take on *pogača*," she told him. "Filled with tomatoes, olives and *panceta* instead of anchovies. Do you remember the *panceta*? Tata had to cook it for you because you wouldn't eat bacon raw."

"It's fair to say my tastes have changed, and now I know the difference. I've eaten more European food."

"So have you travelled much?"

"A little. When Ruth was small we mainly went camping in Cornwall or France, then later we'd have flotilla holidays sailing around the Med. We'd just started on city breaks when Jenny got ill."

"You say a little, but it is far more than me. We would sometimes visit Milo's relatives in Campania, and he took me to Venice for our honeymoon, but apart from that I have not left the country. Barely left the island, in fact."

"But you always wanted to travel."

"With the restaurant it was not possible."

"Surely in the winter…"

She shrugged. "All right. With Milo it was not possible. He was happier at home."

"I'm sorry."

"Again, Lloyd, it is not your fault." Her dark eyes flashed, then she looked away, taking plates and plastic boxes from the cool bag. "But if I am honest, it was one of the things that made me most angry when I saw you outside the *konoba* – the idea that you had stolen our dream of travelling the world, then come back to see if I was still here, waiting."

"It wasn't like that at all."

"I know that now, of course I do. But it was how it felt to me. I couldn't bear the thought of you on the island, lurking around any corner, so when I saw you talking to Kristina and she came straight into the *konoba* afterwards I asked if she knew you, and she told me you'd be coming to Korčula every week…"

They gazed in silence over the bright turquoise waters that

faded to the deepest of blues further away from the land. Lloyd so wanted to make it right for her. He wanted to show her London and all the other places she'd dreamt of more than thirty years before. Paris, the pyramids, New York... The strength of feeling rocked him to the core. Could he be falling for Mirjana all over again?

She handed him a slice of *pogača* and a bottle of beer, then opened one for herself, taking a deep draught.

"It's hardly enough Dutch courage," she told him, "but you'd better give me that bag."

He watched as she smoothed the centre of the rug flat, her hands liver-spotted, her finger puffed a little around her wedding ring. It had been barely more than a year for her; far too soon. Even for himself, he wasn't sure he was ready for a new relationship, but when he looked at Mirjana he wondered if he'd be willing to try. Not to take up where they'd left off, of course, but to forge something entirely new.

The idea fascinated him, but he pushed it to one side as she tipped the contents of the bag onto the fabric. Tarnished silver, dull gold, a chip of diamond glinting in the sun. She picked up an earring, a loop studded with the tiniest chips of the stone.

"Tata gave these to Mama the night before they were married. She grieved over them more than anything. They had so little, and he'd saved so hard." Her voice was breaking. "Sorry," she said harshly. "I'm being stupid."

"Far from it. They hold such memories. Such love."

"Shut up, Lloyd," she sniffed. "I'm trying not to cry as it is."

"Why?"

"Because..." She set the earring to one side, then found its partner, before sifting gently through the other pieces until she came across a string of pearls. "My grandmother's. Now I can give them to Krasna to wear on her wedding day. I never imagined…" Mirjana's shoulders began to shudder, and she put her face in her hands. Lloyd edged across the rug and wrapped his arm around her, his own eyes brimming with tears. For a moment he thought she might pull away, but instead she leant into him and sobbed.

She needed to cry. He needed to hold her. Nothing else mattered right now.

Lopud

TUESDAY 22ND AUGUST

Given it was August, Natali knew it was inevitable that Lopud would be heaving with tourists, both those spreading through the village from the hotel as well as the day-trippers who were now returning to their boats along the promenade. Rather than battle against a tide of people, she dived into a side street, and within moments the hustle and bustle was behind her, replaced by birdsong and instant calm.

This was the face of the islands she was coming to love. The peace and friendliness epitomised by an elderly gentleman who looked up from his gardening to call *"Dobar dan"*. The washing hanging out to dry next to a vegetable patch. A terrace overhung by vines. The patchwork of citrus and olive groves, the buildings hunkered down between them. It was hard to imagine the city was only an hour away by ferry.

She may be heading to the community centre to help Lloyd pack up the library, but Natali had left enough time for Obi to dawdle, and once they'd turned down the shaded track that wound between the trees, she slowed her pace even more.

It was just as well she wasn't in a hurry because Obi wanted to sniff every trunk and bush. But that was fine. It was what she did, and it seemed to Natali that it was a whole load better for her than gluing her nose to lamp-posts and bins.

Would she have to go back to Dubrovnik? She didn't want to, but it was where the jobs were. Much as it was lovely of Lloyd to offer her a place to live with him in Ston, where would she work? Ana had said there'd be work near the town during the olive harvest, but they would disappear well before Christmas, and then what? Only caring for Baka offered her any stability, but it was proving a tough decision to make and Dina seemed unwilling to speak to Mateo before she had Natali's answer. She supposed that was fair enough. Why make him angry if she didn't have to?

Part of the problem was that Baka kept talking about her and Valentin being there to look after her, and it built an uncomfortable expectation. When she'd visited Baka on Sunday, she had managed to speak to one of the senior nurses who had explained that the more the tumours multiplied and grew, the worse Baka's delusions would become. While it had made no difference to her as Baka's friend, living with it day after day would certainly present a challenge.

Easier for her, though, than for someone who didn't know Baka and didn't understand. Perhaps that was why Dina wasn't looking for anyone else, but it did put pressure on Natali. Ana had been emphatic that it was tantamount to emotional blackmail to make Natali responsible for Baka's happiness, and that had been an upsetting moment. Was she in danger of being duped? But no, the more she thought about it the more she knew that Dina had Baka's best interests at heart too.

If she did agree to do it, she'd be in the heart of an island community who supported each other, and who would support her. It was a perfectly wonderful thought, to be part of somewhere like that, a place where she was already accepted, just as she was. As Obi nosed around a thyme bush, Natali hugged her free arm to her chest. That was what it would feel like, she was sure. Living in a hug.

But it wouldn't be forever. Natali was used to the idea of Baka dying now. She'd let it seep into her a little at a time, thinking it would hurt less that way. Lloyd had said she should do whatever helped her to cope, but she had the feeling he wasn't sure that anything would in the end. So she'd found a positive thought instead. Maybe Baka would even be reunited with Valentin when she left this earth. Who knew? But believing that it was a possibility gave Natali a great deal of comfort.

At the community hall, Lloyd was waiting for her in the lobby, a slim youngish man with close-cropped curly hair by his side.

"Natali, this is Filip."

"Glad to meet you." She held out her free hand to shake his, while Obi tried to jump up Lloyd's legs.

"You too." The man was really smiley and scratched Obi between the ears, which made Natali grin back at him. "Once I've said hello to the children I'll come back and help you pack up."

Left alone, even by Obi, who had insisted on following Lloyd, Natali studied the library table. She'd read a fair few of the English books now – mainly fantasy, but she'd also tried several romances, as well as one about a young spy that she hadn't much liked. With every book, her English had improved. Not that she had the courage to speak it, but understanding all those words made her feel very proud.

"*Oprostite...*" Natali turned to see a girl of about thirteen standing behind her. "I have a book to return, and I would like a new one." She was holding out one of the dragon rider books that had first drawn Natali to reading and there was a reticence about her that Natali recognised.

"Oh, they're ace, aren't they?" she said. "How many have you read?"

"Just the first two."

Natali scanned the table. "The third one isn't here. Someone must have borrowed it already." The girl's face fell. "I know, how about this one? Lloyd told me the series is based on stories about a legendary English king, and there's this girl who's a super-brave changeling and has to save him."

"Have you read it?" the girl asked.

Natali nodded. "It was hard to put down."

"Then I'll take it. It's great to talk to someone who's read the books. Thank you so much."

Natali hadn't noticed Filip was behind her. "Looks like you chose the right boat, given that you love reading."

"Oh no, I didn't at the start of the summer. I'd never managed to finish a book before, but a fairy tale someone told me started me off, and Lloyd's helped so much." A fairy tale Baka had told her, to be precise. Stories, recipes, friendship ... there was so much to be grateful to Baka for.

"He tells me you're thinking of studying to improve your qualifications."

Of course, it was Filip who'd told Lloyd about the adult education scheme in the first place. "It's difficult. I need to work as well." She turned to him. "This is the problem. You're local, so you'll understand better than Lloyd. The people who need to improve their qualifications as adults are in low-paid jobs. Or seasonal work, like me. We work long hours just to live, so there is no time to study. And no spare money either." She shrugged. "We're still trapped." However encouraging Lloyd had been, that was the truth of the matter.

"But no, you're not, not completely. There is no time limit to complete the courses. You just study when you can. I do know it's hard, honestly, but it is possible." He picked up the first pile of books and put them into a box, Natali following suit. "Lloyd says you really know your stuff as a yacht mechanic. Is that what you'd like to do?" Natali nodded. "Then from next year your practical experience should count towards your qualifications too, which will make it easier to complete the course. If you don't mind finishing up here, I'll pop into my office and print off the information about what mechanics are expected to study."

Once the library was packed away, Natali sat in the shade outside the hall and scanned the paperwork while she waited for Lloyd. She knew most of this stuff anyway, and she was pretty confident she could translate that knowledge into the words and calculations needed to pass the course. How many doors would open for her? A future so different she could barely imagine it. But when she tried, she found she wanted it so much that it brought tears to her eyes.

No, this was rubbish. She knew in her heart of hearts what she would need to make it happen: money, time and a place to live. Caring for Baka would give her all three, so why was she hesitating? Because it was too big, too huge, to risk making Baka's last months miserable if she got this wrong? Because she didn't know if she could do it? Or because she was scared to want to, in case Dina couldn't persuade Mateo it was the right thing for his mother?

When she'd talked it through with Ana and Lloyd on Sunday night, Ana had been understandably cautious, but Lloyd more practical. He'd suggested she turn the problem around: if she decided caring for Baka was what she wanted to do, she should consider what needed to happen to make it a realistic option, such as the help and support she might need to deal with her concerns, or at any rate make them more manageable.

That had to be her next step before she went back to Dina with her answer. Ana was going out when they got to Šipan this evening, but she was sure Lloyd would help her make a list.

Šipan

TUESDAY 22ND AUGUST

It was not often that Ana studied herself in the mirror on the back of the bathroom door, but tonight was an exception. Her hair may be a little damp from her shower, but at least she looked as though she'd made an effort in a short denim skirt and turquoise top with a subtle sequin design. She laughed to herself. Not that she needed to show off her legs to Raš. He'd seen her in a bikini any number of times.

Tonight, another piece of the jigsaw that was her future would be put into place. One way or another. Raš as a lover, or as a friend? She knew which she wanted, not just because he was attractive, but because he was like her. And his acceptance of who he was, and his honesty about the downsides, had shone a light on her own future in a way no one else – not even her *dida* – had.

But rather than blowing her family apart, telling her parents of her plans had made Ana feel closer to them than ever. Having made her own, she felt better able to support Natali in the big decisions she had to make and that was another bonus. She just had to cross her fingers and pray that the library's strong finish to the summer was enough to convince Ivana not only to carry on with the project, but that she was the person to run it.

Lloyd and Natali were finishing their supper in the salon, and it was a joy to hear their animated conversation drift down the stairs. She checked the clock on her phone. Time she was going. She ran up the steps and stopped in front of the table.

"You look stunning," Natali said, her face full of admiration.

Lloyd winked. "You'll do."

She rolled her eyes. "I'll have to."

After ruffling Obi's ears, she headed across the deck then jumped onto the quay, her bag swinging from her shoulder. Would she be back tonight? Most likely, but just in case, her toothbrush and a packet of condoms were nestled next to her phone and purse.

Already the sun had dipped below the islands, the intense heat of the day fading into a comfortably soft and warm dusk. The bar on the edge of the square was buzzing, and children still played on the beach, running in and out of the water and splashing each other amid gleeful cries. Another two weeks of high season to go. Another eight days of the library.

Raš was perched on the wall outside the *peka* restaurant she'd passed on her way to the winery. Seeing that he was wearing a white linen shirt over chinos, she was glad she'd dressed up a bit too. For a moment he looked uncertain whether to kiss her cheek or shake her hand, so she made the decision for him and leant in, brushing her lips over his skin and inhaling his earthy aftershave.

The waiter led them to a table in the far corner of the

restaurant, which was already filling up with locals and tourists alike.

"The *peka* smells amazing," she told Raš. "They were cooking it the first time I walked past and I've wanted to try it ever since."

"Their wines are excellent too," he replied, grinning.

"Then I assume we're drinking something local."

"Very local, given you can practically see my winery from here."

She settled opposite him. "Do you only ever drink your own?"

"Oh no, I taste as widely as I possibly can. In fact, in November I'm heading to Lyon for a massive wine fair and to visit a few growers in the south of France. In some ways their climate's not dissimilar to ours and I might be able to pick up a few new varietals." He stopped. "But I don't want to bore you."

"Why would it be boring? It's your passion."

"The fact is, Ana, it's a very long time since I've taken anyone out to dinner, and I'm a little worried I only have one topic of conversation."

She smiled at him. "Then why not ask me about my day?"

"*Sranje!* I didn't realise I was that rusty. Where are my manners?"

"It's fine. And my day was fine too, actually. We were on Lopud and that's always a busy one for Lloyd and the library. And busy is good."

The waiter returned, and Raš suggested that Ana choose their *peka* and he would choose the wine. It was no choice at all, given there was octopus on the menu, and before long a round, flat metal dish was in front of them, filled to the brim with potatoes, tomatoes, herbs and deliciously soft tentacles.

"Wow," said Ana. "This is one of the best I've had."

"The food or the wine?"

"You're not going to rest, are you? Of course I mean the wine."

"I'm so one-dimensional." He laughed, but his eyes didn't meet hers.

"You're really not. But now we're eating, let's cut to the chase. Tell me why you're not dating at the moment."

"It's because of Manda. I think I said … I'm carrying a fair bit of guilt about the break-up, and underneath it all, I'm pretty sure Jelka is too. Whatever our differences, it wasn't Manda's fault and we want to have as much of a family life as we can for her, which means not introducing extra people into the equation. Jelka went out with someone for a while last summer and it made Manda very insecure, so we agreed that for the next couple of years at least, we wouldn't. Besides which, we spend Christmas together, go on holidays together… It wouldn't be fair on a new partner. Someone like you definitely deserves better."

That did sound like a pretty emphatic no, but looking across the table at Raš, Ana reckoned it was worth probing a little further. She admired the way he knew what he wanted; it was both reassuring and seriously attractive. If he didn't want her, that would be another matter entirely. But she had a sneaking suspicion that he did.

"You can't possibly talk about what I deserve, because you don't know what I want. And, equally important, what I don't."

He put down his fork. "Then tell me."

"I will. But first we need to agree that whatever happens we'll be totally honest with each other about our wants, needs and no-go areas. Not just tonight, but in the future, whether we move forwards as friends, or as ... something else."

"Sure. I mean, why wouldn't we be?"

"Because sometimes people make things complicated by second-guessing the other person and doing or saying what they think they want. I know, because it's a big fault of mine, one of many I'm working hard to get better at. I'm more likely to backslide on this than you, so the promise is as much for me as anything."

"You mean you have faults? Now I'm really intrigued."

But for her, it wasn't the moment for joking. "You have your vines, I have my boat. My work can take me all over Dalmatia and that's just how I like it. I crave that freedom. I don't ever want to settle down to family life in the traditional way. And yes, I am sure about it. I had a narrow escape this summer and I won't even be considering it again. So if dating means chugging along with a view to marriage or similar, then no, I don't date either." She took a mouthful of *peka*. "This octopus is spectacular. How ever do they get it this soft?"

"Don't change the subject."

"Oh, so you want to hear more?"

"*Sranje*, Ana, you know I do. You sit there looking so bloody gorgeous, and I know you have legs up to your armpits under this table, then you tell me half a story that has me absolutely hooked."

Ana burst out laughing. "I knew that day on the beach when you told me your vines were the reason you were put on this earth that I'd found a kindred spirit. I'm happy to be second on your list, third, to your daughter, because that's about where you'd be on mine. I don't want you to put demands on me, and I won't put any on you. We may not even see too much of each other because of our priorities. But I think any time we do spend together could be really good."

"It could ... I know it could." He was looking straight at her, but his eyes were troubled. "Tell me, Ana, do you have a man in every port?"

"No! That isn't me at all, and if you want to play the field and have me around too, then we should just stay friends."

"Well that's a relief. I don't have the energy, or the desire, for those sorts of games. It's just ... oh, I don't know, it's hard to see how it might actually work."

She hadn't quite imagined this much resistance. Had she read him wrong? But having come this far she wasn't giving up now. She gripped her fork harder, but kept her tone light. "In what way?"

"I don't just find you attractive, Ana, I really like you as a person. You're right about being kindred spirits – we have a proper connection. The way you feel about the sea ... it's exactly what I feel about my little patch of land, and I've never met anyone... I felt so bad when I blurted out about dinner that morning, but I didn't want to let you go without ... I don't know." He shrugged.

She relaxed just a little. "And now here we are."

"Yes." But his eyes were still filled with doubt.

"Keep talking, Raš, keep talking," she encouraged him.

"OK, but what if we start, and our relationship develops differently for each of us. What if, perhaps, one of us wants more, or less, than the other. What if, maybe, even, one of us falls in love?"

"But you never know how it will pan out when you start

anything, do you? There's always that risk. I know you've been hurt by how your marriage ended, and you've told me about the baggage you carry because of it, so if you're not ready to try again just yet then I'll honestly respect that and shut up and enjoy the rest of my *peka*."

"But ... I don't want to let you pass me by."

"Look on the bright side, Raš. If it all falls apart, you still have your land and your daughter, and I still have *Dida Krila*."

He laughed. "There is that. Ana, I must be completely mad, prevaricating like this. An intelligent, sassy, beautiful woman is offering me the kind of relationship I didn't even know I wanted, yet will suit me down to the ground, and all I'm doing is questioning it. What I should be doing is grabbing it with both hands."

"If you need time to think it through, that's fine."

He stood slowly, arranging his cutlery on his plate and wiping his hands on a paper serviette. Oh god, he'd taken that literally. A jolt of horror shot through her — she'd felt like she was almost there and instead she'd totally messed this up. He was going to walk away right now. But instead he leant across the table and kissed her full on the lips. Firmly, confidently, in a way that ran rills of heat deep into her belly.

When he finally pulled away, she all but slumped back into her seat. "So you don't need time?" she said, trying to stop her voice from sounding as weak as she felt.

"Only to finish the wine." Still standing, he drained his glass. "Shame to waste it."

She stood and did the same. The *peka* was only half-eaten, but she didn't care. His sudden impatience matched her own, the idea he'd probably keep surprising her taking a delicious hold. Much as she found she wanted to surprise him.

Ana's whole body felt like it was on fire as they left the restaurant, Raš's arm casually draped over her shoulder. Without even asking, he turned right towards the winery, walking in silence along the path until he reached a gate leading into the olive grove. He stopped, putting both hands on her shoulders.

"You're sure? It isn't me rushing you now?"

She brushed her lips against his. "No. Not at all." Stepping back a fraction, she reached into her handbag. "Look, I even brought my toothbrush."

"Oh, you presumptuous—!" He pulled her to him, laughing softly, kissing her again before holding the gate open and following her through.

Koločep

MONDAY 28TH AUGUST

Natali began the climb from the quayside to the upper reaches of the village. Although in the bay below the morning sun caressed the water making it sparkle, at this hour the path was shaded. A woman she knew by sight greeted her from the terrace where she was drinking her coffee, and further on a baby's thin cries drifted through closed shutters, but otherwise all was quiet.

"Well, Obi," she sighed. "Who would have thought this week would be here so quickly?" Obi looked up, wagging her tail. She didn't know their lives were about to change again. Well, maybe not immediately. With the extra work Ana had secured they'd be living and working on *Dida Krila* for the best part of another six weeks, but without Lloyd and the routine of the library, it would feel awfully strange.

But what then? That's what she needed to decide. The three of them had talked about it long into the night, this way and that, and she'd exchanged countless messages with Krasna in recent days too, about what it was really like to care for someone who was dying. It wasn't fair to keep Dina hanging on any longer for her answer, even though the thought of giving her a final yes or no made Natali feel sick inside.

Perhaps Baka's garden was not the best place to reach her final conclusion, because she and Obi loved it so much it would surely sway her, but as long as she was aware of that... And anyway, even if she did come down on the side of offering to look after Baka, there was still a Mateo-sized hurdle to overcome. Dina had said she would handle it, but given his attitude up until now, Natali wasn't so sure how successful she'd be.

If nothing else, she had a practical reason to come here: to water the vegetable patch and pick the glut of tomatoes and aubergines Baka was fretting about. They'd be eating the most wonderful veggie pasta tonight on *Dida Krila*, and tomorrow perhaps she'd make *punjeni patlidžani* if she could find some beef to stuff them with.

The thought of all that cooking cheered her. As did the thought of Obi having a blissful half-hour or so running around under the trees, which was absolutely her favourite thing.

As she opened the gate to the steep track down to Baka's garden, she noticed how quickly the lemons and mandarins were ripening beneath their shining leaves. They wouldn't be ready for another month or so, yet Natali's mouth was already watering at the thought of being able to pick them. She hadn't told Baka at the time, but before the day they'd made the *ajvar* she'd never picked anything from a plant in her life, and there'd been something perfectly thrilling about it.

At the bottom of the path, she freed Obi from her lead and watched as she zoomed off to the far corner of the citrus grove, a tiny tan and black shape bouncing between the trunks. Turning towards the house to collect the watering can, she stopped in her tracks. There, sitting at the table outside the back door, was Mateo.

"When I saw the dog, I thought it might be you," he said.

"I've c-come to water and pick some vegetables. Baka said..." She trailed off. "I didn't know you'd be here."

"I didn't either." His voice was heavy, sad.

"Is anything wrong?" She could have kicked herself the moment she said it. Of course there was – his mother was dying. She hung her head. "Sorry."

Time stretched between them. Neither spoke, neither moved. She should call Obi and retreat. She should get out of Mateo's space, before she annoyed him. She didn't want to annoy him, not at all. His good opinion could matter so much for her future.

Did that mean she'd made her decision? Was her choice to care for Baka, after all?

"I can come back later," she ventured.

"No, no. We should talk, anyway." He smiled a very small smile. "Because until I know your thinking, there is little point in me continuing with mine."

She nodded, although she suddenly felt a little shaky. "M-me too."

"Coffee?" Mateo asked. Natali shook her head. "Then at least come and sit down."

Natali slid onto the other chair and folded her hands in her lap. Mateo gazed into the trees, although she wasn't exactly sure he was seeing them. He cleared his throat.

"I know my duty to my mother. My duty is to look after her, if possible in my own home. But my wife has made me question whether it is, indeed, possible." Another silence. A long one. A bird sang nearby, trilling a couple of octaves above the putter of a boat in the bay below.

Finally, Natali ventured to say, "So you have come here to work it out."

He raised an eyebrow. "Just between us, my wife has sent me. But also there are practicalities to consider if my mother is to return home. Adaptations to the house to make it safe."

Natali's stomach clenched. He was thinking about it, after all. This would make such a difference to Baka. "Small ones, I think, would make it possible. Handrails where there are steps to the terrace and into her bathroom. I do not think she should come downstairs without help, but I worry she might try to put flowers in Valentin's room."

"Ah, yes. Valentin."

"It must be ... difficult for you."

"He could do no wrong in her eyes." Mateo shrugged. "It is the way these things are sometimes, but it made me determined not to make that mistake with my girls. And now Dina tells me that I am, by not giving Petra the same chance to study as her sister had. I do not want that to happen."

"You said my thinking affected yours. Does that mean if you cannot look after your mother, you would like me to?"

"It is a solution that would please her, but you are not a carer. You told me you work on yachts."

This was awkward. Very awkward. Had Dina come clean about their discussion? It was impossible to tell, so best to say nothing.

"I'm right, aren't I?" he persisted.

Natali nodded. "But I have been thinking too. My work is seasonal, unpredictable. I'm twenty-two years old, so that has to change, but I will need better qualifications. If you decide you want me to move in here and look after Baka, I could study as well, so the arrangement would suit us all. With certain…" What was the word Lloyd had used? "P-provisos in place."

"And what might they be?"

"I will need internet. And also … every so often I'll need a couple of days off. So I can stay with my friend to have a proper break."

He nodded. "That doesn't seem unreasonable. I was thinking about internet anyway, so my girls can video call their grandmother. Anything else?"

Only the elephant in the room. When would he tell her that his mother was dying? Should she pretend that someone in the rehab centre had let it slip? Yes, that was a solution. If he wasn't man enough to say it, then she certainly had to.

"It's not as though it's long term, is it?"

He shook his head. "Which makes it harder. I want her to be with me for these last months. I want her to know I care, that I am a good son after all. But the irony is that in making her come to Split I would not be a good son. Or a good father."

"She knows you're a good son. She once said to me that Valentin may hug her, but you make sure her cupboards are well-stocked. She said that you show your love in different ways."

He lifted his fingers and squeezed the bridge of his nose. "Oh." It was a small word. Neutral. Yet full of feeling. "Oh."

"Your mother is a wise woman."

"And so, Natali, are you. Wise beyond your years." Certainly nobody had ever called her anything like that before. Even in these serious circumstances, it was hard not to grin from ear to ear. Just wait until she told Lloyd and Ana!

Natali watched as Obi scampered towards them, panting, and flopped next to her feet. Mateo stood. "I'll fetch her some water."

"That would be kind. You like dogs?"

"Petra's allergic so I try not to get hairs on my clothes, but yes. Yes I do."

"So would it be a problem, Obi living here? Because if so—"

"Mama would be very disappointed if she didn't. Somehow we will manage Petra." He turned at the back door. "If you say yes, that is."

Once Mateo had gone, Natali leant down and fondled Obi's ears. "So what do you think? Shall we commit?" It wouldn't be easy. She'd been over it again and again, with Lloyd especially. How tough it was caring for someone who was dying. How much it hurt when they finally slipped away. And Krasna had had an angle too, having helped to look after her father at the end. But Krasna had also been adamant she'd be there to support Natali. She would be there as her friend.

The hum of cicadas filled the trees in the citrus grove, the bay glistening a silverish turquoise between the branches as Obi nestled closer to her legs. She'd been dreading this week, when the library books came back and didn't go out again, but now she could see it wasn't only an end, but a beginning, too. A new beginning for each of them. Different lives, which had been beyond their imaginations just ten weeks before. And if Ana and Lloyd were prepared to dive straight in and give it a go, then so was she.

Korčula

FRIDAY 1ST SEPTEMBER

Lloyd lifted the last of the boxes onto the banquette and gazed around. So that was that. Ten whole weeks, and now he'd packed up the island library for the very last time. It seemed an age since he'd collected the stock from the tiny shop in Dubrovnik old town – there was certainly no new-book smell now. In fact, some of the more popular titles – German clean romances with pastel covers and the English young adult fantasies Natali loved so much – were looking a little dog-eared.

It had all come good in the end. Yes, they still had some ground to make up on Mljet, but given he'd be teaching there over the winter it was definitely something he could work on. He could still hardly believe he'd be going back into a classroom, working with children of all ages. All right, it was only half a job, but it was a definite start, and he still had some savings that would prop him up until the other half came along, as Kristina assured him it would.

Dida Krila was moving under him, the thrum of her engines

familiar and comforting as she drew away from Korčula marina for the short trip to Lumbarda. Time for him to go and freshen up. He'd check and re-box the books tomorrow, ready for winter storage. He'd be packing his own belongings too because finally, finally, he was going home to see Ruth and he could not wait.

In his cabin he found himself prevaricating in front of the narrow wardrobe. Just a clean polo, or the blue and white shirt he'd bought with Jenny at Marble Arch? He wanted to wear it, yet to do so for another woman felt wrong. And even if tonight was a celebration for the crew, if he was honest with himself, he would be wearing it for Mirjana. And that in itself felt mighty strange.

He sat on his bed and picked up Jenny's photo from the shelf. "So what do you really think?" he asked her. "And how … how do I do this?" Oh, he was being ridiculous. This wasn't even a date. It just so happened Kristina had invited them to Konoba Pecaros. The place that had been the beginning of his Croatian life all those years ago, now marked an end. Except it wasn't; not quite. It was a comma, or maybe a semi-colon, but not a full stop. This time he was coming back.

He searched Jenny's features, the face so dear to him over the years, and still, in so many ways, the one he most wanted to see. But he couldn't, and he'd had to accept that quite some time ago. It was just that now he was more at peace with it, more at peace with himself. He remembered his darling Jenny telling him, quite close to the end, that he was too young not to live, not to love again; that more than anything she couldn't bear the thought of him being lonely for the rest of his life.

He looked at the shirt again, and then at her picture.

"OK," he said. "Baby steps. But I'm going to try."

He kissed her nose, as he did every night, and set it back in its place.

The sun was low over the far side of the island as they set off along the quay towards Konoba Pecaros, the gentle chink and tinkle of the masts of twenty or so yachts accompanying them.

Natali wrapped her arm around Lloyd's waist. "I'm going to miss you so much."

He looked down at her fondly. "I'm coming back in a fortnight."

"I know, I know, but it won't be the same. I don't think anything's ever going to be the same as this summer."

"You can say that again," said Ana with some feeling.

"You sound as though you're glad it's over." Lloyd was only half joking.

"Well of course, in some ways I am. It's been tough. Really tough. For you more than anyone, Lloyd. But of course, I forget, you're practising for your sainthood." She rolled her eyes.

"Not at all. It wasn't Mirjana's fault. Let's face it, Ana, if you found out one of your friends was employing someone you knew to be dishonest, wouldn't you tell them? So they were at least on their guard?"

"I suppose so. I guess I'm just a bit grouchy because we've come to the end of the road. It's been just the best working with you guys." She smiled at Natali. "At least you, me and Obi get to stay together a bit longer."

"And hopefully next summer we'll be doing it all again," said Lloyd.

"The jury's still out on that one." Ana grimaced. "I can't see Ivana making a quick decision either. She'll play me like a cat with a mouse. Get a kick from the power."

Already they'd reached the headland, where a yellow taxi boat was collecting its passengers to take them into Korčula town for the evening. The tourist season was about to change gear, as children all over Europe went back to school. Now the visitors would be the youngest of families, the retired, and empty-nesters like him.

Lloyd was going to have a holiday too. He'd decided to drive from London back to Ston, and Ruth was taking time off to come with him. They'd had such fun on their nightly calls, planning and tweaking their route: Bruges, the prettiest part of the Rhine valley, then the Black Forest and down through Austria to Zagreb, Croatia's capital, with the final night in Split. It was going to be wonderful spending all that time with his daughter. His heart ached to see her and despite all the goodbyes, he could not wait to get on that plane on Sunday.

Konoba Pecaros came into view just along the quay, the fairy lights on the terrace beginning to twinkle as the sea turned a deeper shade of blue and the last rays of the sun reflected orange-pink on the parched hillsides of the Pelješac opposite.

"Never in a million years did I think we'd be coming here," said Ana, "or that Kristina would be buying. What a difference three weeks makes."

"I expect she feels guilty about not believing Lloyd," said Natali.

"Maybe. But she doesn't have to. Hopefully it's just a thank you for the way we kept the library going in the face of it all – even though in the end it was a close-run thing," Lloyd replied. "Anyway, we're here now and I, for one, am looking forward to a seafood pizza."

They climbed the steps and Mirjana bustled forwards from the bar to welcome them. "Kristina's on the terrace and I've put out some Grk wine. You have to go local on your last night."

Lloyd grinned at Mirjana. "Thanks so much. Are you able to join us?"

She shook her head. "Not now. It's much too busy. But it should quieten down later." She touched his arm. "I'd like the chance to say goodbye."

"I am coming back, you know."

"I've heard that before."

"Mirjana…"

"I'm joking! This time I have your phone number, remember? There's no escape."

He followed the others to the table, and once they had ordered their pizzas, Kristina asked Ana about her plans for the winter.

"Natali and I can keep going with chartering and day-boat hire until the middle of October, which is when she expects to start her new job anyway."

"And what's that?" asked Kristina.

Natali smiled shyly. "I'm going to be a live-in carer for a lady I know. She had a stroke and although she's doing quite well she'll never be able to manage alone."

"And Natali's going to study too, aren't you?" Lloyd added.

"Yes. I didn't get good grades at school so I'm going to do one of the new adult programmes online. I'd like to qualify properly as a mechanic if I can."

"Natali's amazing with boats," said Ana. "She can fix anything more or less instantly. It's quite a gift."

"Well, good luck to you, and if you need any help you only have to ask. I know almost every teacher on this island, and the high school in Blato runs a course in mechanics."

"Thank you, that's really kind. I do have Lloyd to help me, but perhaps engines are not his thing."

"They're certainly not!" Lloyd laughed.

"And how about the rest of your winter, Ana?"

"Some of it will be spent sorting out the mess my father always makes of his paperwork, but what's really exciting is I have the chance to tender for a water-quality survey in Malostonski Bay, so I'd be out on the boat a couple of days a week." She frowned. "The thing is, I need a reference from this project and I'm not at all sure what Ivana might say."

"She'll be fine," said Kristina. "Anyway, I'll make sure she is, as long as this new work won't stop you running the library next summer."

Lloyd sat back in his seat. "You really think it might happen?"

"Well my recommendation is that it does, and having spoken to your new boss on Mljet, his will be too. They never even consulted him on where to put it, you know? Idiots."

"And the smaller islands have done very well, on the whole," Lloyd mused.

"Then everything will be fine," said Kristina firmly. "Look, here are our pizzas."

A young waiter brought Ana's and Natali's, Mirjana following behind with the others. She placed Lloyd's in front of him with a flourish.

"Your favourite."

Ana stared at it. "But you ordered seafood."

Lloyd looked up at Mirjana and grinned. "I don't think you'll find this one on the menu."

"My chef nearly mutinied when I asked him to cook the *panceta*. He said frying the egg was bad enough."

Lloyd's eyes were unusually moist as he spoke. "Thank you. Thank you for remembering."

"Right. I'm busy. Enjoy your meals everyone."

As Mirjana walked away, Ana nudged him. "So what's this all about?"

"The day her father asked me to work for him, he cooked me bacon and eggs for breakfast, except, of course, the *panceta* was raw and I was afraid to eat it. In England, back then we thought we had to cook pork until it was hard and dry for it to be safe."

Kristina beamed at him. "I never had Mirjana down as much of a joker."

"Oh, I don't know. When she was younger..." Before. Before everything had happened to change her, but Lloyd knew for sure that something of the girl he'd fallen in love with was still there somewhere. But he wasn't looking for the past. He wanted to get to know the woman Mirjana was now; every layer that life and experience had added and shaped.

"Well I think it's romantic, her remembering," said Natali.

Lloyd shrugged. "I know who's winning in the adoring gaze stakes right now," he said, looking down. "No, Obi, you know the rules. You get the last bit off my plate and nothing before." He tousled the soft fur between the dog's ears. "But I'll make sure it's meaty, OK?"

∽

Leaving the *konoba*'s staff clearing the last few tables, Lloyd and Mirjana strolled along the quayside in the direction of Bilin Žal Beach. A fishing boat chugged from the harbour to begin the night's work, and in the distance, through the islands, the lights of Orebić shimmered.

By silent mutual consent they sat on the bench closest to where they'd first kissed, the gentle movement of the water licking the rocks below.

"I will come back, you know," Lloyd said.

"I know." She paused. "Well, of course I know really, but my stupid head just keeps playing forward all the things that might stop you this time."

"The most likely of which is my car breaking down as it's barely been used all summer. But Ruth's just had it serviced so it should be fine. It'll have to be. I start work again on September 20th, and that's already a couple of weeks later than they asked me to."

"You're really serious about this, aren't you?" By the tone of Mirjana's voice, the question wasn't entirely rhetorical.

"Yes. It won't be easy living away from Ruth, but she needs her own life. She's put far too much on hold for me since Jenny died, and since I've been away she's been going out with her friends, dating even. Like women in their twenties are supposed to."

"Krasna's younger and she's getting married next year."

"Then she's lucky she's found the right man."

"Before Milo died too. It helps her to think her father liked him."

Lloyd sighed. "It makes me sad that Jenny will never know how Ruth's life pans out. More than sad really."

Mirjana's hand crept across the bench and took his. "When

you come back, you must talk to me more about her, and I will tell you properly about Milo. It feels important, although I couldn't say why."

"Maybe ... maybe because ... and I could be getting ahead of myself here, but if we, you know, decide we might try again, we need to recognise what's gone before. Jenny and Milo will always be part of us, always walk alongside us."

She didn't reply, didn't look at him, just gazed out over the dark, shimmering water. God, he was such a fool. He'd already told himself it wasn't that long since she'd lost Milo. What was he thinking? He knew he'd stuff this up. The silence stretched, but then he realised Mirjana's hand was still in his, and it gave him the courage to speak.

"It's too soon for you, isn't it?" he said. "I should never have mentioned—"

"Of course you should. It's what we've both been thinking. I saw it in your eyes the day we went to the old barracks, and I was scared. Really scared. Because I felt it too. That old pull. It hadn't gone away."

"So?"

She squeezed his hand. "You need to come back first."

"And I will."

They sat for a while longer in silence, the deep velvet blues of the Mediterranean night surrounding them, neither of them willing to break the moment.

Eventually Lloyd said, "If I need to come back, then first I'll have to go."

Mirjana nodded and they stood as one, still holding hands as they strolled back towards the village, the full moon guiding their way.

Acknowledgments

I often find people are interested in where ideas for stories come from, and in this case I can honestly tell you it came in the shower. From more or less out of nowhere, except I knew I wanted to write another story about very different people coming together over books. How wonderful would it be if there actually was a library on a catamaran, sailing around Croatian islands for the summer?

Luckily my then editor, Charlotte Ledger, loved the idea – and the characters and locations – so I set to work. I had already planned to be in Dubrovnik, so decided to extend my stay so I could visit Koločep and Mljet (the two islands on the catamaran's schedule I didn't know) and reacquaint myself with Korčula, which I hadn't visited since 2019. Quite frankly, I didn't need much of an excuse.

I had a huge chunk of luck on Korčula, as by some miracle (and it was a miracle, given he spends his summers travelling up and down the Dalmatian islands) Darko Barisic, who helps me with all my books, was there at the same time and we had a wonderful evening catching up and eating far too much *peka*. I could never write about Croatian life without him. Wherever he is in the world he always answers my questions, however random they might seem, and offers me great little insights I can blend into my stories, for example eating raw "bacon" for breakfast. More than all that, he's become the greatest of friends.

Darko is not the only Croatian who helps me with my books. Krešimir Pehar has always been far more than a driver and guide, and it is through him and his love of the Pelješac that I had the idea of Ana being the daughter of oyster farmers from Ston. He was also kind enough to arrange for me to visit an oyster bed to see how it's all done – far more information than I needed for the book in the end, but it was such useful background and a pleasure to visit Malostonski Bay.

More than anything, I needed to go on a catamaran, which took some arranging because of the times I was visiting Croatia. In the end, Mato Knego, the Dubrovnik Defender who influenced *The Dubrovnik Book Club* so much, introduced me to his friend Tanja Grossinger Bosnić, who works with Huck Finn Adventure Travel. They have a fleet of charter catamarans of just the right size and took me and my friends out for a morning with wonderful skipper Zeljko Kelemen and his three Yorkshire terriers. There was always going to be a dog in the story, but these fabulous little seafaring ladies stole all our hearts and one of them, Phoebe, became the model for Obi.

Much as I had a stroke of good luck meeting Darko on Korčula, I had what I thought was a stroke of bad luck too, when many of the ferries between Korčula and Mljet were cancelled because it was late in the season. There was no way I could get to one of my main locations, where I had planned for Baka to live. But a few days later I visited Koločep for the first time and absolutely fell in love with the place. Its small community was the perfect home for Baka.

I know many new readers discovered my Croatian books through *The Dubrovnik Book Club* and I'm so grateful to you all for investing your time and money in my work. Sharing stories is my main motivation for writing, so without readers there would be no point, and I love it when you reach out and tell me what you thought of my characters and their lives.

Talking of sharing stories, a quick word on *Fisherman Plunk*. The tale comes from a collection by Matica Hrvatska first published in 1916 and translated into English as *Croatian Tales of Long Ago* in 1924. Most of the stories are freely available on the internet and they're quite magical.

Naturally I don't write in a vacuum. Most important in my writing life – and my life full stop – is my husband Jim, ever patient, ever supportive. I am so lucky to have him. Then there are all my writing friends: a big shout out to Kitty Wilson in particular, who was my beta reader for this particular book and threw herself into it with her usual enthusiasm. She pulled no punches, for which I love her dearly.

A big thank you too, to my former editor Bonnie Macleod. Her thoughts on the first few chapters made the whole book so much better as I wrote it, and her insightful edits pulled it together at the end. Thanks also to Helen Williams for picking up the baton and running with it as brilliantly as ever.

While I was finishing the book, my cousin, the literary novelist Roger Hubank, died. I will miss him so much as he truly understood the writing journey and gave me no end of valuable advice. Which is why this book is dedicated to him.

I'd love it if you would like to stay in touch:

Newsletter sign up:
https://mailchi.mp/99543ad90bea/sign-up

Website: www.evaglynauthor.com
Instagram: @evaglynauthor
Facebook: Eva Glyn, Author
X: @janecable
Bookbub: @evaglyn

ESCAPE TO CROATIA AND JOIN A NEW BOOK CLUB WITH FRIENDS, FAVOURITE READS AND A MYSTERY TO UNRAVEL...

In a tiny bookshop in Dubrovnik's historic Old Town, a book club begins...

Newly arrived on the sun-drenched shores of Croatia, Claire Thomson's life is about to change forever when she starts working at a local bookshop. With her cousin Vedran, employee Luna and Karmela, a professor, they form an unlikely book club.

But when their first book club pick – an engrossing cosy crime – inspires them to embark upon an investigation that is close to their hearts, they quickly learn the value of keeping their new friends close as lives and stories begin to entwine...

AVAILABLE NOW IN PAPERBACK, EBOOK AND AUDIO!

ESCAPE TO GREECE WITH THIS JOYFUL NEW NOVEL ABOUT FRIENDSHIP, NEW LOVE AND HIDDEN STORIES...

Three women, one writing retreat, endless possibilities...
Bestselling author Jessica Rose needs to escape from a terrible secret that's robbed her of her creativity. Could leading a retreat on a gorgeous Greek island be just what she needs?

Coming home to Santorini was never in Zina's plans, but now she's determined to make her new business a success. And then there's Karmela, who just wants to write her book and make her mother proud.

In the heat of their Greek island paradise, these new friends find the courage to shape their own stories, and write endings they can all be proud of...

AVAILABLE NOW IN PAPERBACK, EBOOK AND AUDIO!

The author and One More Chapter would like to thank everyone who contributed to the publication of this story…

Analytics
Imogen Wolstencroft

Audio
Fionnuala Barrett
Ciara Briggs

Contracts
Laura Amos
Inigo Vyvyan

Design
Lucy Bennett
Fiona Greenway
Liane Payne
Dean Russell

Digital Sales
Laura Daley
Lydia Grainge
Hannah Lismore

eCommerce
Laura Carpenter
Madeline ODonovan
Charlotte Stevens
Christina Storey
Jo Surman
Rachel Ward

Editorial
Rosie Best
Kara Daniel
Catherine Jackson
Charlotte Ledger
Lydia Mason
Jennie Rothwell
Sofia Salazar Studer
Helen Williams

Harper360
Emily Gerbner
Ariana Juarez
Jean Marie Kelly
emma sullivan
Sophia Wilhelm

International Sales
Peter Borcsok
Ruth Burrow
Bethan Moore
Colleen Simpson

Inventory
Sarah Callaghan
Kirsty Norman

Marketing & Publicity
Chloe Cummings
Grace Edwards
Katie Sadler

Operations
Melissa Okusanya
Hannah Stamp

Production
Denis Manson
Simon Moore
Francesca Tuzzeo

Rights
Ashton Mucha
Alisah Saghir
Zoe Shine
Aisling Smyth
Lucy Vanderbilt

Trade Marketing
Ben Hurd
Eleanor Slater

The HarperCollins Distribution Team

The HarperCollins Finance & Royalties Team

The HarperCollins Legal Team

The HarperCollins Technology Team

UK Sales
Isabel Coburn
Jay Cochrane
Sabina Lewis
Holly Martin
Harriet Williams
Leah Woods

And every other essential link in the chain from delivery drivers to booksellers to librarians and beyond!

ONE MORE CHAPTER

YOUR NUMBER ONE STOP FOR PAGETURNING BOOKS

One More Chapter is an award-winning global division of HarperCollins.

Subscribe to our newsletter to get our latest eBook deals and stay up to date with all our new releases!

signup.harpercollins.co.uk/join/signup-omc

Meet the team at
www.onemorechapter.com

Follow us!

@onemorechapterhc

Do you write unputdownable fiction?
We love to hear from new voices.
Find out how to submit your novel at
www.onemorechapter.com/submissions